Witchcraft, Science God: Witchcraft

ANDREW KAITIFF

About the author

In May of 2015, I was involved in an accident that resulted in a trip to hospital, courtesy of The Air Ambulance. To that point I had been a very keen sportsman, and in many ways, sport defined me. As I lay in "Majors" in A&E, my world spinning from a dizzying mix of head injury and morphine, I saw a lot of my world and the pleasure that I took in it, disappear. Nihilistic I know, a little narrow minded yes, particularly considering that in all probability the very worst outcome was that might have lost an eye. It could have been much worse. But I was, nonetheless, feeling quite sorry for myself.

Over the next few days, while trying to ignore overheard snippets of my wife's phone calls to the local eye unit to the tune of, "I'm supposed to put drops into his eye, but I cannot find it, what shall I do?", I decided to write a book. That has now turned into a series.

The first part of the story was 4 years in the making. I didn't specifically set out to write a fated adventure story, replete with folklore and magic, medicine and psychology, but I did want it to reflect the enigmatic, rugged beauty of Cornwall and Devon, the area in which I am fortunate enough to live. The moors and coasts of each are truly stunning... and I believe everyone should go surfing.it makes you feel so alive, so at one with nature, firing all five senses at once... you can even taste it.

I went back to work but continued to write it in my free time. Well, I say "free", technically I should have been looking after the children, or fitting a kitchen or tackling the garden, or any other number of more mundane activities.

I now work as a GP in Cornwall and am back to playing lots of sport, albeit with one slightly dodgy eye. My plan is to continue writing many more books and fund my habit by continuing to practice medicine.

Enjoy the ride!

Also, by the author:

Witchcraft, Science, God: Witchcraft

First published 2020 Frustrated Author Publishing. Second edition 2023

Witchcraft, Science, God: Science [May 2023]

Witchcraft, Science, God: God [2025]

Website: frustratedauthor.com

The moral right of the author has been asserted.

All rights reserved.

Some of the proceeds of these books go towards supporting The Cornwall Air Ambulance [cornwallairambulance.org], The Devon Air Ambulance [data.org] and The Royal National Lifeboat Institution[rnli.org].

I would encourage you to support them as well; you never know when they may be required to save your life.

Witchcraft, Science, God: Witchcraft

In the blink of a blinded eye, I saw much of my world disappear into a painful void. So, I decided to write a book, just in case...

Prologue

A **March 21st, 1941**

The pilot of the Heinkel He 111 bomber cursed. He'd overshot Plymouth on the second run and wasn't going to risk another go. That, he decided, might well be asking too much of luck on this near cloudless night. The cockpit window dropped below the horizon as the plane banked and his stomach lurched with the familiar, almost pleasurable G force. His eyes tracked down... there was his waypoint, the river Tamar, a broadening, silver ribbon below, directing them south towards home. That at least, was good. He gave a disgruntled sniff. Less good was that this would be their third failed mission and there would be repercussions, consequences. But, the pilot reflected, better to keep them all in one piece.

He glanced at the controls and flexed his traitorous hand. Strange, that resistance he had felt when the moment had come to press the bomb door release. It was as though it had not, for a brief moment, been under his control. Still, he wiggled the fingers on the joystick straightening up the plane, all seemed fine now... and his attention was drawn to the ground. Far below a light shimmered in the darkness – an unwitting, careless beacon. The pilot gave it some thought and shrugged, after all he did need to lighten the load to get clear of any chasing fighters. This time there was no resistance.

An hour later, as the fire began to die down, an elderly couple from a cottage in the nearby village hurried along the cobbled track that led up to what remained of the farmhouse. They had got there as quickly as they could, but for them, the two miles was a significant distance in the dark, torch and full moon notwithstanding. The man slowed as the track's gradient eased, and he unhooked the weathered, iron gate-catch, letting himself into the farm's main yard. He looked up, feeling a waft of heat caress his face, a cruel parody of welcome, then swallowed hard, steeling himself and began to pick his way around the unnatural, jagged fragments of what had once been a place of refuge, a place of peace, a home. Smoke eddied from burnt timbers strewn across the centuries-old granite walls, like blackened hawthorn branches on a collapsing tor. He exhaled, it was as bad as he had feared, worse in fact; the farm had taken a direct hit. There was no chance of anyone surviving a blast like that. The farmer's heart sank that little bit further, wearied now not just by the exertion, but also by the certainty of more senseless loss. He had known the three generations of the family who lay somewhere under the smouldering rubble. True, they had kept themselves a bit separate from the community, stuck as they were on top of this hill, but they had been good enough folk and didn't deserve this, nobody did, no matter what their strange habits. He turned and motioned for his wife to wait at a safe distance then, fanning his hand in front of his face as his eyes started to stream, he began his forlorn search.

Why he had felt compelled to circle the whole farmhouse he didn't know. He hadn't been able to get within so much as twenty feet of the place, let alone enter. Clearly this was pointless, futile. Furnace-like heat and dense black smoke had repelled him at every turn and, he thought, shielding himself with his coat, it all looked to have been pretty much flattened anyway. He'd just complete the circuit, then at least he could say that he had tried. Coughing, he trudged on and was almost back to his starting point, about to return to his wife to suggest that they come back in the morning, when a metallic glint caught his attention. It came from a small door that he could now see in the far southern corner of the farmhouse which, on closer inspection, had maybe fared slightly better. A room, or part of one, appeared to remain standing; the walls and even most of the roof were intact. He sniffed, rubbing his sore eyes; the smoke must have blinded him to it earlier.

The entrance was perhaps only five-foot high, and a thumb-sized brass hare hung from a nail hammered in near the lintel. It swung freely, glinting sporadically as its polished surface reflected the flames from the nearby timbers. The old man grasped the latch on the left side of the door, lifted the lever and gave it a gentle push. The door creaked as it swung open, and the man bent forward, extending his torch to look inside. Plaster dust caught in the beam, small particles dancing in the light like a will-o'-the-wisp. He scanned the roof and the rafters, checking as best he could that it wasn't about to collapse. Everything looked solid enough. He pulled his jacket around him; the air in the room felt perversely cool. Probably just the fact he was away from the direct line of the fires, but still...

Maintaining his careful approach, he turned the torch to the floor. There were a few wooden toys, carved animals mostly, scattered between displaced pieces of furniture. A chair had been thrown across the room and close to him a large lump of lime mortar had been dislodged from the wall. That, he could see, had shattered several floorboards and sharp splinters of wood erupted upward like a mini stockade fence. He inspected the room further, leaning in cautiously. Given the fireball that had erupted when the bombs landed and the destruction of the rest of the farmhouse, the fact that there was relatively little damage in here was remarkable. Stepping into the room, his foot nudged a crude rocking horse and it rumbled gently as its curved rockers rolled against the fractured boards. He took another step, placing his foot warily between a rattle and a rag doll... and then, he heard a noise, a different sort of noise. It was a sound not from the crackle of burning wood, or the rumble of settling debris, but a snuffling coming from somewhere ahead of him. His light scanned across the room, flashing across the bare whitewashed walls, and stopped abruptly on another small wooden structure, placed in the very middle of the room. A crib? Snuffling again, coming from that direction. His heart quickened. He felt hope surge within him, and forgetting the perilous floorboards, he moved swiftly towards it.

It was a small cot, he could see the hooded outline now. Plaster fragments, fallen from the ceiling, littered the bedding. He reached in, removing the larger pieces, and saw the top of a small head poking out from underneath a sheepskin. The head wriggled and the child gave a small cough. The man's heart now felt as though it would erupt from his chest. Reaching down, his hand shook, and roughened fingernails caught on strands of wool as he peeled back the sheepskin. A pair of intense dark-brown eyes blazed back at him.

The man stared down at the miracle before him, for that was what this was, must be – a miracle. He just stared. He had seen the bombs land, heard the terrible explosions and felt the ferocious heat from the fires. Realistically, he knew when he arrived, that nothing could have survived that blast. He knew, and yet...

The ceiling above shook, bringing him back to the present. Maybe the room hadn't been as undamaged as he'd at first thought. He slid his arms into the crib and picked up the infant and, shifting its position, cradled it under one arm. He brushed flakes of plaster from the child's hair and, noticing blood on its left cheek, dabbed the small cut with his sleeve. The child frowned but made no sound. There was another creaking from the ceiling, and more plaster fell. Glancing up, the man tucked the child inside his coat and turned. The bundle clutched firmly, he made his way rapidly across the room, speed rather than care the prerequisite now. He stooped to get through the low door, and as he did so, the beam of light from the torch in his free hand tracked over the shattered floorboards beneath him, penetrating well below the floor level of the crumbling building. The coat fell open and the child's eye was caught momentarily by a flash of something white, a brilliant chalk-white, deep in the foundations of the farmhouse. The child wasn't to know it, but his were the first eyes to look upon this symbol of ancient power in over a thousand years.

Chapter 1

A 1997

Dr. Will Cunningham felt slightly awkward as he looked at the carnage surrounding him. There was blood pretty much everywhere. Droplets hung from the curtains, a few splatters decorated the ceiling and rivulets trickled down the wall like peat-stained streams meandering their way off Dartmoor. There were ruby-red specks soaking into once pristine white sheets and several glinted off the glasses of the bewildered patient lying on the bed in front of him. Will turned his head, his nose wrinkling, as he regarded the young woman standing opposite him. She was the person responsible for a scene more akin to that found in an abattoir than a hospital. Her flecked cheeks were flushed, green eyes venomous, and her usually serene features were fused in a mix of acute embarrassment and barely controlled rage.

He reached into his pocket and pulled out a handkerchief to dab down his shirt, realising quickly that it was well beyond salvation as specks became streaks across his front. He sighed, putting it away, knowing that Infection Control would have issues with what had just happened and that the cleaners would be on overtime, but also that medical students had to learn, even if there were unpleasant consequences to that learning. They had to learn to contain themselves at all times, no matter what, even when provoked to their limit by well-intentioned senior house officers. They had to learn to remain professional and not let anything distract them from the task at hand. And, more pertinently, they had to learn that when injecting a syringe full of blood into a culture bottle, to depress the plunger with a slow, smooth, consistent pressure and definitely not slam it down with a temper-driven fist, causing the needle to separate from the syringe and coat anything within a two-metre radius in a fine, bloody mist.

Will smiled pleasantly at the patient. "I'm not absolutely sure that the culture will give reliable results after we have squeezed out the bed sheets," he said. "We should probably do them again."

The patient looked anxiously at the medical student and then back at Will.

"That is," Will continued, "I should do them again." He glanced over to the medical student. "Tamsin, why don't you go and borrow some scrubs from theatre? I'll meet you in the doctors' mess in a few minutes."

He watched her leave the cubicle, her shoulders tensed, her hands clenched and without so much as a "sorry" to the patient. Will hadn't meant to humiliate her to quite that extent, but if she didn't know that the minimum investigations for a patient with a pyrexia, that was to say an elevated body temperature, were a full blood count, liver, renal and C-reactive protein blood tests, with serial blood cultures, then she did now. She would also remember to stick to her original decision and not be swayed away from what she knew to be the correct clinical approach. In this instance, one that did *not* require a routine rectal examination. He reflected on his teaching methods as he parted the curtains to fetch some fresh blood bottles and decided that, in principle, they were sound. That's how you passed on both information and life lessons, wasn't it? It was how medicine had been taught from time immemorial until the present day, the eve of the new millennium. It created backbone and an ability to stand on your own two feet. It was how *he'd* been taught. All the same, he did feel uncomfortable about the whole situation particularly, he recalled a bit too late, given that she had been through tough times relatively recently. Anyway, best get on, no time for those thoughts now. His attention reverted to the patient, "Right, then," he said, "shall we try again?"

Grimacing, the patient nervously tendered his arm.

A short while later, the patient's blood dispatched to the laboratory, ap-
propriately contained, Will headed to the mess, stopping via theatre to get a
change of clothes. While, technically, theatre clothing was supposed to be for
those engaged in operative procedures, there wasn't the option of driving the
ten miles home to get a change of attire, so under such circumstances as Will
and Tamsin had found themselves, it was accepted that one could borrow some
scrubs. Will still retained several pairs of these back at the cottage after similar
incidents involving bodily fluids and made a mental note to try to return them at
some point. Such garments did, however, make great beach or painting clothes,
even pyjamas, so he was a little loath to return *all* of them. He bagged up his
soiled clothes and went to meet up with his errant charge.

The doctors' mess was on the seventh floor of the twelve that made up
the hospital and was situated just along from the canteen. Will took the stairs
rather than wait for the lift and the waft of cooking aromas got stronger the
closer to level seven he got. No time for a doughnut this morning though. He
heaved open the fire doors, wondering if their sturdy presence was less related
to fire prevention and more to deter frail patients from using the stairs and
consequently the services of the orthopaedic surgeons.

Two right-angled bends and he was halfway around the rectangle surrounding the central transit system and he'd reached the unmarked mess door. He
punched in the door code, which was also the pager number for the emergency
crash team, a number one wasn't supposed to forget, and entered the lemon-yel-
low, L-shaped room. There were doors at each end of the "L" and a bank of
telephones hung on the walls next to the doors. Four sofas, in various states of
disrepair, were positioned randomly around the room. There were chairs dotted
between the sofas and medical magazines piled neatly on windowsills, while
back copies of *Surf's Up*, the main UK surfing magazine, lay open on most of the
tables that filled the rest of the space. A vast French window provided stunning
views over Dartmoor and a reminder of why it was that he had chosen to work
in this part of the country. It led out onto a small outside balcony, which allowed
the potential for a breath of fresh air – well fresh as long as there wasn't a smoker
already in occupancy.

One such nicotine-dependent individual, now snoring with a newspaper resting on his chest, lay on the sofa nearest to the window. Headlines about genetically modified foods were clearly not enough to keep his good friend Godfrey Brown awake, though given what he was likely to have been up to the night before, Will suspected that very little would.

He'd had junior house jobs with Godfrey here at Whitehorse Hospital two years ago, before Will had left to work in Australia and New Zealand. Will had arrived back at Whitehorse and was genuinely pleased to find his old mate was still there. They had slipped easily back into their friendship despite no correspondence in their time apart. No matter that Will had been around the world twice, while Godfrey, it turned out, hadn't quite made it past Exeter. In fact, he still lived in the same doctors' residence, much to the frustration of the Scottish manager, Mrs Hammerock, with whom Godfrey had various ongoing differences of opinion over living arrangements. She felt *her* flats were purely a stopgap measure for young doctors before they grew up and moved out into the real world like proper adults. Residences were "*Not* to be viewed as a permanent home."

Godfrey, on the other hand, did not share this stance and had customised his flat in ways that suggested no intention to move... ever, and adaptations that would require more than a vacuum and some paint to restore it to the way Mrs Hammerock intended the flat to look.

He smiled at the balding, hook-nosed, cachectic individual, who undoubtedly still lived off a heady diet of cigarettes, Frey Bentos tinned pies and Jail Ale, also noting his continuing predilection for red theatre clogs.

Will left his friend to sleep off whatever vice he'd been indulging in the previous evening and looked around the room in search of his medical student. There were a few registrars and middle-grade doctors sitting having a coffee at one of the tables, while the more low-ranking staff, junior and senior house officers, crowded around a computer. They were, as usual, playing *Doom*.

Theoretically, the computer was there to look up blood and microbiology results for patients, but it was rarely used to that end, with the demand for the first-person, alien-based "shoot-'em-up" game taking precedent over more mundane matters such as abnormal haematology or biochemistry.

"Have any of you guys seen Tamsin?" Will asked, going over to the crowd encircling the chair.

A ginger-haired senior house officer, Corin, responded without taking his eyes away from the screen. "Which one is she?" he asked, his fingers paused over the keyboard. Then he turned to Will, face screwed up, with realisation apparently dawning, "Not that Trevelyan girl, the one involved in those, er, deaths? Do you mean her?" There was an unpleasant inflection in his tone.

"Yes..." Will replied cautiously.

Corin turned back to the screen just in time to see his character die in a haze of Beretta gun fire. "Damn," he cursed, then swivelled the chair, standing up to allow another of the junior surgical team to take his place. "No, she's not been up here, not in the last half hour, at any rate. She's not stirring things up again, is she?"

"Yes, I mean no," Will floundered. "Well, not really."

"Not really? That sounds more like a 'yes'!" He shook his head, "You'd have thought she'd have learned to keep her mouth shut and head down after the trouble that she caused a few months ago."

"It's nothing," Will found himself jumping to her defence, "we just have to get to a ward round that's all." Then something pricked at his conscience. He *should* have paid more notice to things he had been told about the other day and not be dropping her in it again. "But what do you mean, trouble?" As far as Will recalled, she'd had nothing to do with what happened – well, not directly at least. She hadn't been in 'trouble'?

Corin gave him a questioning look, "You don't know?"

"Erm," Will's response was non-committal.

"But you know about Jen, yes?" Corin asked. "The one who'd hit her head a while ago?"

Will sort of did; an anaesthetist, Jen O'Connor if he remembered correctly, had committed suicide after accidently giving a fatal overdose to a patient. That was the mostly the extent of it, he'd thought. It sounded horrific. The rest he had probably blanked out as he usually did. There were always tales of disaster doing the rounds and the job was hard enough without carrying someone else's mishaps with him.

"A bit," he replied.

"Well, you should know then that she made a very difficult situation a thousand times worse with her accusations, especially for Cadan. All that witchcraft nonsense!" he snorted.

OK, so he *had* blanked that bit out. Witchcraft? Cadan Metern? Will looked confused. He knew of the reputation of this Dr. Metern, a remarkable doctor by all accounts, though had yet to bump into him. But witchcraft...

"What she said about him was –" Corin continued, as his pager went off. He glanced down at the number as he finished his sentence, "– made-up, vitriolic swill. She is just walking trouble that girl." He grimaced, "Urrgh, got to go, the boss is on the ward," and began to walk quickly towards the door. "Catch you later."

Will's gaze followed him as Corin left quickly for the 6th floor. He found himself wishing that he hadn't been off on one of his daydreams when he was being given the now clearly quite pertinent details, relating to his new medical students.

The mess door opened with a slam.

"Where is the idiot anaesthetist who is supposed to be assisting me in Theatre Four?" said a remarkably irate, Will squinted – Mr. Coetzee from reading the name badge. He didn't know who this surgeon was but did have a suspicion regarding to which anaesthetist he was referring. He glanced over at the sofa. However, where Godfrey had been lying only moments before, there was now only an indentation, with a half-drunk cup of coffee standing next to it on the floor. Coetzee, grinding his teeth, was gathering himself like a leopard ready to spring.

A phone rang next to him but was picked up by one of the other doctors. The house officer blanched as he held the phone. "Mr Coetzee," he said, "Dr Brown is waiting for you in theatre and is asking where on earth you have got to. Everyone is apparently waiting to start." From the opposite end of the L-shaped mess, Will heard the soft click of a phone being put down and, looking in that direction, was just in time to see the door closing on a pair of red theatre clogs departing at a sprint.

Chapter 2

Will made his way up to the ward on the tenth floor. He brushed past the double doors, his voluminous scrubs top catching as he did so, and he wished he hadn't put on the first top and trousers he'd laid his hands on. The scrubs were an ill-fitting combination of trousers that were too short and a top that might have doubled as a marquee. He briefly wondered at the average body habitus of theatre staff that required the ordering of so many size forty-eight chest tops and twenty-nine-inch-leg trousers. Grunting, he detached himself and walked up the corridor past a couple of small interview rooms.

It was a ward like many others. The entrance corridor brought you to the main nursing station, with its array of telephones, computer equipment, pens, forms, and piles of stray notes. The notes trolley, where the notes were supposed to reside, was positioned at the far end of the oversized desk. The corridor met a T-junction and aisles disappeared off to the left and right. Each arm had five bays containing six beds and they were divided into 'males' and 'females'. These bays were, as always, filled with patients attached to a variety of machines, drips and, in some cases, large weights connected by pulleys to their legs. They ended in windows that might have offered patients a good view of the moor had they not been constructed halfway up the wall. Most patients, obliged to remain in the prone position on account of their broken limbs, were only able to stare forlornly at the perennially grey sky. For those patients who were mobile, he suspected that the views merely gave them further cause to lament their situation in the hospital and their inability to be off roaming the tors, those high granite outcrops, before them. Will gave an ironic smile as he realised that he had spent many hours standing by those same beds thinking the very same thing.

Standing outside one of the bays was a group of ten or so individuals mostly wearing either white coats, scrubs or nursing uniforms. One individual, a solidly built, man with a greying, full beard, wore a suit and loomed above this crowd. They, for their part, leaned forward, necks craned, all on tenterhooks, visibly flinching with each word he uttered. Today, Mr Stoneman, the consultant, was gracing them with his presence. He was an old-fashioned orthopaedic consultant. That was to say, he used to play a lot of rugby, was involved in the local rugby club, took days off to see the international rugby matches and did orthopaedic surgery because theoretically, it meant he could continue to talk rugby as part of his job. His patients either loved or hated him. Mainly hated. Most of his work, it had turned out, rather than fixing medial cruciate ligaments and shoulders in fit young sportsmen, had tended to be total hip replacements in eighty-year-old women. They didn't tend to follow the rugby and had no idea what being penalised for "handling in the ruck" was, but many felt that a three-point penalty didn't seem harsh enough for such an unsavoury driving offence.

Will had done a preliminary round with Dave Bolt, his registrar, at 8 am, before the morning surgery list had started, so he was reasonably sure there would be no chastisements for him today. He picked up his pace a bit and increased his breathing rate, blowing, to create the impression that he'd done everything to get to the ward round on time. Everything was under control, he knew the status of all of his patients, this would all be fine.

"What did you think you were doing changing the order on this morning's list?" bellowed Mr Stoneman, his whiskers shuddering as the words were expelled. Clearly then, Will had been wrong.

Stoneman glared at Will, whose eyes widened and mouth dropped wordlessly. "If you change the order, you let me know day or night." Another glare. "Got it?"

"Er, yes," said Will, still reeling. He hadn't spotted that one coming. All that he'd done was to alter the order of patients on the operating list by swapping Mrs Jago, who was very anxious and keen to get on with her right total hip replacement, with Mrs Dillan, who was to have a left total hip replacement but wasn't that fussed about getting it over with. He had sent the list down and made sure the change had been clear.

"I need to know whether I am operating on a Doris or an Edna and not be surprised with an Ivy," said Mr Stoneman. Doris, Edna and Ivy were not the actual names of patients, but Mr Stoneman's way of distinguishing between a repair to a right neck of femur fracture, a Doris, and a left, an Edna. Will had no idea what an Ivy was, but it was clearly quite surprising for Mr Stoneman.

"OK, I understand, Mr Stoneman," he said, aware of a subtle smirk on the faces of the assembled medical students, one in particular. There was no way Will would be calling his boss at 3 am to tell him of a list change and suffer even worse outbursts the following day because his boss was tired.

"And Dr Cunningham," said Mr Stoneman, looking Will up and down, "overestimating our physique somewhat, aren't we?"

Will looked down at the top hanging around his knees.

"Right let's get on. Who's first?" said Mr Stoneman. His chest beaten, frustrations vented, he loped to the end of one of the beds, knuckles scraping on the floor. At least in Will's head he did.

Surgical ward rounds were much swifter affairs than the medical ones. Surgeons generally preferred to see how their handiwork had fared and how it functioned, rather than engage with the organism upon which they had operated. This could be done, they felt, by getting the organism to use whatever had been repaired and then quickly move on after success had been demonstrated. Any opinion or conversation content outside this subject, particularly relating to the welfare of their husbands, grandchildren, or pets, would be greeted with a stiff indifference. The medics' ward rounds were the polar opposite. Those seemingly interminable twice-weekly occurrences could go on for six hours or more, sometimes without a break. Medical students, then the junior doctors, followed by the more senior registrars, would offer their thoughts and opinions on every single tiny case detail, and then, God help them, those of the patients were canvassed. Then the consultant would announce joyfully that they were all wrong, and to prove it, serial serum "rhubarb" levels were required and "would the house officer mind doing them every fifteen minutes for the next ten hours". Will had decided early on that he wasn't a medic. Mr Stoneman had, he deliberated, seemingly decided that Will wasn't a surgeon either.

An hour or so later, the ward round was over and there were jobs to do. Will set about showing the students how to fill in X-ray requests and blood forms. Then he went back to the patients from the ward round, who had questions about their case and enquires over who the rude man with the beard had been. A few of the students, including Tamsin, went to 'clerk' a patient: talk to them about what had happened to bring them into hospital. They then waited to present the case to Will. Will would then ask them questions about the patient, their management and what might happen with various scenarios around the case. Robert, a gangly, bespectacled student, went first and led Will to a bay where an eighteen-year-old lay. Robert explained how the youth had been swinging on monkey bars and come off, landing on his elbow, causing a displaced fracture to his distal humerus. K wires had been inserted, realigning, and stabilising the fracture. They looked at the X-rays, pre- and post-op, and discussed how long the wires would be in and what subsequent problems the youth might have.

Next was Jim, a mature student who balanced his medical studies with married life and a young family. He always looked weary. That wouldn't improve with qualification, thought Will, considering the additional sleep deprivation that he would incur as a houseman.

Lastly, he turned to the student standing apart from the group, at the end of the semicircle, Tamsin. She had taken his advice and changed into scrubs as well. Nobody looked their best in these loose-fitting, poorly shaped items of clothing, but she managed to carry off the grunge fashion with style. He couldn't help but notice how they clung to Tamsin's trim form. No such clothing size issues on the women's side then. That, or the prolonged search had been the reason for Tamsin's non-attendance in the mess.

"Now, Miss Trevelyan" – Will smiled patiently, turning to Tamsin – "would you like to tell me about Mrs Craven?"

To give her credit, she returned his smile, though it was visibly lacking in warmth. She described how Mrs Craven, an eighty-year-old lady, had had a fall and broken her right hip. It had been fixed with a dynamic hip screw and then she had been noted to have a persistent pyrexia on the ward round. Will smiled inwardly at the way the world had aligned to allow the reinforcement of lessons learned.

"I think we should re-X-ray her hip" – she looked up at Will – "and get an FBC, CRP, U and Es, LFTs," she said, her eyes seeming to intensify their deep green colour – did they have specks of amber in them? "And blood cultures."

"Are you happy to do that, Tamsin?" asked Will, his face completely deadpan. Tamsin nodded, raising an expectant eyebrow. "I'll notify Infection Control and the cleaning staff then," he said, looking down at the patient's notes, biting his lip furiously.

There was a stifled laugh from one of the other medical students, which received a whip-crack glance from Tamsin. Word of the morning's earlier events had obviously leaked out, but she kept her cool replying to Will, also delivering straight-faced, "If the good doctor is staying to supervise, shall I phone theatre for him and get them to send up a change of frock, or will he just pop along to the women's changing this time and perhaps get one that fits a bit better?"

There were more titters from the audience.

"I'm very sure that will not be necessary *this* time, Miss Trevelyan," he said, bowing his head in acknowledgement and beckoned for the remaining giggling medical students to follow him to the next bay.

Chapter 3

Will dropped fifty pence in the slot and the barrier lifted to let the Toyota Corolla Estate out of the staff car park. The maroon-coloured car joined the queue of traffic that led from the hospital onto the main moor-bound road. It wound down the side of the bare hill upon which Whitehorse Hospital was situated, past a distinctly malodorous chicken farm, into a wooded valley, where it picked up the road heading north-west. The curves in the road weren't severe, but Will couldn't help but think that the frequent turns wouldn't help patients travelling in the back of ambulances feel any better before reaching the doors of A & E. Once there though, Will considered, they seemed to survive well enough. In fact, Whitehorse Hospital was renowned for having astonishingly low mortality rates across the board in all specialities. The hospital's reputation was such that the Department of Health was always sending parties of experts to see what it was that Whitehorse was doing to make their statistics so good. To date, they hadn't come up with much, not even a fiddling of the figures. It couldn't, of course, just be the quality of staff that the hospital attracted, could it!

The drive to the cottage on the edge of Dartmoor was beautiful. It wasn't the awe-inspiring majesty of the mountains in New Zealand or the eucalyptus forests of Australia, but it had an ancient, mystical quality, which on spring days like today, sunny and warm, radiated a tranquil calmness; a calmness however, that belied the fickle and often unforgiving nature of the moor. Will knew that things could change in an instant. There were many legends surrounding those caught out on in wind, rain and snow, the turn of weather appearing seemingly out of nowhere, their lost souls trapped by a supernatural, maleficent power, to roam the bogs and tors for eternity. He shook his head free of these images and opened the windows, breathing in the coconut-smelling fragrance of the yellow flowering gorse that lined the roadside. Today was a mild, benign day, Dartmoor was in one of her better moods.

The village of Valtor lay ten miles away from the hospital, but it was the nature of the narrow twisting roads that the journey could easily take half an hour. A few wild daffodils poked their cowled yellow heads from within the Devon banks and the first delicate fan-shaped blooms of the purple ground ivy sought to trumpet their arrival. These were ancient hedges, constructed centuries ago by building a stone outer wall and filling the centre with mud, loose stones, and often general rubbish. Finding old leather hobnailed boots would not be an unusual discovery and bits of broken pot were commonplace.

Will drove along sedately, not only to take in the beauty, but also because driving down these lanes required one to have a certain understanding and caution relating to the road and other road users. Understanding, as there was only room for one car, and that often meant having to reverse a hundred yards or so into the nearest passing place. Caution, as Godfrey could well be that other road user coming the other way, possibly doing over sixty miles per hour.

He rounded the final bend before descending into Valtor proper. This small village was wedged in a valley between hills that ascended steeply up onto the open moor. At the top of one of these hills stood a fifteenth-century church, unusual in that it lay facing north-east along the line of the rising sun on the longest day, rather than the more traditional east–west. There was a babbling stream running through the middle of the village, its waters tinged a reddish brown from the peat in the bogs upstream. Once, the flow had been sufficient to power the mill that stood to one side of the stream, the renovated water-wheel testament to its history. Brown flowing fluid was still the stock-in-trade of the establishment, but it now came out of pumps connected to a bar and went by the name of Jail Ale or Tribute. The Old Mill was a popular village pub, especially with the numerous hospital staff living close by. It served traditional pub fare, and in winter a couple of roaring fires made the place a perfect stop after a walk on the moor.

Built into the side of the pub were a row of converted barns and cottages. They nestled into the Old Mill's structure as if trying to take refuge from the hostility of the moor. One of these cottages was 'Southside', and its newest residents were Will and Shauna. It was a rented cottage, and for the last decade or more it had been handed down through a succession of hospital doctors. Will approached and drew breath. Admission to the sanctuary of off-road parking required nerves of steel. It lay down a narrow, cobbled lane, bordered on one side by the uneven granite wall of the pub and on the other by a Devon bank possessing stony fingers stretching out to caress the careless or the tired. The few centimetres clearance from the hedge was comparatively plenty, however, when measured against the millimetres given by the gateway to the cottage. Two waist-high pillars waited, the myriad, coloured paint marks decorating them testament to too long spent on hospital wards with too little sleep. Will noted the fresh yellow hue, not dissimilar to that of the Astra parked in the gravel pit in front of the residence; Shauna was home. He braced himself for the literal rite of passage, considering that ironically, there were acres of room to park cars on the gravelled area in front of the house once the entrance had been negotiated.

Will stopped, put the brake on and got out. He looked at the whitewashed, Z-shaped cottage, which had clearly been at least two separate building in a previous existence. A barn conversion at one end was connected to the wall of the pub and what had been an L-shaped neighbouring cottage was joined to the barn with a much later extension. The barn conversion had been fitted with glass-fronted doors that opened onto a grassed area leading onto the gravelled forecourt. Around the walls were flower beds; a trowel and some bedding compost suggested that Shauna had been busy planting something pretty or tasty for the coming summer.

Will walked from the car, up to and through the pine-panelled kitchen door. He was *almost* getting used to the sensory assault that took place on setting foot over the threshold. The brown and lime-green seventies' wallpaper boggled the eyes, just as the heavy aroma of woodsmoke, mixed with damp and mildew, reached the back of the nostrils. The brown lino underfoot was ever so slightly tacky as he walked past the sink towards the barn end of the cottage, where he could hear Shauna practising her violin.

Shauna had been in the year below Will at medical school, and they had vaguely known each other through Will's sister, who had also been a medical student at St Georges. She had needed someone to share the cottage, and as she hadn't known anyone else at Whitehorse Hospital, she had asked Will if he would split the rent. He knew from his previous time at the hospital that the village was well liked by hospital SHOs; there were at least ten more living either in this village or the adjacent one, and he didn't have the same commitment to the residences that Godfrey had, so he had moved in.

Will opened the door to the large expanse of the 'barn' room. It was rectangular with high, blackened wooden beams. The once white walls had been darkened by time and smoke from an open fire. A sofa bed and a couple of armchairs surrounded the fireplace and a TV sat in the corner of the room. A piano, which had come with the property and was the main reason why Shauna had wanted to live in Southside, was positioned against a wall next to the door. Shauna, her fiery, auburn hair jerking backwards and forwards as she bowed, looked up as Will entered the room.

"Hello," she said, her Irish brogue betraying her origins, "a good day?" She put her violin down on top of the piano.

"Not too bad," he replied. "How's practice going?"

"Oh, you know, OK." She gave a depressed smile. "I'm not sure why I'm bothering though. I'll never get anyone to swap my on-call so that I can play in the concert."

"Well, you know I'd offer, but—"

"—But you're doing orthopaedics, and while I'd appreciate fewer patients, having you kill them off is probably not an acceptable way to achieve that."

"Well, I was going to say, but the personnel department aren't keen on cross-speciality cover, but you're probably right," he said. "How are we fixed for food?"

"There's a chicken pie in the oven if you'd like some. Ready in ten minutes."

"That would be brilliant," he said. "I'll cook next time."

"That you will," she said, picking her violin up again.

It was eight thirty when they finished their meal. Shauna, being Shauna, had not only cooked the chicken pie, but she'd also rustled up a quick apple crumble for dessert. She'd cleaned up as she'd gone along so there was practically nothing other than a few plates to wash up. Essentially the perfect housemate. There was a knock at the door, and in walked Godfrey.

"Anyone for a pint?" he asked.

"I could be persuaded," said Shauna, as she put the last of the plates back into a cupboard.

"And how may I be persuading you?" said Godfrey, mimicking her accent and affecting an impish grin.

"Well, I'd start by desisting from murdering my mother-tongue," she said, "and then by ordering me a Jail Ale please."

"To be sure, to be sure," he said, and Shauna launched the tea towel at him. He ducked, though it landed nowhere near him, and then looked in Will's direction.

"Might I be troubling you for something very similar, if not exactly the same," said Will, whose Irish accent was no better than Godfrey's.

"Why t'would be my pleasure," Godfrey replied, "especially if I might trouble you for the use of your wonderfully comfortable sofa rather than suffer the pains of supping but a single pint," he turned to Shauna.

"Oh Jesus," said Shauna getting her keys, "you realise that what you are doing is highly offensive and likely to get you hospitalised in the wrong company?" she informed them. "And deservedly so."

They looked at her blankly.

Shauna shook her head, "Yes Godfrey, you can stay the night, but any more of that accent and it'll be in the shed and not the lounge." Then, turning to Will, "And you'll be joining him!"

"Absolutely," they both replied, the lilt if anything even thicker.

A blackbird disturbed by the trio, fluttered into a nearby hawthorn tree twittering its alarm call as they made their way along the cobbled lane into the pub's car park. There was a grassy area on the bank of the stream with outside benches, for those wanting a bit of fresh air with their pint. The entrance to the pub was via an age-blackened solid oak door. A huge brass latch had to be raised slightly to allow passage over the well-worn threshold. It was warm inside, as it always was. Will had been here numerous times before his antipodean exploits, often when the temperatures outside were sub-zero. The granite walls and modern heating systems created a very welcoming environment. Will looked up, as most people did when they first came in. The beams of the high-vaulted ceiling still had the holes and indentations that marked where pulley systems had been used to move the grain, and subsequently flour, around the mill. He could see the large window at what would have been a second-storey height, where grain was hoisted in from outside. There was also the mezzanine, a prized sitting spot with comfortable leather armchairs from which the goings-on in the rest of the pub could be observed. Relatively new windows had been put in to look out over the stream, and tables were dotted throughout the lower floor. A few of these tables had been constructed from the old cross-hatched mill stones, while the rest were fairly rough-and-ready, wooden affairs. The bar was situated in the alcove where once the system of cogs and wheels had converted the energy of the stream into ground flour. Now all that remained were odd bits of angulated metalwork set into the wall.

Will saw that a couple of other members of Valtor's medical community had had a similar idea for the evening's relaxation. Either that, or Godfrey had rounded up the troops before he'd arrived at Southside. He headed over to the vacant seats where the two other doctors were sitting. Melanie was a medical SHO like Shauna and Kris a slightly overweight anaesthetist with a penchant for computer games. Godfrey disappeared off to the bar to fetch the promised drinks.

Kris grimaced as Will and Shauna sat down. "How did you fare with Mr Stoneman today?" he asked. No one had any secrets for long in the hospital community, and even though Kris was an anaesthetist rather than a surgeon, Will's somewhat tense relationship with his consultant usually made for rich entertainment for everyone, except, Will mused, for Will himself.

"I still think he resents the fact that I fence and surf rather than play rugby," said Will, ruefully.

"It's still sport," said Kris. "In his eyes, abilities in this field far outweigh any capability to do your job."

"Well, to an extent that's true," agreed Will. "But in my case, I don't think it counts for much, particularly as I sort of sold him a metaphorical dummy on my first day. We kind of got off on the wrong foot."

Kris raised an eyebrow.

"You see," Will continued, "he got all excited on our inaugural ward round when I told him that at med school, I had played fly half. When I added that I had a one hundred per cent rate for kicks for the whole season, he almost wet himself with excitement. He was lining me up to play for the Albion, and I maybe should have let him have his dream, the dream of the hours we would spend discussing miss-moves and a drift defence. However, I felt obliged to come clean, in case his misunderstanding ended up with the reality of me being chased around a muddy field by fifteen Plymouthian Neanderthals. So, I added that it was for the third XV and I had missed each of the ten kicks I took. The light in his eyes... well, it just died, and he hasn't given our relationship a chance since that," said Will, the corners of his mouth dropping in mock mournfulness.

"That's the thing about relationships," said Godfrey, returning with the beers, "one tiny misunderstanding, you do your best to correct it, trusting that the truth will smooth everything over in the end, and *bang*, you're dumped."

"Godfrey," said Shauna, "I hardly think that Will's relationship with Mr Stoneman is the same as yours with Jessica Whisper." Then looking at Will, "At least I hope it's not."

"No, it's not!" he replied indignantly, before adding, "Besides, I would never cheat on Mr Stoneman."

There were chuckles as Will took a drink from his pint. Godfrey lit a cigarette, inhaling deeply, then blew the smoke out of the corner of his mouth, away from the centre of the table. Shauna looked on disapprovingly.

"You didn't have a list today. Why were you in scrubs after lunch?" asked Melanie, looking in Will's direction.

"Oh, an incident involving a patient, some blood bottles and a particularly volatile medical student," he replied.

"Not *the* medical student?" said Melanie.

"The very same." Will took another sip. "To be fair, in retrospect, it probably wasn't entirely her fault. I may have pushed a little too hard in developing her as a doctor *and* as a person," answered Will.

"Oh!" said Kris sarcastically. "You have such an holistic approach to learning."

"I think that my duty is to impart life lessons as well as knowledge," said Will, trying to defend himself.

"You mean you feel it your duty to be obtuse, misleading and humiliating," said Melanie.

"You've been to one of my teaching sessions?" said Will.

"Teaching and particularly life lessons from you, I can probably manage without," she said.

"I think it's very important to weigh up the facts," said Will with false indignation, "decide on a course of action and be prepared to justify it. If you can be convinced that examining a patient's rectum is part of the work up for a pyrexia on an orthopaedic ward, against what you believe, then it's my duty to make sure you stick to your guns in future."

"So, you goaded her into doing a PR," said Godfrey, laughing. "Nice one."

"It's OK," said Will, amid horrified gasps from the onlookers, "I stopped her before she had actually put any jelly on the glove. And besides, when the syringe shot off the culture bottle a bit later on, the patient took that incident much better as a consequence of not having had to drop his pants earlier."

"Oh right, so blood everywhere – that explains the scrubs," said Mel.

"Yes, that explains the scrubs," echoed Will.

"You are a bastard," said Shauna. "I'm not surprised Tamsin exploded! There are other ways to teach than by humiliation you know."

"Never did me any harm," said Will.

"Really?" said Shauna, raising an eyebrow.

Will's face twitched, mimicking a nervous tic. "Well, maybe just a little bit."

"Seriously, Will," she continued, "don't you think you might have eased up on the girl, given what she's been through recently?"

"Yes, I suppose so," said Will, pausing with his pint at his lips. "The thing is, I don't *really* know what went on, so knowing where to draw the line with my particular teaching style is a tad difficult."

"Will, you never have had any concept of where lines might exist under normal circumstances," said Shauna.

"Exactly," said Will, pensively, "so I don't think I can necessarily be blamed for her reaction today." He wasn't convincing even himself. "I mean, I got told a few details from her tutor, like she was good friends with the anaesthetist who well, accidentally killed a patient. Jen O'Connor, was that her name?"

"Yes, that's right," confirmed Shauna, with a grimace.

"And then she... I guess... couldn't live with the consequences...?" Will suggested, adding, "It's really poor that no one thought about her though, perhaps get to her in time to stop her."

Shauna and Godfrey exchanged looks.

"Well..." said Godfrey, hesitating, "that's sort of just it." He inhaled on a freshly lit cigarette, pausing to collect his thoughts. "You see Tamsin was the last person to see Jen alive," he said.

Will flinched.

Godfrey screwed up his nose, looking uncomfortable with what he was about to say. "From what I understand to have happened," he said, "Tamsin had spotted Jen leaving the hospital car park in a distraught state. At that point she didn't know what had happened but recognised her friend's distress and jumped into her own car to follow, finally catching up with her on Plymouth Hoe. Apparently, they spoke, Jen explained what she had done and Tamsin persuaded her to go back to the hospital. They were in separate cars so agreed to meet up, back at Whitehorse. However, Tamsin got stuck in traffic and, when she did get back, a considerable time after Jen, she ran around the hospital only to be told that her friend had been found dead down in the basement, next to the mosaic."

Will's blood ran cold, "God, that sounds awful," he said, suddenly appreciating why Tamsin might be struggling to control her temper.

"Perhaps it is an excuse for what happened next," Mel jumped in, "though, perhaps not; it certainly didn't help. Obviously, the police got involved, and it was then that Tamsin made all sorts of allegations against Cadan Metern – you know the obs and gynae reg?"

"Mmm, sort of," said Will. "But what sort of allegations?" he asked, remembering what Corin had said.

"Black magic, satanic rituals, child sacrifice, poisoning, all very unpleasant stuff," said Godfrey, stubbing out the cigarette as it hit the filter.

"What?" said Will. "That sounds very, very odd. Very unlikely."

Godfrey extinguished the last embers and shrugged, "Tamsin maintained that Jen had witnessed Cadan Metern dressed up in some strange costume or other, plunging knives into defenceless infants." He reached into his pocket to light up another cigarette, got a glare from Shauna, then thought better of it.

"Really?" Will puffed out in disbelief.

"I'm just telling you what has done the rounds on the rumour mill." Godfrey gave a flattened smile.

"So, Tamsin made these allegations based on what?" Will asked.

"Based on a conversation with Jen shortly before she died," replied Godfrey.

"And was there any truth to what she had said? I cannot see how there could be." His mind tried to process the information, "And why hadn't Jen gone to the police with what she had seen?"

"Well," said Shauna sighing, "that would be because of Jen's behaviour after her head injury *and* the fact that Jen had been in a relationship with Cadan. No one knew quite what was the truth, and what was the result of concussion... or perhaps malice. She had been doing and saying odd things generally."

"Yeah, like when she tried to swim across the harbour in a snowstorm," Kris interjected, "or popping over the outside 3rd floor balcony to get to cardiology rather than take a more conventional route like the lift."

"And that she said that she was 'damned anyway', so why worry?" added Godfrey. There was a regretful, pained look on his face. "She should have been cared for better," he muttered, "*especially* after her injury."

"Yes," agreed Shauna, frowning, "it *did* all seem to start after her *accident*."

Will narrowed his eyes at the unconvincing emphasis on accident.

"You know," she looked at Will, "after she had fallen and hit her head on the stairs, running to an arrest call?"

Will didn't.

"A proper crack she gave it, as well as sustaining a nasty ankle fracture,' continued Shauna, "and supposedly she would have been in a much worse way had Cadan Metern not come along *just* as it happened."

"They reckon his swift actions made all the difference to her recovery though. Maybe even saved her life," said Kris.

"Mmm, maybe," hummed Shauna again, "I won't deny that given how serious the fall sounded, she recovered very, very quickly – from a physical point of view at any rate." She still sounded doubtful.

"I always thought it was a bit odd that she was running to an arrest *down* the stairs that led to the mosaic in the basement," mused Godfrey. "I mean that's literally the bottom of the hospital; those stairs don't go anywhere else. The arrest was on the 5th floor."

Shauna nodded her agreement.

Will's brow furrowed.

There was a prolonged silence.

"So, it was assumed that whatever she might have said," Kris picked up the main thread of the conversation again, "was just part of her brain's er," he stumbled over his words, "recovery process."

"Which is why what Tamsin said and alleged was not really taken seriously either," Will surmised.

The others nodded.

"They did investigate around the mosaic and in the basement," said Shauna, "where Tamsin says Jen had witnessed the odd goings-on, but with the thorough, deep-cleaning policy that the hospital has, even if there were anything to find to support such claims, it wouldn't have been there anymore. And they didn't take it any further."

"Last orders at the bar," the barman called across the room.

Kris shot out of his seat, "One for the road anyone?" he offered.

A 1948

The young boy hid in the bracken, watching the gathered brethren dance 'sky-clad' around the dying fire. Hands linked, their chant drifted out like mist across the tors, blanketing the hills and valleys of the moor that surrounded them. The circle spun, once clockwise, thrice anti-clockwise, one clockwise, thrice anti-clockwise, spinning, binding, invoking the elemental spirits and summoning the Goddess. Occasionally an individual would break free and run through the heart of the flame, shrieking, to emerge seemingly untouched on the other side, testament to Her power.

The boy had been frightened and had run, fleeing from the sabbat, pulling away from his aunt, whose nails had raked down his forearm in a vain attempt to stop him. He rubbed the arm and then wiped a tear from his cheek. He knew it would mean the birch when the light of the morning sun had burned away the darkness. Then he would be told again of the sacrifice that his parents had made, the ultimate sacrifice, for his benefit as well as for that of all humanity.

He must not turn his back on the 'old ways' of the past, for they were also the future, his future. The boy shook his head and scowled. That fire was hot and would hurt; walking across the firepit to make some goddess who you could not see, or touch made no sense whatsoever. It was stupid. It wasn't just an interest in the "new ways" that told him that, it was his own observations, it was science like he'd learned about in school. Fire was hot it burned; you could experience that. Gods and goddesses were made up and he didn't believe in them. So, he hid as his aunt cast ferocious glances into the darkness.

Chapter 4

The following morning was a Saturday, and Godfrey had picked up the phone to find out what the surf conditions on the north Cornwall coast were like. The Ann's Cottage surf report line was generally fairly accurate, though prone to a certain amount of exaggeration, no doubt to draw in a bit of extra trade. Ann's Cottage was a petrol station in Polzeath that sold a few wetsuits as a side-line but had got fed up with people phoning them to get advice on surf conditions, so it had taken to having the report as their answerphone message.

"Five foot and clean with a light offshore wind," he said, putting the phone down.

"Perfect, let's go then. Shall I drive?" asked Will, knowing full well the answer he would receive. Godfrey pursed his lips, shook his head, and Will went to get his kit to put in his friend's Volvo.

Godfrey's car was a testament to fine Swedish engineering and its ability to cope with anything the driver put it through. In Godfrey's case, that would be sandy beaches, forded Dartmoor streams, muddy farm tracks and the occasional hedge. The exterior of the car was remarkable for having its own ecosystem. Lichen and moss grew out of the wing mirrors and there was a spider living in the left one that must have travelled over seven thousand miles. The car's exterior was officially listed as being white. The interior was, if anything, marginally less well looked after than the exterior. Cigarette cartons, crisp packets and fast-food remnants littered the floor. The leather seats were scuffed and had dubious stains, the origins of which one didn't ask about. What it lacked in sanitation and adequate hygiene however, was made up for by a fantastic stereo system. Godfrey had invested in a minidisc player with top of the range Bose speakers, and by his own admission he had *the* best taste in music. It ranged from Oasis and Blur to Irish folk music, with a bit of Dolly Parton and Simon and Garfunkel thrown in. It was difficult to disagree with him, given he almost certainly possessed some music to your taste too.

"How's your strumming coming on?" asked Will, by way of conversation, as Godfrey wheel-spun up the cobbles of the lane. He was never sure if talking to Godfrey when he was driving was a good idea. On the one hand, if he was talking about music, he tended to drive that much slower. On the other, it did mean he wasn't fully concentrating on the road when travelling at a still ludicrous speed.

"Really well actually," replied Godfrey, who listed guitar amongst his talents.

"I've worked out all of 'Stairway to Heaven', and I reckon it sounds OK." He didn't feel the need to read music just picked up the guitar and played until it sounded how he wanted it to.

"Have you got enough for a set?" asked Will.

"Probably," he replied, "enough for an hour or so at least," he replied, "but no band members yet."

"You know Shauna is a violinist, don't you?" pointed out Will. "*You* play a lot of Irish stuff, I've heard you, but it clearly cries out to have someone playing the fiddle."

"I vaguely mentioned it a while ago," said Godfrey, "but she's classically trained and a bit worried it would ruin her bowing."

Will nodded sagely, as though he understood what Godfrey meant, though he wasn't completely convinced that Godfrey really understood the complexities of bowing either.

"Why don't you try asking again?" he asked. "I know she's having to give up the city orchestra because of her on-call rota. She can never get to the practices. Besides, she can't run away from her heritage forever."

"It's probably not the heritage thing she's likely to be running away from," said Godfrey, smiling ruefully. "But yes, there is the coming from Killarney thing, being a musician and the red hair."

"So, why don't you ask her again?"

"I'm not sure I've been forgiven yet," said Godfrey, the car's speed picking up a bit. Will's grasp on the armrest tightened.

"What, of the many things that you have said and done, do you feel has particularly upset her now?"

"The hair thing."

"Oh, the hair thing," said Will, remembering their most recent, and quite drunken trip to the Old Mill. Shauna was, it had been noted, a little sensitive about her hair. "Yes," said Will, as more details from the evening surfaced in his memory. "A small apology perhaps?"

"Look, I meant it as a compliment, whatever you think – it was a compliment!" insisted Godfrey.

"You compared her hair to your favourite brand of marmalade," said Will.

"I really do like that marmalade," said Godfrey, the corners of his mouth turning up.

"Yes, but pulling the twigs from her hair and suggesting you especially liked the thick shred did strike a bit of a nerve, didn't it?"

"Next time she will bring a torch so that we don't all walk into a hedge though, won't she?" said Godfrey.

They rounded a bend and The Mouls came into view. This basalt island lay about a mile out into the bay, and on big swell days the waves could be seen crashing against its dark granite edge. This attritional force was what had created a series of small inlets that had once been a drop-off point for smugglers. Wreckers had also lured ships onto the jagged rocks, The Rumps, that jutted out from the mainland like blades of obsidian. On top of this twin headland promontory sat an Iron Age fort complex with the Guglane Caves beneath. Will shivered. Basalt was such a bleak, forbidding rock, he thought. The car drove into the hamlet that was Polzeath, past Ann's Cottage petrol station. Nine-foot yellow foam surfboards leaned against the outside of the building alongside wetsuits of varying sizes. Selling petrol and doing a few car repairs in a small seaside hamlet was obviously not paying all of the bills. They passed a small grocery store on the opposite side of the street and then passed over a small bridge. The beach, and in the distance the sea, was on their right. The tide was fully out so there was an area of beach free to park on, and Godfrey pulled to a stop in front of the Ship Cafe. The tide wouldn't reach this far up the beach for six hours or so, so they had plenty of time. Timing errors did occur and cars had been caught out, but it was tourists and not locals who had to explain the circumstances to the insurance companies. Tourists and, on one notable occasion, very nearly a Godfrey.

They got out of the car, stretching as they gazed out along the vast sandy expanse to the sea in the distance.

"Well, at least it won't be quite as far to walk back," Godfrey observed.

"Nope," replied Will. "Last wave should land us right back at the car."

"Er, I'm planning to get back a little sooner than that time," said Godfrey. "Water lapping against the tyres was a trifle close."

They pulled the plastic suit-box from the back of the estate and changed, towels providing intermittent modesty. The wetsuits were done up with a zip at the back and it was traditional to help your surf-buddy out by doing it up for him. A hairy back almost always provided too much temptation.

"Sorry, mate," said Will, as Godfrey yelped. "Zipper accidentally caught a few."

"'Course it did," he replied. "May I return the favour? Doing up your wetsuit, I mean?"

Boards retrieved from the roof rack, the urge to get to the sea was such that they broke into a jog down the beach. The soft sand underfoot firmed up as they got closer to the water, and Will felt the coolness of the water seep through to his neoprene-booted feet. Away from the lee of the cliffs and coastline, on the edge of the water, the wind blew briskly, and Will shut his eyes, feeling the silky soft sensation of it as it passed over his skin and through his hair. It seemed to charge him in a paradoxically relaxing kind of way. He opened his eyes again, looking out to sea, watching the waves. Godfrey stood next to him, but Godfrey's closed eyes, he suspected, were less to do with spirituality and more to do with a lack of sleep. He nudged Godfrey, who opened his eyes and shook his head.

"Woah, nearly dropped off there. Are we ready to go?"

"Seriously, you either need to get more shut-eye or have your narcolepsy investigated," said Will. "And to think I let you drive."

He bent down to do up his leg leash and Godfrey did likewise. They looked for a smaller set of waves to come in to make an easier paddle out, wading into the shallows. When they were deep enough, and had got the timing right, they launched themselves in unison onto the top of their boards and paddled out into the white-water. Arms extended in front crawl fashion, they pulled themselves through the surf, the rhythm only broken to duck-dive under the breakers.

Getting beyond the waves was energy sapping, requiring determination and, if the surf was big enough, no small amount of courage. Set after set of waves pounding on top of you, attempting to flip you over or hold you under; there was barely enough time to draw breath. It could be quite a fight unless you read the sea and the currents. Once past the break line though, there was the peace and calm of being "out back". Here, you could lie or sit on your board and feel the swell that had travelled thousands of miles gently lift you up and smoothly set you down, lulling away all cares and thoughts until it was time to ride.

It was a relatively easy paddle out today, and Will wasn't out of breath as he sat astride his six-foot-six short board. He watched the scintillations of the approaching wave, the light reflecting transiently off the ripples on the water's surface. It disappeared underneath him and his eyes followed it, seeing it rise as the wave formed, flecks of white appearing at the top when it appeared to almost halt, then the crash and spray of it breaking. His eyes flicked back automatically to look for the next one coming in. It was hypnotic.

There was a splash and he turned to see an equally mesmerising sight, but in a very different way. Godfrey had paddled through his final wave and was now pushing himself up to sit on his board. Beneath him, the board's none-too-subtle pattern of a semi-naked woman created images in Will's head he really didn't need. Godfrey had received a certain amount of stick in the past for the design, but he adamantly maintained that he had bought it second-hand for the quality of the board's manufacture, and for that reason and that reason alone. He was blowing slightly with the effort, but the ruddiness of his complexion probably owed more to his fair skin and the weather than his exertions.

"Sun cream?" asked Will.

"Ummm, no," said Godfrey. "Good thing to have remembered about ten minutes ago though."

"Yes," said Will.

They sat for a while, constantly scanning the horizon, watching the incoming sets, looking to see where the wave was likely to break. You needed to be in the right spot. Too far off the break point and the waves passed under you. Too close in and the wave landed on top of you, and you got munched. Pick your wave and time the acceleration of your paddle to match the speed of the wave. Pop up, take the drop, carve your turns and enjoy the ride.

Will looked back again and there it was, time to get going. The swell rose and the wave started to crest. It was quite a big wave, Will thought, really quite big, but he'd committed now. Flat on his stomach, he began to paddle, gradually increasing his speed to get up to that of the incoming wave. He glanced behind him... Woah, really very big. No bailing out now, that would be disastrous.

"Paddle, paddle, paddle," yelled Godfrey, "and whatever you do, don't look back!"

With as much explosive force as he could muster, Will took off. How big must this wave be, he thought to himself as he heard a shriek from his friend. Rapid, powerful strokes pulled him forward, the pointed nose-end of the board cutting through the water. He could hear the wave approaching, feel its face rearing up behind him lifting the back of the board and propelling him forward. Don't look back. From lying on his stomach, in one smooth move he pushed up on his arms and swung his legs under him into a sideways crouch position.

He stole a quick glance at the wall of water behind him. Yep, much bigger than anticipated.

The power of the wave forced the board firmly into his feet, and he was up, OK, not really up, but rescuable, just a small adjustment to his centre of gravity and... uh oh... not rescuable then! He wasn't fully balanced; his glance was going to cost him, and he felt his weight tip forward. It was fractional but enough. The front of the board disappeared under the surface and Will felt a slight panic as he knew what was coming next. He drew his last lungful of air for what might be some time. The mass of water underneath him thrust against the back of the board, as the nose stopped abruptly and Will was catapulted, headfirst, into the base of the wave. The impact drove the air out of his chest and seawater filled his senses. It pulled at his eyelids, roared in his ears, pummelled his body, its salty taste in his mouth. There was no up, no down; they were both the same. He drew his arms up to protect his head and braced, locking them like a roll cage. Somewhere above him was a twelve-kilogram lump of fibreglass travelling at speed, and it would be landing very shortly within the metre radius of his leash... and his head. He waited, and waited, then felt a jerk on his leg. The board had re-entered the water and hadn't added injury to insult. Tumbling over and spinning around, he remained frozen in his protective position, holding his breath until the wave was done with its plaything.

It was probably only a matter of seconds but felt a considerably longer time, especially when his lungs started to burn, but finally the beating stopped, and he floated in the direction now re-designated as up. He hit the surface, gasping, wiping his hands over his face to clear the water from his eyes. He knew he had no time to catch his breath, however, unless he fancied another rinse/spin cycle, and he needed to get back on his board quickly. Reaching down to his right leg, Will felt for the leash, and having located it, he pulled hard until the board appeared on the other end. He jumped on, turning the board to face into the oncoming wave as he did so. Just in time, he threw his weight onto the nose, duck-diving under the wave, and held it down for a couple more seconds, then resurfaced hoping to regain some measure of control. Two more waves hit; he ducked under them, and with a last effort, he surfaced beyond the break, back to the calm of the open sea.

Will lay on his board and saw Godfrey appear from underneath a wave. He had obviously caught a more manageable one after Will and fared significantly better, though Will could see that his supposed friend was laughing so much he was struggling to stay on his board as he paddled.

"Oh, fuck off," said Will, who hadn't yet recovered the energy to do anything other than drape himself on top of the board and moan obscenities.

"That was hilarious," said Godfrey as he came level with Will. "The look on your face as you realised that you'd got that all wrong. Priceless!"

Will just lay there, bobbing up... and down.

As with most things when they go wrong, it takes a degree of courage to try again. A thorough rinsing, such as the one Will had just endured, might have knocked his confidence and perhaps persuaded him to go for something a bit smaller and easier. But Will was an experienced surfer, which meant making the same mistake with more certainty. So, he waited for a few sets to go through before carefully picking out another seven-foot wave to fall off.

It took a while before Will felt a bit more in tune with conditions. A small and friendly looking four-foot wave trundled along, and Will once again lined up his take-off point and paddled furiously, fully committing to the wave this time, no worried backward glances, no checking that the wave wasn't just going to dump on top of him. Just commitment. He felt the rear of the board lift and he popped up, landing solidly this time, watching forward as he plunged down the wave's face. He rode "regular" rather than "goofy", which meant his left foot was forward, so he pulled his weight back a fraction onto his right leg and pushed the edge of the board, leaning into the wave. The fins in the base of the board cut through the water and the nose came sharply around to face up the wave face and the board carved its turn. He shot back up the wave, then carved another turn at the top, this time dipping the right edge into the top of the wave. The wind clutched at his hair, flicking salty strands into his eyes as flecks of spray pattered into his face. He took a final turn and allowed the board to fly along the wave face, always just escaping the white-gloved clutches of the roaring wave behind him. His body and mind fizzed with the exhilaration of truly being alive. This was what it was about, this feeling, this explosion of sensations, this complete "oneness" with the sea.

They spent three hours in the water with only the waves to think about. It was a complete escape from the hospital, release from the incessant screech of a pager, the ping of machines and the bellow of an unnecessarily irate boss. All that occupied Will's being was the next wave. Where was it, where did he need to be to catch it and when to come off to avoid too much paddling through the white-water. Every second or third wave, the pair would meet up out back to laugh at wipe-outs or talk through near misses. Godfrey appeared to be particularly on song today as he caught wave after wave, without the errors in judgement or technique to which Will seemed to be prone.

The last ride in was traditionally one they would both try to catch. It did, of course, have to be the biggest wave, and there was a right of veto. This meant, almost invariably, that actually getting the last ride in could take some considerable time. There would be a debate, floating side by side, about whether it was big enough, whether the next one in the set was bigger, or whether the other's genitals had gone missing because a wave had been judged too difficult. Finally, either agreement was reached, or the veto didn't come in quickly enough and two separate waves were caught. On this occasion they managed to agree. Paddling swiftly in unison, they both popped up onto the boards and stood, grinning at each other, as the wave carried them towards the shore. It broke, and they bounced around in the white surf before dropping to lie on their stomachs, the last of the wave's energy bringing them onto the beach. Will jumped off his board and tucked it under his arm before the board's fins incurred any damage, and he saw that Godfrey had done the same. They walked back through the shallows, water pushing at their legs, then bent to undo the Velcro of the ankle leash, which gave with a satisfying rip.

The walk back to the car was half what it had been, but it still seemed like a significant distance to Will's tired body. Godfrey, however, almost skipped along beside him. Will could never quite work out how it was that despite the fact that Will was the one who went running, fenced and played cricket, it was the essentially sedentary, pie-eating smoker who always looked the fitter after a three-hour surf. It wasn't that Godfrey didn't catch as many waves, he did, and surely it wasn't technique, was it? Will concluded that half drowning on his first wave had probably taken an unnecessary toll on his stamina and resolved not to go too big too soon in future. Maybe a change in diet and lifestyle as well.

Across the road from the beach was a toilet block and a rudimentary shower poking out from the side. It was a cold shower, colder than the sea, but fine for rinsing off salt water and cleaning the suits. Will turned on the tap and stood underneath it before taking a deep breath and undoing his zip. The icy water hit his skin, and there was a strange burning sensation before it went completely numb. He hurriedly pulled off his wetsuit, to leave him standing in trunks and neoprene boots.

"I can't imagine why it is you find it so hard to find a girlfriend," observed Godfrey dryly. Will stepped out from under the shower and looked down.

"You step under this icefall and see if 'little Godfrey' fares any better." He rinsed off the wetsuit and offered his place to Godfrey, who was getting out of his own suit.

"Do you know what?" said Godfrey, his face scrunched as though he were chewing a lemon. "I think I may give the waterboarding torture a miss this time." He stripped off his suit outside the shower and dangled it half-heartedly into the stream of water.

"Explains one or two of the odours in your car, I suppose," said Will.

"And the stains," said Godfrey.

"All of the stains?"

"Not quite."

"I won't ask."

"Best not."

Godfrey held his suit at arm's length, and a trail of sandy water followed him as they crossed the road and made their way back to the car.

Another tradition, established as junior doctors, was that of enjoying a post-surf chilli, cheese and chips from the Ship Cafe. This cafe nestled into the cliff on the left-hand side of the beach, protected from the prevailing south-westerly winds. It therefore provided warm shelter as they sat on the wall outside in board shorts and hoodies, tucking into a mound of chips covered in minced beef, chilli sauce and melting cheese covering the top. It very much hit the spot, washed down with a large mug of sweet tea or, on this occasion, hot chocolate, and they sat, red-faced, a serene sense of calm enveloping them. There was no more beautiful place in the world than Cornwall on a warm, sunny day. Granted this tended to be the exception rather than the rule, with 'liquid sunshine' a more frequent weather condition as the Southwest took the brunt of whatever the Atlantic sent. But that was what created the stunning landscape and gave it its rugged beauty, which made your heart sing on days like this.

Will mopped up the final spots of sauce from his plate with his last chip. "We should organise a surf trip," he said, putting it into his mouth.

"What do you mean?" asked Godfrey.

"Well, we should book a backpackers' hostel and get a whole lot of us out for the weekend."

"Sounds like an idea," said Godfrey. "Where did you have in mind? I'm not sure Polzeath could cope with a Whitehorse invasion."

"How about Newquay?"

"Newquay would be great. Good surf, good pubs and a bit of nightlife," said Godfrey, shooing away a gull as it landed next to him.

"OK," said Will. "Let's put the word out and see who would like to come." They swigged the last dregs from their cups, and binning their rubbish, they made their way back to the car.

Chapter 5

Monday arrived all too soon. Will awoke and, staring at the Artexed ceiling, contemplated what was going to be a busy week. Depressingly, he was on call for the Monday and the weekend. That meant taking the calls from the general practitioners and accepting referrals from A & E, as well as doing all of the usual duties. He admitted patients to the ward if required and, having stabilised them, they were then reviewed by the registrar before being prepared for surgery. All manner of fractures could come his way; if there was a bone, people would find a way to break it. A significant proportion of his work, however, came in the form of those little old ladies who had broken a hip bone, the neck of their femur. They were often referred to as NOFs. The fracture itself was relatively simple to fix, but these ladies often had multiple co-morbidities and were on an orthopaedic surgical ward, where, Will had found, knowledge and understanding conditions outside broken bones was a bit "hazy" for the senior staff. In fact, the more senior, the hazier such knowledge was. It fell to Will, therefore, to make sure that while these little old ladies had their bones fixed, they also got to make it out of the hospital with no deterioration of their diabetes, heart failure or respiratory disease. Part of this entailed trying to rationalise the numerous medications that these ladies brought in. Tablets were religiously brought along by these patients when they were admitted, which they knew were necessary to treat their medical conditions. What these conditions were, the exact details on their drugs and how they were supposed to take them, was not infrequently something of a mystery to them. Will suspected that it was a certain random attitude towards this medication that was probably responsible for their hospital attendance in the first place. Some he had known had openly admitted to having a bowl on the living-room table into which they put their medications. Then, a few times a day, they would take a handful and wash them down with a nice cup of tea or, if evening approached, perhaps a small sherry.

Lying in bed wasn't going to make the week go any quicker. Will looked at the clock. Damn, he was already running late. He showered quickly, deciding to skip breakfast then jumped into his car, avoided scraping the gate, and shot off up the road out of the village. The normally beautiful drive to work now turned into a snaking, stop-start, tyre-depleting ordeal, and that was before reaching the queues on the main roads proper. Scenarios began running through his head, ways in which he might arrive on time, but he had really cut things fine this morning and that looked increasingly unlikely. Having run through the 'on time' scenarios and dismissed them as now impossible, he moved on instead to the excuse scenarios, but as he did so, he felt an unease, and images of his car by the side of the road formed in his mind – was he driving too quickly? Was he going to crash? He checked his speedometer; he was only doing thirty miles per hour. His foot went to hover over the brake... then the car started to lose power, the engine cut out completely and he realised that excess speed wasn't going to be the issue here. He snorted to himself – how ironic. It was all very well having a heightened sense of foreboding, but a second before the event was stuff all use. The good news was that he was on a downhill section of road and there was a car park at the bottom into which he would be able to coast before his momentum ran out.

Will got out of the car and then he did what you did under these circum-stances; he went to look under the bonnet. Will was reasonably sure that what he was looking at was an engine. That was, however, the full extent of his knowledge. Humans he could fix. Cars, no idea. He was a bit stuck, and he was trying to decide on what to do next, when a white Peugeot 309 Style pulled into the car park. Tamsin wound down the car's window and he walked over.

"Would you like a lift?" she asked. Was there a little frostiness in the tone?

"Um, yes please," he replied. Tamsin's impassive face hinted that her good Samaritan actions night well be at odds with her internal desire to just drive on. Not completely forgiven for the previous week's teaching session then. He retrieved his white coat from the back of the Toyota, which contained the tools of his trade: his stethoscope: a tourniquet for taking bloods and an assortment of loose bits of paper with patients' names on, then locked his car. He smiled at Tamsin, without reciprocation, and got in.

"Thanks, I owe you one," he said, putting the belt on, "I was wondering how I might get in today."

"You owe more than one," he thought he heard her say under her breath. He wasn't exactly sure what she meant, or even whether he was supposed to have heard her, so he settled on looking around the car. He was struck by the fact that there were no wrappers or drink cans littering the interior and that he could see the floor. There was a string of coral and cowry shells dangling from the mirror that jangled slightly as the car moved off. It also smelled, well, pleasant, in direct contrast to both his and Godfrey's cars. That, however, was where pleasant atmospheres ended; Tamsin's jaw was set rigid.

"I'm really grateful that you stopped," said Will, repeating the sentiment, hoping a little conversation might break the tension and prevent him ending up in the windscreen. She wheel-spun the car out of the parking area and he grabbed involuntarily at the seat as they took off up the road. It was almost as frightening as having Godfrey at the wheel. Almost, but not quite.

"No problem," said Tamsin, and she left the silence hanging.

"I'm on take today and already a bit late. I suppose this will at least give me a legitimate excuse," Will continued, uncomfortably. Maybe she just wasn't a morning person. His eyes tracked around the car again, looking perhaps for a subject of neutral conversation: leather seats, roadmap in the side pocket, lipstick by the dashboard, the way Tamsin's skirt had ridden up, revealing a well-toned, very shapely, tanned thigh. He realised that his gaze had lingered rather longer than was acceptable and his head snapped forward. Oh, that's really going to smooth the situation, he thought, getting caught copping a look. Brilliant! Fortunately, Tamsin had been concentrating on the driving and just flicked a puzzled glance at the sudden movement. Will decided that the air needed clearing.

"Er, look, I'm sorry about last week," he said. "I may have been a little..." – he searched for the correct word – "... overzealous."

She turned fully this time and looked at him, fury burning in her eyes.

"Overzealous!" The word was growled back at him.

Overzealous was probably not the correct word then.

"I mean, what I did was perhaps a little... unfair."

"Unfair?" She spat.

"Yes."

"In what way do you consider that your so-called teaching method was 'unfair'?"

"Well," Will blustered, "I might have got a bit carried away, and—"

Tamsin interrupted him, apparently having had enough flannel. "—And decided that humiliating me was a perfectly acceptable way to pass an otherwise tedious half hour."

"Well, not exactly. I was trying to make you trust in yourself and what you've learned. Not get thrown by erroneous suggestions."

"Oh really!" she said.

"Yes, really," replied Will, not even convincing himself.

"You seriously think that the way you went about teaching me about pyrexial patients, i.e., by humiliating me in front of them, was a good way of imparting information?"

"You seemed to remember the next time I asked you about it," Will pointed out. Tamsin shot him a glance. Wow, quite scary! "OK, point taken."

"And how many of your mates have been educated by your story?" she asked. "Cos it's important that they learn too, I suppose."

Will winced. "Ummm."

"Yes, thought so."

"Sorry," he said.

"Oh, you've got a way to go before your apology can be accepted," she said. They drove on in silence for a bit. It felt a little less tense now, and Will stole another glance over at Tamsin. Her gear changes were less violent now and her grip on the steering wheel less tight. Her face relaxed, a smile flickering at the edge of her mouth. "You almost had me doing a PR on that man, you bastard."

"I know," said Will, "but I did stop you in time."

She shook her head, and he could see she was desperately trying to suppress a smile through gritted teeth.

"Oh, you are *so* going to pay for that," she said.

They went through the barriers into the car park. Will's pager was already going off. He thanked Tamsin again and ran off into the hospital. There were internal phones just inside the main entrance and Will got to one to answer the call. It was the sister from Equus Ward, the main orthopaedic ward, informing him that they were waiting to go around the patients. His pager went again and this time it was a GP sending in a rugby player with a locked knee. Well, at least that might brighten Mr Stoneman up a bit, even more if the chap played in the front row.

Will took the lift up the ten floors and joined Stoneman, who was waiting by the main desk with the rest of the team. Will gave a brief apology and explanation as to his tardiness and they set off around the patients. Tamsin stealthily slid in to join the round at the rear of the group a few patients in. Medical students rarely made much impression on Mr Stoneman, unless of course they were the pretty ones.

"Good of you to join us, Miss Trevelyan," he said. "I hear we have you to thank for the presence of our SHO this morning."

"Yes, Mr Stoneman, his car had broken down," she replied, meekly clasping her hands in front of her.

"What *was* wrong with your car, Dr Cunningham?" he asked, sarcastically.

"Er, it stopped working," Will answered.

"So, we know as much about cars as we do orthopaedics. Marvellous! Miss Trevelyan, perhaps you had better accompany Cunningham on take today, in case he needs rescuing again."

"Yes, Mr Stoneman," she replied, and looked at Will, who just shrugged.

The ward round continued with Will episodically running off to answer the insistent call of his pager. One of the students was copying what was supposed to be happening to the patients into their notes, so he could catch up later, and another wrote up the blood request forms as they went. Orthopaedic surgeons rarely requested very complicated bloods, limiting themselves to a full blood count, kidney function and the occasional CRP to measure inflammation or infection response. Anything more and there was a strong chance they would find something they had no idea of how to treat, which meant calling in the medics, and that wouldn't do at all.

The round finished. Mr Stoneman and the registrar went off to fracture clinic and Tamsin went to start clerking the first patient who had arrived. Will would catch up with her after he'd checked through the notes of the patients he'd missed. There were also the endless forms, drug charts and discharge summaries to be written, as well as bloods to be taken.

Chapter 6

The morning drifted into afternoon, and the demands on Will's time were relentless. He had, of course, tried to down tools for lunch, which might have been a smoked salmon and cream cheese baguette. One of his golden rules was that unless a patient was actually about to die, then getting a bite to eat and a cup of coffee superseded any other requirements of his time. If you didn't get a break for refuelling, you started to make mistakes, and no one cared that it was because you were hypoglycaemic, with no sugar getting to your brain. Your patients, your consultant and the lawyers didn't give a monkey's that it was your dedication to your job that meant 10 pm had arrived and your entire sustenance for the day had been a bag of crisps. "I was too tired and hungry to think," is apparently not a legal defence when you accidentally kill someone. So, Will always made a point of getting at least a sandwich somewhere around mealtimes. Disappointingly, the ward had fast bleeped him up to the ward halfway through today's meal, hence the 'might have been'. The reason given was because a patient's relatives wanted to talk to him about their granny and it had to be immediately because their parking would be running out. His baguette was left behind in the mess. Dealing with the complaint paperwork just wasn't worth it.

The medical students were doing their best to help, but they were a mixed blessing. They were great for getting words on paper, the patient clerked, but tended to be a lot less focussed on the actual problem at hand in their recording of the patient's 'history', so everything got included. Will then needed to listen to the history and then talk to the patient again to hone down the exact nature of what was wrong and why. Determining what might be broken was relatively easy, what else might be going on, which might affect a general anaesthetic often wasn't.

Will stood, his mind scrolling through the numerous tasks he had to do, only half paying attention, as James, one of the more loquacious students, even by their standards, warbled away. Gradually he became aware that James had become silent, waiting expectantly for Will's pronouncements, and jolted back.

"So, she's probably got a broken hip?" he summarised, his brain playing back the last thing he could remember James saying.

"Yes," said James, who looked like he'd been expecting a more thorough questioning. Will looked over to the patient.

"Do you agree with all of that?" He smiled at the old lady lying in the bed.

"Yes, dear," she replied. "It's going to be alright, isn't it?"

"Of course. We'll have your leg fixed in no time." Will went on to determine why it was she had fallen to break the hip. Straight forward this time, she had tripped over the dog... not an uncommon cause.

"Do you mind if I just take a quick look at you?" he went on to ask. The patient nodded and he quickly examined her respiratory and cardiovascular systems before pulling back the bed sheet to reveal the shortened, externally rotated left leg. He gently moved it slightly and the patient winced. He also noted that she had a bit of a skin infection, cellulitis, in her non-broken leg. That would need to be sorted with some intravenous antibiotics before her leg got fixed.

"OK, are you happy to put up a drip and get some bloods?" Will turned to James. "And don't forget to group and save." It was important to have the potential to refill the patient with blood if the surgeon let too much of it escape.

James nodded.

"Good thank you. I'll go and do the forms." Will wandered back to the ward desk with the notes and slumped into a chair. It was five o'clock. Most of the medical students would be heading off home, except for those supposed to be on take with him. He would tell them to go home at eight. They had revision and exams to do and hanging around a hospital at night only taught you how to be tired. They would learn that soon enough. He started writing up the notes on the patient he had just seen. Presenting complaint, history of presenting complaint, drug history, allergies, skip social history — it was orthopaedics after all, relevant exam findings, differential diagnosis, investigations, and management. He was transferring the medications onto the drug chart when a blonde staff nurse in her pale blue uniform distracted him.

"Mrs Wren says that she's in pain and wants something done about it immediately," she informed him. The nurse looked fed up too. Mrs Wren was one of those patients for whom one could never do enough. She was middle-aged, had paid her taxes all her life, was disappointed that she had to be on the main ward and not in a more private room (after all, the chief executive of the hospital was her good friend), and she had buzzed the feet off the nursing staff during her stay. Will had no doubt that her repaired fractured tibia was sore, but then there was going to be some discomfort — it had been broken, hadn't it. Will left the desk to go and determine the nature of the pain, considering whether, or not, to relieve her pain to the point of unconsciousness. Tempting.

He returned a short while later having placated Mrs Wren, for the time being at least, and tried to pick up where he'd left off. He had been in the middle of writing up the patient's notes... no, the drug chart... or was it a blood form?

James approached.

"I've done that lady's bloods and there's a line in. Is it OK if I go now? It's just that I have a presentation to do tomorrow and I need to write it up."

"No worries," said Will, "and thanks for your help."

James sauntered off out of the ward. Will stared after him wishing his shift might be over. He'd been in the hospital for ten hours and there would more than likely be another twenty-four more before he got to go home, probably with only a couple of hours' sleep. He spotted Tamsin on her way down the ward. She moved gracefully, yet purposefully, her braided ponytail flicking out from behind her shoulders with each step.

"Hi," he said as she arrived. He still wasn't sure if the air had been completely cleared between them yet. She smiled, though, and he asked, "Are you off now?" She looked at the piles of notes surrounding Will.

"I can give you a hand if you like. You look a little frazzled."

"That's really kind, but you don't have to. I get paid, remember, you don't."

"Many would pay handsomely for the privilege of receiving the bounty of *your* ministering," she said, with thinly veiled sarcasm.

Will screwed his face up before looking back at her. "You make me sound like some sort of cult leader," he said.

"Something like that, yes," she said, dryly.

"I tell you what," he said. "I've got to give the first dose of antibiotics to that lady in bed six. You can help me with that."

Will wrote up the co-amoxiclav before obtaining the keys to the drug cabinet from the ward sister. Tamsin fetched the needles and syringes and then Will double-checked the details on the vial with her – drug, strength, expiry date – before adding water to the antibiotic powder to reconstitute it. He carried the antibiotic syringe and some water to flush it through the IV line over to the lady's bed. Tamsin picked up the notes as she passed the desk.

"I'm just going to give you some antibiotic to help treat the infection in your leg," he said, arriving at the patient's bedside. His voice was raised to help the lady to hear what he had to say. So much for patient confidentiality. She just smiled at him. He took the saline flush and injected it into the line that James had put in earlier. It went in smoothly. Well done, James. Tamsin's sleeve brushed against his wrist as he reached past her for the syringe containing the antibiotic. Her attention, however, did not appear to be as much on this momentary frisson as his, as she flicked through James' notes, seemingly oblivious to him. Will drew up the antibiotic, expelling the remaining air from the syringe, and fiddled to align the syringe and IV port. Damn thing.

"Stop!" shouted Tamsin, and grabbed his arm, pulling the syringe away from the port. Will jumped.

"What?" he said, a bit stunned.

Tamsin's finger ran under a line in James' written notes. It was underlined and in capitals: <u>PENICILLIN ALLERGY ANAPHYLACTIC REACTION</u>. Will stared at the note, then up at Tamsin, before turning to the patient. "Mrs Trevellis, are you allergic to penicillin?"

"Oh, yes, dear," she said. "Last time I had it, it nearly killed me."

His hands shaking, Will put the syringe down – fuck, that was close. He re-read the note, clear as day, and he'd just not seen it. He excused himself from Mrs Trevellis and went back to the desk. Tamsin followed.

"Thank you," he said as they reached the nursing station. "I cannot believe what I almost did." Tamsin smiled sympathetically and touched his arm.

"That's number two," she said.

Will shook his head, trying to clear it, before going back to the drugs cupboard to get some IV erythromycin, the alternative antibiotic, to give to Mrs Trevellis and one that wasn't contraindicated by a penicillin allergy. Tamsin again did the checks. He glanced at the allergies box again, with 'penicillin' clearly written. How could he have missed it the first time around? How could he make such a stupid, dangerous error? He knew how, of course. He hadn't had a proper break in nearly twelve hours and his mind was busy trying to do multiple things at once, including working out one particularly tricky medical student. Stupid, stupid mistake. What sort of example was that to set? And why did it suddenly now seem to matter? He looked down at the syringe containing the new and hopefully less lethal drug in the syringe and began to walk past the desk and towards the patient, turning to give a 'Stan Laurel' look at Tamsin. Bizarrely she started to point behind him, a smirk on her face.

Will was knocked flying, as a bed, just brought up from theatres by the porter, rounded the corner and hit him full on. He felt his legs crumble and was aware of the erythromycin, needles and syringe all flying across the floor, as he was deposited, ignominiously, on his backside. Dazed he looked up and was relieved to see that the bed didn't contain a patient. The porter looked horrified.

Tamsin walked over. His eyes followed her from his sprawled position on the floor.

"Three," she said, barely suppressing her mirth. "Er, watch out for the bed."

"Yeah, thanks!" Will replied, rubbing the elbow that had broken his fall as he got up. "Anything else going to go wrong?" he asked the world in general.

"No, that'll be it for the time being," said Tamsin. Will looked at her. He hadn't really expected an answer.

"Rule of three," she said.

"Pardon?" said Will.

"Have you ever noticed that things tend to happen in threes?" she said. "Three pieces of bad luck or good luck, all at once?" Will looked a bit blank.

"Whatever good or bad energy you put into the world you receive three-fold in return."

Will stared up at her, brain whirling, "Are you suggesting that because I made you look a bit daft the other day, I've suffered the consequences of this due to some cosmic balancing of forces?"

"Couldn't have put it better myself," she said, smiling. "You seem to have grasped the concept remarkably quickly. See you in the morning." And, with that, she turned and walked away.

Chapter 7

The following evening, after his thirty-three-hour shift was finished, Will called the breakdown service, the AA, and arranged to meet them where he'd abandoned the car. Kris offered him a lift back to the car park and gave him a look when he realised exactly *which* car park it was.

"Car couldn't take the session?" asked Kris, referring to the infamous nature of this particular car park. Its reputation had been acquired owing to the rather frequent and unusual nature of the 'accidents' that seemed to happen in this spot. The nearest casualty department was, of course, Whitehorse Hospital.

"That's right," retorted Will, "the driver's seat got stuck in the recline position and I'm not even going to tell you what happened to the gear lever." You may start doing an A & E job as a naive and innocent twenty-five-year-old, but you certainly didn't leave as one.

The AA man was already there, sheet of paper and clipboard at the ready. Will described what had happened and was then asked to open the bonnet. He tried to start the engine, which just clicked, and the man took out some electrical contraption and put it across the battery. He nodded and then fiddled with a bit of the engine that looked a bit like an octopus. He grunted in satisfaction.

"Your alternator had become detached," he said, his Janner's lilt marking him as a local man, "so your battery isn't charging."

"Oh," said Will, trying to come up with an intelligent follow-up question but failing.

"Thing is," the AA man continued, "it would have taken one hell of a bump to displace it. Much more likely to have been put on badly. Has anyone been messing around with your car?" Will thought for a moment. It hadn't been serviced in several years, so a garage error was unlikely. He often left his car unlocked because it wasn't worth anything, so theoretically it might have been tampered with. But who would do that?

"No," Will replied, "but the car does get taken over some rough ground. Was it dangerous?"

"Other than the fact that it would slow down and stop in the middle of traffic, no, not really," the man said. Then he scratched his head. "Well, I suppose it's *possible* that it might have shaken loose on its own," he said, but he looked unconvinced.

"Is it going to cost much to fix?" Will asked. The AA man put his hand into the engine, twisted the octopus, and turned to Will.

"All fixed," he said, wiping his hands on a rag from his pocket. "I'll just put some charge into your battery." Then he disappeared back to his van and brought out a black box, then connected the leads. "You'll need to drive it around for about half an hour to get your battery fully charged again, but it should be fine after that."

It took about five minutes to charge and then the AA man disconnected the leads and dropped the bonnet.

"Thanks," said Will, still slightly puzzled.

"No problem," the man said. "I'll just follow you up the road for a mile or two to make sure it keeps going." Getting back into their respective cars, Will gave Kris a thumbs-up and they drove off in convoy.

Realistically, Will considered, anyone could have disabled his car, but equally, with the hammering the car took, it was also possible that it had just shaken loose. Perhaps Godfrey would be able to shed some light on matters.

"No, definitely not guilty," responded Godfrey, slightly affronted and wafting a hand in front of his face. "And no one has owned up," he added.

Shauna was sitting next to Godfrey on the sofa, a mug of tea in her hand. She'd also baked a fruit cake and lit the fire. Will noted the way the small air currents caused the smoke to swirl in spiral eddies before drifting up to the ceiling.

"Well, I suppose it was a lack of maintenance and my off-road driving then," Will said, coughing. He looked the few metres across to where Shauna was rapidly disappearing from view. "I suppose I should really lock my car from now on." His eyes were becoming increasingly irritated and a tear trickled down one cheek.

"I suppose we all should," agreed Shauna, who took a bite from the cake.

"Shauna," said Will, wiping his eyes, "do you think that we might have to rethink our heating strategy for something, I don't know, less carcinogenic?"

"I have no idea what you mean," she said, taking a sip from her tea to wash down the cake. It was the last view he would have of her for a while as another downdraught sent smoke from the fireplace billowing into the room.

"Well, it's just that I don't think the chimney is drawing very well."

"I thought it would be a nice idea, a warm fire to come home to," she said indignantly.

"He may have a point though," said Kris's disembodied voice. "Don't get me wrong, it's lovely and warm and all, but I can't actually see you, and I'm only sat three feet away."

"And I wouldn't want to damage my lungs," said Godfrey, pulling out a cigarette from his pocket.

"You're all making far too much fuss," said Shauna, but reluctantly she got up to open the windows. "You, though," she pointed to Godfrey, "can still smoke that thing outside."

Godfrey started to protest but thought better of it and went over to the now open French windows, muttering something about hypocrisy, olden days, smoking-jackets and women, before lighting up in the garden.

Will sensed another debate into yet another of Godfrey's bad habits, so he brought up a more peaceable conversation topic.

"Godfrey and I wondered about organising a surf trip," he said, "for anyone who wants to go."

"Yes," said Godfrey hovering outside, "we thought, a group of us could go down to Newquay, say in a couple of weeks' time, stay in one of the backpackers near Fistral Beach, do a bit of surfing and have a few beers. That sort of thing?"

"Sounds like a really great idea," said Kris. "I'm on this weekend as well, so I'd be free the following week. How is everyone else fixed?"

"Trevor and Izzy are on for medicine, and neither of them are into much, other than each other, so we're fine to go," said Melanie, looking over at Shauna. Shauna nodded.

"So, is it a general invite?" asked Kris.

"Just use word of mouth," instructed Godfrey. He looked over at Will, the space now clearing of smoke. "Are you OK to book one of the dorm rooms that sleeps twelve, perhaps at Waves backpackers?"

"I can do that," said Will. "We can firm up numbers a bit later."

Chapter 8

The next week passed with little incident and Will didn't get nearly so close to killing someone as he had on the Monday. The weekend take wasn't too bad either, and he got more than average sleep overnight, that was to say four hours. Much better, he reflected, than medical jobs, whose doctors didn't expect to get any sleep at all. Tuesday morning saw him in the mess with a free run to the weekend. There was quite a lot of surfing-related conversation around, and Will suspected that word of the surf trip had got out and he might need to revise numbers for the trip up a bit. He walked over to a group of junior staff where the debate over coffee was regarding the best beaches for the varying surf conditions hitting the region.

"Bantham is good," said Mel, whose parents apparently lived in the picturesque South Hams, "if you live on the Channel coast."

"Yeah, but that's only if there is actually some swell," said another scruffy-looking house officer. "It's more miss than hit, and the river running out can create scary rip tides. I nearly ended up at Start Point on one of those once."

"If you want surf, you have to go to the north coast, Devon or Cornwall,' suggested Jess, who Will had bumped into once down in theatre. He wasn't even sure what she did, was it gynaecology? Godfrey might have mentioned her. "Croyde, Ilfracombe, Bude, Widemouth, and then you get to Watergate Bay," she continued, flicking her long ponytail over her shoulder. "That huge expanse of sand at low tide goes on for miles and gets good consistent waves."

"You know what, though," said Mel, "if you do want to go down that far, I don't think you can beat Polzeath. It's never the biggest, probably not the best, but the chilli, cheese and chips afterwards makes any surf worthwhile."

There was someone who would obviously be welcome on the trip, thought Will, and he wandered over to get another coffee.

"Where do you reckon has the best ride, Tamsin?" he heard Mel ask. Will looked over to the armchair into which a hitherto unseen Tamsin had curled herself.

She pulled her attention away from her *Handbook of Clinical Medicine*, seemingly having been oblivious to the preceding conversation, and paused before replying to what appeared to be an inexplicably expectant crowd.

"All of the beaches have their days," she began, "and it's all dependent on conditions and what sort of swell there is that day. The southern beaches tend to have a smaller, less reliable, wave, but it can be fun. The northern coasts of Devon and Cornwall pick up better conditions, and the most reliable is probably down in Newquay where you've got many, many beaches all catching slightly differing swell directions. And," she said, smiling grimly, "Newquay has the Cribbar."

They all looked slightly bemused.

"What's that?" asked Mel.

"Very rarely," she answered, "when there's a low-pressure system sat out in the Atlantic and the tides are right, the swell hits the Cribbar Reef just off Towan Head. Waves build and can easily reach twenty or thirty feet."

There were a few wide-eyed looks. "What, a wave that big in this country? It sounds more like The Pipeline in Hawaii," said Adam, another medical student.

Tamsin nodded.

"And you can ride it?"

She exhaled slightly with a half laugh. "Yes, it can be ridden, but only a few have done so successfully. It has something of a reputation."

"Of what?" said Adam, now enthralled along with the rest of the room.

Tamsin looked at him with the patient kind of look that a parent gives a child who has seen a lion at the zoo and wants to go and pet it. "It's called the Bonecruncher or Widowmaker locally, which sort of gives you an idea."

"You surf, Tamsin?" asked Will, caught up in the conversation but clearly not in possession of all the facts.

"Does she surf?" snorted Adam on Tamsin's behalf. "She came in the top ten in the Rip Curl Boardmasters a year or two back, and that was alongside the professional surfers. Does she surf?" He laughed again. Will looked from Mel to Tamsin, who merely smiled back at him.

"Have you ridden it, Tamsin? The Cribbar?" asked Will, slightly awed by the concept of the concealed talents of his errant charge.

"No... not yet," she said, her gaze drifting back to her coffee. "But one day."

There was a bang on the door and it burst open. A tall, dark, tousle-haired doctor stormed into the mess. His tanned face was flushed and he had a small scar on his left cheek that glowed lividly with the fury he emanated. Will stole a glance at the name badge.

"Where the fuck is she?" seethed Dr Cadan Metern, registrar in obstetrics and gynaecology. His eyes darted left and right, scanning each face in turn, searching out whoever his unfortunate quarry might be. He prowled the room, halting as his gaze came to rest on Tamsin's diminutive form, who had buried her face even further in her book than before and was shrinking back into her chair. Metern strode over to stand on front of her, a hand outstretched, clutching what looked to be a bundle of green cloth. With barely controlled rage, the hand trembled as he leaned forward. His free hand shot out, ripping Tamsin's book away from her. He threw it down and it hit the floor with a muffled slap, dislodging some loose sheets. Tamsin put her hands up defensively. The green bundle shook mere centimetres from her face. Will moved forward ready to intervene, noting as he did so that the green cloth was, in fact, a poorly stuffed doll of some sort, complete with rudimentary face and limbs. Protruding from the doll and rocking with the movement was a twelve-gauge green needle. Tamsin remained still, her eyes fixed on the doll, frozen like a cornered mouse.

"This supposed to be funny, is it? An amusing little game?" Metern's lowered voice had a cutting, icy edge. "Or did you actually intend me harm with this fucking witchcraft shit?"

"What...? N-no," she stuttered. "I-I don't know what you mean."

"Don't know what I mean, my arse!" The words were spat out. Tamsin looked at the doll, then back at Metern, forehead wrinkled, shaking her head blankly. The look seemed to infuriate Metern even further, and Will thought Tamsin was about to be dragged from the sofa. He decided it might be wise to intervene at this point, so eased himself between Tamsin and her prospective assailant. The backs of his calves pressed into the cushioned fabric, leaving him nowhere to go, and he was suddenly distinctly aware of the much bigger and very much more solid frame in front of him. He'd have to bluff this one out... or perhaps backflip over the sofa from a standing start if bravado failed? It was bluff then.

"Wait, wait, wait," Will said, "its Cadan, isn't it?"

Metern turned his glare to Will.

Will smiled in what he hoped was an appeasing manner. "Let's see if we can settle this a bit more quietly. Whatever has happened, you can't just come in here shouting and losing your temper like that." He looked his colleague in the eyes, which required more than a few degrees of neck extension, and Will was made even more aware of the physical disparity between the two of them. He certainly possessed presence. Metern stood firm for a moment, staring Will down. Will was glad of the sofa behind him in case his legs gave way.

"Yes, I am fucking well can," he replied coldly, glaring at Will, but maybe some of the fury was defused. He looked at the doll in his hand and tossed it in Tamsin's direction. It rebounded to the floor off a protective forearm. "Thirty-six hours on call, three crash sections, and when I go back to my on-call room to try to get some sleep, that thing is lying on my fucking bed." Metern stepped back further, pointing towards the offending toy then directing his index finger at Tamsin. "You put it there. We both know you did."

Will risked a glance behind him. Tamsin had drawn her legs up under herself. "Is that what you think?" she said, and looked at the object on the floor, adding weakly, "But it's only a doll."

"You know damn well what this is, you stupid witch," he said.

Tamsin just stared back at him, and they stayed locked for several seconds.

"I know what you have been up to. That is not something that you can hide from me." His jaw tensed. "No more of this, do you understand?' The intensity of his brown eyes seemed to bore into Tamsin, who to her credit, returned the glare with equal ferocity. Will was ignored.

The stand-off continued for a few more very uncomfortable moments before Metern turned abruptly and left the mess; a tissue dropped from his pocket as he did so. The door slammed behind him. Will watched him go before returning his attention to Tamsin, squatting down in front of her. She had tears in her eyes and she was shaking.

"What a complete prat," he said, putting a hand on her shoulder. "Are you alright?"

She took some time composing herself before nodding and wiped her eyes with her sleeve. Will noticed her empty coffee cup on the floor.

"Come on, I'll get you another one." He stood her up and took her to the quieter coffee-making area away from curious eyes, picking up the doll on the way. He glanced down at the two very roughly cut pieces of felt that had been stitched together. The seams were very loose, and he could see it was stuffed with tissue paper. It had a poorly penned face, but no hair or clothes, and it didn't look as if it would last five minutes in a child's hands. In fact, it looked as though a child had made it. The green needle was still protruding from the middle of its abdomen. Will removed it and put it in the sharps bin, which rather unhygienically sat next to the toaster, then set about making a fresh cup for Tamsin.

"There you go," he said, handing it to her. He looked at the tear-streaked face as Tamsin thanked him for the drink. "Tamsin, I don't know what that was all about, but whatever it was, he can't go around acting like that. I can maybe go and have a word with someone?" He wasn't sure who.

"No!" she said quickly. "I mean... it's very good of you, but no, I don't think that would help." She paused. "Look, it's complicated, and I just don't want any more trouble." She wiped her eyes again. "It was probably someone's funny little joke."

"Not that funny if that was the reaction," Will observed, toying with the doll in one hand. He put it into a bin and reached for the biscuit tin. There were a couple of Nice biscuits, the chocolate ones having long since been eaten. Tamsin shook her head, sniffing, and indicated that she needed another tissue.

Will pulled one out of his pocket and offered it to her. "It *is* clean," he said, smiling.

"Thanks," she replied, then added, "Actually, I will have a biscuit."

Will turned around to get the tin, knocking Tamsin as he did so, causing her to drop the hanky. She bent to pick it up as he apologised, then, retrieving the biscuits, he proffered the tin. She straightened up and took one. There was a few moments' silence. He was aware that the normal chatter of the mess had resumed, but there were a few glances cast in their direction.

"Look, I know I haven't done very well so far, but if I can help in any way, do anything, just say. OK?"

Her eyes moved to meet his. There *were* flecks of amber. "Thank you," she said, "that's really kind."

"And I promise I'll try to refine my teaching methods."

"Really? You will?"

"I said *try*."

"No, really — you *will*," she narrowed her eyes and smiled.

Will raised his eyebrows putting his hands up in mock surrender, and laughed, "I will, I will." His eye caught the time on his watch, "Woah, best hurry or we are going to be late for the ward round. Then he had a thought. "Hey," he said, "there's a surf trip to Newquay at the weekend, you may already be aware of it?"

She nodded.

"It would be great if you could come along." Then stuttered, "All of the students, I mean."

"Do you know," she said, smiling, "I was sort of hoping that you might ask."

Chapter 9

Hours later, Godfrey, Shauna and Will nursed their pints in the Old Mill. "So, just to be clear," said Will, "regarding numbers for this surf trip. I've invited the medical students. You, Shauna, have suggested that a couple of the nursing staff *might* like to come. Mel you aren't sure how many people who you have asked, have definitely said that they would come. And you, Godfrey, have asked along pretty much everyone you've met in the hospital, including the attractive young woman whose C-section epidural you did this morning."

"To be honest," said Godfrey, taking a last drag on his cigarette, "I don't think she's going to be able to make it. Something to do with wound healing and infections, or whatever."

"And the new baby?" said Shauna.

"Oh, yeah, and that," he said, grinning.

"So," said Will, "we have twelve beds booked in the backpackers and no actual idea of the numbers turning up."

"I think it'll be more than twelve," said Mel grinning.

"Another room more than twelve?" asked Will.

"Quite possibly, but maybe not," said Godfrey. Will cast a frown over at Godfrey, who wasn't in one of his more helpful moods. Godfrey smiled back.

"It's a bit academic really," said Shauna, "because there were no more rooms available at the hostel – I phoned them earlier. The girl did say we could put a few mattresses on the floor. And we can tell people to bring carry-mats."

"Or share!" said Will, only half-jokingly.

"Always happy to share," said Godfrey. Then, thinking it through, "Within reason, obviously."

"Would anyone not paralytic with alcohol really want to?" said Shauna. Godfrey looked up from his pint, a pained look on his face.

"Well then," said Will, "I'll just give the backpackers a call and let them know that we have absolutely no idea how many are coming, or at what time, but we will be there on Friday for two nights, probably."

"That about covers it," said Shauna, sarcastically. "What about kit?"

"You mean wetsuits and boards?" said Godfrey. Shauna nodded.

"There are loads of hire shops, so those not wanting a dawn surf can hire their kit on Saturday morning, but most people down here have their own," replied Will.

"And the surf report and weather forecast?" asked Godfrey.

"Saturday's weather forecast looks good, but Sunday is a bit gloomy. The telephone surf report line suggests the swell may be dropping off a bit."

"Oh well, there's plenty of other stuff to do," said Shauna. "Shops and pubs and cafes."

"And the aquarium," said Mel.

"Aquarium? There's an aquarium?" said Godfrey.

Mel smiled and nodded.

"OK," said Godfrey, standing up. "One more?" he asked, turning to Will and Shauna. "Assuming I'm booked into my usual room."

"I don't believe anyone else reserved the sofa bed," replied Shauna. "It's all yours."

Chapter 10

Friday saw Mr Stoneman in a particularly good mood, one usually associated with the possession of tickets to one sporting event or another at the weekend. His bonhomie meant that he dispensed with the usual quips at the expense of his junior staff and fairly whipped through the ward round. Instructions were left suggesting that calls should be directed to his registrar. Should he be required, he could be reached on his pager. The implication, however, was clear. "You may call, but it *will* be considered a sign of weakness should such an instance occur." Fortunately, Dave Bolt, the registrar, was very competent and there were no particularly sick individuals on the ward. Dave was about to sit the final part of his surgical exams and was no doubt looking forward to an exciting weekend of revising. Still, he wasn't much of a surfer anyway.

The mess was buzzing with the trip, and Will fielded numerous questions on weather, surf conditions and the weekend's itinerary. He wasn't sure he'd ever talked to at least half of the people who came up to him with enquiries. It was quite possible this trip was going to get a bit big on him, in the way that some waves he had chosen recently seemed to do.

Despite this additional demand on his time, he managed to leave early and was pleasantly surprised when Shauna arrived back at the cottage only half an hour behind him. Always meticulous and diligent, she would have undoubtedly made sure all of the patients were completely sorted before she left. Plans and just-in-case scenarios would have been worked through and documented in the notes and all blood forms and X-ray requests for the following week would have been done, even though she would be back on the Monday. Nurses and relatives would have been spoken to and yet she would still return and worry about something.

Will was reasonably sure his patients were alright. None of them felt like they would "go off" over the weekend. His method of patient care wasn't quite as fine-tuned and by the book as Shauna's, nor, if he was honest, was it quite as likely to stand up as well in a court of law were something to go wrong. But, to date, Will's instinct for picking up on a potentially sick patient had been un-erring. The textbook couldn't predict the often, random way in which patients presented, or at times sift the myriad potential diagnoses quickly enough. Will had found that he just could, and he never worried about a patient after having left the hospital.

They were taking Will's car, which seemed to be running well after its mishap. It was the sensible choice, given that it had roof bars, a large boot and wouldn't cause Shauna to have a fit were a little sand and seawater to find its way onto the upholstery. Having been in Shauna's car on a few occasions, and now Tamsin's, Will could see how having a nice-smelling, clean car to get into made for a more pleasant driving experience. He was fairly sure that the secret to this pleasantness did not include leaving un-rinsed sandy wetsuits for a week or so in the back of the warmed vehicle, or the lingering presence of half-eaten sandwiches in the footwells. A trashed car, however, did mean that there were never any immediate concerns over finding a bin, or forgetting protective a plastic container for wet... surf kit.

Will strapped the boards to the top of the car, taking care to pad the areas of direct contact between fibreglass board and metal roof bar. Putting a "ding" in your board was a disappointing start to a trip. The suits were loaded into the boot and they were ready to set off.

The trip to Newquay and, more specifically, Fistral Beach was slightly further than to Polzeath. The drive crossed Bodmin Moor, a much bleaker and boggier moor, than Dartmoor. It was, nonetheless, magically enigmatic, with its rugged tors, rocky outcrops of granite shrouded in mist, its smuggling and highwayman history and, not forgetting, tales of Arthurian legend. They passed Jamaica Inn, made famous by Daphne du Maurier, proudly flying the flag of St Piran, a white cross on black background representing the seams of tin found within the granite base-rock. Coming down off the moor, the road took them past more of Cornwall's history, the Cornish Alps, huge hills formed by the excavation waste from the clay pits. Amongst these clay pits now, a new enterprise was due to be developed. Huge biodomes were to be built to provide controllable climates, such that tropical rainforests or plants from the African savanna might be grown within them. It was going to be called The Eden Project.

They turned off the main A30 and headed through picturesque villages to Newquay. A lack of a car radio was one of the consequences of leaving wet garments in the car for prolonged periods, so as they drove along, Will imparted what he knew of Newquay to Shauna. He had completed a project at school comparing a coastal town's history with that of an industrial town, and Shauna was now reaping the full benefit of his studies. He told of how Newquay was a town of a few thousand that swelled with holidaymakers and surfers in holiday months. The town, based originally around the natural curve of the headland, had a well-protected harbour at its centre. Up until the early twentieth century, this had been the site of the fishing industry that was the town's lifeblood. The town's insignia was still that of four herring, though the industry was now a fraction of what it had once been. As they passed through the outskirts of the town, by the golf course, Shauna pointed to a huge building that dominated the headland.

"Is that the backpackers'?" she asked.

Will laughed. "I wish. No, it's The Headland Hotel. An old Victorian building. Caused quite a bit of trouble when it was being built."

"Why's that?" asked Shauna, showing a little more interest than had been elicited by explanations of clay extraction from the quarries.

"Well, it precipitated the Newquay Riots at the turn of the century. You see, it was built on what the fisherman believed to be common ground. They used to dry their nets all over that headland and felt it was impacting on their livelihoods. Building went on anyway, so the fishermen started destroying the scaffolding and intimidating the local workers. They used any means possible to disrupt proceedings, including, it is said, witchcraft."

"What do you mean?" asked Shauna, gazing at the structure.

"Well, local witches were supposedly engaged to curse the building and all those involved with the project. Spookily" – Will turned to Shauna and gave his best demonic face – "accidents and misfortune seemed to befall anyone associated with its construction."

Shauna returned his expression with a mildly incredulous one of her own as he continued. "The architect's wife, for example, was killed in bizarre circumstances when she visited the site. She was taking a walk on the windward side of the site when the wind apparently caused a loose piece of masonry to be dislodged from the top of one of the main walls and it landed directly on her. No one was working up there at the time, and as I said, she was walking on the windward side of the building, so the wind would have been blowing the wrong way to cause it to fall onto her."

"How terrible," said Shauna, wrinkling her nose.

"It's said that her ghost still roams the hotel," Will continued. "A woman in a long, dark, sleeveless coat wearing a small, white hat." He saw Shauna shiver.

"Anyway, from that point on, the locals refused to work on the site, and in the end hundreds of miners from Redruth were drafted in to complete the build." Shauna stared up at the austere, isolated hotel, silhouetted against a greying sky.

The road took them past rows of terraced house on the right, with the golf course and the sea on the left. They passed a few surf shops and The Golden Lion Pub and then turned left onto the beach road that took them to the headland and Fistral Beach itself. The Waves backpackers was halfway along this road on the right. Will parked the car and they got out and looked out over the dunes to see the lines of swell coming in from the Atlantic Ocean.

"Two to three foot and clean," said Will, leaning on the car bonnet. "That will do nicely."

"If it lasts," said Shauna.

"Well, it'll be fine for tomorrow at least," said Will. "But as long as there's something to surf on, we'll be fine." They both watched the surfers who were out there, carving turns on their short boards. One in particular, caught his eye. Hair flowing out behind her, she flew up and down the wave, balance perfect, turns crisp and sharp. Even from this distance, Will had a strong inkling of who it was and the talent she clearly possessed. He looked on a while longer, itching to get out there himself and join her, but he was aware that someone would have to be around to deal with the imminent chaos, and heaven forbid it would be Godfrey.

Shauna obviously sensed this. "Not going to be time tonight," she said, looking over her shoulder as a couple of cars pulled up along the road. Then, in typically empathic fashion, she added, "The residents are just going to love us. We've brought Valtor to Newquay." The road, while not narrow, could only accommodate parking on the one side road, and with who knows how many cars from the hospital to come, spaces would be limited.

They went into the backpackers, which consisted of two joined mid-terraced houses. There was a long, dark corridor with the odd poster of well-toned Hawaiian surfers adorning the walls. Doors led off to rooms on either side; there had been some major interior redesigning done to reconfigure the houses in such a way. The reception was at the far end, by the back door, which was open. Beyond this, they could see lines of wetsuits hanging out to dry and a rack of boards.

"Hi," said a blonde-haired girl who appeared from behind the desk as they approached. Her dreadlocks swung rigidly as she placed her hands on the counter.

"Hi," replied Will. "We're part of the Whitehorse party."

"Excellent. Good trip down?"

Will nodded. The blonde girl reached for a registration book. "One of you has already arrived, but any ideas on total numbers yet?" she asked. The upward intonation at the end of her sentence gave away if not her origins, then time recently spent in Australia.

"Um, no exact figures as yet," he replied.

"The nearest two or three?"

"Um, in all honesty, I'm not sure I could give you the nearest ten or twenty. I'm really sorry."

"No worries," she said." You've got the whole dorm anyway, and there are a few spare mattresses in the store. Do you know your way around?"

"No," said Will.

"Well, I've put you in the dorm on the ground floor, first door on the right, the red one. I can give you several sets of keys. Please try not to lose them." She continued in a well-versed patter. "There's a shower out at the back. Come in that way if wet, and if you can hang your stuff up outside, not in the bathrooms if you don't mind, that would be appreciated. The boards should be safe there too. If I can get you to sign in just there..." She handed him the book and he signed himself and Shauna in. "And there are your keys. Give me a shout if you need anything." They took the keys as Godfrey stepped through the entrance door with a couple of, if Will remembered correctly, physiotherapists. Shauna looked skyward.

"Sign in over there and best be quick before all of the beds go," said Will to Godfrey, as he saw more cars pulling up outside. Will and Shauna went into the dorm, which was a good size and contained six sets of bunk beds. There was already one pack on the top bunk by the door. Will put his stuff on the bottom bunk so that he could leave with a minimum of fuss if he decided to go for a dawn surf. Godfrey and the physios came in and there was more movement outside as the other medics shuffled through the door. It didn't take long to realise that the mattresses from the store would be required after which time it was felt that the pub beckoned. Will just hoped that it would be able to cater for all present without a booking. As they were sorting themselves out to leave, the dorm door opened, and Tamsin entered wrapped in a towel.

"That *was* you out there, wasn't it?" Shauna greeted her as she came in. "You looked really good."

"Thanks, there were some fun waves," Tamsin replied with a smile. "Are you guys on your way for some food?"

"Yes, we're just off to The Lion," said Will.

"Excellent," said Tamsin, reaching for the pack above Will's bunk. Will tried to give the impression of not watching, but he was impressed as, within a minute, she had stripped off her swimsuit and changed under her towel in a clearly well-practised manoeuvre.

The Golden Lion Pub was perched on the harbour wall on the opposite side of the headland to Fistral Beach. It was a large open-plan pub with a central bar area. The bar had a decent selection of beers and specialised in cocktails. There were pine tables dotted throughout the floor area, which were placed to make the most of views through the large plate glass windows overlooking the harbour. It was a couple of hours or so before low tide, so there wasn't much water left, and boats lurched to one side as their keels grounded on the sandy harbour floor. The sun was just starting to dip below the skyline and the sky was streaked with hues of orange, red and purple. It was a view of which it was worth making a feature.

The group entered the pub en masse and moved over to several the tables in the middle of the room, the best ones by the window being already occupied.

"Are your mates coming along as well?" Mel asked Tamsin as they approached the biggest table, which would seat at least ten.

"Yes, they're intending to, but Adam had a dentist appointment. So, as he was driving, they're going to set off a bit later with the others. They should be here soon, and I said we would probably be..." Tamsin trailed off and Will saw her stiffen. He followed her gaze across the room to where a few individuals were playing pool. He recognised them as obs and gynae SHOs, and then he saw the cause of Tamsin's reaction. Cadan Metern was lining up a shot along the side cushion into the bottom pocket. The cue slid smoothly through his bridging hand, sending the white into the last striped ball, which cracked into the pocket. The white then halted for a split second before the screw took it fizzing back up the table to land perfectly behind the eight ball. There were shrieks of appreciation from the surrounding entourage. He got up from his cueing position and walked around to take the final shot.

Will couldn't help but be a bit envious. He'd found out a bit about the guy over the last few days after events in the mess. He was thirty-five, having got a first-class honours degree from Cambridge in physics. Then he moved to doing medicine, collecting a BSc in medical genetics along the way, and went on to become a highly respected obstetrics and gynaecology registrar. *And* he gets to look like that, thought Will, observing the well-muscled body, poorly covered by a tight-fitting T-shirt. Will watched as Metern leaned over the winning shot, his lips resting on the pendant that dangled from a leather cord around his neck. The ball disappeared into the pocket and he permitted himself a small smile before taking his applause. He straightened up and, looking round, spotted Will and then Tamsin. He handed on his cue and strode over to their table.

"I hope you don't mind a few of us tagging along," he said, indicating the others over at the pool table. "Godfrey told Jess about the trip, and it seemed like a great idea. We've booked up at the Seabreeze to give everyone a bit more space."

The Seabreeze was a slightly more upmarket hotel along the beach road. And, Will realised, Jess *was* on the obs and gynae rotation. He diverted his gaze to where Godfrey was already talking to her by the pool table. Boy was *he* in for a complicated weekend. Will returned to Metern and was about to reply, but Metern's attention was on the medical student stood opposite him.

"Look, Tamsin," Metern said, "I owe you a huge apology for the other day." Was that genuine sincerity and a look of concern in his eyes? "I had just had the worst, and I mean *the* worst, on-call. I was tired and behaved inexcusably."

Tamsin's expression tightened, her lips drawn in and her eyes like firebrands. Metern persevered with his apology. "I took a trip up to the paediatric ward and clearly one of the children put the doll that she had made into my pocket, probably as a present. And" – he paused – "I can remember losing track of a needle when sticking in an IV line. Really careless. That obviously ended up in my pocket too, and hey presto, one voodoo doll falls out when I take my white coat off." He raised his eyebrows, waiting for some reaction from Tamsin, but she remained steely faced. "I *am* really sorry."

Will could see Tamsin's clenched fists by her side, her nails digging into the palms of her hands. "There is a cycle, Cadan Metern," she said, her soft voice laced with thinly veiled malice, "and your turn will come around. Justice will be served. You *cannot* be forgiven."

Their eyes locked, before Metern nodded, dropped his gaze and backed away. Tamsin remained unmoved.

"I *am* sorry... for everything," he repeated. There was a moment's further silence. Metern shifted uncomfortably. "Look, can I get you a drink... in fact," he said, addressing the table as a whole, "can I get anyone a drink?"

With the unerring timing that only medical students short of funds but with a passion for beer possess, in walked the rest of Tamsin's cohort with their hands raised. Will watched Metern go to the bar then looked back at Tamsin. She appeared less tense but the fire in those eyes was unmistakable. Will felt a chill run through him. Not one to cross, that girl.

Metern brought a tray full of drinks over, which was cheered by the contingent present. His performance in the mess the other day didn't seem to have dampened his popularity. He handed the drinks around before placing an orange-coloured cocktail in front of Tamsin.

"White rum, Lapponia Lakka Cloudberry liqueur, white crème de menthe, orange and lemon," he said, then, "a 'Forgive me' and no, I have no idea what a cloudberry is either." He smiled wanly and left to return to see what was happening at the pool table.

Tamsin stared at the drink.

"Well, he could have brought you the 'Salem Witch'," said Will, looking down the cocktail menu and unable to control his tongue.

Tamsin twitched, then responded, "Or the 'Witch Hunt'." The sparks in her emerald eyes flashed with more than just humour.

There were twenty-four members of the party in the end, which made for quite a cramped dorm on their return to the hostel. After two to a bed was vetoed by a few the party, and not just because the upper bunks didn't look like they would handle one, let alone two people, mattresses and carry-mats were laid out to cover the entire floor surface. Shauna, whose pack had mysteriously fallen off her bed, was in the bed Godfrey had originally claimed. Godfrey had made a noble sacrifice and gone to sleep on the floor, finding himself sandwiched between two physios; he appeared very dealing with the consequences of his grand gesture very well. The boy was on fire, Will thought, as he rolled over in his comfortable single-occupancy bunkbed.

Chapter 11

Will awoke at 7 am and announced to the room that the dawn surf patrol was leaving. There were a few groans, a few comments of "be with you in five", and the odd "shut the fuck up, it's still night-time". The bunk above his was empty. He left the room, stepping over a stray limb hanging out of a sleeping bag, and went to the kit room where he had put his board and wetsuit. He found Tamsin already suited up and about to go.

"Morning," he said, holding his head as it threatened to send him off balance.

"Morning," came the reply. "A little wobbly, are we?"

"Just a tad," he said, trying to gather himself. He squinted at Tamsin. "You don't have to wait if you want to go. I may take a little more time." He pulled at his wetsuit, tipping his board onto the floor with a crash.

"Do you know, I think I will. I'm not sure you're in a fit state to make it out of the kit room on your own, let alone cross a road to get to the beach," she replied.

Will clattered into another surfboard.

Tamsin laughed. "Besides, some mornings are for surfing alone, but others it's much nicer to have someone with you." She looked on curiously as Will dropped his dry wetsuit onto a wet sandy floor and cursed. Picking it up, he overbalanced trying to put his leg into the appropriate hole and started hopping madly to avoid falling over. Finally regaining some stability, he pulled first one, then the other leg through the suit, grimacing as he became aware that the suit hadn't dried from the last trip, then he pushed his arms down the sleeves. That was the easy bit done. He started twisting and contorting himself in an effort to catch the zip-cord that would allow him to do the suit up at the back.

Tamsin just stood back laughing, before saying, "Oh, for heaven's sake! Would you like me to do it?" She grabbed him and spun him around to pull the flaps of the suit together.

"It's amazing how they shrink," Will said, sucking in his stomach.

"It is," agreed Tamsin, though Will noted a distinctly flat abdominal panel to her wetsuit, which suggested that she really didn't know anything about shrinking wetsuits at all. He felt her reach down the back of the suit to pull the neoprene flaps straight, allowing the suit to be closed more easily. The cool touch of her hands was almost like an electric shock as they brushed his back, and he had goosebumps that weren't at all cold related. He heard the zip whirr as she fastened him in.

"Ready?" he asked.

"Have been for ten minutes," she replied.

"If you had drunk more, you would be more understanding and sympathetic."

"I didn't drink more so that I wouldn't have to be," she said.

"Fair point," said Will, shrugging.

They left via the back. Will stopped briefly to wax his board and threw the interestingly named Sex Wax back into the car. The wax gave the surfer better grip on the board and stopped him slipping off in turns. He put the car key under the wheel. No one had yet discovered this cunning hiding place, though the state of the interior was such that he suspected if he left the key in the ignition, with the engine running, the car was likely to still be there on his return.

The road stretched a hundred yards or so, before turning left and dropping down into a rough gravel car park on the edge of the beach. The expanse of sand stretched far off into the distance, to end abruptly at imposing sheer cliffs. The two surfers paused for a moment, taking in the sweet smell of land as it mingled with the salty sea air blown in by a light onshore breeze. The sun was up but it was still spring, and so the air was cool, feeling fresh and enlivening. Songbirds were declaiming their territorial rights and mating potential, their plaintive melodies juxtaposed by the harsh cawing of a raucous seabird. The day felt new and exciting, bursting with life and the joy of existence; different from any other time of day, and that's perhaps why surfers, even the most hungover ones, loved a dawn surf.

Will stood, Tamsin by his side, letting nature wash through him, before turning his attention to face the waves. He could feel Tamsin doing the same, her head still but her gaze flicking across the water. They looked for how the swell was coming in, the time between waves and their size. They watched where and how the waves were breaking, where the rip tides that could be perilous if they caught you out were; but also, where they might provide an easier paddle out. They watched the way the white-water from the broken waves drifted laterally, indicating any longshore currents. Finally, casting a sideways look at one another they bent to strap on their respective ankle leashes.

Tamsin broke first, jumping up, board tucked under one arm and running down the beach. Will followed at a canter, accelerating with the gentle descent of the shoreline. The waves seemed to pull them ever faster towards the water, and they hit the sea almost at a sprint, leaping over the first ripples and then, reaching greater depth, they flung themselves onto their boards and began paddling out. The water was cold, and the initial shock removed any sluggish, beery, hungover feelings left in Will's brain.

The surf was a decent size, four foot or so, with about a twelve-second wave interval, and Will felt the rip he was in accelerate him into and through the breaking waves. Tamsin got beyond the break line a minute or so before Will, having hit fewer waves full on, and sat straddling her board as Will arrived. No one else was out; the ocean and the day were, for this moment at least, all theirs. A few sets disappeared under them, the swell first lifting them up a couple of metres and then gently dropping them as it passed through. It was such a calming motion, and Will closed his eyes, feeling any remaining tension in his body drain away.

There was a splash next to him, and he opened his eyes to see Tamsin off to catch her first wave.

"See you in a bit," she exclaimed, shooting away, arms pumping and board cutting smoothly through the water.

A wave passed under Will and dropping into the trough he briefly lost sight of Tamsin as she disappeared under the water that was being pushed upwards. He tracked the line of where he thought she might be and was rewarded with the sight of the top of Tamsin's head as it bobbed in and out of view in front of the wave. Ten or so seconds later, he saw her rise up the wave and jump backwards off her board to land behind it. Getting off early avoided having too long a paddle back.

Will turned seaward; it was his turn. A nice easy first one, just to get going, and here it was, a good set coming in; he'd have one of them. He passed on the first two waves and then spotted his wave. It wasn't the biggest of the set; he'd decided that he needed a few waves to warm up before picking anything bigger. A good middling wave would be just fine. He spotted his take-off point, dropped to his stomach and started paddling. His wide front crawl stroke pulled him through the water. The board's speed increased and he felt the wave lift the rear of the board up, pivoting his head down and pushing him forward. He put his hands onto the rails of the board and popped up, bringing his feet to land between his hands. The Sex Wax felt tacky and firm underneath him; he wasn't going to slip off this board today. He transferred his weight back a fraction but felt the board's nose dip as he did so. He looked below him; the board's angle was now at forty-five degrees and pointing straight down the face. He needed to turn the board at an angle to have it run parallel. All good so far. A little more weight on his rear foot, lean in... and a bit more... a bit more... quickly...oh no! His weight transfer back was not enough and too late. The nose dipped and caught in the smooth green face, stopping it dead in the water. The board's tail pushed violently behind him, and he felt the all too familiar feeling as, once again, he was propelled at velocity, head-first, into the bottom of the wave. The impact of hitting the water and the wave landing on top of him felt like being hit with a sledgehammer. There were bubbles everywhere and a muffled roar in his ears. He was tumbled over and over, the weight of the water holding him down. He kept still, protective arms up and he waited... and waited, waiting for the rotation to stop. Still he rolled. The surf here seemed stronger, more powerful, probably because of the direct line to the Atlantic and the shape of the ocean floor. His lungs began to burn. Don't panic. It seemed like an eternity before the spinning stopped and he floated to the surface, gasping for breath as he hit air.

He was greeted with screeches of laughter from Tamsin, who, like Godfrey, almost fell off her board as she paddled over to him. He wiped the water from his eyes and the snot from his nose, coughing a couple of times as he did so. Not terribly impressive. He really did need to sort out this first wave of the day thing that seemed to keep happening. Perhaps something really, really small in the white-water to get warmed up next time.

Tamsin reached him. "Are you OK?" she asked. "That was one awesome wipe-out!"

"I'm just fine!" he replied. "I always like to see what the seabed is like first. It gives me a much better idea of how the wave on top is going to break."

"Right?" said Tamsin, eyebrow cocked.

"Oh absolutely," Will said, almost coughing his guts up.

Will's next wave, however, was much better, not least of all because he avoided nearly drowning. He popped onto the board, distributed his weight effectively, steadily traversed the wave, avoiding any complicated turns, and was carried a hundred metres or so into the shore. He hadn't come off the wave early, just enjoyed the ride, so he had a long paddle back out again. In the distance, Tamsin nodded her approval and then set herself for the next wave coming in. Will watched as, with a few powerful strokes, her arms propelled her up to speed and then in one fluid movement she was up on the board, tiny against the looming wall of water behind her. She took the drop down the face, then, with a fractional weight change, incised her turn back up the wave with surgical precision. He watched the white scar of her wake cut clean against the green translucent water then merge into the crest of the wave breaking moments behind her. Reaching the top of the wave again, she then glided, weightlessly, across its top, seeming to ride the horizon itself, and then, with a flick, the nose of the board shot skywards, launching her off the top of the wave. Will was awestruck. She was good, so very, very good.

They continued to surf for another hour and a half or so, Will doing his level best not to embarrass himself further with his efforts. Tamsin made appropriate whooping noises as he caught his waves, yelling encouragement and, when everything went a bit wrong, dissolving into fits of giggles. She made no mistakes, at least none that Will could see. She was in her element, completely at one with the ocean.

After a while, other surfers joined them, none were from the Whitehorse contingent, and as Will was nominally supposed to be directing things, he decided that they ought to get back. They caught the last wave in together, riding it into the white-water then dropping onto their stomachs and letting the ocean wash them onto the beach.

They sat unstrapping the leashes. Will felt the serene calmness descend on him, a feeling that only seemed to exist walking out of the sea after a surf. He looked over at Tamsin and knew he wasn't alone in that sensation.

"It's a good to be alive day," she said, sweeping back her hair from her eyes and sitting back in the sand. "All that matters is here and now. No past, no future, just now, this moment. Just this beach, these waves, this feeling." She stared out to sea. Will knew. This was why you got up early, why you braved the cold, why you took your near drownings. This was why you surfed, this feeling.

Their reverie was broken by a shout from Kris at the top of the road. "Oi, you two! Breakfast!" Succinct and to the point. They picked up their boards and headed up to the backpackers.

A 1966

The young man just managed to catch his balance as he was jostled from his position in front of the results board: a First. Surprisingly, relief was what he felt, not joy or elation as might have been expected, but relief. Maybe his emotions were tempered by the fact that he had no one with whom to celebrate. It had been a lonely three years, once they had found out about his rural background and even more unusual upbringing, but he had been asked a question and given a straight answer. He would learn from that... Sometimes it was better to hide the truth, hide who you really were because you couldn't expect others to understand.

He walked away down the corridor wondering what was next. He would go home briefly, of course, but they still hadn't come to terms with his decision to leave in the first place. It was a decision that saw him turn his back on their ways, superstitious ways that bore no scientific scrutiny. He chose science, the tangible, logical evidence of his own eyes. It was the true way, he was sure of that, and he would live with the consequences of that choice.

Chapter 12

The smell in the dorm, a mixture of alcohol, sweaty bodies and, if he wasn't mistaken, kebab, was almost overpowering. It didn't seem to be bothering Godfrey too much though, as he remained oblivious, curled up, with his head buried inside his sleeping bag. Either not bothered or dead, thought Will. He wondered whether the smell inside Godfrey's sleeping bag was somehow more pleasant than outside but given the nocturnal proximity of both physios, he doubted it.

Will and Tamsin got changed quickly, hoodies and board shorts being the order of the day, and after deciding it was best to let sleeping Godfreys lie, they left the room to get some sustenance.

They walked back along the beach road and then turned right, heading down the hill and into the town proper. To their left lay Towan Beach, and through a gap in the houses, Tamsin pointed out to sea.

"Do you see a crest of white-water," she said, "about half a mile out there?" Will strained his eyes.

"No," he said. She got closer to him so that he could follow the line of her arm. He was suddenly finding it very hard to concentrate on what she was trying to show him. Breathing in, he caught the light aroma of flowers from her shower gel, but underneath was the fresh, clean smell of the ocean.

"Hey," said Tamsin, turning her head towards him – their lips were mere centimetres apart – "out there!" She smiled and then turned her head back indicating the direction in which his attention was supposed to be focussed. A few hundred metres out from the edge of the headland and a long swim out from the beach, there was a small disruption to the incoming swell line.

"Oh yes, I see," said Will, focussing now on the intended target. "What about it?"

"*That* is the Cribbar Reef," replied Tamsin.

"The one you were talking about the other day."

"That's right."

Will looked again at the slightly white patch of sea. "Doesn't look much at the moment," he observed.

"No, but the conditions aren't right."

He looked out to sea again, imagining the huge wave, then, pondering, asked, "And it gets very big from what you said?"

Tamsin nodded.

"So, who was the first to ride it?" he asked.

"Three Australians did in 1966, and there have been a few since. It's a bit easier now that you can get towed with a jet ski onto it though. You used to go in down the old lifeboat rails and then paddle out from there."

"And you said it's not been back in a decade, right?"

"No, it hasn't, not in a really big way," she said wistfully.

"And did you see it then?"

She looked down. "Yes, I saw it" – she paused – "with Jen. It was the most incredible, awe-inspiring sight; the sheer immense power of the ocean." Her eyes seemed to light up. "We vowed that when it returned, we would ride it together." Her eyes narrowed, locked on the point in the distance, and the wind gently tugged at strands of her hair as though gently persuading her towards the bay. She blinked and her head flinched almost imperceptibly. "No, it's not been back since, and I guess now, we will never get that chance."

Will stared intently at the distant patch of water, straining his eyes to conjure some sort of image of how majestic such a wave might be. Maybe too intently, as he felt his vision swim. He staggered back a step and the scene formed in his mind, a massive, green wall of water, pounding the headland, testing the strength of all that lay before it, testing the resilience of the land — testing it to destruction. He felt nausea rise within him, then panic and sense of complete and utter helplessness, as the vastness of the wave engulfed him.

A hand grabbed and steadied him as he refocussed on reality. Tamsin gave him a quizzical look.

"Hangover catching up with you?" she asked.

"Er yes," he replied and rubbed his temples. His rather too vivid imagination was beginning to get the better of him. It could be useful when running scenarios on the ward, it even helped pick up the sick patients early, but sometimes it definitely got a bit carried away. "Thirty feet is a really big wave..." he said, "... too big."

Tamsin released her hold on his arm.

"No," he said, eyes intent upon hers, reading her thoughts, "I really wouldn't — not ever."

She briefly turned her head facing back out to sea, her lips tightened, then she started to walk, "Come on, I'm starving," she said, and they headed off for the fullest full English breakfast that could be found in Newquay.

They located the others in the first cafe they came to walking from the hostel and judging from some of the complexions of those around the tables, they had done well to get that far. Will and Tamsin pulled up a couple of seats and joined them. Those who had already started to tuck into the sausages, beans, mushrooms, bacon, tomatoes, and fried bread looked slightly more functional, and snippets of conversation suggested that cocktails were never to be touched again. Well, at least not until the coming evening at any rate. A couple of plates piled with "the works" arrived promptly and Will set about demolishing his while Tamsin gave a rather too honest appraisal of Will's surfing abilities between mouthfuls. He took the criticism in good spirit, accepting that it was probably no less than he deserved.

There was essentially one main street running through Newquay, lined with either places to eat, places to get surfing or beach equipment, or places to gamble away your money. Those needing kit filed into a shop replete with boards lined up outside like eight-foot white and yellow dominoes. The inside had the distinctive smell of neoprene and board wax, a scent not dissimilar to bubble-gum. Will wandered in after them and fielded any technical questions, such as, "Does the zip go on the front or back?" from the uninitiated. The answer he gave was, of course, "the front". There were stifled sniggers from individuals who had surfed before. Diving wetsuits tended to do up at the front, but surfers who spent time lying on their fronts didn't need to be lying on an uncomfortable zip, so the zip on the suits generally went on the back. It was entertaining to watch people go through the dilemma of whether it was really worth all that effort to get the suit off again and turn it round just to avoid a bit of discomfort and ridicule.

One of the guys ran back to the backpackers to pick up a car, returning in it to transport the big yellow foam boards to the beach car park. The party headed off after it, and Will and Tamsin stopped off at the hostel to get changed back into their cold, wet and slightly sandy wetsuits. Godfrey was clearly still pacing his day, head tucked well under his pillow.

A warming sun climbed in the near cloudless sky, its light reflecting off the waves as they rolled into shore. The beach was gradually filling up, the striped walls of windbreaks and mushroom-shaped umbrellas marking out territories and making it look a little like a scene from *Alice in Wonderland*. A blue Surfers Against Sewage banner fluttered and flapped against its pole above a food shack. It bore testament to a problem that was shared by many beaches, and not just in Cornwall. This organisation, formed by passionate surfers from the villages of St Agnes and Porthtowan, had campaigned from the early 1980s to improve the quality of water at Cornwall's beaches. A lot of beaches were marred by the raw sewage that flowed straight into the sea, which wasn't only unpleasant, but it also represented a significant health risk to anyone entering the water. Surfers Against Sewage brought it to the attention of the media and local government, and its campaign was having quite an impact.

On the beach, Will gave an impromptu lesson on surfing for those who required it, extoling the virtues of the yellow "foamies" for beginners to learn on. They were very buoyant and stable, so gave a surfer plenty of time to get themselves balanced before standing up. Of course, turning them was almost impossible, but that didn't matter to anyone riding their first wave. The exhilaration of getting to your feet and riding on top of the wave for the first time was probably a better feeling than an aerial stunt pulled when you were more experienced.

Tamsin lay by her board, basking in the mid-morning sunshine, largely ignoring proceedings and Shauna and Mel, who preferred to bodyboard, wandered off in the direction of the sea, boards under one arm, fins under the other. Bodyboarding, they had suggested, felt slightly safer given that you had something to hold on to when it all went wrong, and you knew it wasn't going to land on your head. The fins to put on your feet also allowed you to catch more waves, more often.

They had gone out between the red and yellow flags that marked the area the lifeguards covered for swimmers and bodyboarders. Surfers went in a separate area designated by black-and-white chequered flags. The lifeguards tended to get whistle happy if you strayed into the wrong zone.

Godfrey meandered his way absently onto the beach, the empty leash from his board dragging behind him, looking for all the world as though he had yet to discover that his dog had escaped. In the hand not carrying his board was his breakfast, a Silk Cut cigarette, from which he took a final drag before stubbing it out. He flicked the remaining filter into a bin, not even appearing to look in its direction. Far too well practised. He grunted at Will, pointed to the sea and, yawning, turned to head down the beach. Communication from Godfrey tended to be on a pretty basic level for the first hour or so after he got up. Reaching the water's edge, he bent down and tied his leash, swaying as he got back up, appearing to still have his eyes closed. He waved behind him, an indication that Will was to come and join him, so Will picked up his board, wishing his tutor group a fun time in the surf.

Gingerly, Godfrey shuffled forwards as a wave lapped over his feet, hesitating as they got wet. Visibly taking a deep breath, he waded in deeper, emitting a shriek of "Holy Mary, that's cold" that caused several heads to pop out from behind their protective screens.

Laughing, as his friend's somnambulant reverie was shattered, Will ran past him into the sea and began paddling furiously before the next set of waves came in.

"Sun cream?" asked Will when Godfrey finally joined him outback.

"Oh cock!" replied Godfrey and flopped across his board.

A couple of hours later, Will sat cross-legged on his beach-towel, wetsuit stripped off to the waist. He watched as Tamsin danced nymph-like with the waves; a much lighter, more symbiotic style than that of the herculean form of the surfer next to her. He'd wondered how Tamsin might react when Metern had arrived, but it seemed to have spurred her to an ever more impressive show. Metern too, he had noted, was a highly talented surfer. It seemed to take him little effort as he powered his way through the surf. He watched as Metern caught another wave, agilely landing on his 'thruster' short board and 'shredding' his way up and down the face of the wave. His turns were more acute and abrupt than Tamsin's, more powerful, sending spray careening ahead of the face, whereas Tamsin tended to caress the wave with her board, breezing softly across the lip, sensing the wave and going with it. He watched them going head-to-head, noticing that Tamsin always set off before Metern had got back to his take-off zone. She seemed to ignore his presence to the point that Will was slightly worried she was going to run him over, but she always turned just in time to avoid any — accidents.

His stomach rumbled. Smells from the food shack drew his attention away from the water, his body suggesting that he may not have had enough to eat despite the large breakfast earlier in the day. He looked back: the 'pro surfers' were on their way in, so the show was over anyway. Off to the shack then, which would provide you with anything you wanted, as long as it was a burger, a hot dog, or chips. Not the healthiest, but it would fill a hole. He ordered the standard burger and went back to sit by his board taking in the beach scene and the once more recumbent form of Godfrey, on whom the morning's exertions had obviously exacted a considerable toll. Shauna and Mel were busy discussing their best rides and Tamsin had arrived back on shore and was removing her wetsuit with her back to him. She seemed to be muttering something, but he couldn't hear what. There was a flap of wings and a squawk, and he pushed his arm up, just managing to rescue his lunch from an opportunistic herring gull. He swore at the bird, suggesting it tried somewhere else for its lunch.

"Ouch, fuck!" There was a shout from his right and Will twisted around to see Metern hopping up and down in the water clutching his foot. Jess, who was next to him, grabbed him as he winced, clearly in pain.

"Ow, ow, fuck, my foot," Metern cursed.

Will started to get up to help, but Jess and Mel were already ahead of him and Metern was helped onto the sand by Mel, who lowered him to sit down. Blood streamed all over the wetsuit as Metern brought his foot up to rest across his thigh. Will came over to see a large gash on the sole of the foot.

"It looks very nasty," said Mel, screwing up her face. "Glass?" It must have been several centimetres across.

"Yeah, I think so," said Metern, brushing away sand from the area.

"Is there a first aid kit anywhere?" asked Mel, twisting around. "Perhaps at the shack?"

Shauna, who had been hovering, ran over to the food shack, returning with a rudimentary medical kit.

"Here," she said, pulling out some gauze, "put this over it." Metern thanked her and pressed the gauze against the wound to staunch the flow. He grimaced. Jess came over with some bottled water and Metern lifted the pressure off so that the wound might be rinsed.

"Do you think there is any glass still in it?" Shauna asked.

"Doesn't feel like it," Metern replied. "I think it was one big chunk, so no fragments.'

Will looked up to see some of the group hunting around for the offending piece, without much success.

"It looks quite deep," said Mel, examining the wound. "It will need stitches."

"No, it'll be fine," said Metern, gritting his teeth as Mel prodded him a little more.

Her brow furrowed. "I'm not so sure it will be," she said, opening the cut up to flush it through some more. "I'm not sure that you will be able to walk on it for maybe a week or so. Look, we can run you up to the local casualty quickly and I'll do it. They'll have all the bits up there."

"No, really, just stick a couple of plasters over it and it will be fine. Honestly," replied Metern.

"I really think—"

"—No... thanks," said Metern, in a tone that suggested no debate. "It will be fine."

Reluctantly, she allowed him to reapply the pressure and then bound the foot with a temporary bandage.

"We'll take him back up to the hotel and sort him out from there," said Jess. Metern swore again as he was helped to his feet. His board had been rescued from the shallows, and he was supported, hopping, up the hill to the Seabreeze Hotel. Shauna collected the soiled dressings and put them in the bin by the shack, giving the man some money to buy a new first aid kit as she did so.

"Well, that was a bit of excitement," said Tamsin, without too much in the way of sympathy. "Does anyone want anything else from the shack? To eat, I mean." There were no requests, and she went and got another burger and drink. Godfrey raised his head, looked around, then let it drop back onto his towel.

Chapter 13

Some hours later, back at the hostel, the logistics of getting everyone through the showers had been dealt with. A few self-sacrificing individuals had foregone a shower, a few other, even more self-sacrificing souls had had a cold shower, the hot water having run out after the tenth surfer through. Godfrey observed that there was little sense in putting yourself through the suffering inflicted by a cold shower when all you were going to do was get covered in beer and smoke later in the evening. Shauna suggested that he try the oral, rather than topical application of his pint of Jail Ale, and she got covered in deodorant for her trouble, and then they headed out.

Newquay wasn't short of shops, and various parties went off to look around the town in the late afternoon. Will, Godfrey and Kris set off fully intending to do a bit of shopping themselves and investigate town a bit, but in the end, they decided that the best use of their time would be to go and sit in a pub. Very conveniently, they reached this decision at the precise moment they were passing The Golden Lion. They sat on the outside balcony, drinking their pints of finest ale, basking in the sun and their post exercise glow. Will loved this part of the day, where he had pushed his body, seemed to have used all his muscle groups, and now there was time to relax. His body almost hummed.

He watched the comings and goings of the harbour folk, some setting off to collect their crab pots, others to get a few hours' fishing in before dark. He watched the small boats make their way out of the walled, protective entrance, engines chugging away and heading out around the headland. It seemed such an enviable way of life, particularly on evenings such as this, with fine weather and benevolent water. Just you, your boat and whatever the ocean wished to give up. He knew, though, that this sort of evening was the exception rather than the rule and the weather more frequently consisted of wind and driving rain. These men still went out though, for the moment at least, risking their lives to scrape a living that didn't even earn them enough to live in the town in which they'd been born. Many had been persuaded to give up, selling to wealthy London bankers who would inhabit their homes for only a few weeks per year. Yes, the small-time fisherman's days were numbered, as were the souls of the fishing towns, that now relied almost exclusively on the tourist industry for four months to generate sufficient finance to last the rest of the year. It didn't, though, and so the young left which further killed the town. It could be very depressing in the winter months.

Will focussed his mind back to the present, where another pint had materialised in front of him. Kris leaned back in his chair. "So, Godfrey," he began, "which one is going to be the lucky lady tonight?"

While he pretended not to, Godfrey did like to be the centre of attention, and this was his opportunity to wax lyrical. Will sat back knowing full well what was coming next.

"Well," Godfrey replied, inhaling on his cigarette thoughtfully, "that is a tough one. You see, there are certainly several potential lucky candidates, but as yet, I'm undecided. I sort of feel responsible for Claire and Jill, as I brought them – "

" – What, both of them?" asked Kris.

Godfrey just smiled, before continuing, "And then there's Mel or Steff and..." He proceeded to name pretty much every female on the trip, with one notable exception, Will observed to himself.

"Godfrey, did it occur to you that this attraction thing does sort of have to go both ways?" pointed out Kris. Godfrey looked slightly blank.

"Honestly, I don't think it has," Will replied for him. "He'll maintain it's all about timing rather than personality and the ladies to have time with their friends. Don't bother them until it's an appropriate time to do so" – he shook his finger; a stern look on his face – "and don't turn on the charm too early."

"And too early is...?" asked Kris.

"Often not before –" Will started to explain but was interrupted.

"– Taxi time," said Godfrey, grinning.

"Explain," said Kris. Will shook his head. He had heard Godfrey's "Sermon of the Taxi Provider" before, many, many times.

"Most women," Godfrey began, "and when I say most you may assume all, are very much wrapped up in their own world, and it's largely a female world. They notice other women, respond to other women, talk to other women. They, for the most part of the evening, prefer the company of other women. In fairness, why wouldn't you? I mean look at us! Obviously, there are exceptions, but that's a separate talk. If you're a bloke in a nightclub, unless you have unnatural dancing abilities and you know how to use them, you tend to get in the way of a lady's good time with her friends. They don't like, and who could blame them, 'grinders with two left feet'." He swivelled his hips in an uncomfortable fashion to demonstrate. The concept of a gyrating male pelvis, particularly Godfrey's, certainly did nothing for Will... or Kris from the expression on his face.

"So," Godfrey continued, "as a chap, you can drift around on the peripheries having a good time with your mates – this doesn't include dancing but does include drinking, until it's time to return home in the rarest of commodities, the taxi, which *you* have conveniently mustered to be at your and a significant other's disposal."

"Really?" said Kris, looking puzzled,

Godfrey turned to Will, who knew what was coming. "Who had the higher trap rate at the GX as house officers, you or me?" he asked. The GX was actually a nightclub in Plymouth called the Jesternellium Club but was referred to as the GX, or "Groin Exchange", by locals.

"You did," said Will, resigned.

"And who seems to be in with all of the ladies before midnight, engaging them in wonderful repartee that none of them can hear because the music is too loud?"

"Me," said Will, his head going into his hands.

"And who struts their stuff on the dance floor with fancy salsa and jive moves?"

"Me again," said Will. Godfrey, when he had a point to make, made sure to press it home.

"And who appears to do nothing until closing time and then appears with a taxi?"

"That would be you."

"And who left, often with not one but several ladies in his taxi?"

"Ah, that would be you again. And can I just say I am still upset about you repeatedly surrendering my seat to so-called 'damsels in distress'."

Godfrey gave a pitying smile. "Generally, it boils down to taxis and their limited availability," said Godfrey, "and doing your talking in the cab on the way back to theirs."

"Taxis!" snorted Will. "And there was me thinking I left those places on my own because of rumours that I had a small knob and am a crap shag." Godfrey winced and Kris spluttered into his beer.

"Small knob *and* a crap shag," a now familiar voice chuckled from behind him. "Poor Dr Cunningham," said Tamsin, who appeared from over his left shoulder alongside the other medical students. Godfrey and Kris were having trouble staying on their chairs.

"My capabilities as a doctor, my surfing prowess and now my reputation as a sex god in tatters. I truly have no credibility left with you at all," said Will with a wan smile.

"No, Dr Cunningham, you don't!" said Tamsin, pursing her lips. She shifted her gaze to her left. "And Godfrey, I shall be alerting all of the ladies not to enter into any 'taxi' negotiations with you unless a drink is forthcoming right now."

"Ah, yes," he said, looking guilty. "A *Doom Bar* for the lady?" She nodded. "Anyone else?"

The other medical students all grinned and Godfrey picked up the empties and went to the bar, to return a short while later having delivered his forfeit. He sat down with a sigh as Kris got up to visit the gents. "What do you make of her?" Godfrey asked, nodding in Tamsin's direction.

"I really don't know," said Will.

"You like her though, don't you?" said Godfrey.

"Yes," replied Will cautiously, "I think I do, but it's so difficult to keep up with her. One minute she's all beguiling smiles and laughter, and the next... well, it's as though I'm something the cat just coughed up." He recalled the way she had left him lying on the floor of the hospital ward. "Then there are times when she drifts away no doubt fighting some internal demon."

Godfrey gave him a look.

"OK, poor choice of metaphor."

"You need to remember she has been through a lot," said Godfrey. "Jen was her best friend, and I guess she feels very guilty about what happened."

"Why guilty?" asked Will.

Godfrey hesitated a fraction, then rubbed his nose. "I spoke to her once at the GX," he began.

Will looked alarmed.

"It's OK," said Godfrey. "She beat me in a race to the taxi that evening and then told the driver to drive off. I can still see her grinning out of the back window."

Will relaxed a bit.

"Anyway, earlier I had found her in a corner of the nightclub, and we... God help me... started talking. Probably why I failed to score that evening. She seemed quite low and was on the edge of tears – needed to offload I suppose. She told me that she feels she could have done more to prevent Jen's death somehow." He reached to pull out a cigarette. "And she holds Metern responsible for what happened." He looked up at Will. "You know that he and Jen had been going out?"

"I think I knew that," said Will, puffing his cheeks out. "But why responsible for her death? It was suicide after all, wasn't it?"

"Yes, it was," said Godfrey. "But" – he hesitated – "for some... reason, she blames him. Maybe for breaking up with her or not stopping her, I don't know."

"Do you think that Jen killing herself was about more than just the drug error with the patient then – that Cadan Metern was partly to blame?"

"Yes, maybe. And Tamsin's stories..."

"But they're an odd thing to make up," mused Will. "I mean, Metern's pedigree as a scientist is about as unquestionable as it comes. Everybody always mentions his publications – genetics, wasn't it?"

"You've read those papers?"

"No, obviously not," said Will, as if the mere thought was beyond him. "But if you have any grounding in science at all, magic and the occult is nonsensical. And as for child sacrifice, or whatever it was that Tamsin accused him of..." Will shook his head. "I presume there were no missing children from the neonatal unit and no dismembered bodies found strewn throughout the hospital!"

"No more than usual, and none that got a mention!" said Godfrey sarcastically, then he hesitated, looking down at his beer. "There *is* something else you ought to know," he said, but his attention was drawn by Kris returning from his ablutions and he let out a resigned breath, "Though it's probably best if she tells you yourself... if she wants to."

Kris arrived back at the table fiddling with his flies. "Bloody thing," he said. "I can never get the damn buttons to match the right bloody buttonhole! It's not just me, is it?" Will and Godfrey both laughed, and they made sure he knew that it *was* just him.

The Indian Spice was situated towards the far end of town, slightly further than anticipated by Will and the others, who hadn't made it past The Golden Lion. So, this misjudgement, and the fact that they had left at half seven, to be at the restaurant for half past seven, meant they arrived midway through the poppadum and had to squeeze in on the end of one of the allotted tables. It was cosy in the restaurant, whose walls depicted vibrant Indian scenes of dancing women, their red and gold dresses swirling against mountain range backdrops. Will settled back into the heavy red-velour-upholstered seat and listened to the high-pitched twang of the sitar music, remembering his student days. Curry had been a staple in the diet of most students, though it had been perhaps as much as a year at med school, before he personally had had one sober and truly appreciated how tasty they could be.

A very patient waiter returned to take the orders of the latecomers and Will opted for a chicken Rogan josh. There was a general excited hubbub around the table, with chatter about waves and rides and wipe-outs. Shauna and Mel were once again extolling the virtues of bodyboarding and Godfrey was offering to teach the physios how to play the sitar. Did Godfrey really possess a sitar?

Metern seemed none the worse for his foot injury and appeared in very good spirits, leading the conversation, and keeping the group on the other table riotously entertained with tales from his physics lab.

"So, did you voluntarily switch to medicine," asked one of the group, "or were you essentially forced to leave in order to preserve both the structural and moral integrity of the Faculty of Physics?" Will had overheard snippets of a tale about a Professor Gwendoline Jones, ethyl chloride, an electrical current and a not insignificant amount of hair loss, site undisclosed.

"It is true that I had trouble concentrating in Professor Jones' tutorials after that and there were letters exchanged but making mankind's existence better seemed a more worthy pursuit than just the professor, so I opted for medicine." The captivated group laughed on cue, except, Will noted, Tamsin, who just stared out of the window.

"Bananas" looked to be a run-of-the-mill club, Will thought, as he entered through a black door closely guarded by two very solidly built bouncers. He supposed it would have to do now that the pubs had all shut. They had disposed of a couple of very pleasant, if quite beery, hours in a number of local hostelries before meeting up in this randomly chosen nightclub. A few plastic tropical fruits dangled from the walls of a darkened corridor, lit only by fairy lights hanging from a palm tree. There was a hatch to relieve the patrons of their cash and coats, then a bend in the corridor gave entrance to a room about the size of a tennis court. Strobe lighting flashed away and the walls were daubed with splashes of fluorescent pink paint. Spotlights reflected off the glitter ball dangling from a low ceiling above a lit dance floor.

The DJ was warming up playing a variety of eighties songs, the current one being by the Pet Shop Boys. There were a few curious looks from those Will guessed to be regulars who were propping up the bar in the far corner. Will's attention was caught by Godfrey, who had staked a claim on a large table underneath a neon "Tropicana" sign not too far away from the slightly raised dance floor. A few people were already up and dancing, prompting some of the girls to join them. Godfrey hurried off to the bar, keen not to get involved in anything that might interfere with his drinking for now. He returned a short time later with two large green drinks containing fruit, an umbrella, and a curly straw.

"What the heck is that?" shouted Will above the music and looking at the absurd concoction.

"They did have bottled beers at ridiculous prices, but these little beauties" – he indicated the glasses in his hands – "were two for the price of one!" Will looked sceptical. "It's a 'Twisted Serpent' apparently, and I think it contains most of the top shelf."

Will took the proffered drink and tried a sip. "Wow!" he said, eyes widening as the drink burned its way down his throat. Will took a guess at the ingredients. Grenadine, crème de menthe, lemon, and who knew what else, but, having had a sip, it wasn't the worst cocktail he'd had, but there was no way he was going to drink it just to be certain that it wasn't. He got up to fetch a beer and saw Tamsin wandering in with the medical students. They made a beeline to where he stood at the bar and, shortly, his wallet the best part of thirty pounds lighter,

Will made his way back to the table, still puzzling at their impeccable timing. Tamsin came to sit next to him and gave him a quizzical look.

"Who chose the club?" she asked.

"Erm, we just picked a name that Godfrey had seen as we came into town. Why?"

"Oh, nothing," she replied, a smirk now playing on her lips. The DJ expertly mixed Kylie's "I Should Be So Lucky" onto the sound system, punching the rhythm with his right hand as he did so. He wore a tight white T-shirt and jeans with a leather cap on back to front and seemed to be doing the trick as far as the patrons were concerned; the dance floor was filling up a treat.

Tamsin leaned over to shout in his ear again. He could feel her breath on his ear. "Not noticed anything about the clientele, for example?" He looked about him and toward the dance floor. She was right, some of those guys could really move, maybe professional even.

He nodded at Tamsin. "Yes, they're really good dancers, aren't they." She just smiled and turned her attention back to the centre of the room. He'd seen that smile before. In fact, it was one that he was aware he wore at times as well. Was he missing something? It was just like any other nightclub. Usual decor, expensive drinks, jobbing DJ. There was a reasonable mix of folks too, fewer women perhaps, but that wasn't so unusual.

Tamsin leaned over. "The name of the place not a clue?" Will looked around some more. "Or even the music... The Communards, Culture Club, Kylie?"

Will pursed his lips and frowned as the penny suddenly dropped. As he did so, the lights dipped to a very low glow and the DJ asked for the dance floor to be cleared. "You Sexy Thing" started to play over the system and a spotlight spun around the room flashing briefly across a very shiny individual making his way sinuously onto the floor.

"Please welcome the smooth and rippling, the dark and delicious... and that's not a Flake in his trunks... it's Hot Chocolate!" The spotlight steadied and rested on an exceptionally well-muscled black man, wearing what remained of a sequinned shirt, some very tight shorts, a smouldering look and little else. Will looked over at Godfrey, who looked down at his drink, then rapidly around at his surroundings and finally at the cheering, clapping crowd of onlookers. His head jerked upright like a meerkat on sentry duty.

"Crikey," he mouthed at Will, as a few strange looks from his group were cast in their direction.

Tamsin cupped a hand to Will's ear so he could hear her. "I must say that explains a lot," she said, and laughed. Will just sat there, and his jaw dropped as Hot Chocolate started to swivel to the music. Will looked over at Godfrey, who was drinking his Twisted Serpent far more quickly than was good for him. Hot Chocolate began slowly divesting himself of what little clothing he was wearing. The shirt was removed and swung around his head, before he transferred it to between his legs and, in essence, "flossed" with it. The shirt became a lasso, dragging some unfortunate from the crowd to participate in a light whipping, before both got discarded, and Hot Chocolate eased a thumb down either side of the very tight shorts. Off they came and, to Will's relied at least, he had concealed an even tighter and even smaller pair underneath. Will saw Godfrey wince and then shut his eyes. The routine went on for quite a long four minutes before Hot Chocolate finished with his infamous, he was informed, "Chocolate Banana". The girls around the table were all laughing hysterically, and the males all looked a bit stunned. Hot Chocolate left the floor to rapturous acclaim.

Tamsin got up. "Coming to dance," she asked, as several of the group got up.

"I'm not absolutely sure I can compete with that," he shouted above the music.

"Best keep your clothes on then," she suggested, and she pulled him up from the seat.

Half an hour or so later, after Will had exhausted both of his jive moves, they went to sit back down. He looked about just before seating himself and noted that they had left Metern on the dance floor. Metern was on the dance floor! Miraculously, he didn't appear to be suffering any ill effects from the accident earlier in the day. The anaesthetic properties of one of those nasty green drinks? Metern would be sore in the morning and Will hoped that his sticking plasters had held.

Time drifted on, and after a beer and another dance, Tamsin sidled over. "Do you fancy leaving?" she shouted, struggling to be heard above George Michael. Will had been thinking as much himself. He'd never been a great one for clubs. While there was always a temptation to stay on in case you missed something, there rarely was anything to actually miss and Will suspected that the double act of "Peaches and Cream" might be the sort of performance that he wouldn't regret missing.

Chapter 14

The air was cool as they left the nightclub, refreshing and revitalising after the heavy, smoky atmosphere of the club. "Well, I'd never been to a gay strip club before tonight," said Will, taking a deep breath.

"You have now," said Tamsin, grinning, then she took his arm.

"In fact, I don't think I've ever been to any strip clubs before," Will continued, the fresh air and alcohol making his head spin, but in a comfortable way. He swayed slightly, brushing against Tamsin. "I should probably go and see a 'real' strip club just to balance things out."

She caught his arm, steadying him, then linked her arm in his. "That was a 'real' strip club," she pointed out, laughing.

"Oh, you know what I mean – that one doesn't count. I mean one where I... er... well, I er..."

"Have more of an interest in the floorshow?" she said.

"Yes," said Will. "I mean, I already see more male anatomy than I like every time I get changed to play sport." He paused thoughtfully and turned to Tamsin. "Do women run around changing rooms naked, flicking each other with towels?" he asked as innocently as possible.

"What do you think?" she replied, patiently, as though dealing with a child particularly slow on the uptake.

"Yes," Will decided, beaming a self-satisfied grin. Tamsin looked skyward.

"Come on," she said, shaking her head, "I have something to show you," and she began to head off up the hill to the beach road. Will's ears pricked up.

"No, wrong guess!" she said, mildly exasperated. "We're going to the dunes."

"The dunes being...?"

"You'll see," she said, grabbing his arm.

Will wasn't exactly sure what he was about to be shown but was more than happy to go along with whatever Tamsin had in mind. His head felt pleasantly floaty now and his balance had got much better with Tamsin's support. His mind tottered a little behind his mouth, but Tamsin didn't seem to care, and though there wasn't exactly an urgency in the way she led him up the road, he could still feel the keen pull on his arm. His usually overactive mind also seemed to have taken the night off. It hadn't even bothered to concern itself with where it might be being taken, content to just be in the company of a really, very attractive girl and one who appeared to have at least a slight interest in him. Not bothered that was, until they reached the top of the gentle rise and he looked out across the expanse of the shoreline. Then he stopped dead in his tracks.

To the left, dotted amongst the dunes, between the beach proper and the golf course, were pockets of light emanating from a multitude of small fires, glinting like stars on a moonlit cloth. Silhouetted against this backdrop were groups of figures, some seated, some standing, some swaying, some dancing, all to the rhythm and beat of music, the notes of which now drifted up to him on the wind. His eyes attuned to the darkness and in the nearest group he could make out guitars, flutes, a violin and, if he wasn't mistaken, a bodhrán. The furious beat of the Irish drum, accompanied by the intricate melody of a penny whistle, spun and wove a reel, while ghostly forms spiralled like tendrils of smoke curling away from the central fire. He felt a further tug on his arm, and Tamsin beckoned him on, smiling at Will's reaction to this mystical scene. He started walking again, eyes drawn to the distant lines of bobbing torches, fireflies seeking their promised, eternal nirvana.

The rough gravel car park became a gateway to this land, and Tamsin, once on the beach, reached down and slipped her shoes from her feet. Will did likewise. The cool sand felt like strands of silk between his toes, soothing after misplaced heels on the dance floor. The lightest zephyr played with smoke from the charcoal and driftwood fires, sending it first one way, then the other, teasing it apart until it dispersed to nothing.

As they walked, every so often one of those gathered around the fires would look up and shout a greeting to Tamsin as she passed, some inviting her to join them. She smiled at the first few, acknowledging them with a wave or a "Hi", but not stopping. Instead, she headed mid-way along the beach to join a ring of dancers as they circled a small fire. They parted to include her as she arrived.

She glanced towards Will, who suddenly felt very self-aware, unsure about joining the ring. He pulled back and felt his hand slip from Tamsin's. She gave him a challenging look, but Will pointed to the circle of exclusively female dancers. He motioned to the fact that he wasn't wearing a skirt, she shrugged, and he sat down in the sand next to another male onlooker who offered him a cigarette. He declined with a polite shake of his head.

A bodhrán player started to beat out a rhythm, the double-headed stick flicking over the taut drum-skin, striking in different areas to produce differing volumes and depths of pitch. The bodhrán was joined first by a fiddle player, then by a penny whistle, which came in with the melody. The dancers swayed in time, their feet picking up the rhythm. It wasn't possible to hit every beat, to tap it out in the way that traditional Irish dancers could do, the sand prevented that, but they timed the foot movements to the first strike of each bar, that the bodhrán player emphasised as he played. Will focussed back on Tamsin, her graceful, lithe form easing slowly into the tune. Then, gaining speed, she began spinning and twisting, her hair flowing first one way then the other, like a kelp forest caught between two currents. Round and round she spun, arms above her head shaping the turns, the hem of her dress – ever chasing to catch up, wound itself tightly around her thighs with the spin, then flared out as her direction changed, its green and red colours trapped for but an instant in the firelight. She was absorbed, taken by the music, and Will watched her, transfixed, oblivious to all the other dancers as she moved. She blended into the music, her feet blurred by the sand kicked up and her body flickering in and out of the darkness. She pirouetted, a leg extended, toes pointed, before stamping down, then smoothly and slowly turned until she faced him side on, arm extended, finger pointing, she reached out. Her chin rose from her shoulder and she looked down the straight line of her right arm, directly into his eyes. A heat welled within him, a deep burning within in his chest; an ache, a desire, an intense and desperate need. Fire flashed in her eyes as her hands traced intricate patterns in the air and a thin mist wafted in, drawn from the sea. Her lips moved but he was unable to hear what she said. He didn't care, she was so utterly, mesmerizingly beautiful; he could not take his eyes off her.

The rhythm quickened, she adjusted without effort, split stepping to cover the change, small spits of sand kicking up as she did so. He watched her face as she danced, lost again in the freedom of movement, her eyes now drawn to the central focal point of the fire, lost in the motion and the music. He felt a strong pull, a yearning from within him, urging him to join in. She joined hands with the other dancers as the music slowed then, abruptly, the ring turned out and invited the gathered onlookers in to join the dance. Tamsin turned to face him, extending her arm once again and her index finger hooking, beckoning him in. He rose before he even knew what he was doing and took Tamsin's hand as the circle closed once again.

They began to move anti-clockwise, slowly at first, each step matching the soft beat of the bodhrán. The penny whistle blended in, the trill notes soaring high then plummeting away; long drawn out, piecing the darkness, as lodged somewhere high up in the dunes, a violin wove a haunting melody; Will felt the hurt, the betrayal, the loss as tears came unbidden to his eyes. Without knowing why, Will lowered his gaze into the fire.

The whistle quickened up and instantly the tenor changed. The beat of the drum became faster, heads came up and the ring started to rotate. The pave increased and he found himself having to cross-step to keep up. The music became louder, more intense. He felt his mood suddenly lift and energy surge into him, flooding his body, cleansing it of the day's fatigue, banishing everything except the now. The drumstick clicked against the frame, demanding a greater, faster rhythm, beating out two, three, four times the rate. His feet began to fly across the sand. A fleeting, distant thought worried that he might trip, or fall, but he sensed the strength of the circle, knowing it would keep him buoyed. He needn't worry; he couldn't fall, this wouldn't be allowed to happen – and that small thought too, evaporated in the flames of the fire.

The ring flew faster, the drum reverberations flowed though him – so much energy, so much power, it seemed he was flying. There was a rushing in his ears. He no longer felt the sand beneath his feet, only wind currents. Dimly, he was aware of the hands clasped in his, their grip tightening, desperately holding on as the ring spun ever more rapid. The music washed through him, touching his heart, his mind and his spirit, and he felt himself propelled upwards, cast towards the night sky...

Woah, this didn't feel right; he was on the edge of blacking out. His head was spinning, the circle was going too fast... Or was it? Or was this just one of his episodes? He felt disconnected, dissociated. This was a bit like what had happened before, but much, much more intense and then he would see...

He was overcome by a hollow fear; an impression of impending, inescapable inevitability, as though trapped between two twisting serpents from which there would be no getting away... really unpleasant, not nice! And then his vision cleared. Well sort of cleared. Images began to swirl and cycle before him. Wizened creatures their stooped bodies ravaged by time and sorrow walked forest paths surrounded by humming insects. Animals walked in verdant pastures as family groups tended their crops, their basic woollen clothing just enough to protect them from the chill air. OK, this was odd. He looked around him; birds flocked in reddening skies, as metallic suited beings wandered awestruck among blue-barked trees. Had his drink been spiked?

His vision shimmered once more and he was in the middle of a storm. This was more vivid, more real. Winds whipped along a rugged coastline before him and waves smashed into a promontory, a narrow headland, their impact sending spray spiralling out in twisted helices far beyond where the eye could see, out into the infinite.

Will's mind was just, as usual trying to work out if he were going mad, when there was a sudden sharp pain in his right hand. The world lurched as he felt himself flung back to the physical reality of the beach. Fingernails dug into his palm and he heard high-pitched shrieks. Aware for the first time that his eyes had been closed, they flicked open. The fire appeared to shoot away from him and he saw the circle of people fly off in all directions as though mud flakes jettisoned from a spinning wheel. The penny whistle held a long shrill high note, getting shriller and he realised that he was travelling backwards at speed. His feet couldn't catch up and he lost all contact with the ground. Time seemed to stand still; was it really seconds before existence caught up? It did and it took his breath away as he hit hard into the base of a dune. Next to him he heard a thud and a flash of red and green. More sand sprayed over him as Tamsin suffered a similar fate. The whistle stopped and there were a few moments of stunned silence... Then the laughter started. Will shook his head, again trying to clear it, unsure what had just happened. He looked over at Tamsin, whose hair was strewn across her face. There was a wild look to those fire-specked eyes.

There were a few moments stunned silence as everyone looked around. No one appeared any the worse for the experience and a raucous laughter burst out from the dancers as they picked themselves up. Tamsin got up, a wicked smile on her face and brushed herself down, giving Will a playful kick to do the same. He did so but still feel disorientated. The power he had felt within the circle was like nothing he had ever experienced, and while his mind often played out scenes in his head, the images he had experienced had seemed more real than usual. He flicked the remaining sand from his shirt, noticing that his hand shook. What *had* just happened? He looked over at Tamsin and felt a jolt within his chest as she linked her arm in his and set them off wandering down the beach towards another group of people and another fire, this one nestled between two dunes set in a sort of amphitheatre. Will's mind settled, dismissing any concerns, focussing once more, solely on the heat of Tamsin's arm through his thin shirt.

Glowing embers bathed the surrounds in a warm and welcoming light. A number of individuals were curled into impromptu seats created in the banked-up sand and a musician took centre stage by the fire. Tamsin seemed to know the musician, who wore an Australian bush-hat. He nodded to her as he strummed "The House of the Rising Sun" on his guitar, singing as he did so. His audience joined in, providing an enthusiastic, if not melodious, accompaniment.

Tamsin led Will and they climbed up the dune behind the fire, burying themselves down into it as others had done, the sand moulding perfectly to the contours of their bodies. Tamsin settled herself into the crook of Will's arm. He rested his chin gently on her head; her hair still smelled fresh and floral in spite of the smokiness of the nightclub and bonfires. Looking over the fire and out to sea, he watched the light from the moon dance across the water as the waves washed onto the shore.

"This is such a beautiful, magical place," he whispered, realising that they hadn't exchanged so much as a word since arriving on the beach.

"Yes," she murmured. "Almost as though you've left your physical self behind and entered an alternative realm."

He knew exactly what she meant. Although what he was seeing and experiencing was real, it just didn't feel like it; it was like entering a sort of dissociative state. The softness of the sand cradled his body such that it did become difficult to actually feel anything at all. Anything, that was, except the warmth from the woman curled into his body, that was very real. He looked about him at the grey hues, the blacks and whites of the moonlit night, together with the faerie figures which still spun and danced next to other fires, creating an otherworldly, ethereal scene.

"Is it always like this here?" he asked, as the singers built for a final verse.

"No," she replied, "not quite like this. There are, of course, always people coming down to the beach at all times of day or night, but once in a while, a long while..." She trailed off.

"...there are nights like tonight?" Will finished for her, and Tamsin nodded. "And did you know it would be this night?" Will asked.

She looked up at him, sparks of firelight flashing in her emerald eyes. "Might have done," she said. Will smiled ruefully. She had seemed quite keen to leave the nightclub, but it hadn't been just about him after all, had it.

"You seem to know a lot of people," he observed, as another reveller waved in her direction.

She returned the gesture. "My family... we used to live here once," she explained, then her head dropped, and she hesitated. "Jen's and mine." A glowing ember from the fire drifted upwards, and Will tracked it as it vanished into the night sky. "I still have a few contacts," Tamsin continued, "who let me know if anything is happening."

Will looked over to the musician in the hat, who had moved into his Simon and Garfunkel repertoire.

"That's Bruce," she said, following Will's movement and laughing with clear affection. "He's as Cornish as they come, in spite of the name, but yes, he spent some time in Australia, hence the hat."

Will laughed as well, but felt a strange twang of, was it, jealousy? "So, you and Jen must have been quite young?"

"Yes, we were only fifteen. We used to surf all day," she continued, her attention thankfully returning from the Cornishman, "then grab a bite to eat at home, or even just raid the fridge for something to stick on a fire and come out here to the dunes. It was so exciting!"

"Your poor parents," said Will, looking at an unkempt youth walking past offering to sell a box of Black Magic chocolates. "I mean, it's a fantastic party, but I suspect *he* didn't get those from an auntie who hadn't realised he didn't like dark chocolate."

"Oh, Will!" she scoffed. "Yes, there is a rule-breaking element here, but it's a small community and everyone looked out for everyone else. We were in no danger."

Will looked sceptical. "So, your mum and dad approved of your nocturnal adventures then?"

Tamsin shrugged. "Actually, most of the time we sneaked out of our bedroom windows, so there was no actual approval or disapproval."

Will snorted. "Well at least it meant that they didn't worry, I suppose."

Another older youth walked past offering "something to smoke" and Tamsin waved him away.

"So why did the family move?" he said.

"Dad got a job at the dockyard in Plymouth and I'd shown some academic aptitude. Schools back then weren't great here, so everything directed us towards Devon."

"And you were sad to leave?"

"Absolutely. It was a long drive over to Bantham for a surf, not like here where we used to just walk out of the front door onto the beach."

"That must have been hard," he paused for a moment. "And you'd have had to leave your friends. Jen, what happened to her?"

"She ended up going to Truro and yes it was. We drifted apart for a bit."

"And yet you both ended up doing medicine, but three years apart. How was that?"

"Jen was always set on doing medicine, so her path was clear. Sciences at A level, got the grades, and then she went to Bristol Medical School. I was less certain. I'd always been interested in the past, why things happened and how they influenced today's world. I was good at sciences as well, so did history, biology and physics at A level. Then I went on to read history in Cardiff. It was a really good course, really interesting, but I found myself increasingly regretting that I wasn't doing anything to help humankind in the present and for the future. And, whenever I spoke to Jen and heard how much she enjoyed medicine, what she was doing and where it might take her, I sort of wanted to do it too."

"You didn't just drop out of the course and start again?"

"No. I spoke to the med school and convinced them I was serious, so they agreed that as long as I got a 2.1 degree and did A level chemistry at the same time as my degree, they would take me. So, I spent a few months at a local crammer as well as uni. I'm not going to pretend I understood much of the chemistry at any point, but I ticked the box that needed ticking."

"It took some guts to do that, not to mention a brain like a sponge."

"Well, I just got my head down and did it. I'd decided that medicine was where I was going in life and those were the hurdles I had to jump."

"Still, really well done."

"Careful," she said, flashing him a smile, "that's dangerously close to a compliment."

Will wrinkled his nose and they watched a few of those at an adjacent fireside standing to link arms as the bodhrán player began to beat a fresh rhythm and the flautist started a new tune. Will drew Tamsin closer with his arm.

"So, what happened... to Jen, I mean?"

She didn't reply for several moments, and Will felt her head turn to gaze out to sea.

"I'm sorry, I didn't mean to –" But she cut him off.

"– No, it's fine." She exhaled deeply. "But if I tell you what happened, you must believe it's the truth. Too many people have said horrible, wicked things about Jen." Then added, "And about me."

Her breath smelled sweet as she turned her face up to his.

"I will," he replied, returning her look. "I promise."

Tamsin took another deep breath. "A number of months ago, Jen phoned me in floods of tears," she began. "She had been seeing someone for over a year and was besotted. He was an obstetrics and gynaecology registrar whom she'd met over an emergency caesarean section. He was apparently, amazing, wonderful, caring, intelligent... it sounded as if he was going to save the world the way she went on about him so much. She loved him and, it seemed, he loved her back. He was the one." Tamsin sat forward and ran a hand through her hair.

"You're talking about Cadan, right?" Will asked.

"Yes," she snorted.

"But?"

"Well, it looked as though it would all end happily ever after, in a perfect meringue-dress wedding... except it didn't. He had always been a bit secretive about his life in general, something about being brought up in foster care, or so Jen had thought, and it sounded as though he'd had quite a bad time of it. He'd been very bright and accelerated through several years at school as well, which created tensions with kids of his own age when growing up. I think all of that had made him quite a hardened, isolated personality."

"And maintaining relationships would have been difficult for him?" said Will.

"I guess so," Tamsin replied. "Most of the time, Jen said, he was really great fun to be with, life and soul, so to speak. Life and soul, that is, right up until he utterly lost it. He had a fiery temper, still does. What you saw in the mess was nothing." Will remembered how terrified Tamsin had looked. "It didn't happen particularly often at first and was never directed at her specifically, but gradually the outbursts happened with increasing frequency."

"What do you mean?"

"Well, he had incredibly labile mood swings. Fine one moment, inconsolable the next, occasionally high, sometimes violent." Tamsin looked at Will. "I don't think he ever hit Jen or anything, she never said he did, but I got the feeling that it might only have been a matter of time."

"That doesn't sound good."

"No," agreed Tamsin. "And to make things worse, then he started having these absence episodes as well; from what I can tell, like petit mal epilepsy. Jen urged him to get help, but he refused, saying he was just tired and had a lot on his mind – told her it was nothing she need be concerned about."

Will frowned. New onset epilepsy in adults often meant a fairly nasty underlying problem. He could see why Jen would have been worried. "Then what happened?" Will asked.

"She backed off a bit, gave him time to come to his own conclusions about getting help, hoping he would realise before it got too late. But then at work she came across a thirty-year-old with very similar symptoms who turned out to have a brain tumour."

"And that would have worried her more and set her off again."

"Yes, she insisted he get help, then threatened to tell the hospital, the police and pretty much anyone who might come down on him to get help. She was doing it for his own good, because she loved him," Tamsin asserted.

"And did he see someone, get help?"

"No. Instead, she got dumped."

"Oh!" Will snorted. "So did she let anyone know or act on her intentions?"

"No, she didn't. She held out hope that he would come to his senses or there would be a minor incident, in which case she would go and pick up the pieces. But he held it all together."

"Poor Jen," said Will. The youth with the chocolates walked past again, chewing. Maybe he'd got over his dislike of dark chocolate. "So how did she cope?" he asked.

"Really badly. It was as though he'd stolen away her very essence. She barely functioned, not eating, not sleeping, didn't turn up for work. It was awful, and nothing I, or anyone, did seemed to bring her out of it. Finally, as a measure of desperation, I thought a skiing holiday might be good for her. Next to the surf, she loved the mountains and snow. A chance to get away for a bit, do some partying. She was happy enough to go along with the idea and her mood even lifted slightly."

Tamsin bit her lip forming a tiny droplet of blood which glimmered like a black pearl in the firelight. "But then she had her accident. It was really serious, or at least appeared so at first. We think she was trying to catch up with Metern having followed him down to the basement, to the mosaic. He'd apparently decided to go and have a look at it between cases. It was, he said, a place that he found relaxing, and he visited it to unwind." She shook her head, and Will felt her clench her jaw against his chest.

An odd choice, Will thought, the basement of a hospital, rather than, say, the mess balcony, where you might get some fresh air. There *was* quite an impressive Roman horse depicted down there, he'd been himself once, but it was hardly anything that might be considered relaxing.

Tamsin continued. "Metern *said* he'd heard a pager go off and then heard a scream, presumably that of Jen as she fell. He said he'd turned and run to see her lying at the base of the stairs, unconscious. When he got to her, he *said* that she had stopped breathing. He called the crash team and started CPR. When the team arrived, she looked in a bad way, head laceration over her temple, ankle at right angles, but Metern *had* managed to resuscitate her, and she was breathing again spontaneously."

"He saved her life then?"

Tamsin's bloodied lips reflected a thin smile. "Perhaps, if you believe what he said."

The wind picked up and swirls of smoke from one of the fires blew across them. Tamsin wafted her hand in front of her face, clearing the smoke.

"Jen got whisked away to A & E, and after all of the tests, she seemed to have got away very lightly, given what was reported to have happened. Despite all the blood, there was now only a tiny nick to her head, and scans suggested that she may have had an old injury, nothing new. Her ankle was a mess, of course, but not life-threatening.

"So, she was very lucky," said Will. "What happened then?"

"Her ankle got fixed and she had a bit of time off."

"OK," said Will. "And generally... her recovery? The skiing holiday?" He remembered what Shauna had told him in the pub about the almost miraculous recovery.

"Well, that's just it, I'd written off our holiday. I mean, I'd thought there was absolutely no chance of going. None whatsoever. Three weeks after surgery, however, and she was carving huge turns into fresh powder snow." Tamsin's eyes glistened, pools of reflected fire welling up as she recounted the story. "God, she was good. If there was no sea, the mountains and snow were a pretty decent second option for her. Watching her snowboard down a mountain was like watching a swallow in flight, twisting and turning, effortless traverses, utterly in her element."

She was silent for several moments as the fire crackled below them. "For most of the holiday it was as though none of it had happened. No Metern, no morbid obsession and bizarrely no accident. Mentally, she seemed like a new person, as if the blow to her head had knocked out all of the bad stuff and knocked some sense in. The days were great, wild even – she was awesome fun. You should have seen the attention she got in the bars afterwards. But," Tamsin said, pausing, "then I woke one night thirsty and went to get a drink. I found her, also out of bed, staring out of the window into the darkness. Her expression was blank and there were tears trickling down her face. She was opening and closing her fists, rhythmically, seemingly unaware of where she was or what she was doing. At first, I thought she was just having trouble sleeping and had become upset, or perhaps was just sleep-walking. When I tried to talk to her or rouse her though, I got no response. I shook her – no recognition, no reaction, nothing. I didn't think it was the sleepwalking, but it was just like those episodes she described Metern as having. And it kept happening every night, I checked."

"That sounds a bit odd. It might have been as a result of her head injury, but the symptoms do sound like Metern's, don't they? Had he had a similar injury?" said Will.

"I don't know," said Tamsin, "but I wish I'd confronted her with it. I guess that as she was fine during the day and had had normal CT scans, I wasn't that concerned, or couldn't face being concerned." Her head went to her hands, and Will pulled her tighter in his arms. "I just remembered what had happened when she had tried to help Metern and..." A tear escaped down her own face. She brushed it away, angrily. "I just wish I'd made her go and get help."

"Tamsin, there's no way you or anyone could have known," his voice was calm and understanding. "Head injuries, even minor ones, can change people, but we don't know nearly enough to predict how." The words were meant as comfort, a rational analysis, but seemed so inadequate.

She nodded, taking what he had said in, but then her look darkened. "The thing is," she said, lifting her head to stare straight into Will's eyes, "she gradually started to remember bits and pieces from around the night of the accident. She told me a fragment more each morning. They came in flashes, or she would wake up having dreamed them. She told me how she had strange images of seeing Metern standing in the centre of the mosaic. He wore odd clothes, she said he wore a mask and, in his hands, he held a ball of spinning light... and she remembered voices speaking in a language she didn't understand."

"But the things she remembered," said Will, "do you think they actually happened, or were they just a product of her injured brain trying to make sense of things?"

"At the time I thought that's exactly what they were, and I told her as much." Tamsin cupped her head in her hands, gathering herself. "But then on the afternoon that she died..." She a few stuttering, deep breaths. "I'd been getting some stamps from the bookshop in the foyer, and I saw Jen run out of the main doors to the hospital. I could see she was really upset so dropped everything and ran after her, calling, but she didn't stop. It was a vile afternoon. I remember a storm had blown up and icy sleet was driving against the hospital doors, so I briefly lost sight of her, only to catch a glimpse of her car on the way out of the car park. I had an idea of where she might have been heading and was proven right when I caught up with her on the Hoe, overlooking the sea at Plymouth Sound. She would always seek solace in the sea when she was upset and that was the nearest point." Tamsin's voice was gravelly as she fought back the emotion. "Jen was standing, facing into the wind," she continued, "looking out over Drake's Island. She was shaking uncontrollably; her thin short-sleeve top was no defence against the elements."

Will felt Tamsin shudder.

"And her face, her face… it was all twisted with anguish, and she was screaming and screaming into the wind."

Will felt a drop land on his hand, the coalescent tears now little rivulets of silver tracing down her cheek. Tamsin let out a sob and Will pulled her in closer.

"She told me what she had done," Tamsin continued. "How she'd blanked out during one of her episodes and killed someone, a new mother. She'd never had them during the day before. She swore she hadn't." Another sob. "She didn't remember how she'd done it, only that when she reawakened to where she was, she had an empty syringe in her hand, alarms going off and a patient who wasn't breathing. Jen told me how she had watched as the crash team had desperately tried to resuscitate the woman: arms pumping on the poor woman's chest; the defibrillator jerking her body in a parody of life; the impotent drugs flushing through her veins. The woman should have come back; they should have been able to reverse the diamorphine, get her breathing again, but they couldn't. Fifty minutes they worked, before finally accepting that she had gone. Jen had stood there watching it all. Watching the woman, she had killed. And then she said that she'd just ran, got into the car and driven. She couldn't live with herself anymore."

The scene played in Will's mind as she spoke. He'd been to many arrests himself. For most, it was just part of the job. You either got them back or didn't, and then you went for something to eat and a chat about the surf. Minimal impact on you and best to just move on and enjoy your sandwich. But then he had never actually caused the death.

"Then she started whimpering," Tamsin continued. "She started saying, 'Please get it out of me, it's poison.' She pulled at my collar, telling me, pleading with me, repeating over and over, 'He's injected poison into me, tainted my soul, get it out.' I asked her who had poisoned her and with what. I tried to get her to say more.

"She was quiet for a bit, then I can remember her turning to look at me, hate in her eyes. 'You know perfectly well who,' she said." Tamsin drew up her knees holding them with her arms. "And then she added, 'Does that affect what you do?'"

Wind whipped across Will's face, seeming to suck his breath, before Tamsin went on. "Oh, the hatred in those eyes... but it wasn't for him..." She took a couple of gasps, "You see I –"

A box of chocolates was thrust under Will's nose and shaken. "Want one," the youth asked. "Going free..." Tamsin buried her head in Will's chest and Will waved him away angrily. The youth shrugged and walked on. Will held her, letting her release her grief. He looked about him. The party still raged on around them, as they remained tucked away in their dune, hidden.

It was a long while before Tamsin began again, her voice raspy. "I talked her into going back to the hospital," she said, pulling herself upright, "told her that it wasn't her fault and she needed to return because running away wasn't going to help. Jen just looked at me and nodded." Tamsin hesitated before continuing, a hitch in her voice. "So, we both drove our cars back up to the hospital. We should have just left her car there and driven back together. You see I got delayed, held up. On my way back, a bus pulled in front of me and I lost her at some traffic lights. It kept stopping and I couldn't get past.

I looked for her when I got back to Whitehorse. I looked everywhere. I knew she wasn't herself and wanted to make sure she was OK. I hunted all over the Anaesthetic Department, in theatre, the mess... and then someone came running up to me, I forget who... and they... "Tamsin's breathing was ragged, "... they told me that she'd been found... dead." A sob shook Tamsin.

She took several moments before continuing, "And the police, they didn't believe what Jen had told me, that it wasn't her fault, that she had been injected with a drug and it was a side effect. They said there was nothing found at the post-mortem, nothing other than diamorphine. They just saw that she had killed someone and then taken her own life... out of guilt, they said. They even suggested that it was an honourable thing to have done. Can you believe that – an *honourable* thing?" She was whispering now. "But I know that it wasn't suicide. I know she didn't kill herself. I know that Cadan Metern injected her with something. He killed her and I didn't stop him."

Her voice was cold, and her shimmering eyes blazed with pain, fire and fury. "He *will* pay for what he has done. He will pay I swear it."

Chapter 15

The dorm was in a very sorry state at eight in the morning. Bodies lay everywhere and Will was sure the unholy smell had emanated from the behind of Beelzebub himself. He tried to get up, but the room kept shifting underneath him. He lay back down clutching the sides of the bed. There was movement above him; that meant that Tamsin hadn't made it out for a surf either. Rolling over very cautiously, he pulled back the curtain beside his bunk and peering out, he saw why. A thick fog blanketed everything and visibility was reduced to the tens of metres, he couldn't see even as far as across the road. The surf was likely to be poor underneath it as well, there was no point getting out of bed. He turned gingerly to face the room. Godfrey lay with his head buried under his pillow, Shauna and Mel were tucked up in their respective bunks and the other medical students snored contentedly in their corner of the room.

In spite of the fact that they might be on a surf trip with a murderer, he reflected recalling the previous night's revelation, it was actually going quite well. People had had a surf and a few beers, let off a bit of steam and seemed to have enjoyed themselves. He shifted in the bunk onto his back, the springs creaking as he did so, and thought about the previous night, trying to sort out what had been real and what was the product of an alcohol addled brain. From what he had seen, Metern was a well-respected, decent enough bloke with bit of a temper after long on-call shifts. Could he really have such dark secrets?

Tamsin couldn't be right, could she? And as for his overactive imagination. Not infrequently in recent times he'd had cause to wonder at himself but crikey, last night was another level! He felt his brain lurch. Perhaps the best thing to do as far as Tamsin was concerned, was do as had been suggested and just support her, until time healed her wounds. If anything turned up in the meantime, then he would act. His mind drifted – he couldn't deny that he felt himself increasingly drawn to her.

Nine o'clock ticked round, and after a clear-up, they all descended on the cafe again for breakfast. Thick sea mist also shrouded the town and as expected, there wasn't much enthusiasm for getting into the water again. He hadn't been able to talk to Tamsin properly yet, but her public face was back on. He had mouthed, "You OK?" and she had nodded back at him. She seemed to be tucking into breakfast without reserve, so appeared none the worse for her disclosures. He watched her reaction, or complete lack of it, when Metern walked into the cafe with his entourage and sat at a table. Will looked at him anew. Tall, handsome, fit, smiling and laughing with everyone around him. He exuded warmth and trust. The room seemed to lift in mood when he walked in; there was an air of expectation, and conversations halted to see what he was going to do or say. He certainly didn't look like a murderer. But then, Will reflected, he hadn't known many murderers with whom to compare him. He scratched his head and turned his attention back to his sausages and fried bread; no dilemma about those at least, and he set about constructing what he considered to be the perfect breakfast mouthful, a forkful of buttered toast, sausage, a small piece of smoked bacon and a couple of baked beans. Chewing thoughtfully, Will gradually became aware of a general hubbub from Metern's table. There were snatches of "That's a great idea" and "Why don't you see if anyone else wants to come?"

Metern cleared his voice and addressed the room. "It doesn't look as if there's any chance of going for a surf today, so does anybody fancy going horse riding instead?" He turned to Will, "If that's OK?"

Will nodded. It didn't seem like a bad idea.

There was a general mumble, a number of yeses from a few and some uncertain murmurs from others.

"There's a great riding stable near here," Metern continued, "and it doesn't matter if you've never ridden before – they cater for all standards."

There was a show of hands. Will looked over in Tamsin's direction to see that she seemed intent on going, so he raised his hand too.

The fog seemed to have cleared as they drove inland along the narrow and winding Cornish roads. Journey time was going to be about forty-five minutes. It was difficult to go anywhere in Cornwall without it taking forty-five minutes, even if the distance covered was only a few miles. However, the scenery was always spectacular; from the ancient hedgerows and rolling hills, to the glimpses of granite cliffs towering above hidden coves; from the eighteenth and nineteenth century mine-workings with their chimneys erupting from heather-strewn moorland to picturesque, chocolate-box villages. It was just that you travelled on Cornish roads and one way or another, be it cows obstructing the highway or a caravan, it took forty-five minutes.

The time passed pleasantly enough as Shauna, giggling, critiqued the performance by Hot Chocolate and described her excitement at discovering a secret beach party. She chatted in a way that required no more than the odd grunt or nod to allow her to continue – similarly, he reflected, in the way she did when he waxed lyrical about plants he spotted in the hedgerow or the refining of tin ore. His brain though was struggling with the scatter-topic assault, he decided, as it tried to mull over the night's events alongside lewd descriptions of banana hammocks from the seat next to him. So, in the end he gave up and just enjoyed the ride.

The riding stables stood at the end of a rutted road, a mile or so inland, flanked on one side by fields banked by a traditionally laid hedge and by an area of deciduous woodland on the other. A number of fine thoroughbred horses looked up as the procession of cars entered the slate-chipped parking area. At the far end of the car park there was a short path leading to an enclosed courtyard. Split stable doors marked the homes of their mounts, and a few of the occupants poked their heads out to see who was arriving.

At the far end of the yard was an old farmhouse built from granite, hewn no doubt centuries ago from the surrounding tors. Originally it had probably been long and narrow, aligned east–west to maximise such sun as there was, but over time additional buildings and rooms had been attached and now it was something of an architectural mishmash pointing to any number of directions on the compass. A new slate roof and fresh point work, however, bore testament to a thriving business. Will stretched as he got out of his car, spotting Godfrey, who had generously offered lifts to the physios. They were emerging white-faced and visibly shaken from their ordeal. Will chuckled.

A middle-aged lady with short curly brown hair and a cheerful cherubic face came out of the tack room to meet them. Her tight-fitting jodhpurs evidenced what Will supposed might be described as a good seat.

"Hello," she greeted them. "You all 'ere for the ride?" She had a broad Cornish accent, generations in the making and looked around picking out Metern. "Mornin' my 'an'some. Keepin' well I see."

"Well enough," he said, coming up and giving her a peck on the cheek. He hadn't so much as hopped once, Will noted, despite the incident on the beach the previous day.

"Good to see 'ee again," she said with obvious fondness, and then she addressed the group. "Now, I'm Maggie, welcome to Penworzel. Now afore we starts you mus' come and fill in these 'ere forms, so as I knows how good you is and then we can get you some 'orses." She smiled and gestured for them to follow.

"I've brought a bit of a mixed bunch, Maggie," Metern explained as everyone filed into the stables, which also appeared to be an office, a cafe and a toilet. There was excited chatter as the riders gave their details and were told which horses they would be riding. Metern led them off to get acquainted with their mounts.

Will, a competent rider, got a fine-looking chestnut mare to ride, about sixteen hands high. She had a bit of spirit and bucked her head as Will took the reins and stood by her. She didn't have *that* look in her eye, he was relieved to see, the look that suggested he might want to rethink his intention to sit on the horse's back or suffer the consequences.

As a child, when he had been riding with his sister, there were invariably two types of horse with which they were presented. One, a three-legged, blind old girl named Snowdrop, and one that was solid muscle, black, frothing at the mouth and called Angry Jim. Will never got to ride Snowdrop, and as a result he was confident he could ride most horses with a reasonable chance of remaining seated for the trip. The Angry Jims had also taught him a valuable life as well as riding lesson. You had to be committed to what you were doing. If you decided you were going to make the horse do something – jump an obstacle for example – then you had to mean it. Any doubts and Jim would know and take the decision away from you. He would, however, leave this decision quite late, which was for him, not to jump... You, however, momentum being what it is, would end up taking the fence on your own, no doubt much to Angry Jim's supressed amusement. Half-hearted commitments in life, Will reflected, too often resulted in you landing on your arse, to which a number of failed relationships and an E-grade junior surgical exam bore testament.

Will watched the attentive way in which Metern went around each horse, checking stirrup lengths and girth tightness, even Tamsin's, though she barely acknowledged his presence. Metern didn't seem to take any offence and Will saw that he had made sure that her horse's saddle would remain where it was, as with everyone else's. He knew his way around horses, there was no mistaking that.

With everyone ready and mounted, Will saw Metern leap lightly into his own saddle and go to the back of the ride. Maggie took the lead. She took the group right, out of the stables and onto the farm track. The weather had brightened up, and the fog had disappeared. Excited chatter babbled from those who had never ridden before and those who had, sat back in their saddles, moving languidly in time with the movements of the horse below them, enjoying the slow, soothing, rocking motion. Will was close to the rear of the single-file line and looked ahead to Tamsin, who was near the front. She seemed happy enough, discussing the finer points of horsemanship with Mel, who rode before her. She looked solid in the saddle, though she was, by her own admission, just a novice who loved horses.

They turned off the track and took a path through the woods. The white stars of the wood anemones punctuated the otherwise blue carpet of the bluebells on the wood's floor, while the decidedly less fragrant smell of onions emanated from banks of wild garlic alongside them. Wood pigeons cooed, and in the undergrowth, Will saw a roe deer grazing on the vegetation, unconcerned at the cavalcade passing before it. The path twisted and turned before heading uphill and leading out onto another farm track, this one lined by hedges on both sides. Tiny wings hummed through the yellows and purples of the hedgerow, brought out by the warmth of the sun. Will noted red campions and primroses attracting attention and some herb robert, once used to cure toothache and nosebleeds if his memory served him right. Sitting on top of a horse also meant that you could look over the top of the hedges, and in the adjacent field Will could see that the farmer had got a little ahead of the game and already had his sheep shorn.

Maggie pulled the ride to a halt. "Does everyone want to try a trot?" she shouted. There was a general, if slightly nervous, agreement that they would, and Maggie explained what needed to be done to avoid an uncomfortable ride.

"Stand up as the left leg comes forward and down as it goes back. Up, down, up, down, feel the rhythm of the horse." Maggie squeezed her horse gently and it picked up obediently into a trot. In front of Will he could see the well-schooled horses following suit, irrespective of commands from the rider. His horse was already increasing its pace without his specific instruction. He bounced once to adjust to the new rhythm and then continued, rising gently then allowing his seat to return, his head, shoulder and heel all aligned vertically. He looked down the wobbling procession ahead of him. A few had got it... and a few hadn't. He winced as they lurched precariously from one side of their saddle to the other, mistimed bounces jarring their teeth and no doubt tenderising other regions. The shrieks of mild panic from the middle somewhere were, Will decided, from excitement rather than any real peril. The trot continued for a couple of hundred metres before drawing to a halt amidst several relieved sighs.

"All OK, no fallers?" said Maggie, looking over her shoulder and laughing.

The track ended at a gate that led off into a field. Maggie walked her horse through and leaning down, held it open to allow the others to come through. They all filtered through in turn and headed to the left to follow the edge of the field. Most were through when Tamsin's horse, having had some sort of contretemps with the horse behind, whinnied and hopped forward. It was the sort of thing that horses did, just like humans. Unfortunately, Mel's horse at the front reacted, starting to break into a trot. Mel, a novice rider, tried to pull it back to stop it but that only had the effect of shortening the reins, which her horse took to mean "Let's get ready to go faster". It sprang forward into a canter, and Tamsin's horse followed it. The other horses following behind then started turning, and rather than continuing in single file to continue along the fence line, they became lined abreast all aimed across the field, in such a way as they might do for a cavalry charge. Ears pricked and the trotting got faster. More heads bucked. Too late, Maggie and Metern, who was last through the gate, saw what was happening. A few of the horses broke and went straight from trot to gallop, hooves pounding the ground as they took off.

The hill rose gently before them for a hundred metres, before dropping away into the sky. Will felt his mount pull to be part of this great race, but he was aware enough to place a firm grip on the reins and sit back firmly in the saddle, making it very clear to the horse that they were not going to be joining in. The horse skittered, veering sideways in protest and Will had to grip hard with his thighs, but the horse remained under control. Tempting though it was to have a bit of a gallop, that would probably just spur other horses on to greater speed and inflame the already perilous situation. They would proceed at a controlled canter and pick up the debris. He looked ahead of him up the hill. A few riders had already left their saddles and been deposited unceremoniously on the ground. Fortunately, there had been plenty of rain recently, so the field was a relatively soft, if somewhat muddy, landing. Those riders who had stayed on, headed on up the hill, however they approached the top of the rise, from there it would be downhill and keeping your seat would be more challenging.

Tamsin was one of those still on. Will called out to the fallers as he cantered past. They were ruffled but had no major injury concerns. As he got three-quarters of the way up the hill, he heard thundering from behind him and Metern shot past on his thoroughbred, hooves flicking up mud as he did so. He was shouting something, Will wasn't sure what, but those horses in earshot reacted, stopping dead in their tracks. Most of those riders managed to hang on, with the exception of Godfrey, who somersaulted from the saddle, over the horse's head, and landed flush on his back in a particularly lush patch of turf. He looked bemused as Will cantered to a halt next to him. Godfrey still had the reins in his hand.

"Orthopaedic or neurological?" Will asked he looked down at his friend.

"Orthopaedic, I think, so I'll be fine. Go and get the others," replied Godfrey, sitting up and shaking his head. Orthopaedic was fine, bones and soft tissue could be fixed, and it appeared, as Godfrey shook himself down further before getting up, it was nothing that a couple of ibuprofen and some ice wouldn't sort out. Will kicked his horse on, worried about the remaining bolted horses, one of which carried Tamsin.

Reining in at the top of the hill he was able to see Metern in the distance. He'd managed to catch the physio, Claire, who had dismounted, and now he'd turned his horse to try to get to the last runaway, Tamsin, for whom the end of the field was approaching very rapidly. Will, for the first time, became alarmed. If the horse reached the end of the field at a full gallop, as it looked like doing, it would either try to jump the six-foot stone bank or, more probably, veer sharply as the bank approached. There would be no way that Tamsin would win the battle against Newtonian laws, and Will felt panic at the dire consequences her abrupt stop against a stone wall might have. He could see that Tamsin had given up trying to regain control of the horse and was now just hanging on, arms clasped around its neck. The horse had flattened back its ears, spittle flying from its mouth, and was galloping inexorably towards the bank. She was in no position to take the jump even if the horse decide that it would be the best course of action. She was in trouble.

Metern closed rapidly, his horse barely seeming to touch the ground as it flew after her. It would be touch and go as to whether he would get to her in time. Will watched as the man's shirt billowed out behind him, its crisp whiteness in stark contrast to the black flecks of the soil thrown up by the horse's hooves. Then he saw Metern dig his heels into the horse's flank again. It responded, increasing its already breakneck speed. The thoroughbred absorbed the distance, drawing level with Tamsin's horse, and Will could see Metern's legs around the girth, small movements and pressures guiding the horse in front of Tamsin's. The two horses collided but Metern managed to keep his leg from being squashed between the two beasts by lifting his foot still in the stirrup. He pushed his horse across the runaway, a shallow angle at first, before the proximity of the bank made him drive across it even further. The pace slowed a fraction and Metern pushed harder, forcing both horses on a parabola, taking them away from the hedge and finally sending them back up the field to safety. They slowed to a canter and then to a trot before stopping. Horses and riders stood, blowing hard. Will saw Metern jump off and help Tamsin down from her horse. They exchanged words and he saw Metern shrug in response to whatever Tamsin had said. Will wasn't absolutely sure it was just "Thank you", but he hoped the phrase had been used at some point, whatever else Tamsin supposed he had done. It had been a stunning display of horsemanship, not to mention strength and courage. Metern headed off to check on the other riders.

"Are you OK?" Will asked, bringing his horse alongside and jumping off. Tamsin's hands held the reins loosely in her hand. She looked flushed but otherwise unperturbed.

"Yes, I'm fine." She looked at her horse, brushing sweat absently from its neck.

"You did really well to stay on."

She snorted. "I think if I had come off, I may never have got up again." Will nodded. Soft ground or not, a fall at that speed could well have resulted in a very serious injury, particularly if there was a slate wall involved. Maggie came over to check on her, her face now anything but angelic, its joviality having left some five minutes ago at the far end of the field. Her voice sounded dry and husky. She satisfied herself that Tamsin was in one piece and then barked a series of instructions. Riders, on foot, walked their horses to the far gate, then through as she opened it for them before getting them all mounted up again, Metern helping those who were struggling

Thankfully, no one had more than a bruise or two and some washing to do. Will had a suspicion that a literal, as well as metaphorical, tight rein would be maintained. No more trotting, no more fields, small tracks only with room for no more than one horse at a time. Initially, there was a subdued silence, as the riders, especially those who had parted company with their horses, nursed their injuries and concentrated on staying on top of their animal.

It was Godfrey who broke the silence. "That was brilliant, Maggie," he called to the front. "Can we do it again?" Maggie turned and transfixed him with a stare, to which Godfrey seemed oblivious. "Seriously, I don't know of anyone else whose accelerated learning programme encompasses a gallop twenty minutes into their first lesson. Fantastic!" There were a few nervous chuckles and Maggie just put her head in her hands.

They arrived back at the stables after the hour's ride was up and everybody dismounted in a safer, more voluntary fashion this time. Will tied his horse up and went to help Tamsin down, but she'd already attracted Metern's attention. She indicated for him to help her down, and as she did so, her finger caught on his pendant and it fell to the floor, landing at Will's feet. Metern shot Tamsin a frosty look, but she apologised. Will bent to pick it up for him. It looked like a tiny white bone set in clear plastic.

They paid and thanked Maggie. Metern had had a word with her and she seemed in better humour afterwards. She was, no doubt, relieved that she would still be open the following day and was definitely off for a cup of tea and with a nerve-settling additive.

Tamsin came over to Will. "What are you up to now?" she asked.

"I'm not really sure," he replied. "I had a big breakfast and don't feel up to a beery pub lunch along with everybody else – he indicated to a group who were in the process of determining which pub would benefit from their presence that afternoon, especially as I have to drive."

"Nor me," she said, smiling. "Besides, my insides are still a bit shaken after this morning's escapade." Will chuckled, glad to see that she didn't appear any the worse for her near-death experience.

"How about a cliff walk? The weather seems to have broken," she suggested.

"Shall I see if anyone else would like to come?" Will asked.

Tamsin frowned.

"I tell you what," he said. "I'll see if Godfrey is OK to take Shauna back." Tamsin smiled, and he went over to where Shauna was chatting to Mel and Godfrey. She shot Tamsin a conspiratorial glance as Will explained the situation and he then returned to where Tamsin stood looking slightly furtive.

"That's all sorted," Will said, returning. "She had a relaxed afternoon in mind anyway, and Godfrey will take her back, though I'm not sure she'll be terribly relaxed after that, but never mind. Right, lead on, and I'll follow you." He paused. "But, er, just in case, where are we actually going?"

"How about Boscle?" said Tamsin, getting into her car.

"I've never been," he said. "Fair enough." And he got into his car before pulling out of the car park and heading for the main road.

Chapter 16

They headed north up the coast on the A39 for about half an hour before taking a left turn, following signs towards the village of Boscle. The relatively fast A-road gave way to narrower roads, where much closer acquaintance with the verges and hedgerow was required to allow the passage of two cars. Bare patches in the high-sided banks revealed the herringbone construction pattern in which the slate had been placed before nature had taken over. Will shivered, recalling the close shave Tamsin had nearly had with one such bank earlier in the day. The lush fields that lay beyond these walls descended to wooded valley sides, and the road continued to wend its way down until, abruptly, the woods opened up to reveal the grey slate roofs and squint chimneys of the old granite houses of Boscle. Looking down onto the village, Will could see that a small river ran through the middle of it, flowing down its well-maintained, five-metre wide, stone-lined channel. The main road crossed the river at a bridge, upstream of which there appeared to be an old mill. On the far bank were rows of fishermen's cottages and boathouses, most now whitewashed and pristine, selling ice creams, shells, knitted goods and books to the circling tourists.

Will followed Tamsin's car across the bridge, which took them round to the right and upriver to the flattened car park area on the valley floor. He drew his car to a stop, parking up next to her. She had already got out of her car and then stopped, holding on to the car door for a moment. She had closed her eyes. Still suffering the effects of the morning's ride, Will thought. He got out of his car and she came over to him, flicking him a quick, slightly uncertain smile. "Shall we, er, go up the right side?"

Shops and the mill obscured his view downriver, and while he had no idea whether going up to the left or right would be better, he agreed to her suggestion. She looked more shaken now than she had earlier and Will wondered if she was having some sort of delayed reaction to her ride.

"Are you alright?" he asked as they crossed the road and walked to the right of the river. "It was a narrow escape this morning, you're bound to feel a bit unsteady. We can sit down for a bit if you like, perhaps get something to eat?" An open grassy area above the riverbank was a perfect place for a picnic and a few families were tucking into pasties, eyed hungrily by a raiding party of herring gulls.

"What? Er no, I'm OK," she said, eyes narrowing. "I'm just thinking some stuff through."

"Oh," said Will, puzzled. "Anything I can help with?" Tamsin didn't reply immediately, her eyes cast at her feet, then she stopped abruptly and grasped Will's hand, jerking him to a stop. Something was troubling her and it probably wasn't good.

"Will," she started, but was struggling to find the words, "there are a couple of things that I should tell you... should have told you last night."

He faced her, "Go on," he said, his tone expectantly subdued. He could feel the tension in her body just through her grip on his hand, it had transferred itself to him and his shoulders bunched.

She gritted her teeth. "It's about Cadan and Jen." She shook her head, then raised it, looking at the sky. "I mean, it's about Cadan and... me." She exhaled heavily. Will felt his heart lurch.

Tamsin took a deep breath. "What I told you at the beach was true, all of it but..." She paused, "There's a bit more." She breathed out heavily. "A while after Jen split up with Cadan, I came down to see her, to see if I could help somehow. Listening to her on the phone, she sounded very messed up, and I hoped that me coming down might straighten things out, give her a bit of support." That word again. "We went mountain-biking and did a few walks up on the moors and generally got up to stuff to help take her mind off what had happened. We talked as well, but as a rule, doing something physical tended to work better for clearing her thoughts." She gazed downriver. "We went out for pub meals with her hospital friends and one evening we got persuaded to go to the GX. We'd been there for a while and then *he* turned up."

"Who? Cadan?"

She nodded. "Jen had been relaxed to that point, at least as relaxed as she was going to get, but seeing him sent her spiralling down again. She didn't want to be in the same room as him and immediately went to get her coat. I, on the other hand, having had a lot to drink, decided that I'd stay and give him a piece of my mind, or try to persuade him that he'd made a huge mistake, or... or something. So, Jen ended up going home with one of her anaesthetist friends and I stayed." She shook her head, rubbed her brow and took another deep breath. "I really wish that I hadn't." She withdrew her hands from Will's, clasping them together. "I really, really do."

Will swallowed hard, a sinking feeling in the pit of his stomach.

"I must have had much more to drink than I thought," she continued. "He was so charming, and while I tried to talk about Jen, he kept turning the conversation and I just got sucked in. He suggested that we went with some of his friends back to his place and..." She petered out. Will's sinking feeling got a whole lot worse.

"You slept with him." He'd known even before she answered.

"Yes," she admitted. "I slept with that predatory bastard."

Will was silent for a few moments. He felt as though he'd been dropped out of a window. Tamsin looked at him, pain in her eyes. But was it for Jen? For herself? For his benefit?

"That was one of the reasons the police never took what I told them seriously," she said, "I had to tell them about sleeping with Cadan when I was interviewed. I'm sure *he* would have told them about our sordid little evening."

Will placed a hand on his forehead. It was a lot to take in. "OK," he said, the dry croak in his voice betraying him.

"The thing is that's not all." She winced as she spoke.

"There's more?" said Will, blurting out the question slightly louder than intended.

"I'm sorry, Will." There were tears appearing in her eyes. Embarrassment, sorrow, self-loathing?

"I had to do something Will! I couldn't just ignore what had happened the way everybody else had. I owed it to her. You see, while Jen had said occasional odd things about Cadan and his behaviour, I sort of just listened, without giving it much credence. That's what you do, isn't it, just listen. Then, when she died and no one took what I told them seriously, I started looking into it myself."

"What do you mean?" Will asked.

"Well, there were her descriptions of the child sacrifice, the bizarre clothing, crystal balls."

"Yes."

"I needed to know more, did a bit of research to see if I could make sense of what she had said. Maybe trap the bastard."

"So, what did you do?" he asked. She looked over his shoulder and he turned to follow her gaze. It was fixed on a sign directing the way to a museum, a sign with unmistakable imagery. Underneath the emblematic black silhouette, it read, "Museum of Witchcraft and Magic". The black witch hung on her fixing.

"I went in there," she said.

Will shivered, "And that's why we're here, isn't it?" he said, his eyes subconsciously flicking downriver to the start of the cliff walk.

She nodded and waited; hands clasped in front of her. Will didn't know what to think. His first feelings had been those of jealousy and disappointment. Nothing to do with dead anaesthetists or sacrificed babies. Purely a selfish feeling. But, he mused, everyone had a "history", even him, and it wasn't as if they were going out or anything. Still, the thought of her with someone else was genuinely painful. Will pulled his attention back to the present, there was a choice to be made, a decisive one Will could feel it. Tamsin was obviously filled with guilt over what she had done and grief over what had happened to her friend. There were odd and unexplained events surrounding Cadan Metern. He would do what he had resolved to do and support her.

"I just want you to understand why I think that there's something to what Jen said about Cadan," said Tamsin.

"And I'll find it in there?" he said, scratching his head. Sensing Tamsin's anxiety, and given that they were practically outside the door, he nodded. "OK, let's go in then."

Tamsin looked relieved. "Thank you," she said.

Chapter 17

They walked past some of the old boathouses that had been joined and converted into an art gallery. Beautiful landscapes depicting the rugged coastline hung in the window, and Will felt a pang of regret. Tamsin took his hand again as they walked on. It was cold in his. He squeezed it, intending reassurance. Tamsin squeaked. "Sorry," he said, and she smiled warmly, which took some of the chill from his heart.

The row of cottages continued around the corner and following the signs, they were directed to the last cottage tucked under the cliff. A broomstick hung by the door and an effigy of a witch, complete with a hooked, warty nose, black pointed hat and black, cardboard cat stood by the doorway. Will felt a tingle of apprehension as they approached the entrance, goosebumps plucking at his neck.

A sweet aroma of burning joss sticks greeted them as the arched doorway loomed over their heads. They passed inside, and immediately in front of them was a wooden counter flanked by numerous coloured stones, all labelled as to their nature and purported magical powers. Postcards of Boscle, as well as images of what lay within the museum, adorned the walls in metallic racks. Silver charm bracelets were mounted inside a glass cabinet and cheaper witch-craft-related trinkets were on sale on the counter itself. Will's attention was suddenly drawn to a figure standing partially in shadow behind the counter.

The man, who had been sitting on a stool, stood up. He was late middle-aged, with a tanned, weathered face, not that of one who spends much time sitting indoors. He had greying, straggly, shoulder-length hair and wore a loose-fitting, cream-coloured, heavy cotton shirt. Will caught site of a tattooed forearm, showing what looked like an anchor, and he had a knotted string bracelet on his wrist. He raised his attention back to the man's face to find him watching him. Those eyes were a Cornish, deep brown, and Will felt them heavy upon him, as if weighing up his very soul. It was an uncomfortable few moments before the man's face transformed when his gaze shifted to Tamsin, and he beamed them both a smile.

"Ah, young Tamsin, back again I see?"

"Er, yes, I had some more... research to do." Her reply was a bit stilted, and she glanced over at Will.

"And how is that going?" the man asked.

"Well, I'm struggling a bit, so I brought a friend along to help."

"Good," he said, turning to observe Will again. "And this is?"

"Hi," Will said, a little unnerved at the fact that he seemed to know Tamsin on a first-name basis. "I'm Will, Will Cunningham."

There was a flicker at the corner of the man's eye.

"Are you indeed. Well then, Will Cunningham, you are welcome to this place of enlightenment. If I may help you with any questions, you just have to ask. 'Course, I may not have the answer, but ye can ask nonetheless." He chuckled at his own joke and then explained the layout of the museum, handing them a leaflet to guide them around. "Don't stray off the path," he warned, chuckling again.

Tamsin moved Will along. "No need to look quite like that," she said. "He *was* just joking!" They headed left through a darkened corridor into the museum proper.

"He was..." – Will searched for the right phrase, "...in keeping with his role."

"He didn't have a pointed hat or staff. I have no idea what you mean," replied Tamsin dryly.

As they passed down the corridor, Will noted the generally held, stereo-typical images of witches. There seemed to be two types: the pantomime "evil" witch from the tales of the brothers Grimm, or the alluring, sexually irresistible witch, likely to lead good men to their doom. The corridor led into a dimly lit, low-ceilinged room circled by a number of display cases containing a variety of pictures and artefacts. There was an explanation of what witchcraft, or in more modern terms, Wicca, was and how witches and cunning, or wise men had been misrepresented since the Middle Ages. On the left near-side wall there was a beautifully illustrated "Wheel of the Year", which depicted the festivals or sabbats marking the year's passage. It was fully four foot in diameter and divided into eight segments, each of which had pictures of stars, moons and the sun to represent celestial energies and other astrological influences. Ornately woven into each of the segments were nymphs, animals, and men, set against a seasonal background.

Throughout the world and throughout time, Will read, humanity had attempted to understand what was happening around them and why. Communities had their village elders and wise folk, who knew about the cycling of the seasons and were able to relate them to the position of the sun and the stars. They observed the patterns of weather and learned to predict spells of brighter weather or oncoming storms. Sayings, common even in today's parlance, such as "Red sky at night, shepherd's delight, Red sky in the morning, shepherd's warning", bore lasting testament to this wisdom. Will knew that there were now well-realised scientific reasons for these phenomena, but in times past such predictive feats may have seemed like wondrous magical powers.

These same people would also have been consulted when an individual or community suffered illness or accident. They had learned which plants might help relieve the suffering. Amongst the display cabinets were the shrivelled-up berries of belladonna or deadly nightshade. These, in small quantities, could be used to treat stomach problems or provide pain relief. They could also help with menstrual problems and might well have been made into an ointment to be applied vaginally, perhaps on the end of a broomstick.

The healers used their knowledge to help people live their daily lives, give an explanation to as to why things were the way they were, and ease the uncertainty of existence. They were respected and had status within society, no doubt working hard to maintain this status, with a little secrecy and showmanship added in, just to make sure. Knowledge and observation handed down the generations would only get a healer so far though. Much was inexplicable and beyond the understanding of man, and under such circumstances, it was very useful to have the contrary will of a deity or spirit to blame for any adverse events. So, they also tended to become a link between man and the occult world as an additional job requirement.

Will looked over to Tamsin, who, aware of his glance, pulled away from what she was reading. "What do you think?" she asked.

"To be honest, I'm struck by how similar the job of being a doctor is, especially I suppose a general practitioner, to these folks of the past." Tamsin smiled at this. He continued, "OK, perhaps not the supernatural bit, but, I mean, they do much the same sort of thing, dealing with the sick, helping to sort people's physical, psychological and social problems. It's not hugely different, other than we understand the science behind most of what we do now."

"And we don't get burned at the stake for not getting things right," she snorted.

Will nodded, "It's still interesting that most people will take what doctors say essentially on faith. I mean, they don't have any idea that the motion sickness tablet we give them for car or boat trips is actually scopolamine or hyoscine—and is a deadly nightshade derivative. That the tablet we give them is a tropane alkaloid drug, acting at muscarinic acetylcholine receptors to produce anticholinergic effects. They just take the medicine because they have a problem, and we say it can help."

Tamsin nodded. "And spouting all of that biochemistry, it might well have been some incantation or spell. It sounded like it."

"That's what I thought when I just read it off that card," he said, grinning and pointing to the belladonna section.

"Hey, I knew you didn't just know that. I'm getting wise to your teaching methods, remember!" she said, laughing.

They moved rooms to the next bit, the "Persecution" section. The images that hung on the walls and in the display-cabinets were those of satanic iconography, suffering and death, and demonstrated the horrific beast that lurked within mankind. They described the "witch hunts" and "crazes" rife throughout Europe from the fifteenth to the eighteenth centuries, which conservative estimates suggest may have resulted in over two hundred thousand deaths. Women, and it was mainly women, were portrayed as cavorting with the Devil; serpents writhed across naked bodies and there were depictions of children being sacrificed for the gratification of onlookers. Their subsequent capture, trial, torture and deaths were a supposed lesson to those who sought to engage in similar crimes against God.

The Middle Ages saw the Church, which to this point had taken a fairly benign approach to what was felt to be peasant superstition, subject to a number of changes in Christian doctrine. It began to recognise the existence of witchcraft as a form of satanic influence and therefore heresy, punishable by death. This, combined with an increasing interest in the acceptable and legal pursuit of sorcery by the 'respectable' classes, drove the need to create a distinction between 'learned men', who wielded their powers through scholarly endeavour, and the peasant folk, who derived similar powers from pacts with the Devil.

"A nice little device for keeping the masses in their place," observed Will.

"Yes, burn or drown those who show a spark of intelligence or independent thought," replied Tamsin. "And wide open to petty squabbles or neighbourly disputes resulting in all sorts of false accusations being made against one poor wretch or another."

They walked on through the Persecution section, only exchanging the odd comment or to draw the other's attention to the gruesome fate of another poor woman or the unlikeliness of certain charges. It was very hard to believe that such things had actually happened and were *still* happening in some parts of the world.

Eventually they reached a less harrowing room, with a wall full of bottles containing plants, crystals and bits of stone. Alongside each pot was a tag that explained what it was used for. One particular item took Will's eye. It was the phallic-shaped flint, or "cock rock", which was, not unsurprisingly, used to help infertile couples. There weren't any details as to how they went about using it, and Will observed that there didn't appear to be a slot for batteries. Tamsin seemed less amused by it.

They entered a narrow corridor again that led up a flight of stairs, at the top of which was a skeleton in a coffin. It purported to be that of one Joan Wytte, the Fighting Fairy Woman of Bodmin, who was a wise woman and clairvoyant in the early nineteenth century. She had died in Bodmin Jail and her bones had been kept until they had been given by a Cornish doctor to the owner of the museum, Cecil Williamson, who had put them on display. Will suspected that she may well have been used as an anatomy demonstration for medical students.

A right turn at the top of the stairs brought them into a large open-plan upper floor. It definitely felt less claustrophobic but was no less aromatic. In front of them was a display case, and in it were numerous dolls or replications of the human form. They were made from clay, twisted sticks, wax or rags. Sticking out of each were pins. Some had multiple punctures, others just the one. Will stared at them. He didn't need to read the blurb to know that a good number had been made with malicious intent. They looked all too familiar, and he felt Tamsin's presence over his left shoulder. As he looked at the dolls, suspicion formed into something more certain. He turned to face Tamsin, who met his gaze, challenging him to ask.

"You *did* do it, didn't you?"

"Yes," she replied.

"Why?" he asked, not harshly, but forcefully enough to require a straight answer. She brushed a stray hair from her face.

"Because I wanted to see how he would react. I wanted him to know that I knew, and that I wasn't going to ignore what he'd done."

"And did you intend him harm?"

She fiddled with the zip of her coat before answering. "It was only meant as a warning," she said.

Will stood for a moment looking at the exhibits. These little dolls, or poppets as they were called, had been found in all manner of places, hidden in walls, stuffed up chimneys, discovered on doorsteps, and with pins stuck in the part of the doll that the perpetrator wished affected. Will shook his head.

"You know this is all nonsense, this witchcraft thing, don't you?"

Tamsin looked at him. The corners of her mouth were turned up, just a fraction. "Is it?"

Will returned her stare. "You're joking, right? I mean, wands and spells and potions... and pointed hats and dressing up. You don't really believe in all of that, do you?"

"Well, I'm not saying that I do, but consider this. You find a four-leafed clover on the way into an exam. You feel lucky and go in with more confidence and do better as a consequence. The plant caused you to do better in your exam. Equally, if I were to produce a doll representing you, with a pin through its nose, I'll bet at the very least you're aware of an increase in sensation in that area. Isn't that magic of a sort?"

"Not really," said Will, resisting the intense desire to scratch a suddenly very itchy nostril. "It's basic psychology and the power of suggestion."

"OK," agreed Tamsin, "it's like the placebo effect in medicine. An inert substance is given to help a patient with symptoms, and it does, even though there's no biochemical way that it should have done."

"So?" said Will, not following.

"So, a lot of how we feel about our lives and our health and our body is dependent on our thought processes and psychological make-up, which seemingly can be influenced by a bit of grass or lump of sugar. We understand why this is today, because we understand the way that neurotransmitters work in our brains. But a couple of centuries ago it would have seemed like magic."

"What you are saying then," said Will, "is that yesterday's magic is today's science."

"And today's magic is tomorrow's science, but today's magic remains today's magic…"

"Because we haven't explained it scientifically yet."

"That's right," said Tamsin. "Of course, it might also be that witchcraft is tapping into an occult power." There was a mischievous glint in her eyes.

Will chuntered, "I still don't see how sticking pins in a bit of cloth can actually cause injury."

"But Metern hurt his foot, didn't he?"

"Is that where you stabbed your doll?" Will pointed out.

"Close," she replied, "– a near miss?"

They wandered along the display a bit further. Happily, there did appear to be some poppets with charms intended for good works, which Will was glad to see.

"So, you don't believe in this at all?" Tamsin asked.

"No," he replied, "and there are things in here that will not be explained by science because they don't happen or don't exist. It's no more than coincidence."

"And my doll had no effect on Metern?"

"Not, other than to make him very cross," said Will.

Tamsin rummaged around in her pocket. "So, you're very sure," she asked again.

"Absolutely."

She pulled out the doll that Metern had thrown back at her in the mess.

"I wondered where that had gone," he said, looking at the tatty piece of felt.

"It fell out of your pocket, so I picked it up," said Tamsin. Then she reached back into her pocket and pulled out a scrap of bloodstained material. Will looked slightly horrified.

"What's that?" he asked. Tamsin didn't answer but pushed the rag inside the doll and handed it to Will. He took it gingerly and realised that the material was in fact the bloodstained swab that had been used to patch up Metern's foot.

"And you picked this out of the bin at the beach!" he said, wrinkling up his nose. Tamsin ignored him and walked over to something looking like a necklace hanging from the wall. She removed the drawing pin that held it there and returned, spinning it between her fingers.

"This," she said, "is an experiment, a scientific study. You don't believe that there's any residual connection between that blood and Cadan Metern." She smirked at Will. "Nothing that's done to that doll will have any effect on him, right?" She waited for his reply.

"No..." he replied, frowning.

"So, if I ask you to stab it with this pin" – she held out the drawing pin in her left palm – "you would happily do it, secure in the knowledge that Cadan Metern would suffer no ill effects."

Will looked at the pin and at the doll. It was odd. He knew that there couldn't possibly be any harm done by doing what she asked. It was an inanimate felt doll, stuffed with a bloodstained rag. That was it. It didn't contain the 'essence' of, or 'astral connection' to, Metern; it was rubbish to be thrown away. And yet he hesitated. Something deep inside him was revolted by the idea of stabbing the doll. He felt his hands become sweaty; he was anxious, afraid even. Why would he feel like this?

Tamsin watched him, a smile now playing across her face. She picked up the pin, rolling it again between her right thumb and index finger then tested the point on her left hand. "So, you're not so sure, are you?"

"It just feels... wrong."

"Feels, Dr Cunningham? That's not very scientific." She moved to take the pin back to re-attach the necklace to the wall.

On impulse, Will snatched it from her outstretched fingers. "OK," he said, and stabbed the doll repeatedly over the body. "There, that should about do it," he said, handing the pin-stuck doll back, but he reeled suddenly as the room started to spin. He saw images of Metern in pain, waving his hands violently over his body and grabbed Tamsin to steady himself. He had a very vivid imagination; he hated the way it worked sometimes.

"Hey, careful, are you OK?" Tamsin said, looking concerned. "I didn't actually mean for you to stab the thing. I was just teasing, showing you how thin the veneer of science is, over our primeval being."

"I'm fine," he said, straightening up, the spinning subsiding. "Probably over-powered by the smell of incense and a lack of lunch." He tried to laugh it off but felt somehow uncomfortable, tarnished even. It was really strange.

"Come on," she said, keen to move on. "Let's have a look at those costumes."

They walked along the wooden floor, past displays of costumed dummies, resplendent in their Knights Templar ritual robes of purple cloaks, bead- and symbol-embroidered shirts. They also seemed to be remarkably well armed, sporting a variety of staffs, knives, and swords. In another display, books lay open before a coven of antler-bedecked witches, ready to guide their spells and their summonings and, of course, there was the obligatory crystal ball.

Descending the stairs, they came to a section on charms and seafaring magic. There were various carved pieces of wood, knotted ropes, bits of coral and scrimshaw work all designed to keep sailors safe at sea. It was quite a large section, much reflecting Cornwall's dependence on the sea. Seamen setting sail put themselves at the mercy of the elements. Good seamanship only took you so far. You needed luck as much as anything for a good catch of fish and for the sea to be kind and return you home safely. It was, and remained, a precarious business, a livelihood derived from the sea, and any little extra help, by way of knotted charms in a piece of rope to control the wind or a spell to bring in the pilchards, couldn't do any harm. And what if the elements took against you for not believing? The fisherman had best be safe and carry the charm his wife had got from the wise woman.

They were just about at the end of the exhibit when Tamsin called Will over to a charm section relating to horses. "Recognise this?" she said, pointing to a small bone that had originally been kept in a leather pouch that lay next to it. It was a toad bone, and the wearer was supposed to be able to exert magical control over horses.

"No..." said Will reactively, then he remembered the pendant that Metern wore around his neck. "Hang on, that's–"

"–Like the one Metern wears, yes," Tamsin finished for him.

He looked at the small bones, then an image of flashed into his head. She had looked remarkably calm after the horse ride and he realised, it hadn't been that which had upset her in the car park, it had been confessing what she had done.

"Oh, no... y-you didn't deliberately start the stampede?" Will stuttered.

Tamsin bit her bottom lip, shrugged her shoulders, and turned away.

Chapter 18

Will needed to clear his head, it was overloaded with conflicting emotions. Clear his head and get some food. This part of the world was never short of a shop selling the local fast food, so they purchased a Coke and a Cornish pasty each before Tamsin led the way to a narrow path that led up the cliff. The hawthorn-arched route clung to the right side of the valley as it traversed its way along the edge of a sheer drop, burrowing towards the imposing headland at the end of the harbour. A wonderful, light scent from flowers wafted around them, a welcome, natural smell and not the heavy, oppressive smell of incense that still clung to his clothes.

They walked in silence, step after careful step, ascending gradually, occasionally looking over their shoulders at the view of Boscle. Will was trying to work out what he'd seen and felt in the museum. It was just a building containing artefacts and stories from history, right? Granted, the stories were frequently quite unpleasant, but any history from the Middle Ages tended to be fairly grizzly, what with the plagues, poverty, wars and barbaric ways in which one human treated another. He wondered what drove humanity to do such things. Ultimately, he supposed, man had always been subjected to Darwinian forces, so maybe it was just the way of nature: the weakest or most poorly adapted failing to survive. An increase in population, and therefore more pressure on resources, was usually at the bottom of most human strife, even if it was dressed up as religious persecution, political differences or boundary disputes. Humans, as with life generally, were genetically driven to survive. Life was about competition, and from an evolutionary viewpoint, failing to compete resulted in extinction from a personal, as well as species, position. The human individual, especially a weaker individual, was often left swamped with feelings of impotence, a sense that he was subject to the whims and vagaries of forces beyond his control. Will could see where religion, and indeed witchcraft, might help a seemingly hopeless situation. It could bond and unify a group of individuals for a common cause, giving them a belief that while their own powers to cope were weak, together, especially if they enlisted the powers of the supernatural, they might have a chance. Hope and belief had, throughout history, provided just enough for many unlikely survivors.

They reached the top of the granite outcrop and sat down looking out to sea. The cold of the rock permeated through Will's jeans, contrasting starkly with the warm paper bag containing his pasty, that rested on his lap. He took it half out so that his hands grasped the bag rather than the pastry. Greasy fingers tended to result in greasy trouser legs. He bit into it, taking a moment to savour the peppery mix of steak, potato and turnip. This one had a good ratio of each and he was pleasantly surprised to find it more than adequately filled. Tamsin, he saw, was similarly juggling her lunch. Will sat back. A cool, salty onshore breeze tugged at her hair, which flicked in response, like angry cats' tails and the hiss of the opening can blended with the waves hitting the bottom of the cliff.

It was Tamsin who eventually broke the silence perhaps, Will thought. Concerned about her actions in the museum. "Look, I'm sorry I pushed you into that," she said.

"Sorry for taking me there or sorry for making me stick pins into a dolly?" he said, taking another sip.

"Well, for both, I suppose. I know I sort of tricked you," she said, wincing. "To be honest, I wasn't sure we weren't going on a cliff walk when we arrived, but I wanted you to see that what Jen remembered could at least have some truth behind it. In the end I decided that you would understand and that we should go."

She glanced at Will, "Witchcraft really does exist you know, even in the late twentieth century, and some of the details that Jen gave matched the kind of rituals that we read about in there. The crystal balls, the ceremonial knives" – she hesitated, "the child sacrifice. You can see that can't you?"

Will didn't say anything, not really knowing what to think or believe, but he had to admit that some of what she said was possible. From what Tamsin had told him, Jen had described ritual black magic pretty accurately. That was, of course, what Tamsin had *said* that Jen had said. A frown appeared on Will's face.

"She really did describe all of those things to me, Will. I'm not making it up. You must believe me, you promised."

Tamsin had read his train of thought. Was he really that obvious? There was a nervous almost desperate edge to her voice. "And I'm really sorry for convincing you to stab that doll. I just wanted to make a point to show that even you, a doctor and confirmed scientist, might at least allow the possibility of the existence of occult forces, even if only at a subconscious level."

Will paused before replying, accepting her point, "Yes..." he said, "you are sort of right. I will accept that doing it felt very wrong, very wrong indeed, even if there were no rational grounds for it to have done."

"But, as you have said, what you did cannot possibly have any effect," said Tamsin, trying, he supposed, to reassure him.

He played with the drink can, flicking the ring pull and making a twanging noise, and his mind reeled again as he relived the experience. So many things going around in his head. Jen's death was a tragic waste, as was that of the woman she had accidentally killed, but for her to have then been murdered by a practising Satanist, a man whose evidence-based, scientific credentials were probably second to none in the hospital? The man was a physicist and had been published in medicals journals, for heaven's sake. Plus, hadn't he just saved Tamsin from serious injury, possibly worse, just a few hours ago? But then, had he? Or had Tamsin just set it up to show a link between a pendant and his skill on horseback? His efforts didn't seem to have changed Tamsin's disposition towards the man. Was it vengeance? How could he trust what she said to be true and not just a spiteful vendetta, spawned perhaps from her own guilt? He looked at the beautiful young woman sitting next to him. Her story was so unlikely as to be dismissed out of hand by the authorities, the deanery and her colleagues. She had already done at least one rash thing with the doll, perhaps two, and would no doubt end up doing more. And yet...

He stood up from his seat on the rock, trying to control his racing thoughts, watching a series of waves crash into the base of the cliff. He sensed her get up and walk over to him to stand by his side.

"Yes?" she asked.

Steeling himself, he faced her. He had to know, to quell his suspicion. "Had you or Jen been to that museum before all of this started," he said.

She looked directly back at him. "No, we hadn't."

"It's just that you seemed to know quite a bit about things inside that building."

She looked back at him, almost quizzically, nose wrinkling, a hint of a smile playing on her lips. "So?"

He dropped his head, closing his eyes momentarily before meeting her gaze. "Tamsin, this might seem ridiculous, but I need to ask..." The question had to be asked.

The wind picked up strands of Tamsin's rich dark hair again, blowing them half across her face.

"Tamsin... are you a witch?"

Her smile pursed, the amber-flecked eyes sparkled, "You think *I'm* a witch? *Me*?"

He couldn't read her. She hadn't denied it.

Tamsin reached out a finger to the collar of Will's coat, brushing away a stray flake of pastry. Her hand lingered there before grasping the material and placing her other hand on the opposite collar.

"Me a witch, casting spells, maybe beguiling you in some sorcerous way?"

He lifted his chin, and she looked at him.

"Surely you cannot believe that?" she cocked her head to one side. Then, gently but firmly, she pulled on his collar, drawing him in. The coat rubbed lightly on his neck and he was compelled forward. Her eyes burned into his now with a fiery intensity, the mirth of a few seconds ago banished. He didn't resist; he couldn't. Will felt the warmth of her breath on his lips, the smell of the ocean in her hair and felt that yearning ache within his chest. Her kiss was soft, insistent, slightly salty, tinged with the sweet taste of Coke. A heat flowed through him, a craving and desire for more of this beautiful woman. He placed his arms around her, feeling her body melt into his, and Will's mind and body soared with the same exhilaration as that found only on the perfect wave. All of his worries about jealousy and truth, sorcery and death evaporated away, disappearing like magic. The ache went away. This was right, this here, this now, that much he knew, and he was going to strive to keep it. She might be a mixed-up, volatile, unpredictable, enigmatic, guilt-ridden who-knew-what, but he knew he would help her cope with whatever she had to deal with, help her fight her battles with whatever demons lay in wait and, if necessary, even follow her into oblivion. She released his collar, her arms closed around his shoulders, and he felt the beat of her heart against his.

It probably only lasted a few brief seconds, Will wasn't sure, but as she drew away, he felt the ache return. She brushed back a strand of his hair, and as she held him, she seemed to have sensed his decision. "Thank you, Will, for believing in me," she whispered, "I know you do."

"I can't understand why you haven't been up to the hospital museum," said Tamsin, as they struggled to lick the ice creams before they melted. "I mean, even if it was only because it happened to be next to the library and you stumbled into it after looking up something for a case presentation."

Conversation had lightened a good degree since walking back through the village. Will had admitted that he'd never ventured into the section of the hospital dedicated to the mosaic of the eponymous white horse located in its basement.

Will pointed out, only half-jokingly, that he didn't even know that the hospital had a library let alone a museum.

"Why don't you go and pay it a visit?" she suggested. "It gives a good history of the mosaic and there are a few artefacts to have a look at; the displays are really quite good. Besides, I want to see if you come up with similar ideas about a possible reason Metern might have been using the mosaic."

Will nodded, slightly disappointed that things seemed to have led back to talk of magic and murder again. He would nevertheless drop in, if only to keep her happy. She smiled, stroked his cheek and slid gracefully into the driver's seat. Will closed the door and stepped back, flushed and with his heart racing again. He wandered, slightly dazed, over to his car, got in, started the engine and followed the Peugeot out of the car park. Even the melted Sex Wax on the dashboard failed to annoy him as much as it could have done.

A 1969

The white lab coat snagged on the gas outlet as the man dived over the wooden bench to cut the power. The acrid plastic smell of burning electrical equipment meant another ruined – no, failed experiment. He ground his teeth and shook as the now familiar mix of frustration and disappointment washed though him like a rigor. He slammed his hand on the wooden bench top, sending a test tube skittering across the surface to shatter against a metal tripod. None of this was working, not the experiments, not their direction, not his life. He was supposed to be achieving so much more than this, and yet here he stood in a clapped-out science laboratory, teaching disinterested students, going precisely nowhere, achieving precisely nothing.

He walked over to the window and opened it, hoping some fresh air might clear his head. His attention was caught by the harsh, guttural squawk of a raven, and he watched as it struck out at a hapless dove, mistaken in its belief that the perch in the sycamore tree was unoccupied. Involuntarily he gasped, as the dove, mortally wounded, or so he thought, fell from the branch. It plummeted down, but, in a flurry of feathers, just before it hit the ground, righted itself, merely stunned rather than dead. He watched as its wobbly flight settled out and it sped off along the treeline, up the hill, then disappeared from view against the distant, grey, amorphous form that was the medical school.

Chapter 19

Will pulled into the drive of Southside back in Valtor, to find Shauna and Godfrey wrestling with a large metal cylinder. They appeared to be trying to position it by the back door of the cottage, but it seemed to be proving heavier than expected. Will shot them a curious glance. "What on earth is that?" he asked.

"It's a milk churn," replied Godfrey.

"OK, but what are you doing with it?"

Godfrey looked down at it, and after giving his answer some thought came up with, "Resting it on the gravel?"

Will looked skywards. "I can see that, but why a milk churn and why this gravel?"

Godfrey looked at the churn and then back at Will. "I need a milk churn," he said.

"Godfrey, no one needs a milk churn. Not even the milk marketing board, or whatever it's now called, needs a milk churn these days."

"I need one," he replied.

"But why, Godfrey?"

"I need a, er... doorstop."

"And a small wedge of wood would be too..."

"Small and woody," said Godfrey, as though this was so obvious as to not merit the breath.

"Right," said Will, "but don't you live on the third floor in the residences and have no outside door."

"True, but I do have fire doors that are very hard to keep open, especially with small wooden wedges."

"Godfrey, you know Mrs Hammerock would freak if she saw her fire doors wedged open even on a semi-permanent basis."

Godfrey smiled. "I know, and she did."

"Which explains why you and it are here," said Will nodding.

Godfrey grinned.

Shauna, who had seen this sort of thing play out for literally hours, sighed and intervened. "We stopped at an antiques shop on the way back because Godfrey saw this milk churn for sale outside it and decided he *needed* it. So, we stopped and he bought it."

"OK," said Will.

"Then Mrs Hammerock spotted us carrying it up the stairs –" continued Shauna before being interrupted.

"– And we disagreed on whether or not fire doors really had to stay closed all of the time," said Godfrey. "I suggested that it was important to allow the noxious but perfectly natural odours that build up as a consequence of the room being inhabited by a living organism, to escape. I went on to explain how it was no good opening the one window in the flat, as two openings to a closed system were required to allow the free passage of air through the aforementioned system."

"And Mrs Hammerock suggested that Godfrey, living in a tor on the moor, would allow an even freer passage of air, which she was happy to arrange if the milk churn stayed," finished Shauna.

"She even offered to book the removal van for later today," said Godfrey, sniffing. "I pointed out that it was Sunday, but from the glare she gave me I don't think that would have been an issue."

Will shrugged... no point arguing, "OK, by the door?" He picked up one end and Godfrey smugly took the other.

The week following a big weekend was always difficult. A one-in-five rota left little time for recuperation, but going off on weekend trips, late nights and drinking to excess was essential to keeping your sanity. That did mean that there were occasionally quite shabby-looking junior medical staff running the wards, but the seniors understood this and for the most part tolerated it and prevented any major catastrophes. Will did a very good line in shabby. He was running late again and had only just made it for the ward round in time. Well, almost just in time.

"Good that you were able to spare the time to join us, Dr Cunningham," said Mr Stoneman, looking Will up and down. "Looks like you had a good weekend?"

Mr Stoneman appeared in fine spirits. You could tell because he was being sarcastic rather than vitriolic. A subtle but important difference.

"Absolutely, Mr Stoneman, fully refreshed after a nice relaxing weekend." Will was well aware that his hair was unbrushed, his eyes barely open and he wasn't definitely sure he'd managed to align the buttons of his shirt up properly. The assembled group tittered and Will managed a glance at Tamsin, who was, as usual, looking immaculate. She really needed to drink more.

They set off around the patients, Dave covering where Will faltered, which was less frequently than anyone expected, particularly Will himself. Dave was an excellent registrar, Will had decided, but a little too driven for the Southwest, which was renowned as the graveyard of ambition. Most doctors in this part of Britain were happy to just look after the patients and improve the lives of those who passed through the hospital's doors where possible. Few papers advancing the frontiers of medicine had emanated from Whitehorse Hospital. What the good academics of the rest of the country didn't realise was that the Southwest was a brilliant place to actually have a life. And there was the bonus of having a career that funded your requirement for toys such as surfboards, windsurfers, sailing dinghies or just walking boots. Will's train of thought wandered off to his attempts at windsurfing on nearby reservoirs. Yes, falling off the board meant mouthfuls of water tasting worse than NHS tea. Then jumping back on and up hauling the sail, only to overbalance and fall off the other side, because the wind was notoriously fickle, was irritating, but the sensation of speed as he flew across the water - feet in the straps, leaning back in the harness, all forces in perfect equilibrium... Wow there was nothing like it.

His reverie was shattered by a rude intrusion. "Dr Cunningham, are you with us or shall I get sister to make a bed up for you?" Mr Stoneman looked displeased.

"Sorry," said Will, looking around for some clue as to what it was that he'd missed or whether he was supposed to be answering a question.

Mr Stoneman sighed, repeating what he'd just said. "Mrs Gubbins can go home if her haemoglobin level is high enough. Is it high enough?" Will had no idea and was pretty sure that he hadn't taken blood from this lady, which would explain the lack of results in her notes. He did, however, have a spare tube of blood in his pocket for just such an occasion. He waved it at Mr Stoneman.

"Just need to send it off," he said, hoping it looked as though he had at least been a little on the ball that morning and had thought about the patient's management. He'd just been too busy to have sent it off to the lab, hadn't he? Will would, of course, go back and do the actual blood test immediately after the ward round. Mr Stoneman just shook his head and moved on. Well, he would after a coffee.

Nope, that hadn't helped. He had a pervading weariness that he couldn't quite shake. Maybe a couple of sugars would help this time. It was mid-morning and he wasn't surprised to find the doctors' mess quiet and unoccupied but with the exception of one individual sat hunched at a table in the corner. Godfrey had his hands clenched between his thighs and was rocking back and forth, as though on a chair made for that purpose.

"Are you alright?" asked Will, dragging another chair across the carpet to sit down next to his friend. The rocking got worse. Godfrey did rock sometimes, but it was usually because he was pretending to be impatient waiting for his beer. This was different. Godfrey's lips were pursed and there was a dark scowl etched into his features.

"No, I'm not," he replied. "Those bastards!"

"What bastards, Godfrey?" He really was quite upset.

"Those bastards that are re-organising the department, and by re-organising, I mean ripping up the organising manual and writing a completely bloody new one. One that I do not and will not recognise."

"Godfrey, you are going to have to be a bit more specific."

He bared his teeth and shook his jaw, looking a bit like an angry squirrel. "Those stupefyingly omniscient beings who sit down in London, doing organising rather than an actual proper job, have decided that careers and posts need to be distributed on the basis of merit. Merit, they have decided, is determined by how many bits of paper you have saying that theoretically you know how to do the job. Actually, being able to do it is utterly irrelevant. Those of us who haven't got their exams, hence don't possess the requisite bits of paper, or are not in the process of studying for their exams, will be out of a job. It's training posts only from now on apparently!"

Will exhaled and patted Godfrey on the back. He knew this would be something of a problem for Godfrey. Until now, you could breeze from one job to the next, do some exams eventually when you had the inclination and could stay in the middle grades as long as you liked. You asked the personnel department, or better still got on well with one of the consultants, and bingo, there was your job. However, things were changing into much more of a meritocracy, and this essentially meant you had to get qualifications and posted to rotations that chucked out consultants at the end. Those consultants might theoretically have posts to go to, but the job was almost certainly not at the hospital where you wanted to be, not unless your boss died at a convenient moment. Instead, you were required to uproot your entire life – again, to fill a post in, God help you, Norfolk or the like. Not much surf there. Your future was even more uncertain if those extra bits of paper didn't materialise.

So, Will wasn't surprised that Godfrey was in a state. Godfrey hated exams, really hated them. But there wasn't any other option that he could see.

"Well," he began, "we all have to do more exams eventually. There isn't going to be any way of avoiding them. Why don't you just accept that, apply and do them?"

"Firstly," Godfrey snapped, "I can do my job without the exams to say I can, and secondly, the exam is in three months' time, with the application for it closing in four days' time."

"OK, so there's still time to get the application in then," said Will.

Godfrey snorted.

"Maybe you could try talking to one of the bosses and see if he can help," Will suggested.

"I did."

"And?"

"That's why I'm here in the mess, rocking. He said I had to do the exam. Bastard!"

"Some places don't have that regulation in yet," said Will.

"I don't want to work anywhere else. I want to work here." He looked utterly dejected.

"So… is three months enough time to do the work necessary?"

"I don't know," he said, now pulling at what little hair he had left. "I'd have to wing it."

Will wondered if there was a way around the problem in the short term. "If you were actually down to do the exam then you would satisfy the criteria, wouldn't you?"

"They're wise to that one, and I would have to actually pass it."

"But it would buy you some time, and you might even pass the damn thing." Silence. "Have you thought about becoming a GP?" said Will.

"Don't be ridiculous!" said Godfrey. "I'd have to talk to the patients then. At least as an anaesthetist if they start to bore me, I just put them off to sleep."

"Fair enough," said Will. "It doesn't look as if you have much option then."

"No, it doesn't."

The door opened with a bang and the medics piled in, chattering excitedly. "Yes, he had so many that they took him in for observation. I mean, the histamine reaction can kill you," said Mel. "Extravasation of plasma and hypovolaemic shock."

Will's ears pricked up. "What's happened?" he asked Shauna as she passed him.

"Haven't you heard?" she said, reaching for a chipped mug then putting it down in favour of washing a dirty one. "Metern got really badly stung last night."

"What?" said Will.

"Yes, his rugby ball rolled out of the back of his car into a hedge and disturbed a swarm of bees. Got stung all over. In fact, he got so badly stung he got admitted."

A cold shiver went through Will. "Is he alright?"

Kris walked past. "Oh, he's discharged himself now and gone straight back to work. To look at him now, you wouldn't have known that anything had happened. Not so much as the odd red lump," he said.

"Yeah, he's been very lucky," said Shauna. "A good thing he lives close to the hospital and got to A & E quickly or things might have been different."

"He needed adrenaline, antihistamines, steroids, the lot," said Mel, joining in again.

Will's mind raced, the rational side desperate to dismiss any link between what he had done at the museum and the events that had befallen Metern. The cold sweat and sinking feeling in the pit of his stomach belied the not so deeply buried irrational side and the thought that he'd really been directly responsible for almost killing someone. His head swam and he toppled into a chair. Mel and Shauna didn't seem to notice his reaction and had turned away to drink their tea with the other medics.

Tamsin entered the mess and smiled at him, then, seeing that there was something wrong, came over to where he was sitting.

"You OK?" she said, frowning.

"Me, I'm fine," he replied, "but have you heard what happened to Metern?"

"Oh yes, the bees." She chuckled and then apparently realised that Will wasn't quite as amused so stopped. "Oh! And you feel responsible?" Then she laughed delightedly, a tinkling sound like shattering glass. "You think you caused him to jump into the middle of a swarm of bees, don't you?"

Will sat wide-eyed, his jaw dropping a few centimetres. He was confused and looking for reassurance, not the piss taken.

"It's not just a coincidence then?" Tamsin continued; lips pouted in mock pity.

"Well of course it's a coincidence, isn't it," he said, trying to convince himself as much as reply to Tamsin.

"So, there's nothing to worry about," she said, and stroked his arm reassuringly. "Coffee?" She turned to go to the kettle.

"But..." He trailed off and Tamsin turned, her look the sort that a mother gives her child when he discovers that Playdough may look great to eat, but it most definitely isn't.

"Will, you either believe that this was just a coincidence or that you have supernatural powers."

"That's staggeringly unhelpful," said Will, struggling to regain a little composure.

She smiled at him, a flat, matter-of-fact smile. "Look, he's had a really unfortunate accident and he's disappointingly fine. Everything is OK, so I'll get a cup of coffee and we can talk about a trip to see *The Fifth Element* at the cinema?" Will nodded dumbly as his eyes followed her tightly skirted bottom to the kettle. He shook his head in mild self-rebuke. The male brain was so easily distracted, as he realised all thoughts of his possible magical, homicidal tendencies had instantly vanished.

The barrier to the car park lifted and he drove out. Several hours later and his brain was still addled. Tamsin's pragmatic and logical dismissal of his concerns had helped about as much as her piss-taking. They'd had a chat and he'd ended up feeling like some simple, credulous country bumpkin. He went over events for the umpteenth time, trying to reassure himself that it *was* an unfortunate, freakish accident. It could have happened to anyone at any time. But a bit of him kept coming to uncomfortable conclusions. His mind kept trying to make the association between him stabbing the doll at the museum and Metern's accident. He knew very well that brains, particularly his brain, tended to do this, to make connections between events that weren't really there. This, he tried to explain to himself, was why so many sports people had superstitions or rituals associated with their chosen activity. It might range from having the same peg in a changing room to a pre-match song. Those that watched cricket on TV might not allow themselves to go and get a cup of tea until an interval because they feared that doing so might precipitate an England middle-order collapse. And there were Godfrey's lucky pants, which tended to be any pair that were clean.

There was no cause-and-effect relationship, he told himself, between a man sitting in his living room, with or without a cup of tea, and batsmen four, five, six and seven, all getting out playing loose shots. Equally, Will reasoned, sticking pins in a doll did not cause someone to get attacked by a swarm of bees. He frowned to himself. Godfrey's lucky pants, though, did always seem remarkably lucky. Stupid brain, he rebuked himself, and headed onto the main road.

Chapter 20

Will arrived back at the cottage. Godfrey was at the back door, smoking a cigarette and talking with Shauna. From his animated gestures and none too quiet exclamations, he appeared to be passing comment on the fairness of "the system" ... really quite *un*fair, judging from the way the cigarette was being finished in double quick time. A situation that was not, apparently, being soothed by the exam bunny with whom he was talking.

"Hi," he said, getting out of the car and hoping that he might break the stand-off, "how are things going?"

Godfrey barely looked in Will's direction, glaring instead at Shauna. "She says I have to stop moping, pull my finger out and get down to doing some work. So, not that well."

"If you want to stay working at Whitehorse, then you really don't have any other options," huffed Shauna, glaring back.

Godfrey took another long drag on his cigarette and hit the filter. Godfrey gave a filthy look as he removed it from his mouth. Glancing up at Shauna, she gave him a "Don't even dare flick that cigarette into the bushes" look. It took mere moments before inspiration struck and Godfrey gave a smug, self-satisfied smile. He lifted the lid off the milk churn and tossed the butt inside.

Shauna frowned but accepted this compromise. She continued in a much gentler tone. "Godfrey, go and apply to sit the exam. You know your stuff, and if you work really hard you might scrape through. It's your only chance of staying here."

Godfrey drummed his fingers on the lid twice, turned and stomped along the drive towards his car.

"Please," she said, her voice wavered.

"OK!" he snapped.

The housemates watched him go. "So, we're not going to see much of Godfrey for the next three months," said Shauna as Will walked with her into the cottage.

"I wouldn't bet on it," Will replied. "It may curb his social life somewhat, but he'll still need feeding."

"And a twenty-mile round trip is preferable to cooking?" said Shauna.

"Oh, absolutely," said Will. "Speaking of which?"

"We have a peach, a gherkin and a tomato, because someone hasn't done the shopping," said Shauna. Did her accent get stronger with sarcasm, Will wondered, before suggesting the pub.

Chapter 21

I t was Wednesday, and Will was acutely aware that he hadn't yet made the promised visit to the hospital museum, which was why he now stood before the hospital library, also the entry point for the exhibition.

The library was open to all hospital staff for referencing medical papers and the like, but the general public were also allowed access for a modest fee, which also extended to cover the museum admission.

He drew in a deep breath. The air in the library smelled of musty, aged paper, despite it being a modern space and having been renovated only a couple of years ago. It was a smell that elicited feelings of anxiety and memories of hours spent in these environs studying to pass exams. He looked over the row upon row of bookcases and shelves containing books, journals and papers representing the knowledge that served to prolong the existence of the human condition. He recognised a few faces buried in their revision for the upcoming exams. Some pored over the viewers for the microfiched medical papers that had been reduced in size and placed on microfilm. Microfilm had been used for over a century to store large volumes of information in a small space, but over the last decade computer technology had progressed at such a rapid pace that its time was surely numbered as a reference facility.

Will followed the roped-off walkway that led to the museum at the far end of the library area. Two ceiling-high wall hangings of the mosaic flanked a very solid-looking colonnaded double door. He pushed at the doors, which opened stiffly with a squeak, and walked through. The walls of a long wide corridor had been lined with thin marbled revetments and interspersed with murals depicting mildly lurid scenes from Roman banquets in front of which stood a variety of exhibits. Looking around, Will was quite surprised by the effort that had gone in to making a room in a medical establishment look anything but medical. It was an actual, proper museum with things to read and stuff to see! He surveyed the artwork admiring the detail but found his eye drawn, as everyone's would be to the floorspace in the centre of the room. He found he was holding his breath. It was stunning; majestic, and there must have been thousands and thousands of tiny ceramic squares contained within it. The mosaic of the white horse dominated the room. Pictured in profile, the powerfully built animal stood, head bowed, right foreleg bent, back lowered, almost as though inviting the observer to mount up should they have the need. Beautiful.

It was, of course, white, well, other than the even smaller tiles outlining the muscle in grey tones. The proportions were perfectly described until - Will felt a pull towards its head - until the eye. It seemed oversized; disproportionately large and it was, if he was correct, a single circular piece of black stone. Will walked over to it and stood looking at the nearly one metre diameter circle. It seemed comforting somehow, even though this was only a copy of the real thing in the basement, an impression of how it might have looked nearly two millennia ago.

He wandered on wanting to learn more of its history and had a look at the displays containing belt buckles, brooch pins and ancient leather goods. A lot of coins had also been found, along with inscriptions on pieces of lead imploring the deities to look kindly on a cause or begging for the healing of wounds or ailments. One theory suggested that the site may well have been a religious one or possibly an infirmary, even back then.

Moving on, a sign invited him to an area of seating off to one side, that surrounded a screen, He duly pressed the green start button and began to watch the brief film about the history of Whitehorse.

It started with the bombing of an old farmhouse on Brepon Hill, situated a few miles outside Plymouth. During the war, a German bomber, possibly mistaking a poorly hidden light for an indication of a larger target or perhaps just to lighten the plane to evade being shot down, released its load on the unsuspecting folk who lived on the farm below. The place was all but flattened and everyone inside was killed. Everyone, that was, except for an infant boy, who by some miracle had survived.

The farm lay in ruins for a decade before it was decided that the area needed a new hospital. The site was chosen for its proximity to several major conurbations and the fact that it was the only proposed site that wasn't actually on the new and now legally protected Dartmoor National Park. Initially, it was due to be little bigger than a cottage hospital but plans for Plymouth changed and the footprint size of the new hospital was increased. This resulted in the drafting of more staff, and amongst them was a man called William Rainer. He was driving the digger that unearthed small white tiles and the foundations of a building incorporated into, and predating, the old destroyed farmhouse. He was a keen amateur archaeologist and persuaded the contractors to halt the build temporarily. In truth, with the confusion over the plans, this probably didn't put them out too much. Local archaeologists all flocked to the site and excavated a small section. They uncovered what was probably a Roman villa dating to the second century AD. Very little of the old building was left, the bomb having landed directly on it, but they did find a reasonably intact Roman mosaic floor with a depiction of a white horse. Beneath the disrupted mosaic, further work unearthed deeper trenches cut a foot or so down and filled with chalk. When fully excavated, the trenches were found to form the shape of a horse. What wasn't so clear was why a layer of red breccia sandstone, brought from the cliffs at Teignmouth, lay in traces in the bottom of the trenches.

One feature was consistent throughout all the layers, even being incorporated into the Roman mosaic. A circular trench, sunk to a depth of one metre, whose perimeter was filled with quartz and its inner capped by a polished circle of black marble. It was the eye of the horse. Such carvings, superstition suggested, were supposed to be a life-giving source, a centre of rebirth and healing. Not a bad thing to have under your hospital, Will thought, and certainly not bad for business.

There had been a degree of debate about what exactly to do with the excavation. Often these were just reburied and the building works continued so everything disappeared under six feet of concrete, but it was decided to build around the mosaic and construct the hospital above it, leaving it as a feature on the bottom floor. The name of the hospital then became a foregone conclusion.

The rest of the exhibition described a bit about the Romans themselves and some of the pre-Roman history. The site itself was a reasonably typical example of the way that the Roman civilisation took pre-existing belief systems of those that they conquered and absorbed them into their own. Often the Romans built on top of sacred sites, creating temples at which both Roman and pagan deities might be worshipped. It was thought that this site might have originally been a religious pagan site or Bronze Age statement of power, given its prominence on the hillside. The Romans, whose influence in Cornwall was much less than in the rest of the country, probably erected a temple on the site and constructed the mosaic as part of an acknowledgement of the site's past importance. There were temporary Roman forts based at Restormel and Nanstallon, and this may have been on a road back to more civilised parts. The site probably fell into disrepair in the Dark Ages but found new use as a farmhouse.

Tucked away in one corner of the room was a small section concerning the site's relationship with ley lines. It might have been easy to miss it. Will went over to have a look. Ley lines were, in the ancient sense, networks of straight trackways criss-crossing Britain, and in the modern sense, lines of power connecting features of spiritual significance in the landscape. Although the phrase had only been coined in 1921, they had been of interest well before that. It had been noted that the Whitehorse site was placed exactly on St Michael's ley line, drawn between Land's End in Cornwall and Hopton-on-Sea in Norfolk. It aligned ancient monuments and churches dedicated to St Michael and purported to be the longest of these ley lines in the country. It included sites such as St Michael's Mount, an island off Cornwall's south coast, St Michael's Church in Brentor, Glastonbury Tor, the Uffington White Horse, Wayland's Smithy and the Avebury henge, to name but a few. The line tracked the path of the sunrise on 1st May at an angle of twenty-seven degrees north of east, Will read... His pager went off and he glanced down at it. His presence was required urgently on the ward.

Chapter 22

Well done him, running late again! Will was in a hurry as it was his fencing night. His delay in the library meant an even quicker than usual turnaround from where he was at home in Southside to back into Plymouth. He *had* been keen to get there on time as he was a new member and had hoped to meet a few people before the serious fencing began. Not going to happen now. The gravel crunched under his feet and he reached for the door handle at Southside, pausing briefly to glance at Godfrey's newly sited '*objet d'art*'. Really, a milk churn! Turning the handle and walking into the kitchen, he was greeted by the hiss of Shauna's violin. OK, hiss was possibly a little harsh, she was very good, but solo classical violin tended to lance straight through his head. It, in his humble opinion, needed some other instruments accompanying it to dull its edge, preferably with those instruments amped up and the violin in a different village. He hesitated and listened. He had been *expecting* a hiss. Actually, this evening, she wasn't playing the usual classical pieces. It sounded more like an Irish jig and sounded... pleasant. He smiled to himself. It would seem that Godfrey might be getting his band after all – compensation perhaps for his exam application?

He went over to the fridge and made a cheese sandwich, grabbing a quick cup of tea to go with it before searching for his fencing kit. It was usually fairly easy to locate in whichever wardrobe it had landed. He just followed the stale, sweaty smell to its source. A look at the clock... aargh! His stuff got thrown into the back of the car, he shouted a goodbye to Shauna and set off for the Rapier Fencing Club in Plymouth.

The club took place in Albion College, a secondary education college in the middle of Plymouth. It was a triumph of 1950s' concrete architecture. Huge square grey blocks of the stuff, towering vertical faces, small windows; as uninspiring a place to study as one might find. It did, however, have a large multipurpose hall, and from his first two visits it appeared that it attracted some good fencers. He entered the monstrosity through violent, swing doors, past the unmanned reception desk, and was channelled down wide Lego-like corridors to reach the changing rooms. They smelled little better than his kit bag. He put on his fencing breeches, which ended just below the knee, and pulled on the white knee-length socks and the lightweight trainers. On went the under plastron, designed to stop any blades that broke with a sharp point, and finally the jacket. It was stiflingly hot just getting into the kit, let alone after fencing in it, and it really did need a wash for next time. He picked up the bag with his swords and electric wires and jacket and headed for the hall.

The hall was a white-walled rectangular area, with a raised stage at one end and cricket nets at the other. Four badminton courts had been marked out across the hall and overlying these were the rolled out one point five by four-teen-metre fencing pistes, the area in which the fencers fought. At each end of the pistes were spools from which a wire emerged. The fencer connected his metallic woven jacket, if fencing with a foil, or just plain fencing jacket if fencing with an épée, to the wire. When one fencer hit his opponent, a circuit was made and a light lit up on the control box, along with an audible "beep" registering the hit. In foil, a light and fast, point weapon, a coloured light, red or green, signified a scoring hit on the trunk of the body and a white light indicated that the point had hit a non-scoring area, i.e., the head or limbs, and there was no score.

Épéeists, those who fought with the heavier duelling sword, had the whole body to aim at, and any hit counted. Sabreurs, who fought with sabres, could use the point of the weapon, but it was primarily a cutting weapon. A hit was scored from the waist upwards. Will could and had fought all three disciplines but was best at the foil. He had come in the top twenty in a couple of the UAU Championships for the country's universities and firmly believed if he'd applied himself at all he might have made an Olympic team. He also considered that he might have been an England cricketer, scratch golfer and big wave surfer, but a decent education and common sense had robbed him of all of those dreams.

The room was filled with around thirty fencers, most of whom were in their late teens or early twenties and still in secondary or tertiary education. There were male and female fencers, and they all knew each other. Will, at twenty-nine and working for a living, was slightly out of the demographic. He put his bag down at the edge of the room, then looked up to see the fencing master, Harry de Velte, walking in. He was a fifty-year-old slightly portly gentleman who sported a moustache and goatee beard. Once, he had been one of the country's finest épéeists, but time and a couple too many beers looked to have caught up with him. His blade work was still immaculate, however, and he taught all three disciplines.

Will went through his warm-up, first stretching and then getting his feet moving. Feet at right angles, moving sideways, he moved back and forth, quick, small steps, cross-steps and the occasional balestra, or jump step. Then he practised a few lunges, throwing his weight forward, body upright, sword arm extended, back leg straight, before bending the rear leg and returning to the en garde position once more. This he then repeated with a sword in his hand, practising his point control as he did so.

When a piste became free, Will nodded towards another foilist, Sean, if memory served him correctly, and they donned their metallic thread jackets and attached themselves to the spools. Meeting in the middle, they shook hands with the non-sword hand and, after raising the foil in salute, put the steel meshed masks on.

Fencing, Will thought, was about speed and precision. Speed of thought and reaction, precision of plan and execution. Work out your opponent's preferred strategies: did they like to attack or counterattack; what was their default parry; how fast were their reflexes; were they trying to work you out or just reacting?

Search out weaknesses, exploit them and win. He had found that he had an ability to visualise a fight, to the point where he could quickly anticipate an opponent's next move.

He fired a straightforward lunge at Sean, who reacted with a jerky parry of quarte across his body. He had no intention of hitting his opponent with this attack, but Sean's point veered away from Will's target reactively. The flicked-out riposte didn't even need to be parried as Will stepped backwards out of range. Will lunged again. Again, he was deliberately short, but as Sean's blade came to parry Will's as before, Will looped his blade underneath Sean's, disengaging it, and extended his arm. Sean's sword shot back across in a parry of sixte, just in time to prevent Will landing a hit. It looked like Will had overcommitted, as Sean's riposte flicked out again, especially as Will couldn't step back quite so far this time as momentum carried him forward, but it was the same direct riposte as before. Will had anticipated it, meeting Sean's blade in a parry of sixte and a green light registered his low line riposte on Sean's right flank. Sean acknowledged it and they retreated to their en garde lines.

Fencing recommenced. This time Sean came on the offensive, beating Will's blade and following it with a lunge, the point of his blade circling in order to evade Will's circular sixte parry. Sean had clearly learned from the last point, and it was only Will's quick footwork backwards that took him out of the way as his parry failed to collect Sean's blade. Sean reprised the attack, lunging again, and again circling the blade to avoid Will's parry. This time Will stepped in, raising his hand but dropping the point of the blade to parry Sean's blade in octave. Will's point flicked from aiming at Sean's flank in the low line, where he had hit previously, to riposting in the high line, and Sean was again left looking at Will's point, this time on his shoulder. Another green light.

They continued to fence for another ten minutes or so before their time was up. Sean registered a few hits towards the end when Will got careless or attempted the extravagant. They shook hands again and unclipped from the wire before unzipping their jackets to allow some heat out. Sean went back to his group of friends and Will went to sit at the side. They weren't the most inclusive bunch he'd ever met.

Harry de Velte came over. "It's Will, isn't it?"

"That's right," Will replied.

"A lesson?"

Harry would try to give as many fencers as possible a lesson during the evening. Fencing bouts tended to create some bad habits that a lesson could iron out.

"Please," said Will, standing.

"OK? Any areas to improve?"

Will suggested a few areas to work on, Harry nodded, and they started with some basic lunges and parries, building the speed and difficulty of the moves gradually. He was right-handed but would swap the sword from his right to his left hand later in the lesson, seeming to fence just as well with his left hand, still using the right-handed sword.

Harry advanced and retreated up and down the piste, getting Will to maintain his distance, concentrating on his footwork. Occasionally, he would extend his sword arm and Will was expected to parry and riposte directly. It was all about the distance, and your feet got you to that correct distance. Too close and Will's parry would be too late, too far apart and his riposte would land short. Will was then drawn into lunges and indirect line ripostes. Very rapidly, the lactic acid built up in his legs and he started blowing quite hard. More fitness work required, he thought.

Ten minutes of a punishing lesson later and Will was in the middle of a complicated sequence: lunge, sixte, riposte, carte, riposte, step back, circular parry sixte, disengage, riposte... when a figure, just arriving, caught his eye. A gleaming white jacket and breeches, mask held under his left arm and épée blade in his right hand, Cadan Metern looked about him and the room looked back. All, that was, except Harry de Velte, whose foil point now hit the centre of Will's chest with a thud, knocking Will back a fraction.

"Circular quarte?" he suggested, slightly sarcastically.

"Oh, er, yes," replied Will, pulling his attention from the man now practising his footwork and warming up.

It didn't take too much longer for Will to be reduced to something of a quivering wreck, and he gasped his thanks as he shook hands with Harry. You had to give it to the man, he managed to pack what was probably half an hour's lesson into just ten minutes. He pushed you to be more accurate and quicker, not letting you have a moment to catch your breath. Will took off his jacket and under plastron and sat hunched against the wall, chest heaving. He looked across the room. So, Metern fenced as well. Everyone in the hall seemed to know him and he certainly had all of the kit. But how good was he?

It didn't take Will too long to find out. Metern was on a piste and fought with the épée. He noted that neither he nor his opponent were wired up, which meant that they fought "steam". And it turned out Metern was good, excellent in fact. His precise footwork allowed him to glide over the matting as though on ice. His blade teased his opponent, feinting, drawing parries at thin air, and his point darted almost faster than could be seen, landing hit after hit. The guy he was fencing was no slouch either, but Metern was just playing with him. He was clever too, flicking his point at unguarded toes or wrists, which, if hit, counted just as much as a lunge landing in the middle of the chest. When a hit landed it was acknowledged by the recipient of the hit. Metern's opponent had a lot of acknowledging to do.

The bout finished and the fencers saluted before removing their masks and shaking hands in the middle of the piste. Metern came over to where Will was sitting; he looked to have barely broken sweat.

"Hi," he said. "Didn't realise you were a fencer."

"Nor I you," replied Will, getting up from the floor a little stiffly. Then he cautiously added, "Are you alright, after your... bee attack?" It was only polite to ask, and while Will had finally just about convinced his subconscious that it had been an accident, another part of his psyche screamed, "Ask him if he killed Tamsin's friend."

"Bee attack," Metern said, chuckling, "sounds a bit dramatic. I'm fine," he assured Will. "It was only a few stings, ten or so, but the medics got a bit carried away."

"I'm glad you're OK," said Will. There was a half-smile on Metern's face. He couldn't possibly know... stop being stupid. There was a momentary silence.

"Do you fight épée as well?" asked Metern, glancing at Will's foil.

Will still hadn't quite recovered from his lesson with Harry, but he was keen to see how he measured up against Metern. "I'm a foilist really and don't have an épée with me, but yes I can use one."

"Not to worry," said Metern, and he reached down to pick out a spare sword from his bag. "Here, try this," he said, handing Will the épée hilt first. Will took the sword offered but found his attention drawn to the épée Metern held. Seeing this, Metern flipped the sword around and handed it to Will. Metern's had a French grip, rather than the modern, stronger, yet less precise, pistol grip. The sword seemed to melt into his hand and become an extension of his own arm – it actually felt warm in his grasp. The balance of the weapon was like no other he had ever held. He extended his arm, feeling the point react to the lightest change in pressure between his thumb and forefinger. He moved through a series of parries; it almost felt as though the blade wasn't there, like fencing with air. Will examined the blade itself. It had a gleaming, bluish lustre, quite unlike any metal he had seen before, let alone in a sword, and it was engraved with the name *Anodho Calesvol*. He hadn't heard of that make before either.

"She's not legal of course," said Metern. "Doesn't quite conform to the required modern standards, but she's still an épée, just a very old one." The steel didn't look old. There wasn't a nick or a blemish on it.

"It's beautiful, the balance, the weight..." Will was lost for words, mesmerised by the shimmering surface. "Where did you get it?"

"A lady, lives up by Dozmary Pool on Bodmin Moor, gave it to me. She used to fence years ago and felt it might get more use in my hands. I hope you don't mind me using it. I do have more standard épées if you do?"

"No, it's fine," said Will, handing the sword back and returning to the one he'd been given. They made their way over to a free piste. Will still had the lesson weighing a bit heavy in his legs as he saluted and put his mask on. A small group of onlookers gathered discreetly at one end, no doubt there to see how the new guy fared.

Will stepped forward to engage Metern's blade, who just stepped back. Will advanced again, this time arm extended, testing for a reaction. Metern, again, stepped back and Will reprised the attack, this time with a lunge, disengaging his blade and looping it under Metern's, aiming for his midriff. Metern took a half step back to create the room for a parry of septime, deflecting Will's blade across his body, and Will felt the sting of the riposte landing on his knee. Damn, thought Will, his brain was still in foil mode, where this riposte wouldn't have counted. He acknowledged the hit and they returned to the en garde line. Will took a small step forward, determined to be more cautious this time, and into the step flashed Metern's épée, aimed at Will's forearm. Will stepped back, his blade whirling reflexively in a circular parry of sixte, desperately seeking Metern's épée blade. He did find it, but not in the forte or strong part of his own blade but in the middle of his chest, and it hit with quite a jolt. So fast.

The next hit was more cagey, Will reluctant to commit to an attack of any sort, aware of Metern's speed were he to do so, Metern was waiting coolly, seeking a mistake, a stand-off. There would be no scoring with first-, second- or even third-phase attack, considered Will. Metern advanced, beating Will's sword. Will returned the beat, judging the reaction, biding his time for an opening. He went to beat the blade again. One beat too many, and Metern lunged, taking Will's blade, and he cross-stepped forward, driving Will back, whose desperate parries fended off the insistent reprises of Metern's point. Will fired a riposte back, but it was deflected away, and he only just got back to counter-parry, but Metern's blade wasn't there. He felt a familiar sting in his shoulder as Metern's counter-riposte landed. Will shook his head.

The following minutes were an object lesson in épée for Will, as he was dismantled to the point where he felt like a pincushion. He was breathing hard with the exertion and his legs weren't responding nearly quickly enough. Metern, however, looking unperturbed, was toying with Will. Finally, after Will found himself back-pedalling rapidly, Metern put an end to things. He bound Will's blade, enveloping the foible, the weak part of Will's blade with his own strong forte, and then, with a flick, he ripped it from Will's grasp, sending it spinning into the scattering onlookers, clattering to a halt against the wall. Will looked from his own weapon some feet away to the weapon now pointed at his sternum. Metern lowered the point and removed his mask.

He smiled at Will and held his eye. "Thanks," he said, extending his hand. "Foil next time?"

"Yes," replied Will, bemused and a little embarrassed at his poor showing and dramatic loss. Will had thought he was a pretty decent fencer, even with an épée rather than his foil, but Metern was, well, unbelievable. He walked over to retrieve his épée, returning it to Metern, and was suddenly aware of the stinging spots of pain dotted over the whole of his body.

Chapter 23

The following day was slack on the wards. Mr Stoneman had an outpatients' clinic and the patients from the previous day's operating list were all behaving well. Will was on his way out of the mess, wondering whether he could get away with giving his pager to his registrar and heading for a walk on the moor, but then a look out of the window at the driving rain put him off that idea. He was also toying with going up to the mosaic exhibition again when his mind strayed onto the work that Metern had published. It was bound to be in the library, and many who knew Metern made reference to his previous publications. Maybe it was worth a look to see if it provided some insight into the man. He made the trip up to the library to see what he could find.

The librarian, a shortish, bespectacled gentleman whose skin colour suggested he was rarely to be found anywhere else but the library and certainly nowhere near direct sunlight, pointed him in the direction of *The British Journal of Genetic Disease*. Will found the section amongst the labyrinth of shelving that twisted and turned to make maximum use of the available space. Will had loved libraries as a boy, exploring just this sort of environment, wondering what exciting adventure he would leave with, which mystical land he would explore. Studying medicine at university had put an end to that. He'd had no time for reading for pleasure, and visits to libraries tended to mean research for projects, tutorials, or, even worse, a quiet place for exam revision. The ever-present threat of exams for all medical students meant that there was a relative paucity of good places to revise. The library was an obvious quiet spot, but he recollected that there were others. Being surrounded by books had been comforting in comparison to where he'd had to go if the library was full. A guaranteed quiet spot was in the anatomy specimen hall. This was an imposing, high-vaulted Victorian hall over seventy metres long that had a mezzanine gallery encompassing the entire hall. Around the edge of both levels were shelves containing specimens collected over many decades, possibly centuries. Between these shelves were large desks that were designed for anatomy tutorials but were also perfect for spreading revision notes. It was deathly silent in there, but any noise that was made echoed and reverberated through the chamber, the perpetrator receiving admonishing stares from the cancerous eyeball and the two-headed foetus. No one studied in there after dark.

The British Journal of Genetic Disease came out on a bimonthly basis. When a year's copies had been collected, the library then bound them into weighty tomes that sat on the shelf until required by some unfortunate who had been required to work rather than go surfing. The librarian had given him a list of three articles. A quick look through the index gave the first article, dated 23 July 1990. It was entitled "Gene Therapy: The Potential for a Permanent Cure for Cancer". Will pulled out the relevant bound book and went to sit down in a secluded area of the library at one of the desks.

The article, which Metern had co-written with Dr James Gowen, was produced to coincide with the start of the Human Genome Project. This was to be a multinational endeavour aimed at sequencing the genetic code for the human genome, essentially the blueprint to build a human by decoding the gene sequence on the DNA.

It was a discussion and justification of the project's aims, pointing out the potential for the future of medicine, particularly in the field of cancers and diseases with a genetic basis. Initially it described how most cancers occurred due to damage or faults in the DNA contained within the body's cells. The body did have repair mechanisms that could correct the damage most of the time, but there were occasions when it couldn't. This fault then resulted in the production of an abnormal protein that was often produced more rapidly and in greater quantities than normal proteins, and subsequently a malignancy of one variety or another developed.

A significant cause of damage to the DNA was noted to be radiation, though other things, such as chemicals, like those contained within cigarettes, could also elicit change. Radiation was all around everybody all the time. It came from the earth, the sun, our galaxy and beyond. Cosmic radiation accounted for about eight per cent of a person's radiation exposure per year, and a lifetime risk of cancer caused by this alone was estimated at about one in a hundred. It was a cumulative process generally, and cancer took years to develop. A small crumb of comfort at least.

Metern's article went on to describe the nature of radiation exposure. The whole planet, including all life, was being bombarded by energy particles all the time. Most did no damage, passing straight through matter, but some particles, particularly the heavy, ionising ones, could collide with cells in living entities and hit DNA, which was damaged in the process. Over a prolonged period of low intensity, or one high blast of exposure, the body either missed a repair, in which case genes got deleted, or repaired the DNA wrongly, abnormal proteins were produced and cancer developed.

The article continued, discussing the methods by which a virus or vector might have its own DNA stripped down and have new genetic sequences correcting the patient's genetic anomaly inserted into it. The vector could then be injected into a host or patient, where it combined with the host's own cells. The DNA then replicated in those target cells and transferred the replacement gene into the host's cells, where it could produce the new corrected protein, thus curing the disease.

This would alter the genetic make-up of the individual and was the ethical line drawn by many who deemed it to be "playing God". It introduced the "slippery slope" concept, where initially well-intentioned scientists might create the potential not only to eliminate certain genetic conditions, but also to allow the selecting of favourable genetic characteristics for offspring – in essence, creating designer babies.

The article went on to discuss the ethical problem of who was to say what was a genetic abnormality or disability and what wasn't. While recognising these arguments, they came down very strongly in favour of not only trying to eliminate human suffering but preventing it in the first place.

Will had just finished the first paper when his pager went off. It was Mr Stoneman requesting his presence in his outpatient clinic, suggesting he "might as well do something useful" with his time. Will was quite glad he'd decided against the walk on the moor. He closed the book and put it back. He would return to read the other papers later. It would be a very long and probably slightly light-headed afternoon with the ever-ebullient Mr Stoneman.

Chapter 24

The following day Will was on-call, so was busy admitting patients as well as managing the ones he already had. It never ceased to amaze him how those responsible for scheduling things had decided that it was a good idea to have a routine list for his consultant on the day of his take. Mr Stoneman was supposed to have cover so that his registrar was around to help out Will if necessary. Almost invariably, the registrar ended up in theatre, either with one of the early admissions needing some bone or other fixing or, more frequently, assisting Mr Stoneman. This would have to mean that either Mr Stoneman had supreme faith in Will's abilities or was testing his moral fibre. Will was reasonably sure that it wasn't the former opinion that Mr Stoneman held.

By mid-afternoon, having admitted any number of broken hips, pelvises and knee cruciate ligament ruptures, Will had gone past the point of being worried about getting things done. He had settled into working at a set rate, doing what he could, when he could, and had given up hope of seeing his bed that night. It wasn't so much the sheer volume of work that had to be got through that was mentally destructive, it was the vain hope that you might just create enough time to have a cup of tea. Once the hope had gone, numbness set in. That was much easier to deal with.

One of the students had finished seeing a sixty-five-year-old lady who'd had a fall and had pain in her left groin, lower abdominal region and some lower back pain. Will stood, only half listening to what he was being told about the lady, while considering the myriad other patients he had to attend to. His mind wandered over the fluid charts, consent forms, drip lines and relatives that all still required his attention. He rubbed his eyes, realising that the student had stopped speaking and was waiting patiently for further instructions.

"So... what do you think might be wrong with Mrs Copper?" Will asked.

"Well, she probably has a fractured hip and pelvis," the student replied. "She has some mild back pain, but there's no bony tenderness and no neurology, so I don't think the back pain is the main problem," he said, coming to the obvious conclusions.

"So, what are we going to do?"

"Get an X-ray, a few bloods and put up a drip while monitoring her pulse and BP and give some analgesia," the student replied competently.

"Sounds good to me," said Will. He then went over the history of what had happened to the woman and gave her hips and pelvis a cursory examination. She was sore and might well have a fracture. Get the tests done and work from there.

"Are you OK to put the IV line in?" asked Will.

"Not a problem," was the reply.

Will didn't ever remember being this competent as a medical student, or as enthusiastic. This lad was surely headed for burnout at an early age.

"Good stuff," said Will, keeping his thoughts to himself and walking off to do the drug chart. So many things to sort out and get done. He pulled out his scrap of paper that contained a list of all the things he needed to do against the names of the patients for whom he was responsible. He had that nagging feeling he sometimes got, indicating things were getting a bit out of hand. He knew his registrar would be getting out of theatre soon, probably, which would add some reinforcement, but even so. He spotted Tamsin walking down the corridor, the motion of her hips and flow of her hair in counterpoint. She was carrying a paper packet in one hand and a chocolate bar in the other. She handed them to him. The packet contained a smoked salmon and cream cheese sandwich. Lunch... or supper. Odd really, Will mused. When he was young, smoked salmon had been a special treat at Christmas, now it was just nutrition. He thanked her, smiling ruefully at his first morsel of food in nearly ten hours.

"What is Cunningham's first rule of house job survival?" she asked, dragging him into the nurses' station, and then, disappointingly, just putting the kettle on.

"Unless a patient is actually about to die," he parroted, "sort yourself out first. If they are already dead or have a good couple of hours left, get yourself fed and tea-ed first." The advice wasn't as flippant as it might have at first appeared. It made sure that you had thinking space as well as a glucose-infused brain and allowed for better decision-making. He smiled at her and she rubbed his arm.

"Anything I can do?" she asked.

"No, I just need to get my head down and keep going," he said, biting into the soft white bread. Tamsin brought his tea over as two more students came in to say they had finished with their patients. His pager went. He could see the nurse responsible through the office door, and he closed his eyes. A more observant staff nurse came in with something else to sign and tutted, asking if he was going to contribute to the tea and coffee fund, given that he was going to drink their tea. Will just looked at her blankly and signed the chart. Gone were the days of the NHS providing such things as refreshment for their staff. Will did so through mess fees, but it didn't cover the wards. He had paid on two of the four wards he covered but he couldn't remember which ones. The nursing staff tended to object to doctors pilfering a tea bag for a cuppa on the ward. However, if the doctor wanted a cup of tea, it meant a trip back to the mess, to which, ironically, the nurses also seemed to object. Bad feeling all round resulting from some genius trying to cut costs.

The first medical student came back with an X-ray that showed that Mrs Copper did have a fractured neck of femur. She would need discussing with the registrar and putting on a list. Still that nagging in his head. He felt uneasy, a little bit the way he had when he'd stuck pins in the "Cadan-doll".

Tamsin noticed his unease. "Anything wrong?" she asked, furrowing her brow.

"I'm not sure," he said. "It's that odd feeling again that I get when there's something that I've missed." He shook his head. "But there are so many things, it may just be a cumulative thing."

"Is it normally cumulative?"

"No, there's normally something specific," he admitted, stuffing the last of the food into his mouth and washing it down with the tea. "Look, I'd better get going. Thanks for the sandwich, and is next week for the cinema OK... say the Friday?"

"That would be perfect," she said.

Halfway down the corridor he isolated what was bothering him. It wasn't a eureka moment but more a feeling that he hadn't really examined Mrs Copper properly. Short cuts were often a necessary part of the job. They came from experience and knowing what was and was not a likely diagnosis and therefore what might be reasonably skipped, given there was a finite amount of time in a day and an infinite number of patients to be seen.

Experience however also bred carelessness, and the need to take short cuts had led to many a medical negligence claim. So, Will went back to see Mrs Copper. He ignored his pager, which now seemed to spend more time beeping than silent, and examined her again, this time properly. He started to press gently into her abdomen, getting her to breathe in and then fully out. He moved the exam across, palpating deeper, and there it was, a large pulsatile mass. How had he missed that first time around? She had a large aortic aneurysm, a swelling of the major blood vessel in her abdomen, that if left might rupture. If it wasn't leaking now, it might well do soon, and an operation for her hip would likely have killed her. He spoke to the vascular surgeons, who came up promptly to see her, and she was whisked away with a few more large bore IV lines in her just in case. The hip repair would wait. She was the vascular team's patient for now. Will's niggling feeling had gone.

The registrar finally emerged at six o'clock and did a round with Will, going through the admissions, their results and plans for each. At seven o'clock, Mr Stoneman joined them and they ran through the operating lists for later that evening and the following day. His mood was dark, as even he could see that the sheer volume of admissions would require him to stay on to help. The round ended and he turned to Will.

"Still, at least you've done your best to lower our take numbers," he said. "Sending them off to see the vascular team. A stroke of genius."

"Er, yes," said Will, not sure where this was heading, "an aneurysm. I decided it wasn't very orthopaedic."

"Well at least you've learned something so far," said Mr Stoneman, and then he smiled. Not the sarcastic twisted smile he reserved for his own amusing comments, but a genuine acknowledgement of some competent medicine. He nodded towards the registrar and they headed off to sort out who was to operate on what. Will took out his list of jobs. His pager went off. Only another twenty hours to go until it was time to go home.

At five o'clock the following day, he was leaving the hospital. He'd had three hours sleep, which as nights on call went, wasn't too bad. Mrs Copper had gone to theatre that evening to have her aneurysm repaired and was doing well on the Intensive Care Unit. She had been very lucky, and so had Will. It would have been very easy to not go back and re-examine the lady, and Will still didn't understand exactly why he'd felt compelled to return to her. There were plenty of other patients he'd half examined that day. What else had he missed? Call it luck, skill, guardian angels, whatever, he'd made a difference. He had avoided suspension, a lawsuit and GMC hearing, he thought. Oh yes, and a lady was still alive.

The drive home was always interesting after being on take. The world seemed to go past in slow motion, spinning and shifting slightly. He was driving using "the Force", as Godfrey referred to it, with reference to *Star Wars*. For some doctors on the way home after shifts overnight, the Force wasn't strong enough to keep them on the road, and more than the odd one had ended up back in their own hospital sooner than the start time of their next shift.

He arrived back at the cottage safely though; Shauna hadn't got back yet so, Will decided that a quick lie down for a few minutes was in order. He was asleep in seconds, sprawled across the bed fully clothed in what he'd been wearing for the last thirty-six hours. He hadn't even managed to take his shoes off.

Chapter 25

Two hours later Will was awoken by voices in the kitchen. He felt awful, a thick-headed, disconnected feeling, with a body that ached as though it had been rolled down a cobbled street. It took a few moments to work out where he was, and he groaned as he lifted his body off the bed. The noise in the kitchen emanated from a few of the SHOs who lived in the village. Bleary-eyed and crumpled, he walked through to the kitchen.

"Tough shift?" asked Mel as Will hauled himself over to the kettle. He grunted in reply, not yet capable of verbalising, put a tea bag in a mug and went to sit at the kitchen table. Shauna fished a bowl of what turned out to be pasta bake out of the oven and put it in front of Will.

"Thanks," Will acknowledged, and tucked in. It was cheesy and peppery with chopped ham. Perfect. He looked around the room and wasn't particularly surprised to see Godfrey, until he remembered the amount of work required to pass medical exams.

"Up for the GX tonight?" asked Godfrey, referring to the night club.

"Er, I'm not sure," said Will, who could have thought of more restful ways of spending the evening. "Shouldn't you be studying or something?"

"I've got loads done today," he replied. Will gave it a moment's thought before things added up in his brain.

"But you had a list today."

"Yes, that's right, but the punters are asleep for most of it, so it turns out that I can get loads of revision done."

"Don't you have dials and things to look at and twist?" asked Will, another mouthful of the pasta disappearing rapidly.

"Well, occasionally yes, but only to make the surgeon feel reassured that his patient will remain asleep. It's mostly for show."

"Right," said Will, wondering why on earth he was doing an orthopaedics job.

"So, are you coming? You know it makes sense."

Will knew it very definitely didn't make sense but equally knew he had no resolve left. "Oh OK, but it's not going to be a late one."

"'Course not," said Godfrey. Godfrey's idea of not a late one and Will's, were very different.

"Mind if I grab a quick shower first?" asked Will.

"We will insist upon it," said Shauna, holding her nose.

It didn't take long for Will to spruce himself up to an acceptable level, visually at least. He jumped into Shauna's car wearing the standard blue trousers, white and pale blue striped shirt and deck shoes. Trainers tended to push admission criteria for night clubs, even in Plymouth. Traditionally, before the GX, a stop at the Fish in a Barrel pub on the Barbican was required. It was very much a 'spit and sawdust' pub, frequented by Her Majesty's Royal Navy, NHS staff and a few local felons. Beer was served straight from the barrel, a row of which were stacked behind rickety trestle tables from which it was served. Seating, such as it was, skirted the room, and there were a few wooden tables and chairs dotted around the pitted concrete floor. Generally, however, people stood in this pub, because being seated tended to result in you leaving wearing someone else's pint.

Will had no idea why tradition dictated that it should be this pub that everyone went to first; it was awful. But then that was tradition for you; the unquestioning following of dogma often flying in the face of common sense.

Having parked the car, Will trailed after Shauna, Kris and Mel into the pub. It was packed and, Will thought, very aptly named from this point of view. Kris turned, motioning with his hand to offer a drink. Will nodded. It would be a pint of Bass, which supposedly couldn't be bettered in the Southwest. Again, Will didn't really see it, but he went along with it anyway. The four of them elbowed a valuable area of space in which to stand. There were a few attempts at conversation, but the general hubbub and music from the live band had drowned out anything more than the odd syllable. So, when Kris returned with their drinks, they stood and listened to the Irish folk music.

After half an hour fatigue started catching up with Will. It always seemed like a good idea going out after an on-call, but almost invariably it wasn't. He looked around the room trying to guess who did what. It was an easy game. Naval types, often marine commandos just back from exercises, gave themselves away because their hands had ingrained grime that no amount of scrubbing could remove. NHS staff were undoubtedly cleaner by comparison and had fewer fungal infections. There were a few crossovers, naval doctors and nurses, but they tended to look more like NHS, managing to keep themselves away from the really unpleasant activities. Someone had to remain relatively hygienic and in a fit state to put the broken "grunts" back together after all. There were a number of dubious-looking groups of individuals, possibly from the docks, wearing oil-stained jeans and grubby T-shirts. Not to be messed with as a general rule, and if a fight broke out, and sometimes it did, it was wise to leave as quickly as possible through any available exit. Godfrey had used the toilet window once, he recalled. He yawned as Kris indicated that they were moving on.

The lights of the harbour area, the Barbican, reflected in the still waters of the marina. Mooring lines and ropes clinked against masts and bow rails as the boats swayed back and forth on the incoming tide. Will looked at his watch - eleven fifteen – he had a decision to make. He was almost out on his feet, even the mix of sea air and frying burgers from the Cap'n Jaspers hut had failed to revive him. It was time to call it a night.

"I'm going to head off," he shouted to Shauna. "I'll see you tomorrow."

"OK," she replied, "a taxi?"

"Unless I get lucky between here and the taxi rank," he said. Shauna smiled, turned and headed off to catch up with the others, who didn't seem to have noticed his departure. It was a short walk to where the taxis gathered, made shorter by cutting through the alleyways of the Barbican. The old cobbles and two-storey "cob" buildings bore testament to how Plymouth must have looked before the German redesign programme it underwent in the early forties. Still, it was no worse than what the RAF had done to many of their cities. The difference in the way the two countries had rebuilt was, however, quite stark. The Germans hadn't viewed concrete as a solution to all building issues. His footsteps echoed off the street, but as he walked, he was aware of another set – no, two sets behind him, approaching rapidly. He turned to see a couple of the dockers from the pub.

"'Scuse me, mate, you have light?" said the first man, the oiler of the two, in a heavily accented East European accent.

"Er, no," replied Will, weighing up the situation quickly. His mind was suddenly sharp and he was fully awake, thoughts racing through scenarios. It was telling him that there was a problem here. He knew how this went; he'd spent too much time working in A & E. Next, they would pull a knife and then he would lose his wallet. He looked the men up and down and decision made, he bolted. He might end up seeming to be a bit paranoid, or not; his sprint start gave him a few metres... and the two men gave chase. He'd been right. He knew he was quick enough to shake most pursuers but realised he'd probably lost his opportunity to just hand over his wallet and walk away unharmed if he wasn't. Shouts followed, he had no idea in what language, but he was keen not to spend any time finding out. He ran hard up the cobbles hoping to reach the top of the hill and then cut down to the left with the intention of meeting up with the main road, where his would-be assailants were unlikely to pursue their 'request'. It was an unfortunate fact that port towns and cities attracted violence of this sort, often from foreign crews onshore for one night and off to sea in the morning. By the time victims had been patched up and police reports filed, the perpetrators were long gone. Will looked about him wildly, as he realised, he didn't know these streets as well as he'd thought. Images of the witchcraft museum flew unbidden into his head. It was disappointing that magic doesn't really work, he considered, scanning the street signs as he ran past. A quick incantation to cause incapacitation would have been useful. Then he found himself wondering whether 'incapacitation' would be deemed a sufficiently violent requirement to merit supernatural intervention. Concentrate on your escape!

There was a crumpling noise behind him, and then swearing, with sentiments recognisable in any language. Will risked a glance over his shoulder. One of the men had tripped on the uneven street and clattered into something fairly solid. OK, any help gratefully received, he thought... and then he ran into a blind alley, complete with a skip and some bins waiting to be emptied. No way out, not good. One of the men rounded the corner and slowed his pace to stop at the only exit point. He was relatively short, and it looked as though he didn't get too much exercise on board whatever ship didn't pay him enough to buy his own box of matches. His mate came up alongside him, bleeding from a nasty gash over his head, but still standing. Will decided dryly that next time he invoked the occult he would go the whole 'to be ripped asunder' route, rather than just the minor damage that was evident here. Something that wouldn't allow his foe to get back up. The reality of the situation was, however, dawning on him and he felt panic rising.

"Sorry, guys, no lighter – probably should have just told you rather than running off. Bit rude."

No reaction from his assailants. Humour not going to defuse this one then. One of the men pulled out a knife. Really not very good at all. He looked to his left, to the skip next to him. It was full, and lying on top there was a banister rail, spindles hanging loosely from it. He grabbed one and pulled. It came away in his hand. He now had a three-foot-long, two-inch-thick oak pole with which to defend himself. Well, it would have to do, it was better than nothing. He swung it around hoping that this might deter the sailors, but alas not. They approached him, seemingly unconcerned by the meagre threat posed by wood against steel. The blade glinted as it twisted in the man's hand. It was all so unreal. One minute he was catching a taxi home after a particularly dull night out, the next he seemed to be about to fight for his life. How did this happen? He could feel fear rising as it had only once in his life, when riding a bolting horse in Australia. Fear had given rise to a cold fury then, firing him with the strength to stop the horse before it careered off a cliff. He could feel the same fury now coursing through him. In his hands he possessed the weapon and had the skill to survive this. He felt himself dissociate from reality, and the world again slowed, but not in the dull post-take fashion of earlier – now everything was sharp, and he noticed every move, every reaction from the two men. They walked forward slowly, the one on the left holding a handkerchief to his head, the other knees bent fractionally in a fighting stance. They were within two metres now.

He heard a deep guttural cry and felt his body launch towards the man with the head wound, the weaker individual. His brain worked with the speed of his reflexes. Take out the injured man, take him out with whatever force necessary, strike fear into the remaining man. He launched towards the man, aiming a cut at his head with the edge of the pole. The man's hand reflexively lifted to parry it with his arm as expected. The rib-cracking change of line took place with the merest twitch of his thumb and forefinger, but rather than flicking his weapon, as he would have done in a fencing bout, instead he put the full weight of his body into the strike. Will felt the crunching impact. The man collapsed to the ground, clutching his shattered left ribs. The pole, coming around after the initial blow, then cracked onto the man's now exposed forehead. It was a relatively safer region to have hit, and who knew, some damage to his frontal lobe might cause a personality change for the better. The man collapsed unconscious and in the recovery position, most convenient. The man with the knife had been surprised by events and slow to react but now lunged with his knife towards Will's flank. Aware of this, Will parried this across his body and brought the pole down onto the sailor's right clavicle and heard a snap as the bone shattered, rendering the arm now useless. Just in case, he brought the pole around again and smashed it onto the man's kneecap. The man groaned with pain collapsing to the floor and took several steps back. That had all gone remarkably well. Neither would be running after him now.

Glancing away from his temporarily incapacitated assailants, Will could see clear road and, sidestepping them, he ran for safety. He didn't turn but heard no sounds of pursuit. The spindle pole was thrown into another skip and he sprinted out to the brightly lit main road, and the security of plenty of people milling around. A black cab passed and he hailed it, then jumped in. He was shaking all over, adrenaline still surging through him. He didn't get into fights. Ever. The driver asked where he wanted to go. Will knew that he should go to the police, but he was so tired he just wanted to get home. "Valtor, please," he said, glancing over his shoulder as the cab left the Barbican. There was no sign of any pursuit.

He telephoned the police with the details of the attack when he got back in and they took down the details, asking him to present himself at the station the following day to make a statement. They suggested that they would send a squad car around to the area to have a look at things, but as he had come away injury free, it didn't sound as though it would be a major priority for them. He was also advised as to the potentially serious consequences of hitting people over the head with pieces of wood. Will was too tired to further protest his case for self-defence and the police said they would be in contact if anything developed. This sort of thing was probably classed as a routine scuffle for them a usual Thursday, and as long as no one was seriously injured there were numerous other things for them to be dealing with. Will wasn't absolutely sure that the man whose head he had split wouldn't be classified as a major injury, but that would be the problem of the on-board medic when he got back to the ship. Exhausted, he collapsed onto his bed once more and fell into a deep sleep.

Chapter 26

Will had gone to the police station early, and now, back at the hospital, he
was aware of the possibility that he might stumble across one or both
of his attackers in the course of his day's work. He didn't. A quick check with
A & E failed to reveal any injuries to people consistent with those he'd inflicted
on the sailors. His friends were horrified by what had happened, though they
seemed happy enough to make him go over events multiple times. "Flooding
therapy to prevent post-traumatic stress," Godfrey advised, and "nothing to do
with the vicarious nature of human beings at all."

Will was still a little shaken but viewed himself as very lucky, and there was
the added bonus that Tamsin was gratifyingly concerned – lots of questions and
words of sympathy. Even Mr Stoneman had got wind of it, and after a brief
check that his houseman would not be any more of a liability than normal,
regaled tales of "real" violence that could only be found in the front row of a
rugby scrum.

The next few days passed incident free, but Will did find himself in an oddly
heightened state of alertness, unusual for him, he had to admit to himself. He
found that he was looking over his shoulder, and on one occasion, the sound
of running feet had him whirling around in a crouch position, ready to ward
off another attack. It certainly startled the poor student nurse who shrieked and
dropped the notes that she was carrying, her face the picture of terror. The ward

sister gave him a withering look and he helped the unfortunate girl retrieve her scattered bits of paper. It was with some relief that the end of the week arrived along with the promised trip to the cinema with Tamsin.

He picked her up from her house at seven o'clock. She was wearing a short black-and-white, hooped-pattern dress with a cropped black cardigan and looked stunning.

"All OK?" she asked as she got into the passenger seat.

"Yep, fine," he replied, trying to sound blasé.

"Because I can get us a marine escort, if necessary," she teased. Will frowned. "What, too soon?" she enquired.

"I think you'll find that I was not the one who required the reinforcements," he said, the pitch of his voice rising.

"And they got no less than they deserved," she replied.

They drove down through the very studenty suburb of Mutley, with its interesting mix of pubs, estate agents, mini-supermarkets and tattoo parlours, parking in the multi-story close to the ABC cinema. The cinema was a very old-style complex with a grand entrance, wide foyer and central counter to dispense ticket and popcorn. The heavy, red velvet décor made everything look quite dated. It was, nonetheless, the closest cinema to the hospital and the seats while worn, were comfortable enough. Will stole a glance at Tamsin who noticed and returned it with a smile. Bizarrely, even after the last 48 hrs he felt contented and settled back to watch the film.

"Fancy a bite to eat?" Will asked, as they left having watched a thoroughly entertaining film.

"Yes," said Tamsin, "where did you have in mind?"

"There's a good pizza place around the corner. How about that?"

"Absolutely," said Tamsin, and they turned left and followed the road around to the Pizza Express. It was a large open-plan restaurant with plate glass windows at the front. The chefs preparing the food could be seen deftly whirling the pizza dough between their hands before landing it in a percussive burst of flour on the prepping table. A waitress, eyes etched with black liner, a white apron covering her red gingham dress, came over and they placed their order.

Tamsin leaned over. "Well," she asked, "what did you think of the film?"

Will smiled. "Really stunning. Colourful, vivid good story and you can't beat a bit of Bruce Willis."

Tamsin returned the smile. "Oh, I completely agree, visually stunning"

"...And I did like the way costume had put a lot of time and effort into the design of Lilu's first outfit," added Will.

"It was duct tape and they clearly didn't have much of that!" said Tamsin frowning.

"No, they didn't," grinned Will.

"Oh, for God's sake!" she replied, shaking her head.

The waitress returned with some breadsticks. Tamsin picked one out of the small basket, twirling it between her fingers.

"And how about the other aspects of the film; the way that the pyramids, those crumbling, inert lumps of sandstone paradoxically proved to be anything but that? You know, turning out to be a focal point for the release of an ancient power?"

Will looked puzzled. Where was this leading?

Tamsin pushed back in her chair. "Notice any similarities with the history of Whitehorse Hospital?"

Will investigated her face, searching for some clue as to the correct answer, but she was running the breadstick across her lower lip and it was very distracting.

"Well," he began slowly, his eyes following the movement of the amuse-bouche, "the story as described by the museum is fascinating," his eyes flicked back to Tamsin's which squinted at him intently, "and I can see how the pyramids and the symbol of a white horse on a hillside might potentially have similar religious connotations, though the Whitehorse site has changed significantly over the centuries, whereas the pyramids really haven't."

Tamsin cocked her head to one side. "Do you think that the site has really changed though? Is its purpose so different now from what it used to be?"

Changed, it was an odd word to have emphasised. Of course, it had changed. It had, after all, relatively recently in its history, been blown up. That though, was he suspected not the answer she was after.

"Well," he said carefully, looking for some non-verbal cues, "the geography and natural topography hasn't, I suppose, but the way man shaped the site has."

Tamsin frowned. "Has he? I mean *really* changed it? What about the use of the site, its purpose? Do you not think it's funny how some places appear to be destined for a particular role and continue in it for hundreds, if not thousands, of years, including Whitehorse?"

"But that's human nature," replied Will, not sure what she was driving at; it *was* like finals. He defended his statement. "There are basic requirements for the establishment of a settlement, and those haven't changed much over the millennia. Not until recently at least, and man developed the technology to build in the middle of a bone-dry desert without bothering about the site and situation, only that oil is beneath it. Besides, it makes sense to make use of pre-existing resources, so new towns would tend to get constructed on the sites of old."

"Yes, that's all true," said Tamsin, her body stiffening.

Will knew he still wasn't getting it. Why did this matter so much to her?

"But isn't it odd how some places just *feel* different and do so for generation upon generation?"

Will scratched at the back of his head. "Do you mean as a sort of spiritual site" – then, giving a small snort – "or a farm?"

"A farm can still be spiritual in a way," said Tamsin, patiently. "A place of birth, nurture, death and perhaps even power over those things."

"I suppose so," said Will, his brow wrinkling. "So, by the same token, you're saying that, as a hospital, the Whitehorse site remains a spiritual site, even today."

Tamsin nodded, pleased, it seemed, with the conclusion that he had reached. He felt slightly relieved, as though he now had a chance of passing this viva.

"It was considered a magical place, a place of power, long before the Romans built their mosaic or even the Saxons stamped their white horse on the hillside," she informed him.

"So, you think that Whitehorse Hospital may still be considered by some to be on the site of magical power?" His mouth dropped fractionally as he continued his train of thought.

"Yes," she said, "particularly because it also lies on *the* major ley line in the country." Will remembered the small section tucked away in the museum.

He looked down at his fingers playing with the table mat before meeting Tamsin's gaze again. "So, you're suggesting it makes Jen's assertions about rituals taking place there much more plausible, aren't you?" Tamsin's posture visibly relaxed, and she smiled as she exhaled softly and patted his hand. A pass then.

The pizzas arrived and conversation became easier once they had moved on from the "Jen issue". She had made the point that she wished to and now went on to telling him about her surfing trips all over the world. The worried tension had gone and she giggled as she described the rides she'd had, waves she had fallen off and scrapes from which she had escaped. Will sat unblinking, mesmerised by the beauty of the woman before him, occasionally taking a bite from what might have been a very flavoursome meal.

A full moon lit the veil of silvery mist that hung lightly across the moor as Will drove back down the road to Valtor. The blur of white drifted across the bonnet of the car; the ghostly visage of a barn owl hunting down its unwitting prey, momentarily attracted Will's attention. They sat in a slightly tense silence as Will allowed the car to coast down the lane before timing the turn to perfection, missing the granite pillars and stopping back at the cottage. He had been going to stop outside Tamsin's house, also in the village but she had gestured him on. "No point parking twice," she had said. He got out and went around to her side of the car, opening it for her. He wasn't really sure where things were between them but that was nothing unusual. He would, he expected, just walk her back to her house.

She stepped out and he closed the door behind her then stood slightly awkwardly for a moment.

"Can I er..." began Will.

"... invite me in?" she asked, a whimsical smile playing across her face.

"Yes," he replied. "Would you like to come in for a... tea?"

"That's very kind," she replied, "but..." – she left the words hanging, "...I had something a little more... stimulating in mind.'

"Coffee and cake?" said Will.

Tamsin raised an eyebrow and took his hand, leading him towards the cottage door.

Chapter 27

Will was awakened by the sun's rays streaming through the curtains. Not for the first time since moving in, his first thoughts were to invest in some blackout blinds so he might maximise the precious time spent in bed. This morning's thoughts, however, were jolted back to a very pleasant reality of the sleeping form of Tamsin next to him. Wisps of hair meandered across her left shoulder and ran over her breast, which rose and fell rhythmically as she breathed. The evening had gone... about as well as could have been hoped. Somehow, in spite of himself, there was a very attractive woman lying in his bed. He grinned inwardly as Tamsin rolled over, her eyes fluttered open, and she smiled.

"Morning," she said, stretching, and then she pulled the sheet up a little self-consciously.

"Morning," replied Will. This stage of the morning was always a little tricky to get past. No precedents had been set, and first thing in the morning people had their own little idiosyncrasies. Godfrey's, for example, was to leave as quickly as possible. Generally, 'playing away' allowed him to do this much more easily than a 'home fixture'.

"Mmm," she hummed and shaded her eyes from the light streaming in.

He glanced over at the clock. It was seven thirty. "Sorry. I know I really must invest in some proper curtains."

"And possibly a slightly larger bed?" she suggested. Quarters were quite close in the single bed.

"Definitely a larger bed," he agreed. "You never know when you might have visitors to stay."

She punched him playfully in the arm.

"Though clearly it doesn't happen that often or I might have anticipated things and made some attempt to tidy the place beforehand." He gestured to the pile of clothes hastily scooped into one corner of the room.

Her hand was raised to punch again.

"Just to clarify, is it the untidiness or the suggestion that there may have been multiple visitors that's the issue here?" He caught the fist this time and Tamsin raised the other hand, which Will also duly caught. She pulled him towards her, and they disappeared under the sheets.

At about eight thirty, with a good deal of the morning's awkwardness overcome, Will threw on a pair of shorts and a T-shirt to get a couple of cups of tea. There was a fabulous smell of baking coming from the kitchen and he entered just as Shauna was pulling a tray out of the oven.

"Muffin?" she giggled. "Unless you've had sufficient already?"

"Oh God, we didn't, er, w-we weren't too...?" Will stuttered, reddening.

"No, it's fine," Shauna said, laughing. "These old cottages have thick walls... well, thickish!" She put two muffins on a plate and handed it to Will, who took two mugs in the other hand and went back through to the bedroom. He gave a mug to Tamsin and put the plate in the middle of the bed.

"Thank you," she said, accepting the tea. "Just rustled these up, did you?" she asked, reaching for a muffin.

"No, can't claim that. Shauna's been baking," he replied.

"She is quite some housemate," said Tamsin, taking a bite. "This is fabulous." She looked teasingly at Will. "Pretty, intelligent, cooks..."

"No, we *are* just housemates," he said, cutting her line of enquiry, "and nothing more. Besides, I think Godfrey might be a bit miffed if there were."

"Really?" she said, craning her neck forward and dropping her voice.

"Well, he hasn't said as much, but he's been on fewer successful GX trips than of old and he is round here quite a lot."

"So, he hasn't made any move yet?" she asked.

"To be honest, I think he's a bit scared of her. She does everything pretty much perfectly, and he... well... doesn't. Take their music. She got grade eight in piano and violin and plays in symphony orchestras. He plays by ear because he couldn't be bothered to learn to read music. She gets all of the right house jobs, does all of the right exams and he is about to be thrown out of Whitehorse Hospital for not doing... anything. She cooks muffins for breakfast, and he is going to wake up in a couple of hours and go to MacDonald's."

"So, opposites attracting."

"I suspect Godfrey hopes so."

"And he hasn't said anything to you or talked about it?"

"No. Blokes don't tend to do that. There may be banter regarding our conquests and sexual prowess over a few beers, but it's generally all for show." He paused, looking at her cheekily. "Except in my case, of course."

"Don't you fucking dare!" she said, as she swung a pillow at his head. Will just managed to put his tea down before the blow landed. While the tea survived, the muffin didn't, and crumbs exploded all over the bed.

"I really am going to have to wash the sheets now," he spluttered as he looked at the state of the bedding.

"I should think so too," she scolded, as if there could be any other option. She picked a few crumbs up and put them into her mouth.

"So, the surf line said that there wouldn't be much swell this weekend," said Tamsin. "Any thoughts on what you were going to do?"

"I hadn't really got beyond last night's cinema trip," he replied, smiling awkwardly, "that sort of took up all of my attention."

She wrinkled her nose acknowledging his compliment, then sat back, thinking. "If you wanted, we could go for a swim and take masks and snorkels?" she suggested.

"That sounds great. Where?"

"Wembury Bay on the south coast. It's a Marine Conservation Area and is stunning. The rock pools get covered at high tide and teem with life. So, there's loads to look at with a mask. Then a bit further out there are kelp forests to swim through, with expanses of sand in the bay. I have spare kit if you need it, and you have some bodyboarding fins, don't you?"

"Let's go then," he said, "it sounds great." Then nodding to a clean towel, "You may have first shower."

"Well," she replied, grabbing his T-shirt, "Maybe in a little while."

The drive to Wembury was around forty-five minutes, following the narrow roads through the South Hams. Wembury itself was nothing special by Devon standards, a few shops, the odd thatched cottage and a decent pub, but after turning left and climbing a short hill, a right turn revealed a spectacular view over the iridescent blue bay and of the Mewstone rock half a mile out to sea. Tamsin informed him, by way of conversation, that this small island had been a prison, a private house and had the inevitable smuggling stories associated with it. A T-junction followed by a left turn, led them to an even narrower rutted track leading to the beach, which was cut halfway up a shallow, grassed valley through which a reed-lined stream trickled its way to the sea. Horses munched away in fields, well used to the engine noise of cars, that disturbed the otherwise tranquil scene.

The track had a left split left heading up a slope to a church that overlooked the bay. They stayed straight and made their way to the car park situated on a flattened, slate-chipped area further on. A small grass bank on the far side, marked the edge of the cliff below which the sea lapped around barnacle-speckled boulders surrounding mirrored rockpools.

"This is breathtakingly beautiful," said Will as he got out of the car, spinning around to take in the whole scene.

"I know," replied Tamsin, sitting on the bonnet. "I wouldn't bring you to any old seagull-infested dock. It's one of my favourite places to come and just commune with nature, rather than the usual duel I have with her in the surf. She feels much more benevolent here and less like she's trying to tear me apart for having the audacity to ride on her back!"

"You need to pick smaller surf days," said Will, laughing.

Suited up and carrying their fins, masks and snorkels, Will and Tamsin descended the narrow strip of tarmac past an old, ruined mill, whose long-departed wheel would have been driven by the stream they had passed further up the valley. The stream had changed its course from those days and now ran down the centre of the beach, its constant flow tumbling sand and small pebbles with it into the sea.

A set crumbling set of concrete steps dropped them onto the beach where walking over the pebbly foreshore elicited the odd yelp from both of them, as particularly angular lumps got through the soft neoprene of their boots. To add to the peril was the lethally slippery bladderwrack, a seaweed that grew over the stone and looked at first glance to present a more comfortable footing. It didn't. However, they managed eventually to reach the sandy relief of the shallows and sat down to put on the solid rubber boarding fins. Will spat in his mask and smeared the saliva on the inside before rinsing it out; a trick to prevent the mask steaming up. Tamsin gave Will a nod, having put the mouthpiece in and immersed herself in the water, casting off with a few gentle kicks, out of the shallows onto the Church Reef.

It took a moment or two before the ice-cream headache from the really, very cold water, subsided. He shivered as a trickle made its way down his back and he concentrated on the rasp of his breathing through the snorkel and what was underneath him to take his mind off it. Once a layer of water, warmed by his body, got trapped in the neoprene, he would be fine. His eyes took a few moments to adjust their focus, and then, three or four feet below him, he spotted the seabed. It was sandy with occasional rocky protrusions, from which strands of green and brown weed swayed gently to and fro with the passage of waves above, dancing to the ocean's tune.

He swam out following the line of the reef a few metres apart from Tamsin. Anemones, above water just blobs of red or yellow jelly, had now unfurled their tentacles to waft languidly in the water, patiently waiting for some unfortunate miniature sea creature to stray into their venomous clutches. Small fish darted from rock ledge to fissure, marking territory and evading predators and a shore crab scuttled for cover as Will passed overhead. There was an almost translucent prawn, visible only by the striped markings across its back and black dot eyes. It retreated rapidly into the protective crevice between the conical domes of a couple of limpets. Floating, weightless in the water, Will became completely engrossed in the everyday lives of these small creatures, watching as they went about the business of surviving the day. The initial shock of the cold water was forgotten, and he drifted over this alien world, only occasionally propelling himself forward with a flick of his fins.

There was a tap on his shoulder. Tamsin indicated that he should follow her, pointing further out. The seabed shelved gently as they followed the line where rocks met sand. This was the region where most life seemed to congregate. A few larger fish, rainbow colours shimmering in the sunlight, hovered in seaweed, which grew up in gravity-defying, verdant streamers. Tamsin pointed out a spider crab, its domed shell covered with mini stalagmites and long spindly legs sticking out in an ungainly fashion. She duck-dived and Will followed her sleek form as she picked the crab up off the sandy bottom and then spun to return to the surface. Will lifted his head from the water as well and pushed his mask onto his forehead, removing his snorkel.

"Lunch?" she suggested, having also removed her mouthpiece and grinned. The spider crab wriggled helplessly as she grasped it by the shell.

"I might pass on that if you don't mind, and I suspect that with this being a Marine Conservation Area, the crab may feel a little aggrieved." She shrugged and disappeared from the surface again to return the poor animal to the position from which it had been disturbed. Tamsin stopped on the bottom then gestured to Will, and he dived to see what it was she had to show him this time. She indicated for him to hold onto a rock with his fins and then that he should look around. He managed to get enough purchase on the rock to keep himself from floating to the surface and looked out along the edge of the reef, out into the infinite clear blueness beyond. It really did seem to go on forever, there was such a vast sense of space, a very different space to that found on the surface. His eyes tracked up and above him; he couldn't see the sky, but only the mirrored interface where the water met the air. It rippled like molten aluminium.

He was able to stay submerged for thirty seconds or so before his lungs suggested that oxygen at some point quite soon would be a good idea, and he shot back to the surface. Tamsin appeared a few seconds later.

"That is incredible," said Will, breathless as he removed his mouthpiece. "Absolutely, incredible. I never realised the English coast could be so stunning. Australia and the Barrier Reef, yes, but Wembury Bay?"

Tamsin smiled back. "So far quite stunning, but a little further over there..." She pointed a bit further out where a sea bird had just surfaced – a cormorant, Will thought. Tamsin disappeared and Will followed, finning hard to catch up. Five metres or so above the undulated floor of the seabed, Will made out the puff of sand as a flat fish shot off, spooked by his presence. His attention was so focussed on this, that when he was enveloped by an iridescent billowing mass of silver, green and red, it took a number of seconds for his brain to register that he was in the middle of a shoal of sand eels. He adjusted his eyes and was able to briefly pick out individuals, each five to ten centimetres long, before they became lost in the shoal once more. Their scales caught the light, reflecting it back as a shimmering light show, and there were hundreds, maybe even thousands of them. They murmurated as flocks of starlings did in the skies above them, though for them it was a tactic to foil predators rather than the social event that preceded the starlings' bedtime. It was a truly magical experience that, he realised, few who visited the bay would see, preferring instead to read a book or just sit and sun themselves on the beach.

He had no idea how long they had been in the water when they finally resurfaced and set foot once more on the shore. Will hoped he looked a little like James Bond but suspected the creature from the black lagoon was closer to the mark. Tamsin, however, carried off a decent Ursula Andress, shaking out her hair as she walked up the beach. At the car, they peeled off their wetsuits.

Tamsin changed rapidly and efficiently under a towel, as before. Will was less adept, and predictably the towel he had brought along was one of his smaller ones, which couldn't be made to stay reliably tied around his waist. In the end he gave up on modesty and relied on speed to get into a pair of shorts, hopefully before he caused too much offence to innocent bystanders.

"Fancy a walk?" Tamsin suggested.

A well-worn path led from the rear of the car park and made its way uphill past the church. It was mud-baked and flanked by the green spines of gorse bushes and brambles, wont to prick any bare arm not kept tucked into a side. Will noted that Tamsin had kept her sweater on, presumably to offer some protection, the act of experience. It was also steep and every so often they paused to catch breath, taking the chance to admire a view or point out an exotic-looking insect.

The brow of the hill signalled a change to the flora, and climbing over a wooden stile, the path led up onto lush fields to the left and plummeting cliffs to the right. Yellow-and-black-striped bumblebees bobbed between the white and purple clover flowers, indicative of excellent pasture. Looking out to sea, a few optimistic sails fluttered on the light breeze, in no hurry to get anywhere quickly. The sun was warm and there was a sense of calmness and tranquillity on a glorious spring day.

A mile or so along the coastal path a branch of the Yealm estuary, Newton Creek, came into view. It was a few hundred metres wide with a sand bar ready to snare any unwary yachtsmen too keen to reach for a pint in one of several pubs upriver. They stopped to watch a dinghy negotiate its way between the red and green buoys that marked safe passage, listening to the rhythmic grumble of the ocean and longing cry of a seabird. Tamsin had been quiet for a while and her gaze had shifted, staring out to sea, lost in some previous time. He was beginning to recognise that thousand-yard stare.

"You used to come here with Jen, didn't you?" he said, giving her the chance to share her thoughts.

"Yes," she said, smiling, but her gaze stayed on the horizon. "We used to pester mum and dad to take us here when she came to visit. Of course, it was much closer than the surf beaches, and when we were older, I could get permission to borrow the car for this much shorter trip. It's a good place to come anyway, even when there's no surf around and you only fancy a swim or a barbecue." She smiled. "We even spent the night here on the beach once, just in sleeping bags under the stars." She turned to face him, eyes sparkling. "Did you know how noisy nature is at night? Owls hooting, foxes yelping... and the rabbits! How noisy are those little beggars, hopping around when you're trying to get to sleep?" She chuckled again at the memory.

Will remained silent, just letting her remember, images of how it must have been playing in his own mind's eye.

"It was just the best thing," she continued, a tremor in her voice, "waking up and going straight for an early morning swim. Then, a breakfast of eggs and bacon washed down with fresh coffee done on the Primus stove. Mum had something of a fit the first time we did it because we were only seventeen and I'd forgotten to call her to let her know we weren't coming home that night."

Will walked slowly by her side, listening.

"Yes, we were in quite a lot of trouble as I recall, grounded for a week. Well at least I was." Then she was quiet, her pace slowed and her shoulders hunched. Will put a hand on her arm and she turned to face him, her eyes filled with sparkling sorrow.

"I can't believe she's gone, Will, I just can't." She clenched her fists and bit her bottom lip.

Will took her hands gently in his, his thumb stroking her fingers, before drawing her to him and holding her in his arms. She let out a sob and he stroked her hair. "I'm sorry, Tamsin," he said, "so very sorry."

He held her shaking form tight to him, but after a few seconds she pulled away, a harshness in her tone as she spoke. "I'm not going to let this go, you know. He will pay for what he's done."

"I know, "he replied, "and I will try to help you."

Her frown relaxed, and she nodded, drawing back into him, sighing frustratedly as she did so. "But I just don't know what to do, how to go about proving anything."

Will looked across the estuary; the tide had turned and mudflats had begun to appear at the water's edge. Wading birds gathered in anticipation of a good feed.

Will wondered what *could* be done. They couldn't very well tail Metern for twenty-four hours a day or put an advertisement on the mess noticeboard inviting all Satanists to an evening's sadistic ritual and child sacrifice - buffet and finger-food provided afterwards. Inwardly he searched for options. Realistically, perhaps the best course might be to continue to collect as much information about the man as possible and see what turned up. He shook his head, still struggling with the concept of modern-day ritual magic taking place at all, let alone one of their own being involved in it.

He had a thought, "Maybe we need to try to trace the babies? Look, you can't just make an infant disappear from the ward, involve it in a ritual murder and then return it a bit less active than it was."

Tamsin pushed back on him, frowning.

"OK, dead then," Will said, his attempt to lighten the mood a fraction obviously ill-judged. He pursued his line of reasoning, undeterred, "So, if Jen's story is to be believed and there are strange things going on involving children, maybe he's bringing them in from the outside – you know, kidnapping them."

"I'm sure that would have been all over the news," Tamsin pointed out. "He wouldn't have got away with that."

Will huffed, "You're right," he said, rubbing his forehead, "he couldn't, not on a regular basis. I wonder if his working at the hospital is linked?"

"Maybe," agreed Tamsin, "Metern is an obstetrician, isn't he, which might make access to his victims easier?"

"By having access to neonatal and paediatric wards, yes, but you still can't just steal children. I'm sure that the staff would notice!" said Will.

"Mmm," said Tamsin. "What if he's passing their deaths off as natural causes somehow?"

"That might pass scrutiny, mightn't it?" agreed Will. "But all of what he does gets closely audited, so there must be records, an audit trail, which may show some suspicious patterns if you know what to look for."

Tamsin nodded. "So perhaps it might be worth asking, subtly I mean, about cases in which he's been involved or where there's been an unexpected death?"

"Good thought," agreed Will, brushing away a rogue fly that was threatening to get accidentally swallowed. They both watched it circling them, flicking it away again when it got too close.

"Why do you think he's doing this?" Will asked. "He's a scientist after all, and despite recent 'accidents' that have befallen him, I don't believe in magic and I don't see how he could think any differently."

A wan smile flicked across Tamsin's lips, before her features darkened. "I don't know, but whatever the reason, it could never justify what he's done. Never!"

A breeze picked up, ruffling the smooth surface of water below them like creases in a counterpane. "Hey," said Will, suddenly, "I forgot to tell you. When I was at the museum, I also had a look at one of the papers that Metern had written..." He paused.

Tamsin tilted her head towards him. "And..."

"Well, I don't think there was anything necessarily directly related, but they were quite interesting." Will's brow furrowed. "He was into his genetics, seems to have been quite impassioned actually, going on about how genetics was the future of all medicine." As they walked on, he relayed the details of what he had already read.

Tamsin looked puzzled. "But that was done up in Birmingham, right, and as part of being a clinical scientist?" Will nodded. "So, what is he doing here at Whitehorse? There's no genetics research going on here and it's a long way from Birmingham."

Will nodded. "Yes, it does look as if, for some reason, he had a complete change of career."

"That is a bit odd, isn't it? How many papers did you say there were?"

"Three, I think."

"It might be worth looking at the other two then?" she suggested.

"It might," agreed Will.

"OK, it's something at least. We can do that on Monday." She grabbed his hand. "Come on, let's go and get something to eat."

Will looked at her as he stepped forward, somewhat confused as to where exactly she had in mind, given the sheer cliff and expanse of water before them. Tamsin smiled and started to pull off her sweater. "It's just a short swim, the current shouldn't be too strong. The tide has only just turned to go out." Will looked even more perplexed. He could see the current, a torrent, flowing up the estuary. Then she tied the removed sweater around her waist. "Or we could catch the little ferry that goes from the pontoon at the end of this path." She pointed to a well-hidden track leading down the rock face.

A 1976

It had been difficult going back, telling them that he'd been wrong about the direction that he'd taken. They had thought he referred to his travelling the new and modern path, that he'd returned to follow the path set out for him some thirty-five years ago. It wasn't too late, they had said, there was still time. But they had misunderstood. He wasn't coming to beg their forgiveness, to tell them that he'd learned his lesson and would give himself up to their arcane philosophies and prophesies. He'd had to inform them again that they were wrong. Their beliefs might be wonderful, beautiful, and conceptually beneficial to The Mother Earth, but they were also simplistic, naïve and ultimately doomed to collapse, as surely as the path which humans trod now. He knew that he could change both of those inevitable outcomes, but it would take some sacrifices; he didn't know what or how much yet, but he would make them, whatever they turned out to be. His connection with these people was just one of those things, one of those sacrifices. His desire was to create and heal, not defend and kill as they would have him do. His intention was to progress and benefit mankind, not send it back to the Dark Ages. The cries of their anguish turning to scorn and fury still rang in his ears, as he remembered declaring his intent to become a doctor.

Chapter 28

Will arrived in the library after finishing his work for the day. The librarian, perched motionless on his stool, looked very bored as he stared at the glowing computer screen in front of him. The starkness of the light served only to highlight the sun-starved, ghostly face.

"Know what you're looking for?" he asked without looking up.

"Yes thanks," replied Will.

"Give me a shout if you need anything," said the librarian, his perfunctory tone lacking any degree of sincerity. Will made his way through the labyrinth to the genetics section and found that Tamsin, surrounded by journals and bits of paper, had already got started. She looked up, brow furrowed, as he pulled up a chair and sat alongside her.

"What do you think?" he asked, noting that she'd been looking through Metern's first article.

"Well," she began, "as you said, he is obviously very *passionate* about his subject, summarising the potential for medical genetics and the future of medical practice as it does." Her tone was a grudging one.

Will nodded. "It does, and he seems very convinced that genetic manipulation has the potential to end many of the illnesses that mankind suffers from, and not just the genetic ones."

"Is that really possible?" asked Tamsin. "Isn't it about thirty per cent of our phenotype that's genetically determined, with seventy per cent determined by the environment, which means that for seventy per cent of diseases, altering the genetics will have no effect?" Tamsin was referring to the term for how an organism's genetic make-up and the environment determined its physical characteristics and behaviour.

"Yes," replied Will, "but I had a lecturer at uni who suggested that how the environment affects us is, in itself, genetically predetermined, therefore we're one hundred per cent the product of our genes."

She frowned, unconvinced. "But if, for example, there's no food in the environment, an organism can't mature to its full potential and hence that affects how it looks, i.e., its phenotype."

"True, but what determines what you can eat? Your genetic make-up. Suppose you could get sufficient nutrition from grass, dirt, or even the atmosphere itself by having a gene that coded for that attribute?"

"Yes, I suppose..." she said, not entirely convinced.

"Let's see what's in the second paper," said Will, and he rifled through the files on the desk to get the next journal compilation.

It was titled "Gene Therapy: The Bureaucratic Quagmire Costing Lives". Metern and Gowen were again the co-authors of this article. It lamented the very slow progress that gene therapy was making and, according to them, would continue to make if governments continued to sit on the fence and the scientific community were not more robust in their approach. While some of the problems encountered were technological issues, more concerning, from the authors' point of view, were the increasingly vocal, highly antagonistic media and religious groups.

Will looked up from the paper, commenting on the opening few paragraphs. "He's right, you know. There has been increasing concern to the development of genetically modified food crops with some environmental groups and religious zealots even threatening violence. You can't help but think that it may well interfere with future research and experiments.

"Right," said Tamsin, "it takes a brave individual to continue to do the work that they know might put themselves and their families in danger." They continued to read on.

The article, written in a number of sections, highlighted a variety of media concerns about genetic modification, be that of crops created for higher-yielding, lower water-dependant plants or of the human genome to prevent a whole spectrum of diseases. It surmised that much of the media seemed more concerned with selling a story and filling their coffers than presenting a reasoned and balanced view of the facts.

Religious groups were found to be no better in pushing their own agendas. Alteration of the genetic code, they stated, amounted to doctors and scientists "playing God", which was fundamentally wrong, even if the intentions were principled and designed to relieve suffering. Mankind should play the hand that it was dealt, which meant suffering and caring for those who suffered. That was what made us human. To remove suffering was to remove part of the human soul. It was, the authors pointed out, a centuries-old concept of humanity designed to maintain the dependence on religion as the only means of succour in an otherwise cruel and hostile world. They questioned its place in a modern society, where demonstrably, this need not be the case.

The first section concluded that most criticism was founded upon a poor knowledge and understanding of the concepts and possibilities of genetic engineering and condemned those who would attempt to supress scientific research with threats and violence.

Comparisons with medieval healers and wise women were made, whom a similarly misguided society had persecuted and burned for their activities centuries ago.

It caused a certain amount of ill-ease within Will as he read it, given the similar assertions made in the witchcraft museum, and glancing across he saw similar anxieties reflected in Tamsin's features. He did, however, agree that science was still looking to understand what the potential of new discoveries might be, but only work *now* would produce answers, particularly to those questions regarding the future of genetics in medicine. It had to be allowed to continue, because it was science, not governments, the media or cultural belief systems, that would ultimately maintain the human race. God, or gods were they to exist, had supposedly given man the gift of free will, and they would have to trust that his creation knew what to do with the answers to this wilful questioning.

The second section of the article discussed the technical problems that gene therapy was encountering. The benefits derived in patients in whom this treatment had been tried tended to be short-lived, with their immune systems rejecting the proteins synthesised by the new DNA, resulting in several reactions and side effects. It did though end on a more upbeat note, talking about a radical new approach, firing radiation at the DNA sequences where specific genes were known to be located and causing predictable changes to those specific genes. It also postulated that if the scientists could create known DNA sequences that coded, for example, for cell repair, or to target the 'bad genes' in a cancer, and if this could be directly spliced into the patient's DNA, relative miracles might be achieved.

"It's interesting he's put the scientific bit of the article second," said Will, seeing that Tamsin had finished reading at the same time as he had done. "It's almost as though any technical problems were less of a stumbling block in his eyes than the resistance from society as a whole."

"I tell you what is really interesting," observed Tamsin. "As well as being antagonistic to large swathes of society as a whole, he also seems to be linking your contemporary scientist with medieval healers and witches of the past, probably putting a few backs up there too."

"Yes," agreed Will, wincing, "on both sides of that rift. But he might have something of a point... a lack of understanding creating an atmosphere of fear and hate; various factions with their own agendas, be it financial, as in the case of the media, or bigotry, in the case of the religious community. It doesn't make him a warlock though, does it?" said Will.

"No, but it does show that he has more than a passing interest in that direction, and when added to all of the other stuff..."

Will nodded. It did certainly add another layer of suspicion. He picked up another of the enormous bound books of journals. "The third paper is in here somewhere," he said, flicking through the pages. "Here you go."

They started reading, and it did indeed continue the theme begun at the end of the second article, but it was notable that the form was very different from the other publications, in that, rather than being a commentary on events, it detailed the results of experiments on rats.

"So, as well as the media, the middle classes and the religious zealots," said Will dryly, "the anti-vivisectionists would now also be after them."

The aim stated in the paper was to alter sequences of DNA and specific genes that were associated with cell repair to malignant, aged or damaged cells. This was done by bombarding different cell types with varying frequencies of radiation for varying times while these cells were immersed in a bath of enzymes and the nucleic acids that was the substrate for the deoxyribonucleic acid strand itself. It explained that the radiation energy caused the DNA to vibrate and fracture at specific points and the fracture was patched with new sequences. The new DNA was then extracted and inserted into embryo cells, or pluripotent stem cells, and the resultant serum injected into the bloodstream of rats who had either had a tumour or been injured in some way. The control group was injected with the original DNA sequence.

The results had been promising, with shrinkage of some tumours and more rapid healing in injured animals compared to the control studies. In one case, a rat whose limb had been deliberately broken had not only had the bone heal perfectly, but it was in a fraction of the time it might have been expected to take. While the impressive recovery time had been put down to the effects of the genetic manipulation, it had also been noted that the increased attention shown to the recovering rat by its fellow rats had also aided its recovery.

In the technical discussion it was decided that pluripotent stem cells from the liver of the rats had proved to be the most effective cell for the serum production. These, it explained, were progenitor cells from which all other cells in the body could be made, not just liver but all tissues. These liver cells were even better than the embryo cells that had been used, particularly if taken from very young rats.

The major technical problem encountered, however, was felt to be in determining the exact nature, i.e., radiation wavelength and duration of exposure, correctly. It appeared that a combination of different wavelengths, not just a single bombardment, was required to disrupt the DNA correctly and precipitate splicing, and it was likely to take decades to work these out. The qualitative data, that which had been observed by the authors, the paper stated, was good, but the numbers, the quantitative data, it accepted, didn't make the study a particularly powerful one. They commented on the fact that there had probably been some fortune in such results as had been obtained, but it demonstrated the significant potential of the experiments. The article concluded, once again, that more work needed to be done to provide better evidence.

"Right," said Tamsin, arching her back and running her hands through her hair. "He believes there's a real possibility of doing what was suggested in the first paper and making a difference for humanity. Did he get any further?" she asked.

"It doesn't look like it," said Will, shrugging. "I couldn't find anything more that he, or his associate, had done subsequently. It looks like they just stopped."

"So, what happened do you think?" she asked, gazing at the rows of books as if drawing answers from them. "Metern must have been doing obs and gynae for several years – he's a registrar – so it doesn't seem possible that he continued with the research, at least not here. But he was obviously absorbed in what he was doing."

"Maybe he's one of those people who have complete dedication to something until they fail or have to stop and then can't stand to be near it? I know it happens to sportsmen."

Tamsin pressed her lips together, shaking her head. "No... but I wonder if the research might have just taken a different form, so to speak. It might explain some of the odd and secretive behaviour that Jen mentioned."

"You mean that he turned his back on genetic science and medicine for something he found in the occult?"

"Yes and no," replied Tamsin, looking back at Will. "From what I've just read, he may view them as the same thing and have just shifted his experiments from Birmingham to Whitehorse."

"And Jen ended up getting involved, perhaps being part of an experiment herself," said Will. "That might explain her insistence that she'd been poisoned."

"And it killed her," said Tamsin bitterly.

For a short while it had seemed as though her vendetta had been forgotten. Now a chill ran through Will, but he said nothing. They put the journals back and walked back past the librarian, who was still fixed in the same position.

"Do you think he gets heparin and TED stockings to prevent deep vein thrombosis," whispered Will, but he received only a blank look from Tamsin and a glare from the librarian.

Chapter 29

Tamsin was meeting friends that evening, so Will dropped her off and arrived back at the cottage at around six. He wasn't very surprised to see Godfrey standing outside the front door, cigarette in hand, talking to Shauna, who was busy washing up at the sink by the window. Godfrey gave Will a none-too-subtle wink as he stepped out of the car. Shauna had obviously not managed to keep news of his recent nocturnal guest to herself for very long.

"Oh, grow up!" said Will walking towards his grinning friends.

"Well, Dr Cunningham, I must say your concern for your medical student's welfare is highly commendable," said Godfrey, with no intention of letting maturity get in the way of a salacious story. He lifted the milk churn lid and flicked ash inside.

"It had seemed a long way for her to make her way home so late at night," said Will, adding, "as you yourself can very well understand."

"Did she also find the sofa very comfortable?"

"It would have been most ungentlemanly to allow her to sleep in such a place, particularly given its previous occupant," said Will.

"Ah yes," responded Godfrey, ignoring the jibe, "no time to change the sheets for the young lady I suppose. But that wouldn't have worried you. So how did *you* find the sofa?"

"It can get very cold here at night, Godfrey, so after consideration we decided to share the bed."

"How egalitarian." He paused, considering his next question very carefully. "And was that *all* that was shared?" he asked.

"Godfrey!" shrieked Shauna, for whom it appeared too much information might be forthcoming, "that's enough!" She hurled a dishcloth in Godfrey's direction, missing by at least three feet.

"I mean, did you talk, share information? Were there any learning points, perhaps about leaving home without thermal underwear?"

"Godfrey!" shouted Shauna again. A wet sponge followed the dishcloth, missing by a similar distance. It rebounded off the door frame and landed at Will's feet, next to the dishcloth.

"I am merely attempting to make sure that the young lady's needs were well... catered for," he said. "You know how negative feedback can affect one's subsequent ability to teach." Godfrey's face was the picture of concern.

Will looked skyward. "It is heart-warming to know that you worry so but be assured that no one got cold as far as I was aware and no one was marking proceedings!" said Will, picking up the sponge and cloth. "And if there is any more said..." He raised the sponge.

"It's just –" Godfrey started to reply but the sponge caught him squarely in the middle of his forehead. Water trickled down his face. Shauna laughed but stopped abruptly as the dishcloth flew past her left ear.

"And that is for the muffin comment the other morning," he said, huffily.

"Missed," she said, looking pleased.

"It was a very tasty muffin," said Will, then he walked in to put the kettle on. "Tea, anyone?"

Godfrey stayed for a cup of tea and then decided it was too late to do any more revision that day but that he could do with a bite to eat.

"You see," he was explaining as they all made their way around the corner to the pub, "I sort of know it all already, and the bits I don't actually know, I can work out. If I can't work it out, then I'm sure I'll be able to make a really good guess at any questions related to the topic. Revision just confuses my strategy."

"Godfrey, you can't just guess your way through the first part of your anaesthetic exams," said Shauna.

"It will not be just guesswork. More an extrapolation of existing knowledge, and I can. It worked for medical school."

"But this is a different situation. At medical school they sort of have a vested interest in passing you or they have just wasted a hundred thousand pounds training someone to not be a doctor. These exams, the more people they fail, the more expensively they can decorate their collegiate residences in London."

"I'm still competing against the same cohort of idiots," said Godfrey, opening the door to the pub, "I'll be fine."

Inside the pub there was the usual mix of locals and medics. There wasn't a great deal of socialising between the two groups. The local populous was somewhat disgruntled over the lack of parking in the village since the influx of multi-car medic households. Each house of medics had four cars, and there would often be girlfriends or boyfriends staying over, so they probably had a point. The locals also knew that if they became ill, the odds were they would have to see one of the medics, so any resentments tended to remain harboured.

Will, Godfrey and Shauna sat down at one of several vacant tables opposite some of the mainly female middle-grade obstetric staff. They were all sitting on the edge of their chairs, leaning in, their conversation in hushed tones. They didn't respond to Will's nod in their direction.

"Must have heard you were off the market," said Godfrey, sniggering.

"Don't bloody start that again," Will retorted, getting up. "Three Jail Ales?"

Will crossed the wooden floorboards to the bar, straining to hear what was being said. Odd words drifted up to meet his ears. "Perinatal mortality... high late termination statistics... unexpected pre-term complications." He caught Jess's eye.

"Is everything OK?" he mouthed.

She gave an equivocal smile and beckoned him over, leaning back in her chair to speak. "We had the quarterly departmental meeting earlier today, to review significant events," she sneered. "You know, a chance to sit in cockup corner. Supposed to be supportive, but it usually involves some poor wretch being dragged over the coals by one lot of consultants while the wretch's own consultant tries to defend them at the same time as pointing out the deficiencies in their colleague's approach," Jess explained.

"So, what's happened? You guys are alright, aren't you?"

"Yes, we're fine, but our perinatal mortality statistics seem to have got slightly worse over the last few years; that is to say, we are *slightly* better than average nationally, having been *significantly* better than average."

"It's still above average – that isn't so bad, is it?" Will pointed out.

"It would seem that clinical executives don't have a particularly good grasp of numbers, statistics or be prepared to accept normal variability," said Jess. Then she continued, "Sort of expect to always get better and improve."

"Commendable aspiration," said Will.

"I suppose," she replied, "but we're only here for six to twelve months at this hospital" – she indicated the junior staff at the table – "so trends over several years, for us, are utterly academic."

"So why the closed meeting here?" He gestured to the huddled group.

"It's a debrief really, theoretically to talk about anything but medicine, but you know how things deteriorate." He did. It was inevitable amongst work colleagues, but some people didn't know when to leave such talk alone.

"Anyway," she said, with a sigh, "we've ended up discussing the strange statistical anomalies that have been responsible for our poorer performance. There seem to be very regular small peaks eight times throughout the year, and this appears to have been the case for the last four or five years. It's these blips that would seem to be tipping the stats. No one can explain them."

"They aren't associated with any one consultant or individual in particular?" Will asked.

"No, they checked against the rota and the named consultants – there was an even spread."

"So, what are they doing about it?"

"Oh, you know, checking that protocols were adhered to, change a few flow charts, question some individuals over minor infringements. We all took a bit of flack to be honest, got to have someone responsible. It can't just be the nature of life."

"Or statistics," said Will. "So, who got a grilling... if it's OK to ask?" Jess glanced around the table, but the discussion still raged on without her.

"It was all small stuff really, nothing and no one stood out. I hadn't done foetal blood sampling as often as I might; Ben should have called in the registrar sooner than he did; a few others didn't progress to C-section early enough."

"And Cadan Metern?" asked Will.

She snorted. "Oh, he was fine. Just got a ticking off for upsetting a few patients."

"Really?" Wills voice squeaked. "I mean, he's the last person I would expect to upset the punters."

"Yes. Storm in a teacup, but if there's a stillbirth, then we're supposed to do some tests and investigations and part of this is to offer a post-mortem on the baby. It doesn't have to be done and there are often cultural or personal beliefs that cause people to reject it. Metern was, shall we say, very insistent, to the point he would almost be running away with the corpse. The parents, who, quite naturally, were devastated, felt bullied into making a decision quickly, and a few raised complaints."

"You don't have to do post-mortems that quickly, do you?" asked Will. "I mean, I never heard of pathologists getting crash paged to an autopsy."

Jess laughed. "I think he just wanted them in the fridge before they 'went off'," she said.

The barman attracted Will's attention. "Anything else?" he asked. Will turned to offer to buy Jess a drink, but her attention had turned back to the other obstetrics staff once more.

Godfrey and Shauna had already decided on what they were going to order and handed Will the menu. He chewed his bottom lip and looked over the top of the card. It didn't escape Shauna's notice.

"Everything OK?" she asked, tilting her head.

"Yeah, fine," replied Will. "Er, three steak and ale pies?" he said. They nodded, and Will turned to the barman to indicate the order.

"So, seriously, you and Tamsin?" asked Godfrey, as Will sat back down and rested his elbows on the table.

"What about me and Tamsin?" said Will, still distracted.

"Is it going to go anywhere? I'm assuming that she is a major part of this." Godfrey poked Will's elbow, drawing a smile. "A longer-term solution to your nocturnal solitude? A reason to invest in larger bedroom furniture, maybe even tidy your room?"

Will was finding it difficult to play Godfrey's game this evening. His head was spinning, so many flying visions, flashes of what might have happened, satanic rituals, Tamsin speeding through the streets of Plymouth, Jen with a syringe full of diamorphine. His mind raced to make sense of things, throwing up scenario after scenario, playing image after image, struggling determinedly to work out what may yet be. It was impossible. He closed his eyes, resting his head in his hands, trying to still it.

"Hey, I'm only joking," said Godfrey. "I can leave it."

Should he tell them, open up? His friends knew a bit of what had happened to Tamsin because of Jen's death, and the fact that she held Metern responsible was common knowledge. But they didn't know how deeply it ran. They also didn't know the extent to which Will had inadvertently got himself embroiled in things, and he had to admit to himself, become infatuated with her. Was it going anywhere? How did he answer that question? Maybe they would give him some perspective – rituals, poppet dolls, the lot?

"Well," Will started, exhaling deeply and clasping his hands together, "she is the most intoxicating, wild, exciting, person I have ever met. I'm aware of my thoughts constantly flicking back to her night and day," he said, snorting and feeling uncomfortably exposed.

Shauna gave him an understanding smile.

"It's very annoying. I just want to spend time with her, whatever we do, and" – he hesitated, expelling a sardonic chuckle – "I'd almost rather spend time with her than go surfing and that can't be right!"

"Crikey, it must be serious," said Shauna, blinking in an exaggerated fashion.

"She *is* absolutely great... mostly. But..." He sucked in his bottom lip. God-frey and Shauna remained still across the table; eyes fixed on his face. "I mean, I know that what she has been through is horrific and made worse because she feels partly responsible for what happened, even if she verbally chooses to place that blame elsewhere. She is, though, obsessed by it. It's clearly eating away at her, and everything that we do returns to finding something to prove that Jen's death was Cadan Metern's fault." He paused again, rubbing his forehead. "The problem is, I think she might be right."

All trace of levity had left the table now, smiles replaced by furrowed brows and looks of concern on the faces of his friends.

He went on to explain what had happened on the surf trip and their con-versation in the dunes. He recounted the guilt that Tamsin felt over betraying Jen with the one-night stand, and then her being unable to prevent her friend's death. He moved on to start describing what had happened at the witchcraft museum, a place Tamsin had wanted him to see so that he might understand her accusations against Metern better.

"Well, I suppose it makes sense given what she told the police," said Godfrey, shifting in his seat. "But something else happened at the museum that bothered you, didn't it?"

Will looked up, suddenly aware that he had been staring at a burn mark on the table. His friend could be unusually perceptive sometimes. "Yes... how did you—?"

"Whatever *you* may think, you aren't hard to read, Will. Something has obviously been bothering you since that surf weekend. So, out with it."

It was too late now, so Will recounted more of the details of the museum trip and of his continuing unease surrounding the events that unfolded involving Metern. There were involuntary gasps at Will's admission regarding the doll, which drew a concerned glance from the chef as he placed the pies down in front of them.

"You did what?" Shauna whispered, leaning forward, slightly incredulous.

"I stabbed the doll lots of times with a pin," Will repeated, cringing and disinterestedly making a start on his meal.

"And then he got attacked," said Godfrey, cackling.

"It was sort of a reaction to her teasing, and a kind of experiment," Will said, trying to defend himself.

"But can't you see?" said Shauna. "It's the kind of 'experiment' that will only ever yield a positive result. At some point something is bound to have happened and you would then attribute it to what you had done to the doll. He might have had a needlestick injury, tripped over a step, crashed his car, and the time frame is from the moment you stick pins into that doll, until – I don't know – forever. That's how all of these superstitious occult things work."

"I understand that," said Will, "but there's a bit of me that still feels guilty. Wouldn't you?"

"Nope," replied Godfrey.

"No, I suppose the man who, on his own, ate nearly half of a Christmas cake destined for the paediatric ward probably wouldn't," said Will, sighing.

Godfrey grinned back at him through a mouthful of pie.

He moved on to tell them about the research and experiments of Metern and Gowen and then described what he had just found out from the SHOs.

Godfrey sat back and took a sip from his pint. "OK," he said, "I get she thinks he's a witch or warlock or whatever, preposterous as that may sound. And I can see how awful she must feel about Jen and, wanting to vent that feeling, has decided that Metern is to blame, but I don't see how that means Metern had anything to do directly with Jen's death."

Will took a deep breath, thinking for a moment before putting it together. "Tamsin thinks that Jen found out about, or got involved in, Metern's occult activities but that Metern had some hold over her so she wouldn't seek further help. Jen had repeatedly said that he had poisoned her. Was that her mind, not physically? I don't know. Tamsin thinks that her friend was struggling with this and may, in the end, have decided to go to the police with what she knew, despite whatever this 'hold' was that Metern had. Metern, realising this, lured Jen down to the basement after Jen had killed the patient and took the opportunity to kill Jen by faking her overdose."

"Metern was there at the C-section, wasn't he?" said Shauna. "So, it may be that he even injected the diamorphine into the patient himself during Jen's blackout." Will nodded. They hadn't thought of that.

"But there isn't a shred of evidence," said Godfrey, introducing a note of reality, "and the coroner was satisfied that there was no deliberate malfeasance."

"I know," said Will, "but I think she's been trying to show me that at least it's possible, if improbable."

"And what do you believe?" asked Godfrey.

"Honestly, I just don't know. As you say, there's no solid evidence, but the more we look into Metern, the more I feel there's something odd about him."

"I can see why you might," said Shauna. "But taken as a whole, how likely is it all, really?"

"I know, I know," said Will, "ritual sacrifice, poisoning, murder, all massively unlikely, especially considering that it's the hospital golden boy Cadan Metern, but what if...?"

There was raucous laughter from across the room as one of the locals slipped off his chair. Will chased his remaining chip around the plate.

Godfrey sniffed. "I agree that there are some questions surrounding Dr. Metern. Let's just suppose that he is up to something, leaving aside the whole Satanist thing for a moment. Let's suppose that he didn't give up on his research and it just went underground."

"Why would he do that?" asked Shauna.

"Well, look at the area he was working in," said Godfrey. "Companies aren't prepared to openly fund this area because of the bad publicity it attracts and the problems in getting ethical approval for such experiments. He was, after all, advocating the use of embryonic stem cells derived from living foetuses."

"So, he's just carried on alone?" she asked.

"Not necessarily," Godfrey said. "What happened to his co-author? What is he up to now? Are you sure he hasn't published anything new that could provide any further information? If you're keen to exhaust all possibilities, you might see if he has any separate publications, or even see if you can talk to him. More importantly, you might impress your lady friend sufficiently to get another shag... ouch!" He flinched as a punch from Shauna connected with his shoulder.

Will pondered what had been said, rubbing his nose. "It's certainly worth looking into," he agreed.

Chapter 30

Work the following day started with the usual ward round, and then, as the registrar was away, Will was required to go to theatre to help with the operative list. He had no great love of theatre, but then he recalled that he hadn't had the easiest of introductions as a medical student. He had been presented at the theatre reception with what amounted to a pair of pyjamas and a hat and asked a theatre sister a not unreasonable question regarding exactly how far undressed he was supposed to get. Unfortunately, a passing surgeon overheard his question, broke down laughing, and suggested that that wasn't an offer she was likely to get twice that day and had better make the most of it. The rest of the rotation Will had spent in his own special corner of humiliation as the tale spread.

Helping in theatre was also a quite exceptionally dull experience. It meant standing in the same position for literally hours while the surgeon sweated, shouted and cursed his way through the operation. The assistant was required to hold a piece of metal called a retractor, designed to keep skin guts, or in this case muscle, well away from the surgeon's knife. Daydreaming, fainting or, on the odd notable occasion, actually falling asleep, would precipitate a verbal barrage that, once conscious again, could scar one for life.

For any amount of money, you would have thought Mr Stoneman would be this stereotypical surgeon, keen to lash out at others because the difficulty of the procedure was proving greater than the size of his manhood, except that he wasn't. He often stated that there was probably no other place on earth, with the exception of Twickenham obviously, that he would rather be. He loved doing what he referred to as carpentry, using saws and hammers to cut out old hips and put in new ones, repair ruptured cruciate ligaments in knees, or put large "nails" into broken femurs. The atmosphere in his theatre was generally calm, and in summer he often had the cricket on the radio. It wasn't that he didn't make mistakes, he did, but he didn't lose his rag at others when they did happen. Infamously, he had been operating one afternoon on a hip, and seeing a lump, did what all surgeons tended to do with lumps – stuck a knife in it. Bright red arterial blood hit the ceiling. He had apparently looked mildly surprised at most, put his finger over it, asked for a clamp and then instructed the sister to fast bleep a proper surgeon to come and sort his mess out. He then continued his conversation about whether England would win another test match against the Australians before the end of the millennium. Mr Stoneman was said to have commented afterwards that the anaesthetist hadn't been as chatty as normal.

So, Will went down to theatre to help out without quite so much of the reticence he usually had when asked to attend with other surgeons.

"Ah, Dr Cunningham, good to see you," Mr Stoneman said as he entered. "Two hips and a carpal tunnel release – fancy one?"

"Er, yes," said Will," that would be great." He paused. "You do mean the carpal tunnel, don't you?"

"Unless you're happy to do one of the hips?" said Mr Stoneman.

"Best watch one first. Next time," said Will, referring to the old and not entirely apocryphal adage of 'see one, do one, teach one'.

They went to scrub up. Hands, fingernails and forearms were thoroughly scoured with a nailbrush and Hibiscrub before being dried with a sterile paper towel. Then commenced the tricky process of getting into sterile surgical gowns without touching the outside of the garment and the even more entertaining manoeuvre of putting on the gloves. It was like one of those party games you played as a child, but without the chocolate as a prize. You started by putting your arms down the gown sleeves. Then, with your fingers holding tight to the inside of the sleeves of the gown, you grasped the edge of the wrist of the sterile glove which had been folded so that it was half inside out, fingers pointing back down your wrist. You pulled it on with the other hand, again covered by a sterile sleeve. The hands were then pushed through the end of the sleeve, popping into the glove. If skin touched the outside of the gown or, even worse, the outside of the glove, the whole sequence started again. A theatre sister stood guard to ensure no mistakes were made and tied the gown strings at the back if she was satisfied you were aseptic. Wound infection rather than the procedure was what used to kill many patients who underwent surgery, and while blood down your front as a surgeon might well have been a demonstration of virility in the old days, a live patient had to suffice in modern times. That and your Porsche in the car park.

Will got past the theatre sister without any issues. The unconscious patient was brought in, and all of the documentation was double-checked particularly which hip was being done. It was very easy to get lefts and rights mixed up, and errors led to a certain amount of 'disappointment' from both the patient's and surgeon's perspectives – but not the lawyers. The patient's skin was prepped with a yellow iodine solution, a sterile, sticky-backed plastic was placed over the top of the site and Mr Stoneman was ready to go. He hummed and warbled along to Pink Floyd between telling Will what he was doing and the potential pitfalls. Will held onto retractors and asked pertinent questions where appropriate. He would at least try to show willing, especially if he was to be allowed to do some cutting.

A mere three hours later and Will's name was recorded as the surgeon. A carpal tunnel release was an operation in the wrist that divided elastic tissues, releasing pressure on the underlying median nerve. Pressure on this nerve caused pain and weakness in the thumb, index, and half of the ring finger. It was a simple operation, which was why he was being allowed to do it, but there was the possibility of cutting significant nerves and arteries in the region if he was careless. He had seen some beginners shake with the knife in their hands as they prepared to cut into the patient. Will's hand was rock steady, and with Mr Stoneman watching closely, his incision into the skin of the wrist in line with the ring finger, his dissection down through the palmar fascia and then the division of the transverse carpal ligament, went perfectly. He then sewed everything back up.

Mr Stoneman seemed reasonably impressed. "Very good," he said, "there may be hope for you yet. Not still stuck on that GP thing, are you?" he asked, as they discarded their surgical attire and wandered out of theatre for a coffee.

Will had arranged to meet Tamsin in the library that afternoon, following up on one of Godfrey's suggestions. Tamsin was a little awkward over the fact that he'd been discussing things with his friends, but in the end, she was pleased that it had yielded another line of enquiry. It was almost deserted when they arrived, but the same librarian was behind the counter and Will could swear he hadn't changed position from when they had been in before.

"Do you think we should call the crash team?" whispered Will as they approached the desk.

"Bit late for that. I think rigor mortis has set in," Tamsin whispered back, seemingly happy to play along this time.

The man looked up and raised an eyebrow. "May I be of assistance?" he asked. "Before I shuffle off."

Will winced. "We're looking for genetics-related papers by JB Gowen, from 1993 onwards," said Will, then added, "please" guiltily. The librarian spent a few minutes fiddling with the keys on the computer.

"He's second name co-author of a few in *The British Journal of Genetic Disease*," said the librarian, giving them details of the papers they had already read. "And more recently he seems to have written a few biochemistry text books, but nothing more."

"Are you sure?" asked Will.

The librarian gave him a withering look. "Yes... I just can't be bothered to tell you about the things he hasn't written."

"Sorry," said Will, and he made a mental note to not take the mickey until well out of earshot next time.

"What now?" asked Tamsin, slightly despondent as they left the library.

"Well, I guess we have only one choice," said Will. "We can look this Gowen bloke up and ask him what happened."

"I wonder if he's still working at the Molecular Genetics Department in the University of Birmingham?" she said. "That's where they did their research."

"A few phone calls should soon tell us," said Will.

Will made the phone calls from the hospital mess, while Tamsin went for a tutorial. He managed to speak to the now Professor John Gowen's secretary and explained that he was doing some work looking into the genetic potential of stem cells and would appreciate anything the professor had to offer on the subject. She explained that he was away for a few days and wouldn't be back until the weekend so wouldn't take any phone calls, but in any case, he had moved on to concentrating on biochemistry these days. She was doing a very good job of blocking him, Will felt. Finally, however, he did manage to get her to acknowledge that the professor would, more than likely, be in his office on the Saturday and might agree to their seeing him, but only very briefly. Will placed the phone down, his brain immediately starting to work out the logistics of how that was going to happen, wondering what Tamsin would say to a weekend in Birmingham. Tamsin, it transpired, had friends in Birmingham and was perfectly happy with the idea.

The drive up the M5 was easy enough, coming off at junction 4 and following the A38, which passed close to the University of Birmingham. Parking on site was a thing of the past, so they left the car in Selly Oak and walked through the campus, past the red-brick architecture and 'Old Joe', the memorial clock tower in the centre.

Professor Gowen's room, they had found out, was situated in the tall, grey building that housed all the clinical sciences. It sat at the foot of a hill that stretched away from the rest of the university up to the medical school, behind which loomed The Queen Elizabeth Hospital. They both paused, looking at the austere vastness of the medical complex before entering the significantly more demure structure before them. A porter sent them in the direction of the professor's office, and they headed off climbing seemingly endless flights of echoing stairs to reach the sixth floor.

Heavy fire doors led into a poorly lit corridor, and a strip light flickered off and on, its worn-out starter unlikely to be replaced anytime soon. The corridor wound round to the left and they counted off the numbered doors to the one marked 611, the office of the professor's secretary. It was open and there was a lady in her sixties sitting behind a computer. Her name badge identified her as Morwenna Trevose. Will knocked, uttering a quick, "Hello," before mentioning the phone call and the secretary grudgingly rang through to the professor before motioning for them to go through.

"Professor Gowen?" Will enquired, poking his head around the door.

A man of around forty, sandy-brown hair, wearing a crisply ironed white shirt, was sitting at a desk surrounded by neatly ordered stacks of books and papers. There was a whiteboard on one wall and posters of biochemical pathways on another. The professor peered over the top of his computer terminal, piercing blue eyes not disguising his irritation at the interruption.

"Yes, and you would be...?"

Will opened the door fully and they both stepped in. "Will Cunningham, and this is Tamsin Trevelyan," said Will. He turned slightly to allow Tamsin to squeeze into the tiny room. "We're sorry to bother you on a Saturday, but we can't make it during the week." Will launched into the agreed story, "We're really interested in the work into stem cell research that you did. Do you mind if we ask you a few questions, we're doing a project on it at uni?" They had decided to avoid any mention of Whitehorse for the time being.

"Ah yes" – he indicated towards a couple of wooden chairs alongside his desk – "but you are aware that I lecture in biochemistry these days?"

Will nodded.

"Well then," he sat back in his chair, "what is it you want to know?"

Will told him of "a project" that they were researching about the potential offered by stem cells for the regeneration of tissues and organ repair; similar, in general principle, to the area that the professor might be, or had been, interested in. He went on to describe how they had come across the paper he'd written and expressed surprise that such obviously important work had not been followed up with more publications. Will deliberately steered clear of mentioning Metern's name for the time being.

"So," Will concluded, "we were wondering if you could give us some pointers or tell us of any further research in this area?"

Gowen snorted slightly. "The short answer is no, there hasn't been. At least not here. Our funding was pulled five years ago."

"But there's such huge potential in this area of medicine," said Will, doing his best to look crestfallen. "How is it that no one was prepared to finance any projects?"

"The risks were just too high," Gowen replied, "both financial and personal." Gowen observed their faces. "I'll explain," he said. "While there were technical problems, they were not insurmountable. Granted it was going to take many years to solve them and our research was not going to yield any quick results, but they were solvable and a few companies were still prepared to back us." He rubbed his chin. "You see, we were reliant on the Human Genome Project and the information that it would provide. That was, and still is, years away from finishing. But irrespective of that, it was more to do with the media and public outcry at the nature of our research and the effect that that had on the Ethics Committee. The companies weren't prepared to suffer the bad publicity that its backing might attract."

All research, Will knew, particularly where transgression of core moral principles might occur, had to go before the committee. It was designed in part, to prevent the 'end justifies the means' philosophy, which could lead to the atrocities seen all too commonly throughout history, particularly recent history. It did, however, have the potential to significantly curb or obstruct cutting-edge investigation.

"We had ethical approval for our research declined repeatedly," continued Gowen, "because the research would involve human embryos. They failed to see that the sacrifice of this not yet human ball of cells, would benefit the existence of millions, no billions, of people in the long term. Ironic really" – he shook his head – "given that it is deemed ethically acceptable to 'terminate' thousands of pregnancies every day for the supposed benefit of one individual who 'cannot possibly' continue with a perfectly healthy pregnancy."

The cynicism of his last statement couldn't be missed.

"However," he went on, "we were prepared to weather even that storm, make alterations and keep up the pressure to get approval in the end, in the hope that there would be at least one company with the vision to see beyond a short-term drop in share price." He sighed. "But when our laboratories were attacked, and a large volume of our work was destroyed..." He trailed off, looking down at his desk.

"Who would do that? What happened?" asked Will, taken aback.

"For months," Gowen went on, "our scientists had been receiving what can only be described as hate mail – anything from bits of paper with symbols drawn on it, to full-blown death threats. The police were notified and helpfully they suggested that we 'remain vigilant' and 'fit proper security' to the laboratories and homes. They thought it was the work of anti-vivisectionists or some religious nuts and felt the risks were small. We couldn't afford the type of alarm systems necessary... heck, we couldn't even afford to do the research that we were doing. So, a couple of locks got fitted and that was about it. In all honesty, we weren't overly concerned. People make idle threats all the time and, for the most part, that's all they are. Unfortunately, this group of nutters weren't most people, and our laboratories were broken into and wrecked."

Will could hear the antipathy in the man's voice. "Everything was destroyed, years of work gone in a few minutes. Such ignorant, mindless stupidity. They took sledgehammers to computers, poured acid over backup discs, as well as setting the animals loose... rats, monkeys, the lot. I mean, if you have genuine concerns about genetic experiments and contamination of the gene pool with 'abnormal DNA', what you don't do is release it into the environment! Then finally they set fire to the building."

"I'm sorry," said Will. "It's such a waste, so misguided."

"Yes, it was, particularly since I had thought we were beginning to make some progress." He paused. "We were left with no ethical approval, no research and no building, bad publicity and no investors." He shook his head again.

"Do you really think, given time, you might well have come up with something significant?" Will asked.

"It's always very hard to say. Most research doesn't come up with anything of commercial value. Significantly less than one per cent of chemicals investigated yield a useful drug."

Will nodded.

"Who knows," continued the professor. "Had we been able to splice the DNA with the right radiation exposure, get the enzyme balance correct... maybe." He sighed. "Still, it's all finished now. I washed my hands of it all and" – he sighed again – "settled for the less cutting-edge life of lecturing in biochemistry." Will gave a wan smile, acknowledging the man's disappointment at lost aspirations.

"You wrote your papers in collaboration with a Cadan Metern." Tamsin spoke for the first time, switching the subject and almost making Will jump. "Did *he* do any further research?"

"Ah, Cadan" – the professor sighed and rocked back in his chair – "a brilliant man. No, I don't think that he did. But I haven't heard from him in several years, not in fact since just after the laboratory was destroyed. He seemed to take it all quite to heart, with the pulling of funding and the Ethics Committee refusal as well. He was very passionate and outspoken over it all."

"Yes," said Will, remembering the tone in which the papers had been written. "So, er, what happened to him?"

"He spent a while looking through the ruins of our work the day after and asked me if I thought it was worth going on. I have to say I was quite down but thought at that stage we might try. He nodded and left. But the following day the press was full of the story, putting a damning slant on what we were doing, only just stopping short of actually condoning the saboteurs' actions. That finished it for me and, apparently, Cadan. Didn't see him again. I learned subsequently that he had handed in his resignation and intended to go back to practising medicine."

They were silent for a moment.

"What was he like to work with, if you don't mind me asking?" asked Tamsin.

"He was very, very focussed," replied the professor. "Driven by his work almost to the exclusion of everything else. He would lock himself away for hours on end, sorting out one small part of a problem and woe betide anyone who dared to disturb him. Not really a team player, if you know what I mean – not the gregarious type – and found most social occasions a bit difficult I think."

Will and Tamsin both frowned, which seemed to catch Gowen. "Don't get me wrong, I did hold him in the highest esteem. In many ways I owe my career to him. He was hugely helpful when I was doing my dissertation." The professor elucidated. "He got me funding from within the department, which was unheard of after the cuts Mrs Thatcher had made to tertiary education in the late eighties. Though the manner in which he went about securing it was, shall we say, brusque. I even heard that one of the female lecturers was going to press charges of assault after one altercation but was persuaded that it would likely damage her career more than his." He shrugged. "Different times."

Will was a bit confused. "He helped *you* get a bursary?"

"Yes, that's right."

"But you were *his* boss?"

"Good Lord no! He'd been around the clinical sciences part of the medical school for a good number of years before I turned up."

Will remembered that Gowen had been the second name on the papers. He'd thought it a little odd for the more senior individual to take second billing. This explained that at least. But the chronology was all out.

"But I don't understand. How long had you known Dr Metern?" he asked.

"Well," the professor mused, appearing to count on his fingers, "we published in the early nineties, and I'd done my BSc and then PhD a bit before that, so I guess about eight years." Will and Tamsin looked at each other. She had done the same calculations that he had. The professor reached over to a file on the shelf. "Look, I think I have a picture of us in here." He rummaged around in an orange folder before pulling out a faded colour photograph. "Here," he said, handing it to them, "taken just after we got our new research team together in 1990." Will looked at the photo in the prof's hand and then tilted it so that Tamsin could see. There was a team of five people, three men at the back, two women in front. The professor's image grinned back at them. He hadn't changed much, but next to him, in the middle of the photo, was an older man, stooped and greying at the temples perhaps, but nonetheless it was the unmistakable face of Cadan Metern. Will and Tamsin's eyes widened.

"But he's... he's an old man," Tamsin blurted out.

Gowen looked slightly offended. "Well not that old. A few years older than I am now, actually."

"I mean," Tamsin recovered herself, "I was expecting him to look younger," she finished lamely.

"No," replied the professor, "he'd have been about fifty back then."

They left the building in a stunned silence and walked that way until well out of earshot. Tamsin broke first, forcing a whisper. "He's nearly sixty years old! Sixty! How is that possible?"

"He is if that's actually him and not, say, his very significantly older identical twin."

Tamsin gave him a look.

"Or his father?" said Will.

"It was him you know it was," asserted Tamsin. "We both saw that scar he has on his left cheek."

"Yes, I know," said Will.

"Any rational explanations or suggestions for that?"

Will shook his head. He was tempted, jokingly, to say witchcraft, but in this instance such a comment was going to be much too close to the mark.

"And there is something very fishy about that research," Tamsin continued. "You don't just stop something with that much potential."

"Well, it looks as though Professor Gowen has," replied Will. "I saw some of the papers on his desk, and none of them had anything to do with genetics. Nor did anything on his wall."

"Maybe Metern has continued with the research."

"Without funding?" said Will.

"Without the approval of the Ethics Committee," said Tamsin.

"So why switch to obstetrics and gynaecology in a backwater like White-horse?" said Will, tight-lipped, well aware of the answer.

A 1992

Cadan Metern looked over at his colleague. He could feel time slipping away. He had dedicated his life to genetics, seen that it was the only way to safeguard humanity. The physicists would get them off the planet, but the distances were so great, and bodies degraded so easily, that they, on their own, were doomed to fail. They needed help; an improvement in the physiology of the human species and then the physicists might make their work count. He and Gowen were on their way to providing that assistance. What they had done could change the future of medicine, offer mankind a chance of surviving beyond any future disasters and catastrophic world-ending events, and there would be some. Why couldn't the dullard see how important their efforts were? Had they got to him, scared him away from pursuing their achievement to its logical end?

Well, he would go it alone, hidden in plain sight. The small scar under his left eye reddened with the burning desperation he felt inside. He needed to control it, not let his burgeoning intentions show. He closed his eyes and breathed out slowly. So be it, a different path then, and, he realised, one that combined not just modern technology, but also the wisdom of the old ones.

Chapter 31

Monday morning and the ward was its usual fraught self. Will sat next to Tamsin at the desk and just watched as the nurses flitted between patients like moths, from red light to red light. The call buttons were pressed with seeming impunity, the expectation being that one of the six nurses on the thirty-bed ward would be there instantly, irrespective of what they were already involved in. They dealt with all manner of need with the same patient demeanour, from the physical, to the psychological, to the unreasonable. And just the six, while two floors up there were legions of bureaucratic management staff. The only thing that seemed to concern *them* was whether the care plans had been filled out and all the boxes been ticked.

Nursing, for nurses, was becoming very much a secondary requirement for the job. Having a qualification to say that you knew how to plan the nursing management of a patient and record data relating to a patient was deemed far more important than actually looking after, or indeed nursing, them. Who cared if the patient suffered or even died, as long as the paperwork was all in order! Clearly not the higher echelons and Royal Colleges. His mind was wandering off again, disappearing at tangents. Today's displacement brain activity appeared to be picking fictitious fights with the state of nursing and the NHS in general.

Will tried pulling his attention back to his work, but it was proving difficult to control, no doubt a consequence of not sorting out the problems at the root cause of his brain's wanderings. Was it possible that Metern had continued his original research? The rate of perinatal mortality had gone up. Was he somehow responsible for this but hadn't been caught? And what of Tamsin's assertions of witchcraft? Should he report it to some senior person in the hospital or go to the police? Sorting out the NHS and its shortcomings suddenly seemed a much less complicated pastime.

Tamsin was perched on a stool at the nursing station next to him, and she looked up from her blood form. "I know I've written it at least twenty times today, but what is the date?"

"It's the err..." he tailed off, mouth agape, "...hang on, I've just had a thought". He put his pen down and looked at her. "The obstetricians mentioned those odd spikes in their perinatal mortality data, didn't they, eight times a year? Don't wiccans have their special dates... you know, like Halloween, when their powers are supposed to be at their greatest?"

"They have pagan festivals, yes," she replied, "celebrating the equinoxes and solstices. I can remember seeing diagrams on the wall at the witchcraft museum."

"And how many of those are there?"

"Four of each," she said. "Why?"

"Eight then... a bit of a coincidence. When did Jen have her accident?"

"Just before Christmas, the twenty-first or second, I think," replied Tamsin. "Why?"

"And she..." he hesitated, the word getting stuck.

"...died," finished Tamsin, "on March twenty-first."

"Might that tie in with those festivals or solstices or whatever they're called?"

"Maybe, I'd have to look it up." She frowned. "Do you think there's a link?"

"I'm not really sure, but it's worth a look," said Will, "and we should definitely have a chat with the obstetrics guys again." He grimaced. "And maybe we should also head back to the witchcraft museum — and no nonsense this time," said Will earnestly.

Tamsin's eyebrow only flickered slightly.

They went up to Boscle the following weekend, Will was driving and the going was tediously slow behind a farm vehicle with a large metal frame attached to its rear. It was coming into holiday season, which meant that the roads also tended to fill up with cars and caravans. Will suspected that by way of revenge on the city folks, farmers deliberately took their tractors out during the hours of 10 am to 4 pm, just to drive around, so getting anywhere took even longer than the statutory forty-five minutes.

"What did you find out from the obs and gynae lot?" asked Tamsin, drumming her fingers on her knees.

"Well," he replied, keen to pass on what he had gleaned, "I managed to get Jess to give me a list of those spikes – there's a list in my coat pocket... on the back seat!"

She retrieved the piece of paper and looked down it. "Last year it seems there were unexpected peaks on or around the beginning of May, mid-June, the beginning of August, mid to late September, October thirty-first, December twenty-first, the beginning of February," Will was aware of her looking over at him, "and March twenty-first."

"Look at the other pieces of paper from past years." She did, and there was a similar data profile.

"OK," she said grimly, "then let's see whether they correlate with anything in the museum."

They parked in the same car park at the end of the village as they had before. It was noticeably fuller than on the previous visit and they wandered along to the museum. It had been a bright day when they set off, but the weather, on arrival, had taken a turn for the worse, not an unusual scenario in this part of the world, except that often the day didn't even start off brightly. The sun was cloaked by dark clouds, and a wind, a little more chilling than you might expect for the time of year, blew an empty crisp packet along the bank of the stream. Will caught it and put it in a nearby bin. Tamsin smiled at him and took his hand. Hers felt cold in his.

The same man sat at the desk. He smiled at them and just waved them, despite Will's offering to pay. The claustrophobic atmosphere pressed on Will again as he felt a familiar, disconcerting prickle run through him on entering the darkened corridor. He wondered briefly if he had some sort of allergy to joss sticks.

It was only a few metres and Will stood in front of the Wheel of the Year, the main reason for their return visit. He was again taken by the intricate beauty of the artwork, which almost brought the animals, nymphs and sprites depicted, to life. The swirls of roots and branches, interlocking in endless twists and knots, eventually drew your eye to the wheel's centre point, to disappear to infinity. He realised that the last time he'd looked at it, he had been so engrossed by the mesmerising patterns that he'd failed to glean any actual information, so he studied it differently this time.

The Wheel of the Year had eight points and represented the cycle of the year and its festivals. At the top was the festival of Yule, the winter solstice, and at the bottom "Lithia", or summer solstice. These were the points at which the sun's rays hit the earth for the shortest and longest durations, mid-winter and mid-summer. The spring and autumn equinoxes of "Ostara" and "Mabon" were in the nine o'clock and three o'clock positions, when the lengths of daylight and night-time were equal. These were termed the solar festivals and marked the seasons. The so-called 'cross-quarter' festivals were Imbolc, Beltane, Lammas and Samhain and were the fire festivals and marked significant agricultural dates during the year for, for example, planting and harvesting. Each of these festivals took on a symbolic meaning and were associated with both the cycles of the year and the cycle of time and of life itself. Listed next to each of the festivals were its dates and some details surrounding them.

Imbolc, a festival celebrating the first signs of spring, occurred on 2 February. Ostara, on 21 or 22 March, marked the spring equinox. Beltane was 30 April or 1 May and was a fire festival celebrating the turning out of the cattle to the pastures. Lithia, 21 or 22 June, was the summer solstice and when the Sun God was at his most powerful, only for him to sacrifice himself for the good of his people on the festival of Lammas, 1 August. Mabon was on 21 or 22 September, marking the autumn equinox. Samhain, or Halloween, everyone knew about on 31 October, and Yule, the winter solstice, marked the rebirth of the sun and was on 21 or 22 December. It went on to explain that the dates varied due to leap years and the earth taking three hundred and sixty-five and a quarter, days to go around the sun, but for Will and Tamsin those dates had far more sinister connotations.

"That's no coincidence, is it?" said Tamsin, firmly.

Will stared at the exhibit. "No, no, it's not," he said.

"We've passed Beltane," said Tamsin, running her finger along a line of text. "This festival was midway between the equinoxes and associated with invoking protection. In times past, fires would be lit, the village devotees would dance and lead their animals through the smoke."

"Protection from thieves, wolves and pestilence, but not lung cancer," Will observed dryly. "Well, that festival was on the first of May, a few weeks ago." He looked up at Tamsin. "So, the next one is Lithia, the summer solstice, when the sun is at its farthest point north and its rays hit the earth for the longest time, creating the longest day and shortest night."

"So, if Metern is involved in some freakish occult rituals, then isn't it reasonable to expect him to do something on the twenty-first." Tamsin turned to face Will. "At which point we may be able to gain some evidence to attach to what Jen had said.

"What, catch him at it?"

"Yes," she replied. Then she looked concerned. "But where is he going to be?"

"The mosaic?" said Will.

She thought for a moment. "The mosaic is on a ley line, right?" said Tamsin. "Along which lie significant spiritual sites."

"So, he might turn up anywhere along the St Michael's ley line," said Will. "Wasn't there some info on ley lines further on in the museum."

"Yes, there was. Come on." They walked briskly through the corridors, past several alarmed-looking people and past the poppet dolls, Will's heart lurching as they did so. He hadn't really paid that much attention to the ley line section before, understandable perhaps, given that he might just have cast a malicious spell at the time.

There was a map of lines that criss-crossed Britain, which then extended to a map of the world. Will sought out St Michael's ley line, which ran through the Whitehorse Hospital. It gave similar information as found in the hospital museum, but there were a few extra details.

"Did you know that St Michael's ley line is also known as being the line of dragon sites?" said Will, turning to Tamsin, and pointing out a small section on the chart.

"No," she replied, studying the map more closely.

"See, there's Avebury henge and Dragon Hill, just under the Uffington White Horse, where St George was supposed to have killed the dragon. There's a bare patch of chalk where no grass will grow, which is supposed to be where the dragon's blood was spilled."

Tamsin smiled, nodded, and read further. "It says that the white dragon was a symbol of the Anglo-Saxons or modern-day English. They arrived in AD 450 and pushed from east to west, defeating the Celtic Britons and forming the basis of what is now the English nation. As a symbol of power or warning to others, they often carved images of horses or... dragons into the hillside, most into white chalk."

"Do you suppose that Whitehorse Hospital should really be White Dragon?" said Will.

"Possibly, but the site predates the Anglo-Saxons."

"So, who was in charge before them then?" asked Will.

"The Britons and the Celts."

They looked at each other. "And the symbol of the Celts was..."

"...a *red* dragon," said Tamsin.

"The underlying red stone," said Will. "Do you think that it might be that, symbolically, the Anglo-Saxons, having defeated the Celtic Britons, placed their stamp over that of their vanquished foes by digging out the red breccia stone and replacing it with white chalk?"

"Could well be," said Tamsin, "but whatever, I think it makes it a significant site for rituals if that's what you're into."

"And now apparently provides a ready supply of sacrificial victims," said Will. "So, it makes it very unlikely that Metern would go to anywhere else along the ley line, does it?" he continued. "I mean, he's unlikely to be, well, sacrificing at Stonehenge in front of the hundreds of people gathered to watch the sun rise. You have to feel someone would notice and object, perhaps even the constabulary."

Tamsin smiled and hugged Will. "He is going to be there at the next festival, at the mosaic, he must be. And we are going to be there too, to get the evidence to take to the police. Then they'll have to look at Jen's death in a different light." There were tears in her eyes now. "Thank you, Will," she said.

Chapter 32

Will had dropped Tamsin back at her house and was standing by the table in the kitchen, tucking into a piece of fruit cake that Shauna had just baked. It was stunningly good.

Shauna, however, was standing at the other side of the table, open-mouthed, hands on hips. "So, let me get this straight," she said in her exasperated Irish tone. "You have been back to the museum where you accidentally cast a spell that you didn't believe could work. You have now decided that while you almost certainly don't believe in magic, you feel that Cadan Metern does, and that he is a witch, or warlock, or whatever, and you need to try to catch him in the act of performing a ritual. Supposedly the last time he was observed doing this, the consequences were that two people lost their lives. And your plan is to hide in the cleaner's cupboard, leap out, say, 'Look, evil!', take a photo and then leg it?"

"Well, put like that" – a few crumbs fell out of Will's mouth – "it doesn't sound completely fool proof, but as long as we reach the next floor up and get out of the fire doors, we'll be in an area with other people and should be safe. Anyway, there's no way he would be able to cover the distance from the mosaic to the cupboard before we got up the stairs. We'll be fine."

"Well, how are you going to get into the cleaners' cupboard?" she asked.

"Oh, that bit's easy. There are well-labelled keys in the porters' room. I'll just say I've spilled something and am happy to clean it up myself and take the key.

There's a key-cutting place just down from the hospital, so I can nip out and get a duplicate cut. Then I'll be back in less time than it takes to" – he paused – "I don't know, clean up a dropped blood sample."

"And you'll let yourselves into the cupboard and just wait there all night?"

"With Tamsin, in the cupboard, yes."

She looked highly dubious. "You are sure he'll turn up?"

"As sure as we can be. He only gets a few times a year to do whatever he's doing. He can't afford to miss one."

"Eight, yes, you said." She shook her head. "What has that girl done to you? You are completely bonkers, both of you."

There was a screech of brakes and the sound of skidding tyres on gravel. They moved quickly over to the kitchen window to see Godfrey leap out of his car, tripping as he did so.

"The bastards!" he shouted. "Bastards, bastards, bastards!"

"The neighbours, Godfrey!" said Shauna, opening the door.

"Bollocks to the neighbours," he replied, taking a kick at thin air.

"What's happened?" said Shauna. Her tone rose as she realised this might be more than the usual Godfrey tantrum. He was frequently gratuitously rude, but he usually apologised, backtracking quickly.

"They have terminated my contract and are bloody well chucking me out."

Shauna stood a look of bewilderment on her face, before collecting herself. "But I thought if you did the exam, you'd be alright."

"Well so did I, but apparently not. Even if I do the exam and pass with one hundred per cent, I'm still not going to get onto the registrar rotation because they've already filled the positions with people who have the exam."

"Come in and sit down," said Shauna, putting an arm around him and leading him to a seat in the kitchen. "I can't believe they would do this so close to the exam. When is it anyway?" she asked.

"The twenty-second, just a few days away," he replied.

"You are still going to take it?" she said.

"Not sure there's much point," said Godfrey.

"No, Godfrey, you misunderstand. You *are* still going to take it," she said, gently, but forcefully.

"Oh," he replied.

"There's always next year's rotation," said Shauna, "and you will still need the exam."

"But don't you see? I'd have to move away from Whitehorse. I don't want to work anywhere else. In fact, I will not work anywhere else."

"I'm not sure you can demand a job," said Will. "You know what the NHS is like. They don't feel any genuine sense of duty or responsibility towards the welfare of their staff. As long as they have someone to fill a post who has the right boxes ticked, that's fine by them. If you had a home and family down here, and been dedicated to the hospital for years, that still wouldn't hold sway regarding their selecting for a post."

"Thanks for explaining that. I now feel so much better!" said Godfrey, then he rubbed his eyes. "Sorry, I didn't mean..."

"It's OK," said Will.

"But I'm not going anywhere else," said Godfrey, slumping into his seat.

"At least do the exam," pleaded Shauna. "Then if someone drops out, you'll have the requisite piece of paper." Godfrey grunted, then got up, deciding to visit his milk churn outside.

"When is your contract up?" asked Will, following him, as the familiar rasp of the lighter signalled another twenty minutes off Godfrey's life expectancy. Godfrey inhaled on his cigarette and blew a stream of smoke into the air.

"Few weeks' time," he said, "just after the exam."

"Are they chucking you out of the residences as well?" asked Will.

"Oh, fuck," said Godfrey, alarm spreading over his face. "They will, won't they." Things seemed to be going from bad to worse. Godfrey removed the churn lid and flicked the ash into it before closing the lid again. Shauna looked over at Will, who nodded.

"Look Godfrey," she said, "if they do insist that you leave, the lounge is huge and the sofa, as you know, doubles as a bed. If you want, you can stay here until you sort yourself out."

Godfrey's parents lived on the other side of the country in Norfolk, and while they were undoubtedly very proud of him, Will knew that they would probably sell the house and move to an undisclosed location if they thought for a moment that Godfrey was going to make a return home.

Godfrey gave a half-hearted smile. "Thanks," he said, "that's really kind." Then, in a rare moment of insight, he added, "I promise I wouldn't be here for too long. Just until I secure another job and can move back into my flat."

"They'll probably have given it to someone else by that time," pointed out Shauna.

"I doubt it," said Godfrey. "It'll take them months to repair then redecorate the place." It was probably true. Godfrey, against all tenancy agreements, had put up shelves, attached a bracket for his TV to the wall and had painted "artwork" in the bedroom. The boxes for his home cinema system had been piled up against a wall that hid a mould forest sustained by a leaking tap that hadn't been repaired quickly enough. The electrics also needed an overhaul, particularly after the incident with the heavy-duty drill, the thin stud wall, and the mains circuit box on the other side of the stud wall. It was a wonder Godfrey was still alive.

Will turned to put the kettle on again as Shauna stroked Godfrey's head. His demeanour picked up a fraction and was further improved by a slice of cake.

"So, tell me," said Godfrey, turning to Will as he was handed a mug of tea, "I'm in need of a laugh. Anything new with this lady or yours?"

Shauna let out a most un-Shauna-like snort and relayed her version of Will's plan to catch Metern.

Godfrey blinked several times as his brain got up to speed. "Suppose you do catch him in the middle of a ritual of some sort," he said, "and suppose that you even get a picture, what then?"

"Well," Will began, "we would go to the police."

"OK," said Godfrey, "and tell them what?"

"Show them the picture as evidence that he was lying about at least one aspect of his story."

"It's not illegal any more to practice any religion you like," said Godfrey.

"Provided you break no laws in doing so, and I have a suspicion that there may be one or two more than grey areas to look into."

"They've already had the coroner's inquest, and Jen's death was suicide. A photo of a bloke dressed up, waving a wand around, isn't going to get them to reopen it, especially coming from a person who reported that he'd been assaulted and got away without a scratch on him but admitted he may have caused grievous bodily harm to his supposed assailants. Combine this with a wild-child surfing chick who made some very bizarre claims about a man both she and her best friend slept with, and you can see how they may remain sceptical."

"I know," said Will, ruefully, "but hopefully the nature of the photos taken will be sufficiently incriminating so that they might change their minds and take a fresh look. Speaking of which..."

Godfrey groaned, "You want to borrow my very expensive camera."

Godfrey didn't do things by halves, apart from exams perhaps. Photography was no exception. His camera had, on a few occasions, been the subject of envy by professional paparazzi.

"Yes, you may borrow it," he said, "but be very, very careful, especially running away from satanic murderers. Remember, it's save the camera first, then your life!"

Will laughed. "OK," he agreed.

Chapter 33

The following Tuesday, Will and Tamsin went down to the basement to scout the mosaic area. The stairs, the ones which Jen must had fallen down, were situated next to a lift, both were recessed into an alcove. Turning right the space opened into an area half the length of one of the wards. On the left was a double door set into the wall, behind which was a broom cupboard. He walked over to examine it and assess angles. Hiding there provided a view directly onto the mosaic area approximately ten metres away. Not only would the broom cupboard provide an excellent vantage point, but Will could see that there was a gap in the double door of the cupboard wide enough to look through. It would need to be a fraction wider to accommodate a lens, though he should be able to get several shots off before needing to run, if necessary.

The mosaic was surrounded by a protective glass wall, the door to which was situated at the far end; that would inhibit any chase were they to be seen. Anyone leaving the mosaic would have to do half a circuit of the glass wall before they reached the open area in front of the mosaic. Plenty of time to get out of the cupboard and sprint up one flight of stairs to safety if necessary. The door, Will presumed would be locked, although its keys, along with all other keys would be in the porters' lodge situated by reception.

They walked past the whitewashed walls adorned with pictures of Roman art and looked down at the tiled artwork that lay behind the glass. Involuntarily, Will felt drawn to the eye.

"He must have been a magnificent sight, red or white," said Tamsin, brushing Will's shoulder as she placed her hands against the glass wall. "Majestic on his hillside, a symbolic statement to all who would enter this land."

"And now he lies in a glass cage, looking up at a white ceiling where once there were stars."

"If we're to believe the pagan concept of the Wheel of Life, all things come around, so it's only a matter of time before he's free again," said Tamsin.

"It took a massive bomb last time," said Will, ruining the mood somewhat. Tamsin laughed all the same. Then he put his hands to her shoulders, his voice serious. "Tamsin, I'm happy to do this alone if you'd prefer. It is possible it might be dangerous."

"No," said Tamsin. "I need to know. I have a duty to be there."

"OK," said Will, not pushing it further, he knew it would be pointless but he had to ask. "I guess we should go and try to get the key from the porters' lodge then."

The plan was relatively simple. Walk into the lodge, get the key, make a copy, and return it. Will knew that they all hung on well-labelled hooks in the lodge, just by the main entrance to the hospital. It was also where broken pagers got taken after they had 'stopped working' having 'fallen' out of a pocket, really hard, against a wall. Tamsin wished him luck and went to wait in the main entrance hall, ready to go and get a copy cut.

The hospital foyer was filled with more pleasant smells than in times past. Gone was the acrid stench of bleach and detergent, now replaced by the aromas of coffee and pastries. He glanced in the direction of the counter. To go with the coffee, one might enjoy a bacon tasty, puff pastry layered with cheese and bacon: a sausage delight, sausage wrapped in puff pastry or a simple cheese twist, cheese wrapped in pastry. To follow, one might enjoy a Danish swirl or jam doughnut. Conveniently, the cardiac unit was situated on the same level as these outlets, so you didn't have too far to travel, or have stairs to negotiate, when you had your heart attack.

Will strode confidently through the door to the switchboard room, staffed almost exclusively by women sitting in front of banks of phones. Women had been found to manage better here than their male counterparts, given their ability to deal more sympathetically with the somewhat testing nature of the calls received from both the public and the staff within the hospital itself. These women were obliged to be considerate, caring, understanding and patient, while they received dog's abuse throughout the day. The caller would hold them personally responsible for anything from a doctor not answering their pager, to test results not being back and even the cancellation of Aunt Bessie's operation. People failed to realise that these long-suffering women operated the switchboard and not a scalpel. Nor were they responsible for the lack of car parking space, the attitude of the consultant they had just seen in Outpatients, or the appalling state of the NHS in general. Male switchboard operators had a tendency to offer reasons why the caller might have suffered such indignities, which probably had more than a ring of truth but were not deemed acceptable as responses when trying to help the individuals concerned.

Having given it some consideration, Will had decided that the art of being in a place that you weren't supposed to be, was to either move too quickly to be apprehended or saunter along in such a relaxed fashion that you couldn't be up to no good. He'd opted for the former method and fairly fizzed through the room. No one so much as lifted an eyelid, the operators were all too busy on pacifying duties to be particularly bothered with a slightly flushed doctor sprinting 'innocently' through the room. He made it to the porters' door, knocking and entering in one movement. A bearded gentleman wearing the standard grey-blue short-sleeved shirt and dark blue trousers greeted him as he entered.

"May I have the key to the mosaic basement cleaning cupboard please?" asked Will. "There's been a bit of a spill." He hoped he portrayed a confident air of no-messing. Behind the porter he could see hundreds of keys all arranged according to level, and there were at least two keys per hook, one presumably a spare.

"I'm sorry, sir, we can't just give keys out, but if you tell me the nature of the spill, I'll send someone along to clean it up."

"It's really nothing much," said Will, trying to maintain his self-confident performance. "I just dropped my coffee cup. I'm perfectly happy to do the cleaning."

"No, it's not a problem, sir," the man replied patiently. "I can page one of the guys. They'll be able to sort it out in a bit."

"Well," said Will, shuffling his feet, "it wasn't just coffee, there was a bit of blood as well." He hoped this might mean it needed cleaning up that bit sooner, and if no one was available to do it...

"Coffee" – the man paused – "and blood?"

"Er, yes," said Will, looking down. "I went to look at the mosaic and a blood bottle fell out of my pocket, and it smashed. As I tried to catch it, I spilled my coffee." He looked up. It wasn't going quite as well as he'd expected. "Look, there's really no need for any paging. I made the mess and am perfectly happy to clean it up. I *ought* to clean it up as it's my mess. Your guys have much more important things to do."

The porter raised his bushy, greying eyebrows. "That's highly commendable, sir. Am I also to understand that the bottle of blood shattered in the fall?"

"Um, yes," said Will.

"So, that'd be broken glass as well. Sounds like quite a spill."

"It's not that bad really," said Will, hoping to rescue the scenario that was rapidly slipping away from him.

"But given the hazardous nature of the substances involved, best get one of the lads to clean it up, eh?" said the porter. It wasn't so much slipping as cascading.

"Honestly, there's definitely not much to it," Will said, trying to keep the pleading out of his voice. "If you just let me have the keys, I can have it sorted in a jiffy."

"Sorry, sir, but it does sound quite a spill, and besides, I'm not allowed to just give keys out to anyone."

"Not even for doctors?"

"Especially not for doctors, sir."

"It's just a cleaning cupboard."

"Not even cleaning cupboards. Besides, there are special fluids required for cleaning up that sort of mess." Will looked blankly at the man, wondering what tack to take next.

The door cracked back on its hinges, as in rushed Tamsin, breathless and flustered. She didn't appear to see Will as she skidded into him, almost knocking him off his feet and sending a pen she'd been carrying flying across the room.

"Oh God, Will, I'm r-really sorry!" she stuttered uncharacteristically. "I've, er, well, I've managed to drop your, er, pager into the toilet." Will felt down to his belt, realising that it wasn't there. The bearded porter groaned.

"My pager?" he said, looking back at her.

"Yes," she said. "I've contacted the ward and they say they need you up there right now."

"They, er, did?" he said.

"Yes," she said, her eyes imploring him to just go along with things. Then she turned to the porter, who had guessed what was coming. She smiled prettily at him.

"I'll get the long gloves," he said, shooing them out of the room. "Keep an eye on the room for me a second will you, Betsy," he said to one of the switchboard women. She nodded. They were halfway through the switchboard area when Tamsin turned suddenly.

"Oh, I'm sorry," she said. "I dropped my pen in the room." Before the porter could say anything, she had disappeared back into the room and emerged, almost immediately, with her pen, wiggling it in her hand.

"Sorry," she said apologetically. Will shrugged and excused himself, departing at a convincingly brisk pace to get to the ward. On the way through the entrance hall, with Tamsin and the porter filing off to the ladies' toilets, he picked up an unattended half-full coffee cup and checked his pocket for the ever-present filled blood bottle, then headed for the basement.

Tamsin joined him on the ward about an hour later. He shot her a questioning look, and she produced a shiny new key from her pocket, smiling. Will gestured to her and they disappeared into the back office.

"How did you manage that?" he asked, admiring the key.

"Well, I suspected that things weren't going very well when you'd been in there for five minutes and not reappeared, so I came up with plan B." She perched herself on the edge of a desk. "Get the man out of his room and take the key at your leisure. Pagers, like many electrical toys, don't do very well when immersed in water, but get them out quickly enough and there is a chance they may survive. I'm sure our porter chap knew that he had to act quickly to prevent another pager meeting a watery end, quite literally." She giggled at her joke. "When I entered the room, I looked at the keyboard, so I knew which key I needed. Then when I returned to the room to retrieve my 'forgotten' pen, I took the key."

"But when the porters went down to clean up the carnage I'd left down in the basement, they would have noticed that there was a key missing, wouldn't they? There would have only been the main key there and no spare."

"I moved a key from another hook underneath the remaining key so that it would appear that there were still two keys. The cleaner would take the top key for the basement cupboard and be very unlikely to notice that the second spare key didn't match."

"So, what happened when you went to the toilets?" said Will.

"I obviously had to go into the cubicles first to check that there was no one in there, dropped your pager into the toilet bowl, then called the porter in to fish it out."

"Oooo," said Will, wrinkling his nose.

"It's OK, I picked a flushed one," said Tamsin, grinning.

"Oh, that's fine then!" said Will. "'Cos otherwise *that* might have been a bit unpleasant!"

"I've rinsed and dried it," she said, handing him a small rectangular parcel wrapped in toilet paper, "and it still works."

"Well done then I suppose," said Will, taking the pager gingerly between two fingers. He reattached it to his belt. "And the real key has been returned?"

"Yes," she said. "All keys on their normal hooks under the cover of a 'thank you' Danish pastry for the porter."

"That was brilliant, Tamsin," he said. "If medicine doesn't suit you then MI6 may have a vacancy."

She smiled. "I guess that all we have to do now is wait until the twenty-first."

Chapter 34

As broom cupboards went it probably wasn't the worst, Will thought to himself as he sat in the darkness. It smelled very clean for one thing – very 'piney', though occasionally he caught a floral waft of Tamsin's perfume... and it was quite spacious once the vacuum, mops and bucket had been moved out of the way. There was even just about enough room to lie down. The floor was a little hard, but they had borrowed a couple of blankets from the ward to allow a degree more comfort.

Sunrise on the twenty-first of June was at four forty-three. It was now three thirty in the morning and Will and Tamsin had been in the cupboard for over three hours. While initially there had been tense excitement, now it was just very dull and required a big effort not to drop off to sleep. A few hushed whispers had been exchanged, but any disturbance at the wrong time might mean their cover was blown, so silence had been maintained. Tamsin, disappointingly, had been keen to point out that there was to be no nonsense to pass the time.

So, he just sat there in the dark. There was of course, every likelihood that no one would turn up to sacrifice children, hold black sabbats or do whatever warlocks did at these things, and if he was honest, Will really hoped that would be the case. But being in the broom cupboard for the moment did represent their best chance of gaining some evidence to prove that what Jen had told Tamsin and then Tamsin had subsequently told the police was true. It was evidence that Cadan Metern had had more than an indirect hand in Jen's death and was also possibly responsible for the deaths of a number of children. He was aware of Tamsin shifting her position on the blanket that had been borrowed from the ward.

"You alright?" he whispered.

"Yes," came back the reply, but then they both froze as a heavy fire door was opened at the top of the stairs. Footsteps approached the descending flight and then came to a halt. Will held his breath. He could hear no sound from Tamsin, who was probably doing the same. A scraping shoe, indicating that the individual had turned around, could be heard going back through the door. A few moments silence, a breath taken, and then Will heard the whirr of the lift going up in the wall next to them. It stopped, and above the faint squeak the familiar rolling sound of a hospital trolley could be heard being pushed into the lift. Were there two sets of feet? Doors closed and the lift creaked and whirred, this time descending to their floor. They both shuffled next to the double doors of the cupboard, the lift covering any sound they might make. The gap through the doors, only a couple of centimetres, was just sufficient to provide a good view of proceedings. Will had the camera in hand, and it really was a monstrosity, but Godfrey had said it would do the job and even fitted a telephoto lens.

The ping of the lift's arrival in the basement echoed like a gong through the previously silent room. Will heard the doors open, clattering against their mechanisms, and the trolley was rolled out. The man pushing it grunted.

"Er, this thing's worse to drive than a supermarket trolley," a voice said from the lift. In the light from the lift, Will could see the trolley and its macabre load. It was a coffin, the sort used to transport the departed, not so inconspicuously, from the wards. Will shivered. "What shall I do with it?"

"Oh, just park it in front of there, that cupboard. We won't be able to wheel it down the side to the door anyway. We can carry the kit over."

Will felt his pulse race, and he shrank silently away from the cupboard doors, feeling Tamsin do likewise. The trolley wheels squeaked as it was bumped against the doors, then he heard the brake being applied, blocking them in and narrowing the gap between the doors. Will's heart sank. There would be no quick escape, and even worse, there was now insufficient gap for the camera to get a shot off.

Light from a torch bounced through the crack in the door as one of them came around to the side of the coffin. A gloved hand reached over and pushed up the coffin lid, which collided with the cupboard doors, causing it to shake.

"Shhh, you muppet, we really don't need security down here," said the man furthest away.

"Sorry..." The reply was whispered.

There was a rustling as both men rummaged inside the coffin. Will elevated himself on tiptoe and risked moving closer to the gap. Over the top of the coffin lid, he could just make out the backs of the two men as they carried items towards the glass mosaic chamber. Both were relatively short, about five foot seven, one quite stocky, the other thinner. Both sounded Cornish, and neither was Metern. As they turned the corner to go up the side of the chamber, Will could just make out that the men carried packages wrapped in plastic. He found himself oddly disappointed to see that it wasn't a body being unpacked, well not unless they had dismembered it and had it vacuum-packed.

It took four or five journeys before all the packages were placed beside the rear door entrance to the mosaic itself, and only the echoes of the men's footsteps broke the silence. It was fully ten minutes before the thinner of the men spoke. "Right, shall we get ready," he said, "it's about time."

"OK, but I hope he gets a move on," the other replied. "We don't need another screw-up."

Will saw him glance at his watch. This wasn't their complete contingent then. The thin man fetched a key from his pocket and unlocked the door to the mosaic then stepped inside the chamber. The stocky man then passed the packages to him, which were duly lined up against the back of the glass wall. The stocky man stepped inside with the last package and the door was closed. Once inside, they selected two of the packages, removing the plastic wrapping, and pulled out all-in-one vibrant orange boiler suits, complete with head-masks. Will stared intently, racking his brain for what the suits looked like. He'd seen them recently on the news, to do with the recent outbreak of a virus in the

Far East. Then he had it – they were putting on biohazard suits. He heard the ripping of paper and saw that the men were removing sterile gloves from their envelopes and then they continued unwrapping the rest of the packets. The men were being very careful not to directly touch any of the items, using aseptic technique. Will shifted his attention to the large array of instruments being laid out on a small table next to the eye of the mosaic: scalpels, needles, syringes, a tube of some sort, metal tripods, dishes, a freezer box and what appeared to be a crystal ball – all were carefully arranged.

"Four twenty," the stocky man said, a worried edge to his voice. "He's cutting it a bit fine."

"He'll be here, don't worry," said the other.

Will watched as they set the crystal ball onto a tripod directly over the eye of the mosaic. A glass Petri dish, glinting in the reflected torchlight, was positioned a carefully measured distance underneath the ball. Everything was being done with huge precision. Both men worked steadily, with the calm assurance of a well-practised routine. One of them, it was difficult to tell which in their suits, retrieved a vial from the freezer box and held it up to the light. It contained a pale-yellow liquid. Carefully, he set it down next to the Petri dish. One man, the one not in charge of setting up the tripod, waited by the closed glass door, his torch trained on the foot of the stairs.

Will wondered what Tamsin was making of all of this. Even from his sceptical point of view, it certainly seemed to confirm their suspicions that something was going on, but was it a satanic ritual? It would be odd to take so many precautions to maintain conditions as sterile as they appeared to need it. He remembered reading a section in the museum above them about the now ironically described 'hermetically' sealed chamber that allowed perfect conservation conditions within to be maintained. Near perfect conditions for a genetic experiment? He cursed silently that he had no way of recording this, but the gap was too small.

The doors at the top of the stairs opened. A man in theatre greens dashed down the steps, and in his arms was a bundle wrapped in a theatre sheet. Will heard a gasp from Tamsin next to him. It may well have been the knowledge of what that bundle might contain, or she too might have caught a glimpse of the white bone pendant that danced around the man's neck. Cadan Metern passed not two metres from them; they heard the click of his clogs as he ran. He reached the mosaic entrance, which was opened, and he handed the bundle inside. It was placed on the table and the sheet drawn back to reveal the form of a new-born child. It lay there, bluish in colour and streaked with blood – so tiny, so silent, so unmoving.

Will focussed on the scene at the far end of the room. A scalpel was taken off the table, and it glinted as one of the suited men held it above the child. Metern and the other man looked on. The blade was lowered, and it was Will's turn to stifle a gasp. He couldn't see any reaction from the baby as the knife cut deeply into it. It didn't move or react in any way. Forceps dug down, and with more cutting, a small piece of tissue was excised and then passed to the second man, who placed it into a test tube containing a fluid and it was shaken violently. Picking up the vial containing the pale-yellow liquid, the "surgeon" poured them into the Petri dish under the crystal ball.

"Time?" he hissed.

"Four forty-one and twenty, twenty-one, twenty-two..." The surgeon's assistant counted the seconds off, and at four forty-two exactly, the contents of the first tube were added to the glass Petri dish to join the other liquid. Another two minutes were counted off before the tray's contents were syringed into another vial. This was held up, and in the torchlight, it gleamed a golden colour. The man grunted, satisfied, and placed it into the freezer box. As he watched, the surgeon then returned his attention to the infant, still unmoving on the table. He picked up a tube and glued the wound together, holding it to make sure it took. When he was satisfied, he rewrapped it in the sheet and handed it back to Metern, who dashed from the mosaic chamber. He reached the stairs but faltered momentarily and appeared to sniff the air. Will and Tamsin stiffened, withdrawing again from the door crack. Metern, however, took off up the stairs again at a sprint.

The other two men took great pains to tidy away all the plastic wrappings in which the implements had arrived. All was packed away into the coffin along with their biohazard suits. Will had become worried that they may choose to do a slightly more thorough job of cleaning and, having located Tamsin in the dark, had whispered a suggestion to hide under the blanket at the back of the cupboard. As quietly as possible, under cover of the noise being made by the men cleaning the chamber, he had then placed a brush and cleaning utensils close to the door, so that it might, if required, be easily obtained. They wouldn't be using the vacuums, he hoped, for fear of attracting attention, too noisy. However, there wasn't enough room for them both in the corner, and if the door was opened, he was certain to be caught.

The men were halfway across the basement heading to the trolley. Will looked above the doors. There was a small shelf directly above them with another foot or so to the ceiling. Using a small stepladder propped against the wall, he climbed up to above the doors, resting as lightly as possibly upon a shelf situated above the lintel. He dared not put too much weight through it, so he partially braced himself against the parallel walls. Below him outside the doors he heard the men putting the last of the equipment back into their macabre suitcase. The doors rattled again and swung open a fraction more. The trolley moved away from the doors and a hand appeared, pulling the door open further. A torch shone around the cupboard's interior, underneath Will as he tensed, remaining rigid above the door frame, his muscles screaming with the effort. Then, to his relief, the doors closed. There were the sounds of the lift being called and steps going back up the stairs to the main hospital. He hung on for a minute or two, as long as he could, then his muscles gave out and he let go, landing with a thud on the floor.

He heard Tamsin come out from her hiding place and flicked the switch of his torch on and looked at her. Her face, though pale in the torchlight, stared past him and was one of vindication and steely determination.

"I will make this right, Jen. I swear I will," she whispered.

They waited for another half an hour before carefully opening the doors and creeping up the stairs. Tamsin had left her bag up in the mess, which had her house keys in, so they made a careful tour to the seventh floor. Will opened the door with some trepidation and peered in, but the mess was empty. Someone had rather carelessly thrown their bag on top of Tamsin's, and the contents – books, pens and a stethoscope – had fallen out. Tamsin tutted and Will helped replace the items in their owner's bag, blowing away a few stray black feathers that surrounded her rucksack, the result no doubt of a childish impromptu pillow fight. It was no wonder the mess's cushions were in such poor repair. They decided to exit the hospital via a side entrance on the first floor, passing no one other than a security guard on the way, and were thankful not to bump into Metern or one of the other two men.

The freshness of the cool morning air was a stark contrast to that of a stuffy hospital broom cupboard. The sun was bright in the sky and birds were in full voice, the seesaw call of the chiffchaff, the blackbird's beautiful melody and the odd wood pigeon cooing its amorous advances. They hadn't exchanged more than a word while walking through the hospital, and Tamsin's pace quickened as they walked back up past a wooded area to the car park. Will waited until they were back in the car before speaking.

"What did we just witness in there?" he asked, starting the engine. "I mean, that was definitely Metern, wasn't it?"

"Yes, it was," replied Tamsin, staring through the car's windscreen, "and it explains what Jen saw, the odd costumes and the ritual."

"But it wasn't witchcraft or satanic ritual, was it?" said Will.

"Does it matter?" said Tamsin.

"Sort of," said Will. "It looked like some kind of experiment or process to create whatever was in the vial – the golden liquid."

"Whatever he was doing, it was evil," said Tamsin, her features set hard. They drove on to where the road opened out onto the moor. There was a clarity to the light in the mornings that wasn't found at any other time of day.

"What about that child?" he asked. "It was already dead, wasn't it?"

"I'm pretty sure it was," she replied.

"And it was really small, looked considerably pre-term." A thought then occurred to Will. "Do you suppose that Metern has been running off with stillborn babies... and using their stem cells in his experiments?"

"A good way to source his stem cells, but what was all the kit for... his crystal ball, for example?" said Tamsin.

"Maybe the crystal ball was a focussing device. His paper suggested that specific wavelengths of radiation were required to splice DNA into the stem cells. Maybe that's what it did. After all, there doesn't have to be direct sunlight. Radiation can travel through a building as though it weren't there "

"But why eight times a year?"

Will gave it some thought. "That will probably be to do with harmonic frequencies. Suppose that to splice the DNA you need the resonant frequency of radiation energy produced on the longest day of the year, which occurs on the twenty-first of June. This is the fourth harmonic. The lower harmonic frequencies can be boosted to this level using a focussing device, in this case by probably varying the size of the crystal balls."

Tamsin didn't appear interested in Will's hypothesis. Instead, her reply was focussed on the perpetrator of the evening's event. "I'm still going to make sure he comes to justice." Her tone was slow and clipped. "I know now that Cadan Metern killed Jen. One way or another he will pay."

Chapter 35

Will made his way into Whitehorse separately from Tamsin later that morning. She had got up well ahead of Will to shower and change at her parent's house. They hadn't had much of a chance to talk through the events of the night, sleep engulfing them as soon as their heads hit the pillow. Will still felt in that vague dissociative state that characterised too little sleep. His brain was struggling to just keep the car on the road, let alone deal with the night's revelations. He supposed that the best course of action would be to go straight to the hospital's chief executive... Robert Jilks, was that his name? He felt a pang of anxiety. It wasn't going to be an easy day. He was a bit late. It was nine o'clock, technically the time he got paid from, even though he was expected to be on the ward usually by eight. But coffee, that's what was required first this morning, he thought, pulling into the car park.

Will took the lift, up to the seventh floor – the stairs seemed too much like effort – and went along to the mess. Even his bag weighed a tonne today. Bleary-eyed, it took him two attempts to punch in the correct code and he pushed the door open. He got halfway through before looking up and seeing the delegation of suited gentlemen standing before him, arms crossed with grim expressions on their faces. Mr Stoneman was one, there was a security guard, and wasn't that the Jilks bloke he'd been thinking about in the car only a short while ago? There were a few other doctors in the mess, but no one was talking, and the silence was only broken by the stirring of a coffee cup. Looking further around the room, he saw Tamsin, sitting hunched up in one of the chairs, her head in her hands. Had she already told them without him? Tamsin looked up. He could see she had been crying.

"Right," said the man who Will had assumed to be Jilks, "you two follow me." It was a barked order rather than a request. Tamsin got up from her chair. Stoneman and the guard also moved to follow.

"Is this about –?" Will began but got no further.

"– Just follow me!" The atmosphere of the situation and the tone of Jilks' voice suggested that whatever Tamsin had said had not gone down well... but then it wouldn't have done, would it. He looked worriedly at Tamsin, but she just stared at the floor.

They went over to the lift in silence. The ping from its eventual arrival was like a glass shattering on a tile floor. The button was pressed for the desired floor – "0": Basement. So, Tamsin had told them, and they were going to look over the scene. Was that it? Shouldn't the police have been called though, to do forensics or something? Granted they may not find much with the biohazard kit that had been worn, but there might be a bit of evidence left.

The lift slowed in the gentle, protracted way that hospital lifts did. The doors opened with a clack and Jilks stepped out in front of Will. He took two steps forward and stared aghast at the scene before him.

It was more reminiscent of a 'Hammer Horror' set than an archaeological site within the confines of a hospital. Blood and black feathers smeared the floor surrounding the mosaic and there was an unpleasant slightly metallic smell, like that of a butcher's shop, pervading the space. The owner, or rather ex-owner of the blood and feathers, a cockerel – Cornish Black by the looks of it – dangled upside down, suspended by a piece of string from the ceiling. Its throat had been cut. Congealed blood matted the feathers on its head, the rest now a red pool on the floor.

Will's attention moved from the floor to the glass wall of the chamber that faced them. A pentacle had been drawn a centimetre wide in blood, its symmetry marred somewhat by the points dripping and running towards the floor. Situated in its centre, affixed solidly with clear tape, was a wax doll, a poppet. The tape, Will noted, had rucked up like waves over the top of the effigy, squashing it slightly. A rivulet of blood had run from the uppermost point of the pentacle onto the doll's head. Encircling both the pentacle and the effigy, written using a feather dipped in blood, were the words "Cadan Metern killed Jen O'Connor". It was pretty gruesome, and while the blood and gore didn't upset Will particularly, the smell was beginning to get to him.

"Well," said Jilks, hands clasped in front of him, resting on his paunch. The word was spat out and he glared at Will.

"Well, what?" said Will. Then the realisation caught on. "Oh, hang on, you don't think I... we," he said, looking over at the taut-faced Tamsin, "had anything to do with this, do you?"

Tamsin looked blankly ahead of her.

"Did you?" asked Jilks. "You were in the hospital last night. Billy here" – he indicated the security guard on his left – "saw you leaving hospital premises at five thirty this morning, and you weren't on call."

Will hesitated for a moment, looking again at Tamsin, who just stared blankly into the room. "I... we were here last night, but because there's something really awful happening in this hospital. New-born babies are being –"

"– Killed, yes," his tone was dismissive as he cut in. "So, Miss Trevelyan was saying. *Again*." He emphasised the "again".

"That was looked into thoroughly at the time and the police were perfectly happy that nothing untoward was found."

"But," Will spluttered, "last night. A stillborn baby, at least I assume it was stillborn, was dismembered. Right there." He pointed to the middle of the chamber. "And it was done by Cadan Metern and two other people."

Jilks' face reddened and he exhaled forcibly. "Dr Cunningham, I'm not sure exactly what grievance *you* have against Dr Metern. We understand that Miss Trevelyan has some personal problems, some of which relate to Dr Metern. But you?"

"I'm telling you we saw something very concerning here last night." Will couldn't believe the way this man was thinking. "You must believe us. Yes, we were here last night, and yes, we saw something pretty horrific going on, but no, we did not do this, or have anything to do with it!"

Jilks shook his head. "We will, of course, look into what happened last night on the delivery suite, however, I'm afraid that the evidence suggests that you did."

"But I'm telling you we had nothing to do with this. You're missing the point here." Will's tone rose with his insistence.

"You were both here in the early hours of this morning, while, I would add, Dr Metern, who was vouched for by several different staff, was working up in the delivery suite. Miss Trevelyan, I believe, had a well-witnessed altercation with Dr Metern in the mess a few weeks ago, involving some sort of effigy or doll *and* Miss Trevelyan has allowed us to examine the contents of her bag, which was found to contain black chicken feathers. That would seem very much to be the point, Dr Cunningham!"

"I have no idea how those feathers got into her bag, and I doubt she does either, other than that someone else put them there." He couldn't keep the tremor from his voice. She wouldn't have been so stupid, would she, not again?

"Really?" said Jilks. He looked down at his shoes before licking his lower lip. "I understand you had another accident only a few days ago involving blood."

Will's head dropped. "Yes, I did, I dropped a bottle of blood."

"Down here?"

"Yes, down here," said Will, snorting. He felt frustration welling up inside him.

"In the basement?" Jilks paused. "And what, exactly, were you doing down here in the basement?" he asked.

Will looked over at Tamsin, wondering how much and exactly what she had told them. "I came to look at the mosaic and to look for a suitable hiding place. I'm sure Tamsin told you."

"She did, and how you came by the key, which in itself is a disciplinary offence." Jilks looked around the room at the assembled hierarchy. "Dr Cunningham, Miss Trevelyan, I think there are some very serious issues here. We will look into this matter further and see if we need to get the police involved or press charges."

"But wait, you have to –"

"– As I said, we will look into this fully." Will was cut dead once more. "But for the moment you are both suspended until further notice."

Will gasped and looked over to Mr Stoneman, who was just shaking his head and turning to go up the stairs. He looked over at Tamsin, who now gazed unflinchingly ahead of her. He was given a firm push in the middle of his back and headed off, dazed, to get his bag from the mess, accompanied by the security guard.

Chapter 36

They were called in a week or so later to see the chief executive after what he repeatedly referred to as a "full investigation" of the facts had been made. It was obvious that Mr Jilks was keen to avoid further tarnishing of the hospital's reputation, especially given recent events and well-publicised, worsening performance statistics. The police were not called in. Will and Tamsin had both been required to present written statements of the evening's events. Then they had been asked to amend their statements or provide some evidence for the serious allegations against Dr Metern. There was of course none.

The investigation had found nothing out of the ordinary that evening on the wards. Dr Metern had been involved in the sad case of a medical termination of a pregnancy. A routine scan at twenty weeks had revealed a foetal heart anomaly incompatible with life, and the mother had elected to have a termination, which at that later stage of pregnancy meant having to go through an induced labour. The poor mother had gone out of her way to praise the care and attention that Dr Metern specifically, had shown even working beyond his normal hours, such was his dedication. He had discussed the taking of biopsies from the baby to look for any chromosomal anomalies with the mother and father and done so with their full consent. Obviously, any trauma that the body had suffered was directly related to this, and Dr Cunningham should be aware of the importance of getting as much information as possible from such catastrophes. Any statement pertaining to the practice of witchcraft or occult rituals was to be rescinded, and no further mention of such nonsense was to be made.

It was understood that Tamsin in particular, had been through a very rough time recently, and this mitigated her actions somewhat but did not excuse them. They would endeavour to help her through it, perhaps with some counselling. Will had let his feelings for Tamsin get in the way of common sense; he should know better. Their actions down in the basement would be treated as a practical joke in very poor taste. Further misdemeanour, it was pointed out, would have significant consequences for their medical careers.

They had little option but to agree. Metern, for his part, was happy to accept an apology and guarantee that nothing like it would happen again; he agreed to say no more about it.

There was nowhere they could go, nothing they could do without risking their futures. The injustice irked Will, but Tamsin had taken it much more severely. She went through the motions of turning up on the wards, attending lectures and went to her counselling sessions, as she had been obliged to do. She didn't talk to Will much about it, if, in fact, about anything at all. She had locked herself away, emotionally if not physically, cocooning herself from the pain she was in. They still "went out", but Will was often left wondering if it was because she lacked the will or drive to do or change anything. It began to have a perfunctory feel, rather than anything that could be called a meaningful relationship. Yet despite this, he had continued to try to help, tried to get her to talk, to understand her thoughts, get her out of this downward spiral, but nothing had got through her wall. He loved her, he knew that, but now his heart ached for what might have been, not what was. All he could do was watch as she was swallowed by the waves of grief and guilt, destined, it seemed, to be cast up and dissolve away like the foam on a beach.

Chapter 37

It was 1st August and a low-pressure system had sat out in the mid-Atlantic for several days, with an area of high pressure off to the east. The full moon, spring tide and strong, westerly winds had combined, creating a powerful swell with mountainous waves that smashed against the coastline of the Southwest, ripping into the very fabric of Cornwall itself.

Will sat in the passenger seat of Tamsin's Peugeot as the wind pummelled and buffeted the car. Eerie, watery shafts of sunlight filtered through the blackening skies and droplets of sea spray peppered the windscreen. They turned into the beach road, then took a right turn just before Fistral Beach. It took them over a gentle rise before descending into a small, sheltered dip. Nestled at the bottom was the old lifeboat station, once the last hope of those at the mercy of the sea. Lifeboats hadn't launched from the building since 1934; more recently, it had served as an art studio. The grand wooden double doors, once big enough to allow the passage of the lifeboat, had been reduced to a fraction of the height and the lookout window above them had now been made into a property feature. The station stood on the leeward side of the small granite spur that rose gradually to the heather-clad headland and the octagonal lookout hut at its summit. Spray cascaded over this small peninsula that extended like a fist, towards the Cribbar Reef and a pounding like thunder shook the earth as a wave named The Widowmaker, hit the rocks at its tip offshore. Even sitting inside the moving car Will could feel the impact of the wave; the immense natural power and it filled him with a mix of awe and fear.

They pulled into a parking space on the right, one overlooking Newquay Bay, next to the lifeboat slipway. The isthmus at this point was only a few dozen metres across, and it felt as though one big wave may, on a whim, obliterate this thin strip of land in its entirety, toppling the headland into the sea. Tamsin switched off the engine, rested her hands on the steering wheel and stared out along the shoreline. It was that gaze into nothingness that Will had become all too accustomed to in recent times.

"Well, we're here," he said, forcing jollity into his voice in an attempt to break his girlfriend's fugue. She had been very quiet in the car on the way over, even more than usual. He'd thought, hoped, it was just the early hour. Receiving no acknowledgement, he followed with words that he seemed to have used a hundred times of late, "Tamsin are you OK?"

"Yeah fine," she replied, rubbing her forehead, "let's get out." She pulled the handle, and her door flew open as it caught the wind, dragging her out. Will had to push hard on his side to create a gap big enough to get through, and the door slammed shut as he got clear of the car. It was as though the elements only wished for the presence of one of them. Showers of watery splinters bit into his face as he rounded the bonnet and fought his way round to where Tamsin stood a short way away from the car. The wind clawed at her hair, whipping it behind her into an angry, serpentine frenzy. He walked in front of her then turned to offer some little protection from the wind. Her eyes narrowed and looked past him to the huge waves rearing up in the distance, manes of spray streaming off their tops. Will watched her, following her gaze. She had scanned Fistral Bay and was now tracking back past the headland and the jutting granite crags, out to the open sea, to the Cribbar Reef. He nudged her, trying to get her attention, but she was oblivious.

"Come on," he said, "shall we take a trip to the top of the headland and get a proper look."

She didn't move, remaining fixed on that point on the horizon. He walked forward a step, tugging at her coat this time.

"Tamsin?" he said again. "Are you coming?" She remained focussed ahead, unmoving. "We *have* driven all this way. We should have a look."

There was still no reaction, no movement. Was she deliberately ignoring him, the way she had been of late? "Tamsin, are you sure you're OK? Is something wrong?"

A gull landed precariously on the rocks in front of them, but unable to maintain purchase, it took off and headed for the relative safety of the town.

"Tamsin?"

Her face was wet with the sea spray, but she remained unflinching, unblinking, disconnected, deathly still.

"Tamsin!" His voice was raised now, piercing above the wind, and he put his hands to her shoulders, turning her to face him.

It broke her concentration. He was about to speak again but she put her hands up and softly, very gently, lowered his arms. "Will," she said, her eyes meeting his for the first time, he realised, in weeks, "I can hear it summoning me."

Will felt a chill inside, the hint of a realisation.

"It's telling me that it is time," she said.

A dread began to worm its way through him. "Time? Time for what?" Will looked back at her, strangely desperate not to know, not to have an answer, to maintain the pretence that she would merely suggest that they should go back into Newquay and go for a coffee. Don't tell me and it doesn't have to be.

"It's time for me to go," she said.

This cannot be happening, surely she cannot be thinking this. He felt sick; it was the way she was staring beyond the headland. Why hadn't this occurred to him before this moment in time, so that he might have had some way of preventing it?

Because this is how it must be.

He'd agreed to put the surf kit in the car, but only because that's what you did if you went to the beach. It didn't mean you were definitely going to use it. There might have been the unlikely chance of a paddle in the white stuff, close to shore but...

"Go where?" he heard himself say.

"Oh, you know, Will."

"I don't," he replied, stubbornly, "I *don't* know what you mean."

Her smile was thin, her reply, patient, "You know that I must go out there." Her eyes flicked out into the bay – her lips continued moving and he thought that she might have mouthed, "We both must," but he wasn't sure. He decided not to trust his lip-reading skills and responded dismissively, "You aren't serious?"

"I am Will, very serious. A trial must be held and in the ancient way now. Judgment must be passed, and penance paid; a sacrifice."

"You're talking nonsense," said Will, snorting. "Tamsin, honestly, I don't know what you mean. What trial? I don't understand..." He heard his voice crack and reached out putting a hand on her shoulder, but she felt rigid in his grasp, and he immediately let go. "Please Tamsin," his tone was softer, "you haven't done anything wrong; you have nothing to stand trial over. You have nothing to answer for. You're just... confused."

She looked down and ran a hand through her hair sweeping it back before looking him in the eye again. "Will, my sweet Will," she said, a deep sadness in her voice, "can either of us really understand what it is to have poison seep through to your very core, eating away at your soul, twisting and destroying your mind."

Will shook his head and frowned, not quite following.

"No, I don't think that *we* can, but Jen could," Tamsin continued. "You see, I know now that she had worked out what Metern had done to her after her accident – once she had managed to piece together her fractured memories. I know that she realised that he had taken the opportunity to inject her with his potion when she was unconscious. She was his little experiment," Tamsin sneered. "Sure, he maintained that it had been the only way to save her life, when she had confronted him but that was just a lie. It was really just a convenient way for him to test out the serum and any side effects would be put down to her fall and nothing more."

She rubbed a palm on her brow, "It was obvious that night when we saw what Metern was doing with the stillborn infant, saw the purpose of his rituals, looked at that hideous golden vial and I knew that what Jen had tried to tell me was true. It wasn't her accident; it wasn't her memory playing tricks. I knew that what she had told me *was* true." Her eyes closed momentarily, "I just didn't try hard enough to believe her... to understand... when I had had the chance."

A gust of wind hit, nearly taking Will off his feet. Tamsin remained fixed, the wind seeming to pass straight through her.

She dropped her head, "I didn't listen to her. No, I was too wrapped up in betraying her, my best friend." Tamsin spat out her self-loathing.

"She knew that I'd slept with him, you know –" Tamsin looked Will hard in the eyes, almost in a challenge, "– her reaction when I arrived on the Hoe and..." Tamsin stared off into the distance again, a choked laugh sticking in her throat. "And I... I suggested that she shouldn't make up such lies, that it was her head playing up again." A single tear escaped, rolling down her face, losing itself in the sea spray on her cheek. "She would probably still be alive if I'd just confessed, owned up. My cowardice was the reason that I said we should take separate cars back from Plymouth and why I lost her in the traffic. I *wanted* to lose her because I didn't want to face her or support her when she needed me the most." Her head dropped. "It's why I wasn't there to stop Metern silencing her. Ultimately, all I did was betray her. I am as much to blame as him." She looked down at her feet.

Will put his hands on her shoulders again, turning her to face him, lifting her chin. "Tamsin, look at me. Whatever happened *isn't* your fault. You can't have known. With what Jen was saying, you would have *had* to think it was as a result of her accident. I think that she must have suffered a serious brain injury despite the negative scans. You know that they don't always show up positive, particularly if the scan is done too soon, and you know that such injuries can have all sorts of after-effects: hallucinations, mood disorders, as well as epileptic absences."

"And my betrayal, Will," her emerald eyes glistened, "you haven't said anything about that?"

Will sighed, "We all make mistakes, tell lies, often to the ones we love the most. We can't always see or know the consequences of our actions..." He put his hand up in case Tamsin was about to protest.

She was not.

"... But we must live with them and try to make amends," Will finished.

Another forced smile. "And that is what I intend to do," she replied.

Wrong conclusion. This wasn't working. He felt his throat tighten and waved his arms in a gesture towards the sea, "Tamsin, going out there and throwing away your life will not bring her back, or do anything to stop Metern."

"No, it won't bring her back, but you're wrong about Metern," she said, with some force, "that is exactly what will happen." She paused. "Do you know what the date is, Will?"

"No, why? Why would that matter?"

"It is the first of August, Lammas," Tamsin said, "the day when a single sacrifice may be made, so that the many may benefit."

"Oh please!" said Will, more sternly than he'd intended. He felt angry now. "That's just rubbish! All of that witchcraft stuff is. It's messed your head up and your ability to think straight."

Her lips pulled thin, "No, Will, I didn't expect you to understand yet, but you will. It is what must be. It is what has been demanded of me." Her voice was firm.

Will looked into her eyes; the tears had stopped, to be replaced, it seemed, by a fierce resolve. The anger in Will's heart melted away, an icy physical pain replacing it. The wind howled about them as another squall blew in.

"I *am* going to ride the Cribbar," she said.

The ground vibrated with the impact of a wave and water showered over the top of them.

"Tamsin," he said, trying one last time, "just wait for one moment, listen to what you're saying. You can't go out there, look at it."

Another massive surge hit the granite cliff, shaking the earth, drenching the vegetation.

"I must," she replied.

"Please, no." He took a step towards her, "Just think. The wave will still be here in a few hours. It may even be a bit more manageable then. When it drops off, you could go in then."

"But that's why I have to go now." She reached up and gently stroked his cheek, wiping the tears that he now realised fell from his eyes. "It's OK, really it is."

Will stood, eyes burning, his mind reeling. Scenes flashed before his mind's eye, all of the futures, all at once. Possibilities, probabilities all invaded his head. Images of Tamsin flickered before him, the shadow of light and dark engulfing her. None of them helped. None told him what the outcome would be. Whether she would survive. He toyed with the idea of grabbing her board and jumping on it, snapping it in two.

You must let this happen; this is what must be. He felt rather than heard the words within him... *It must be now.*

"Right then, I'll come too," he heard himself say.

She looked up at him, then dropped her gaze to the ground. "OK," she said.

The sky seemed to darken as they returned to the car. Greyness had turned to black and gone were the shafts of light. Tamsin turned the key in the lock, springing the doors open, then climbed lightly onto the footboard to untie the board straps. Will pulled the wetsuits from the plastic box in the back of the car and laid them out. The boards were lowered carefully, onto the tarmac beside him, to be partly sheltered by the car. He was aware of Tamsin stepping down, the car rocking slightly as she did so. She picked up her suit and reached past him for her gloves; there was the hint of her perfume on the wind. As he stripped off and put a leg into the suit. It was still damp, and he felt the little grains of sand rub on his skin. He looked over at Tamsin, already putting her arms into the sleeves. Was she really so keen to go? He zipped himself up.

A gull cried forlornly overhead. Was it the same one as earlier? Tamsin picked up her board and she locked the car, putting the key under the rear tyre. She looked up at Will as she did so. So that I know where it is, he thought.

They walked the short distance to where the old lifeboat slipway led out to the sea. The old, rusted, ironwork track, cemented into the rock, led steeply between the rocks and down into the churning water five metres below. This was the place to get in. A rip current would take them up the leeward side of the headland and reduce the distance and effort to get out to the reef. It would be much more difficult, maybe impossible, to go from the Fistral side. They clambered down the slipway, lifting the boards clear of the rocks, before reaching a flat ledge off to one side, a metre or so above the waterline. The ocean's roar seemed magnified, echoing back off the small amphitheatre created by the rock face behind them.

"Tamsin, don't go," he said quietly. Tears smeared his vision. She turned to face him, tears too in her eyes.

"I'm sorry," she said, "but I have to."

"You'll die," he said.

"Maybe, but if I don't go, I'll never truly be alive again." She brushed a wisp of his hair from his face.

"Then at least promise to *try* to come back."

She bent down and attached her leash to her ankle, and as she straightened, he saw the spark – that fire he had thought dead, re-ignite in her amber-flecked eyes. They blazed with a certainty and belief that he had never seen within her before. "I will," she said, and then, kissing him, "I promise." She picked up her board, turned, and without looking back, launched from the earth into the air where the water rose to meet her, engulfing her and sucking her out into the churning black maelstrom below.

Will didn't even go to the pretence of picking up his board. He wasn't going in, something inside him stopped him. She, it seemed, knew he wasn't going to be following her. Was he guilty of cowardice too?

He watched the small figure paddle out, her metronomic stroke slicing through the water until, with a wave approaching, she threw her weight forward to sink the tip of the board as deep as possible, timing the duck-dive as it arrived. Will found himself counting the seconds, five... six... seven... until she surfaced and began paddling again before the next wave hit. She was being carried quickly by the rip current, and he ran back up the slipway to the car park, dragging his board behind him, then throwing it down by the car, no care for any dents that he put into it. Facing towards the headland, he sprinted along the well-worn path between the heather banks that tracked the cliff edge, his eyes fixed on the bobbing form. God, that rip was fast, he was struggling to keep pace. Rocks and heather on the rough, uneven path disappeared under his neoprene-clad feet and he strove to more his feet quicker, be faster, to keep her in view. Taking his eyes of the path he saw that she was opting to go over the top of the next wave travelling up the face and then out of sight once more as she disappeared over the crest. He strained his eyes, half blinded by driving, stinging spray desperate to follow her, holding his breath in empathy as she went under, gasping as she surfaced once more.

He didn't see the root that felled him. There was just a searing pain in his right foot and an audible crack as it stopped abruptly, and he hit the ground hard missing the potential cushioning of the heather, instead landing on solid stone. He let out a yell, cursing his carelessness, then gritted his teeth and picked himself up to continue up the slope to the point. There was a sickening crunching sensation coming from two of his toes as he did so.

Hobbling badly, he managed to get himself up the hill to the lookout-point and he gripped the protective railings as he scoured the water beneath him. It took thirty seconds, maybe more, before he finally spotted her. The rip had carried her around to the tip of the headland before casting her out into the true fury of the Cribbar. He felt nausea rise within him: the sea was mountainous. She duck-dived, seeking any meagre refuge in the wave's base, away from the barrelling lip, knowing that a miss-timing would mean being caught under a huge weight of water, plenty enough to shatter every bone in her body. A wave thumped into the rock face and he felt the percussive effect shake his whole body as he was deluged with salt water, but wiped his eyes and resumed his vigil, his heart pounding as he saw her rise only to disappear from view.

Minutes passed. His eyes flitted up and down each wave in turn, tracking its progression as it grew, crested, and broke. Occasionally, the swell would drop a fraction and he could see slightly further, but still there was nothing. More minutes passed. He moved around the headland to the Fistral Bay side. Where was she? Where?

As he searched, his mind again played with the past, how he might have recognised what was going to happen, foreseen the pattern, maybe tried to change it. That was, after all, what he did, wasn't it? It was what he had come to rely on, his mind throwing up all the potential futures so that little or nothing surprised him? He'd already worked out the solution to a problem before it arrived. So how had he missed this?

Except he hadn't. He hadn't missed this. Buried deep, he knew that whatever he had foreseen or done, he couldn't have stopped her. Not with what he had known, with the way his mind had interpreted events. And now, she was testing fate or destiny or whatever she chose to call it. Placing herself in the balance between life and death, an ancient trial by ordeal, catharsis. A part of him did understand. The irrational, non-scientific, intuitive side that made decisions based on a hunch, not a set of data: what would work and what wouldn't, a feeling of what was right and what was wrong. It was the same side that knew when there might be no course of action, other than for a soul to visit hell itself, to feel cleansed of its wrongdoing: maybe the side that made you human. That was why he hadn't picked up on it. Events had already been set in motion a few months before he had arrived at Whitehorse, maybe a long time before that. There was nothing he could have done.

He scanned the waves. Another set hammered through, and then there was a lull, another set, then a lull. He kept looking.

In the distance beyond the break, he saw a figure, *her figure* sitting on her board. He watched, losing sight of her as the swell sank underneath her, dipping deep below the horizon, before she appeared again, driven up, propelled over the peak. She sat poised, glancing over her shoulder, readying herself to harness the might of the ocean. Stamina and determination had got her out there. Skill, balance, and courage would get her back.

From his elevated position, Will could see another huge set coming in. It was monstrous. Not this one, Will thought. You haven't recovered enough from the paddle out. Not yet, it's too big. But he could see from the way she was setting up that she intended to take it on, the first wave, the biggest of the set. He held his breath as she paddled to get up to speed, her arms powering through the water. He saw the wave lift her, and the board seemed to climb backwards, defying the natural laws of gravity as it travelled up the face and he watched as she popped, effortlessly up onto the board, immediately angling it into the wave, the rail cutting into the face. She was a silhouetted speck against the immense black wall now chasing behind her, like Satan's maw.

The angle gained her some height, flying her up the wave in time to avoid being trapped in the wave's base, then she shot back down as the lip furled, the white crest beginning to barrel, teeth in closing behind her. She cut back up once again, seeming to dance in front of the Devil as he pursued his quarry, hunting her down... but Tamsin stayed just out of reach. Will could hear the roar, watched the spittle fly, felt the pent-up power. She hurtled across the face, a streak of white against the all-consuming mass, the challenge thrown down, daring it to catch her if it could.

The wave hit a shallower outcrop of the reef, slowing its base, and sending its mass steepling upward. Momentum carried this mass forward and gravity pulled the apex over and down as its centre passed beyond perpendicular, beyond the vertical plane of the base, and the lip dropped. The small figure, he could see, had anticipated this, and now sank lower as the tubular vortex barrelled over the top of her. The apex crashed into the base, throwing up a huge white plume, and Will held his breath as Tamsin was swallowed. He watched as the barrel closed behind her, eyes skipping to the open end, where the pressure of air compressing inside the tube would spit her out... should spit her out. He waited... and waited, mentally tracking her progress through the tube, watching as the barrel closed from left to right... and then to his horror, he saw the far end of the tube closing prematurely and the wave began to collapse. Tonnes and tonnes of water began to land like wet cement, the tube crumpling like a drink can under foot... it was a weight, Will knew, that would be flattening anything contained within it. It would flatten Tamsin.

Will felt something rip deep inside him, well aware of the consequences of that mass of water landing on a fragile human body. The power and forces involved were immense and that did not consider the fact that a person would, more than likely, be held under the water for far longer than a breath might be held. He let out a cry; it was deep, guttural, and primeval, the rawest of basic emotion, and it felt as though his soul was being torn from his body. He screamed again and collapsed to his knees, the rock cutting into his wetsuit, and he vomited, spewing his pain and shock over the unfeeling, uncaring granite in front of him. Reality struck. Until now, he had felt as though all of this was some bizarre nightmare from which he would, at some point, awaken. None of this had seemed real. And now he had, and it was. His mind spun. Had some part of him really expected her to ride the Cribbar? Pop up, ride the wave and see him on the beach. Really, despite all those images and scenarios that had played in his mind? Really?

Yet he had.

Will lifted his head and looked at the sea.

You need to act now.

This was no good. Stop this, get up, pull yourself together and do something. Maybe it still didn't have to be this way; maybe he would see her emerge on her board, having somehow avoided being crushed and she would shoot out in the white-water on the other side of the isthmus. He had to hang on to this hope and started off again, limping along the cliff edge, staring intently at the water as he went, head jerking left and right, back and forth across the sea in front of him, willing his senses to work harder, become more acute, pick up any signs of her. His pulse raced and he could hear his breath rasp as he shouted impotently into the wind, called out Tamsin's name. He tripped, and a sharp jab of pain shot up his leg from the injured foot, but, blowing hard and gritting his teeth, he carried on, the foot dragging behind him. He made it to the Fistral Beach side of the outcrop and stopped to scan the surf once more. Just a sign, just something, give him just... something.

Several hundred metres offshore his attention was caught by a different movement in the water. There was a solid patch of white – not surf or foam, it was too well defined, didn't appear to shift or disperse with the sea's motion. He strained his eyes. It seemed to bob on top of the water, there was definite shape to it, but it wasn't quite right. His brain processed the image and he felt his heart sink. It was her board... or what was left of it. Tossed and thrown and in the process of being given up by the ocean; it was snapped almost in two, its leash flailing free. There was no sign of Tamsin.

Will knew that somewhere he had played this scenario in his head, and in it he had gone back to call for help. Get the coastguard, do the sensible thing. Maybe he should already have called them; why hadn't he done so? But now he knew; the coastguard would be too late. It was pointless. Without her board she would be pulverised by the waves, held under, and drowned. All that they would be doing was collecting a dead body... that was if rescuers could get here at all. He looked about him as the storm seemed to increase in strength: the wind howled around his ears; the rain now being driven horizontally. He knew there were limits to what the services could go out in themselves.

She was in the white-water somewhere; he sensed it – a hundred metres away, maybe two. He looked at the waves still hammering in. He took a deep breath. There was only one option left, the one he had never really thought he would take, had never seen himself taking. He turned and went to fetch his board. He would ignore the pain in his foot. He would ignore it and he would go. He would try to bring her back.

The board by his feet, he bent to attach his leash and saw blood oozing through the neoprene sock. The foot was broken, possibly quite badly, but he would just have to cope. He surveyed the rocks, looking for the easiest place to get in. His timing would have to be perfect, or he would end up smashed against the granite wall. He glanced up. He could still see Tamsin's board being played with in the way a cat plays with a dead mouse, for practice, for sport. Another wave pounded the rocks. He would go on the next one. He crouched, board in both hands, ready to throw it under him and land on the outgoing water. Ready, ready...

A hand grabbed his shoulder as he was about to leap and pulled him back. He was twisted around and caught off balance, once again jarring his foot, and he cried out with the pain. It took a moment to steady himself before he was able to turn fully... and then he did so... to look directly up into the face of Cadan Metern.

The hand held Will firmly, preventing any intention to move. Metern looked back at Will, his eyes brooking no argument.

"No," he said, his voice calm, clear. "Not you. Not now." The wind whipped at the man's dark hair, tousled and unruly. Will started to open his mouth, to protest, but then he looked at the knife in Metern's hand as it moved towards him, then watched as it dipped to reach for the tail of Will's board and its leash. He sliced through it easily and snapped a fin for good measure, rendering the board useless.

"Go and get help," Metern instructed.

Will stood for a moment, uncomprehending, watching Metern as the man bent down, replacing the knife in a sheath at his ankle. Metern's board lay a few metres away and he retrieved it, attaching his own leg strap, then he urged Will, "Quickly! Go!"

Will looked in the direction of The Headland Hotel and turned just in time to see Metern take two strides and leap off the rock and into the ocean below. Will froze for a moment, trying to work out what was happening. There was no following Metern in, not with the state his board was now in. He would have done but, he realised, that would almost certainly have left at least two people floating around out there knocked off their boards... drowned. So, he did as he had been told and set off towards the hotel.

Will burst through the doors at the rear of the grand Victorian building, sandy, wet, bloodstained footprints trailing in his wake. The smartly uniformed woman sitting behind the oversized reception desk looked up, her face a mix of bewilderment and horror. She looked to be about to admonish Will for any number of transgressions, but he didn't give her a chance. He heard himself demand rather than ask for the phone, stating the emergency, and she just reached across the desk and thrust the receiver into his hand.

There was no let-up in the wind as Will ran back to the top of Fistral Beach, if anything it was getting even stronger. It drove into his back, now bitingly cold, and he could see it picking up the waves to greater and greater magnitudes. He stood at what he had worked out was the most likely point at which Metern would get back to the beach. If he got back to the beach. There would be no risking a return to the rocks. It would be like jumping out of a moving car and landing on shards of broken glass.

The surf still pounded in, the white-water still seethed and fumed, angry that its journey should be halted by its nemesis, the land. Will came to the edge of sand and stood motionless, watching, helpless to do anything more. How long had it been since Metern went in after Tamsin? How long had she been out there, on her own with no board? It might have been five minutes; it might have been fifteen – he had no idea – yet time was critical. How could he lose track of something so vital? He felt his muscles taut, primed with adrenaline, adrenaline with which he could do nothing. There was a tightening sensation in his chest, his head felt floaty, and the world became unreal. Surely this wasn't happening.

His mind drifted, searching for answers... arriving at Metern. What was he doing here? The same as them, just come for a look? Why did he go in to try to rescue her? An alarming thought occurred to him. Maybe he'd gone in to make sure she never came out again. But, he thought, his heart sinking, there was little chance she would be making it out anyway. Why risk your own life when the odds were stacked so heavily in your favour to start with?

He squatted down, face in his hands, wishing that somehow Tamsin might be saved – save them both, now it came to it. Seconds, or was it minutes, ticked by. It had been so long. The panic he had felt was turning to something far worse. A tremor shook his body. He felt bile rise again. Somebody, somewhere do something. Where was the coastguard, the ambulance, anyone? Wind drove into his face, stripping his skin. He shivered and had never felt so alone, without hope.

Another gull flew overhead, its mocking, pitiless shriek driving a rapier through him. Nature herself had turned against them. He looked at his wet hands, now icy cold, mottled blue, covered in sand and so numb. He let out a sob, and his mind, normally so active, providing comment and advice about everything that he did, went silent. There were no images, no scenarios; it was empty; there was nothing.

Will looked about him, body and mind oddly detached. He looked up at the sky and down at the beach, then at the sea, dispassionately registering the elemental power and natural forces to which he bore witness. So raw, probably quite spectacular.

No one can survive out there, not without help, but you must ask. You know how to ask.

His inner voice spoke to him again as he stared out at a fixed point, the waves passing through his field of vision unnoticed. Minutes passed. He was feeling nothing now, registering nothing. Numbness stroked at his mind and body, a comforting blanket. It would be so easy to give up, just no longer care. The numbness beckoned him in. His shoulders slumped and his jaw relaxed. He knew his foot still hurt but it didn't seem to hurt *him*. The crashing waves, the howling wind – they were around him but weren't part of his world any longer.

His vision closed in, and he felt as though he were looking down a tunnel. Dimly, distantly, he became aware of another voice, much quieter, it seemed, than the first. It wasn't informing or instructing him – there were no words. In fact, it wasn't addressing him at all. It felt like a... prayer – that was it, a sort of prayer. He listened. It didn't seem to be to any specific god or deity and didn't concern any specific religion or faith. He became aware that his lips were moving. The voice, he realised, came from him. It *was* him, and it called to whatever *might* be out there, around him; unseen, hidden, occult. The voice beseeched that *if* it were out there and could see their plight, to take pity on them, on Tamsin and Metern, not to take vengeance, not to judge, not to kill, but to help, protect and save.

The voice died away. Will's senses rushed back to him and he dropped to the ground. His hands fell upon a sandy piece of rope, flotsam discarded from some fishing boat, and he twisted it around his fingers. He felt the strands tighten, felt them bite sharply, cutting white-edged incisions into his flesh, and he watched as blood tried to well up in the cuts. He felt the pain bring him back.

His mind switched on and the images started to return. A picture in a section of the museum: "Charms and Spells of the Sea". He could see bladderwrack, coral, aquamarine, rope. He felt the rope in his fingers and twisted harder; it bit in further. He saw sailors and witches, charms and knotted rope, rope to bind the wind. Untie a knot, release the wind. It had to get in there in the first place, he thought, tie a knot to bind it. He took the rope again, and with all his might, he willed the wind to cease as he looped the rope around itself and tied the knot. Grabbing the loose end, he then tied another knot, then another and another, knot after knot. In his mind he bound it with the seaweed, the coral and the semiprecious gem. He felt the grains of sand run through his fingers as he did so, felt the drops of seawater squeezed from the hemp mingle with his blood, which now ran freely from his wound. As he pulled each knot tight, he felt the wind blowing through his hands and around the rope. He forced the wind to be bound, each tightening loop, each forming knot trapping the power of the storm. *His* concentration, *his* will forcing down nature, he felt energy surge through his body, banishing the cold, and then channel through his fingers and down into the rope... and he saw an image of Tamsin. It spun and reeled just like the dancers on this same beach several months ago, but there was no colour, no gaiety, only a flickering form, writhing through shades of light and dark.

He opened his eyes, looking at the bloodstained knots he'd tied, and was aware of the stillness, the absence of noise. Yes, the sound of the ocean was there, but the deafening roar of the wind... had gone, replaced by a light breeze. The storm had, for the moment... eased.

A distant movement caught his eye, there off the point. A flash of brilliant white, brighter than any foam. His eyes strained... He could see a figure kneeling, hands clutching the rails of the board, fighting to keep the board from being tipped. Will watched it battle to stay upright, then awareness fully returned to him and he started to run down the beach. Hope sprang up in his heart. The board got closer and he could make out a second figure lying face down on the board, arms pinned in place by the knees of the upright figure. Will started to sprint, all pain, all numbness forgotten, hurtling down the beach. Metern had her. He had reclaimed Tamsin and was bringing her back from the sea.

Will waved, shouting, and skirted the shoreline ready to run in and help, his eyes fixed on Metern, willing him to safety. A secondary breaking wave took the board, shunting it forward, spray flying up around it. Metern fought the top-heavy vessel's inclination to tip and kept it on course, dropping his weight back to keep the nose up. Then, suddenly, as though something gave, the sea released them, allowing them to go, propelling them gently on a smooth, calm, white wave to the land. Will rushed forward as Metern jumped off, unstrapping the ankle leash as he did so. Will steadied the board and looked down at Tamsin's unmoving form.

"Take her in," Metern said, urgently, breathing heavily, "and start CPR. She was just about conscious when I got to her, but I don't think she's breathing now." He thrust the board into Will. "I'll be back very shortly." He sprinted off up the beach as Will pulled the board aground and picked up the unconscious girl. He carried her to shore and lowered Tamsin onto the sand. The training, practised hundreds of times, kicked in. He checked her airway. Clear. He checked her breathing. Nothing. Circulation? There was no pulse. He started with two mouth breaths and then the chest compressions, fingers interlocked pressing just below the centre of her chest. Fifteen compressions, two breaths. Check pulse... breathing... nothing... fifteen compressions... two breaths. Where was the rescue service? Where was Metern? Thirteen, fourteen, fifteen... two breaths. Check for breathing... pulse... nothing. Continue.

Will worked on automatic. How many times had he done this in hospital – hundreds? He didn't know. How many had been brought back in those ideal circumstances? One or two in ten? But he wasn't in hospital and he had no drugs and, more importantly, no electricity. It was the defibrillator that made the difference and saved lives, an early shock. He looked at the pale, blue-lipped face, streaked with seawater and sand, and it hit him. It was like a punch to his stomach. This wasn't some faceless drunk swept up off the street or some generic businessman found collapsed in his room. This was Tamsin Trevelyan, vibrant, beautiful, Tamsin Trevelyan, his Tamsin. He knew this person, and he loved this person. It was all wrong. This didn't happen to people *he* knew, *he* loved. People *he* knew didn't die. Thirteen, fourteen, fifteen... two breaths. Will looked at her as he was happening to Tamsin.

He heard feet behind him and Metern landed next to him, spraying up sand. In his hand was his knife, a syringe and a vial, a familiar vial, containing a golden fluid that he'd seen several weeks ago. Metern looked at Will, who continued his compressions.

"Will," he said, softly, placing a hand gently on his arm. "Will, listen." Will looked up but continued the compressions. He was afraid to meet those eyes. "Will, she isn't going to make it, not like this." He paused, searching Will's face. "It's been too long." He hesitated again. "I... we, *can* give her a chance, the possibility of life." He held up the golden liquid in the vial. "What is in here can give her that chance."

Will stared at it, watched the liquid roll around the inside of the vial, the satanic fluid brewed from death. That vial was why they were here now.

"Will, whatever you think of me, have heard or seen, know that what is in here is her only hope, but we need to act quickly. There isn't much time."

Tears of desperation filled Will's eyes, and the tube seemed to swim before him. He knew Metern was right about one thing. He'd been witness to this scenario many, many times. She wasn't coming back. Whatever he did he would lose her. Whatever emergency service turned up now, she was dead. This time he wouldn't be able to nip off and have a cup of coffee and discuss the latest advances in wetsuit technology without sparing a second thought. This time it would be he who would receive those pitiful condolences, those inadequate words. It would be his existence that would be ripped apart, never to fit together again, no matter how much time passed. Whatever was in that vial, it couldn't make things worse, could it? Death was as bad as it got, wasn't it? He looked at Tamsin then into Metern's eyes again and nodded.

The knife slipped through the neoprene of Tamsin's wetsuit, edge uppermost, and cut up the front, exposing her neck.

"Keep up the chest compressions," said Metern, as he drew up the contents of the vial into the syringe. He flicked at it a couple of times to dispel any bubbles and palpated the side of her neck. The needle sank in and there was a red flush indicating he'd located it in the internal jugular vein. Will watched as he depressed the plunger, sending the liquid into Tamsin's cardiovascular system.

Will kept up the chest compressions: fifteen-two... check... nothing. Fifteen-two... check... nothing. Then, as Will completed another set and felt for the pulse, there was a flicker and he saw colour flood her face. A moment later she coughed. He rolled her onto her side and she coughed again. Will looked at Metern, who sat back on his haunches.

The throb of a Westland Sea King helicopter, in the grey and red colours of the Royal Navy, drew Will to his feet, and he waved furiously, signalling that they had Tamsin. The message got through and it circled before coming in to land on the headland by the hotel. Will watched as two men got out carrying equipment packs on their backs and walked slowly down towards them. Will controlled the urge to scream at them to hurry.

"Probably best not mention anything except the CPR," said Metern as he stood up.

Will looked back at him, pausing before nodding. "OK."

The airmen arrived. One of the team went straight into action, going through the advanced life support algorithms, got the oxygen on, cut off the rest of her wetsuit to get ECG leads on and wrap her in an insulation blanket. The other team member, probably more senior, went through events and timings. Will skipped over the events that had led to Tamsin "going for a quick surf", but he could see the ill-disguised look of disbelief on the guy's face, that anyone would even contemplate such an act of stupidity in these conditions. It took a couple of minutes, no longer, and at one point, Will turned to confirm a few facts with Metern. He was nowhere in sight.

The senior airman finished taking his history and went to check on Tamsin's status. Will stood back, letting them get on with their job. It was what they were trained to do. He looked down at the diminutive face, now cocooned in silver, a few strands of seaweed like stray, green ribbons running down her cheeks under the oxygen mask. She looked at peace. In the background, the sirens of a terrestrial ambulance announced its arrival and a couple more paramedics made their way down onto the beach. Snippets of conversation suggested that they were surprised that the helicopter had got through - the weather had broken very fortuitously. Will found he was still clutching the rope in one hand. That question would have to be considered another time. He tied it loosely around his wrist.

There was discussion between the two crews and a decision reached that she was stable but precarious, so they would fly her to hospital. This would most likely be Whitehorse, but the helicopter crew would contact control, who would let them know once in flight.

Will stepped back and watched as the rotor blades spun and the engine whine heightened into a deafening roar. Slowly, it lifted vertically into the air before spinning the fuselage around and heading into the clouds. There had been no room for passengers in the helicopter and Will was forced to watch it disappear, wondering if he would see Tamsin alive again.

He turned to find out where Metern had gone. Hunting around, Will caught sight of the tall figure watching from the crest of the beach road. He had retrieved his board, which now stood planted at his side. It gleamed against the backdrop of the pitch-black sky, a beacon of white against the darkness of the storm beyond.

Chapter 38

Will's foot hurt like fury as he hobbled up the hill to where Metern stood. Now that the adrenaline was wearing off, sensation was flooding back. Man, it was sore. Metern made no move towards Will, or to speak, but he stood upright with his head bowed, one hand still clutching his board. The man's face was drawn, the scar on his face shimmered an angry red. Water dripped from the matted ends of his hair and he seemed to be studying the ripples made as the droplets landed in the puddle at his feet.

Metern looked up, and Will looked again into those salt-reddened eyes; narrowed, resigned.

"Thank you," said Will, breaking the silence, "for going to get her, I mean, and..." – he hesitated – "and giving her a chance."

Metern nodded, offering no reply.

Will observed the supposed murderer of infants, the minister of satanic rites, the orchestrator of their fall from grace and the man responsible for Tamsin now lying on a stretcher, hovering above the earth, somewhere between life and death.

"Why?" Will blurted out. He hadn't consciously formulated the question.

Metern drew his foot through the puddle. "Why what?" he asked, then shrugged. "Why go and get her, risk my life, save her?" He puffed out his cheeks.

Will waited. Was that the answer to the question that he had wanted to ask?

Metern dipped his head, "I did what I did because I" – he paused, looking at Will – "couldn't let her… or you, die. I didn't feel either of you were destined to die today. Besides," he sniffed, "it was a calculated risk for me. I was always likely to make it back again."

"Oh?" said Will – but no one was that good a surfer. His brain spun the possibilities. Then it hit him. "The vial, you've injected…?"

Metern nodded.

That might explain why he went in, but it didn't explain his presence on the beach in the first place. "Cadan, why? Why were you here? You *were* coming here already, right?" Will said, "Of your own volition? I mean," he hesitated, "no one had asked you? Tamsin hadn't…"

Metern snorted, "No, she hadn't… not *directly* asked me. However, I was," he was struggling to find the words, "compelled to be here," he said and dropped eye contact.

"You mean that you felt drawn to surf the hardest wave?" said Will, conscious of what had really caused Tamsin to put her life on the line, but not willing to divulge anything about it. "But you weren't seriously also going to ride it were you?" He would not have got out beyond the break from the Fistral side, yet that was where he had been.

Metern flattened a resigned smile, "No, not really," he replied, "I was probably only going to have a paddle in the white stuff."

Will raised his eyebrow. That wasn't true.

Metern gave him a thinly veiled smile in return. He knew Will knew that there was something more but wasn't, Will thought, prepared to say. He let it go, his concern returning to Tamsin. "Is she going to be… alright?"

Metern exhaled, brushing his hair back from his face. "Do you mean will she live? Yes, probably, but…" He looked down.

"But…" said Will, searching the other man's face intently.

"But more than that I don't know."

"Don't know, as in she may take some time to recover, or don't know as in she may spend the rest of her life on a ventilator?" His voice rasped and sounded harsher than he'd intended.

Again, Metern seemed to carefully consider his answer. "Will, whatever happens, I don't think she will ever be the same." He looked at him. "She was, to all intents and purposes, dead. What we did will have brought her back, and physically," he paused briefly, "her body may well be better than it ever was…" He trailed off.

"So, healed and…" said Will, images from his trip to Birmingham flew into his head, "… younger?"

Metern smiled. "Ah yes, Morwenna told me about your visit to see John. He showed you the photograph, didn't he?"

"Yes, he did," said Will. "Which makes you at least sixty years old."

A thin smile again. "At least," said Metern, an amused tone to his voice. "But, in answer to your question, no she will not be younger, not in her case. Just, shall we say, optimised at her peak."

Will wasn't put at ease with the answer and searching Metern's face stated, "There's another 'but', isn't there. You only said *physically*."

Metern bowed his head, eyes failing to meet Will's. "I don't know how her mind will react, Will. Most of the data that we got from animal studies before the lab was destroyed…" He looked up. "John told you about the lab?"

Will nodded. There were more moments' silence between them. "Cadan, what was in that syringe?" Will said, finally, "What is it? What does it do?"

Metern breathed out a long, tired breath and gazed out to the sea beyond Will. Remnants of the dying wind whistled in Will's ears. "Pluripotent stem cells containing genetically modified DNA," said Metern. "Essentially the blueprint and the apparatus to rapidly repair or heal any tissue, provided that the damage has just occurred and isn't too extensive."

In a way it confirmed what Will had pieced together and he knew that there was more. That was why Metern had been so hesitant, or one reason at least. "But there are side effects. Which is why you have never gone public."

Metern nodded, "Such data that survived suggested that most subjects slowly and specifically reject the new DNA in repaired brain tissue."

"Which means what?" said Will.

"It means that as antibodies attack the modified cells in the subject's brain, they begin to develop symptoms – vacant episodes a bit like petit mal epilepsy. They were also noted to engage in more risk-taking behaviours and exhibited," he swallowed, "self-destructive tendencies."

Will closed his eyes and breathed out slowly, "And that's what happens in humans. You know that now too, don't you? You gave the serum to Jen when she had her accident. She had all of those symptoms. She turned into a guinea pig, a convenient experiment."

A look of pain etched itself into Metern's features. "It has only been given when there's been no other option. A chance at life where there was none. That has been the only entry criterion for this 'experiment'." Metern looked awkward. "Besides, I don't really know if those side effects *always* happen, that was just one individual. Including Tamsin today, there have only been three of us. It's not exactly been widely trialled!"

He let out a forced laugh. "I didn't want to involve Jen in what I was doing you know, but she kept pressing me for explanations. That's why I finished things with her, to try to keep her safe." Another forced snort, "But fate, it seems, had different plans."

"So, what actually happened?" Will asked, trying to control his feelings.

Metern chewed his bottom lip, staring down at the puddle again.

Was he considering what story to make up, the truth... some of each, Will wondered?

"That night," Metern began, "the one of her accident, we were both on call. She hadn't given up on us and wanted to talk things through, but I had no time. I had to make more serum and had things to organise, so I just brushed her off. It was the early hours of the morning and I'd thought she had got the message or was in theatre but she obviously hadn't. She probably saw me disappearing down to the basement and followed, so was there watching us make the serum," – he gave Will an acknowledging look – "likely hidden in the stairwell. Her pager went off. We heard it and then her footsteps running up the stairs; one of the guys began to give chase. She must have tripped, because we heard a scream and a horrific thud as she hit the floor." He closed his eyes. Will could hear the imagined thud himself.

"When I got to her, I noticed her foot, was at a horrible angle and then I saw her head. There was a huge gash over her right temple, and she wasn't breathing. She must have fractured her right temporal bone and, I'm sure, the arterial vessel underneath. CPR just wasn't going to make any difference; she was going to die unless I did something. So, I did the only thing that I could and gave her all the serum we had. It needed refining, spinning down, but there was no time for that, so I just gave it. And, for a time," he drew breath, "I thought it had worked. She made an incredible recovery."

"But the side effects," said Will.

"Yes," Metern sighed, "mixed with the effects of a head injury. She had amnesia, but it didn't last."

"And as she began to remember and confronted you?" This tallied with what Tamsin had said.

"Yes, and I explained what had happened and why I had given her the serum, I thought that she would understand. Except she didn't and took it really badly; couldn't accept the way that the serum was made, and it seemed to feed into her symptoms, make her paranoia much worse." He paused, staring off to sea again. "Then she killed that patient during one of the absences and that I think must have tipped her over the edge."

Metern put his face in both hands; he seemed genuinely upset.

Will gave him a few moments. "Will what happened to Jen happen to Tamsin?" he asked, when Metern looked up. That was the most important thing to know now.

Metern ran his hands back through his hair, shifting his attention to Will. "I don't know. Jen had a severe brain injury, physical, anatomical damage, not just hypoxia like Tamsin, so a more complex repair. And Tamsin also got the refined serum."

"That will reduce the side effects?"

"Might do," said Metern.

"And how long does it last?"

"Well, the altered DNA can go on manufacturing proteins for weeks or months. It really depends on how long it takes for her immune system to identify them as foreign. Often all these genetically altered cells get lysed, killed, in the end, but the healing effects will persist." He considered for a few seconds adding almost to himself, "But if her immune system accepts the new cells, then it's possible that there will be none."

"You have the serum in you don't you, that's what Jen observed, and your system hasn't accepted the cells? So does that mean you need a constant supply of serum?"

"I do, yes. My cells are older and more prone to react, and I too, had an old batch of serum."

Will hesitated, then asked, "And this serum, these stem cells, where do you get them from?"

Metern half snorted his reply. "Oh, I think you know that already."

"From stillbirths and terminations?"

Metern nodded. "Just incinerating or burying the poor things is such a waste. At least their lives, such as they were, can have meant something."

Maybe Metern had a point. Then concern spread over Will's face, given the potential implication. The ends justify the means. "You weren't deliberately causing miscarriages, were you, Cadan? A bit of surreptitious methotrexate at antenatal clinics? Is that also what Jen was so upset over?" He felt horror well up inside him. "Tell me you weren't deliberately precipitating these foetal deaths to supply your need for the stem cells?"

Metern's eyes felt like they burned into Will. "No!" he replied, fiercely. "No. I won't deny that I did try to arrange for terminations to come in on specific dates. But the DNA, stem cell, enzyme mix needs exactly the correct magnified radiation exposure, which happens to be just after sunrise at the equinoxes, so I had to do some manipulation." Metern shifted his gaze to meet Will's eyes – was that a fraction too long? Again, Will wasn't sure. Was that the truth?

Metern continued, "Everything needs to happen at very specific times. I needed to control that." He laughed again, grating and with no humour. "I spent years trying to work out the correct balance of radiation harmonics you know, only to discover that the ancient religions had worked it all out long before me. That's why, throughout the world, in almost all cultures these festivals exist."

"And why so many are seemingly associated with human sacrifice?" Will said.

"Yes, unfortunately so. Back then, one individual's sacrifice benefited many others. Now at least we don't actively kill anyone."

"Unless you count terminations as such," said Will. "As I assume Jen did?"

"Yes," replied Metern, "unfortunately, she was vehemently opposed to them; felt they were morally and ethically wrong. We did discuss it and I couldn't persuade her to think differently. But" he defended himself, "*society* has decided terminating pregnancies is OK, even if Jen hadn't."

"Poor Jen," said Will. "It would explain her abhorrent reaction to what was in her. And I suppose the witchcraft thing." He looked a Metern and said sarcastically, "You don't believe in mixing a little witchcraft and pagan ritual with science as well, do you?" He was really only joking.

"Actually, I do, yes," replied Metern, clearly deadly serious.

Will gawped, lost for words.

Metern smiled, raising one brow. "But what about you, Will?"

Will took a step back, involuntarily.

"What do you think? That wind dropped very quickly" – he looked to Will's wrist, then back to his face. "And, you have quite the way with insects."

Will's jaw dropped further, taken off guard. "Oh, I'm really sorry if I..." He placed a hand over his wrist to cover the rope, subconsciously looking at Metern's abdomen. "If I accidentally..." Then he shook his head, desperately trying to clear it, "Hang on, that's... how did you –?"

"– Know? Maybe I'm attuned to magic... can sense it being used, see it in people."

Will screwed up his face.

"Or maybe stories of your antics filtered through, disclosed by other sources," he laughed. "And it's fine, by the way," he said, before Will could defend his actions. "I know that you meant no harm, did you?"

"No, I didn't," said Will, adding reflexively, "but I don't believe in that witchcraft stuff."

Metern began picking up his board. "Oh, but you should, Will," he said. "Believe, I mean."

"What?" said Will, as his brain tried to keep up.

Metern wound up the leash. "You should believe. Witchcraft, science, God, they all exist, even if only in the minds of humanity. All most definitely have the power to care, nurture and heal, or cause suffering, destroy and kill." He smiled warmly this time, "It's up to the individual to choose what they believe in and how to act, though often the choice isn't as simple as black and white, scientific or magical, life or death. There is often a choice between the greater good or lesser evil. Knowledge, understanding and being open to the concept that you do not know, or understand, everything, is the key to making the best choice."

Will stared at him.

"Never close your mind to possibilities, Will, never." Metern began to walk away.

"Why tell me all of this?" asked Will. "What do I do now? What am I supposed to tell Tamsin?"

"Like I said, it's your choice, Will, your belief. Follow the path you believe to be the right one." And with that, he turned and began the walk over the brow of the hill.

A 1994

He could feel it working, feel it surging through his veins, a beautiful warmth flooding his body and mind; maybe he had injected himself in time. His stomach was still cramped and his whole body felt weak. Saliva clogged his mouth and his head throbbed, but he was able to think straight now, and his breathing was easier.

Even if he hadn't been alone in this isolated cottage in the middle of Bodmin Moor, measures in hospital would only have been supportive, he knew that. Ironic really, that with all of the advances in pharmacology and medicine in general, they still had no antidote for that most ancient and infamous of poisons, hemlock.

He lifted his face from the cold, slate tiles on the floor and dragged himself to a sitting position, propped against the whitewashed cob wall. He looked over to the table where three cups sat, one half-drunk, the other two still full. If only she had waited, given him a chance to explain that in many ways she had been right, that he was sorry. But instead, she told him that they had started again and just left him there.

His head swam, tables and chairs mingling into a leggy, wooden tangle, and there was a sensation of the floor dropping out from under him, of his world falling away. For a moment he thought that the vial had failed, that they had managed to kill him after all, but the warmth returned, and with it, realisation and understanding flooded his consciousness. His eyes widened, and truly, for the first time, he shed some of the scales that had weighed him down and blinkered him for all those years, and he understood.

Chapter 39

Will drove down the hill into Valtor. His foot still throbbed, but it had only been twenty-four hours since it had been sutured back together. He had suffered a three-centimetre laceration through the webbing of his toes and broken two of them. Fortunately, they didn't require K wires and had just been strapped. It still hurt like heck, but he had convinced all concerned that he was still safe to drive.

He had gone straight to Whitehorse from the beach and down to ITU. Tamsin had been intubated as a precaution and was being monitored for any signs of secondary drowning. There weren't any, but the consultant had put the ECMO team on standby, just in case. They had machines to oxygenate blood outside the body if required. What happened after that with stuffed lungs would have been a matter for the lung transplant team... but it wouldn't come to that. Every indication was that she would survive. How well she would be... well, they didn't know. The conversations with her mother and father had proved difficult. What did you say to them? Yes, I allowed your daughter to go and surf an unrideable wave, and no, I didn't go in or stop her because I'd injured my toes. He had kept details to a minimum and would have stayed with them in the unit until Tamsin was de-tubed, but the ITU only allowed two people per patient at a time. So, he had driven Tamsin's car back to Valtor and picked his own up, briefly stopping to tell Shauna what had happened before driving back to Whitehorse Hospital once more. He had stayed in one of the on-call rooms but needed to return home for a change of clothes.

Now, his car passed over the bridge and past the pub, then along the narrow, cobbled lane to Southside. He was curious rather than surprised when he saw Godfrey and Shauna carrying a mattress – no, his mattress – out of the front door. They took it further along the lane, Godfrey tripping from one cobble to the next as Shauna marched on at the front and disappeared round the bend out of site. Will negotiated the gateway without incident and parked up before following them. They had, it seemed, taken it into the house that backed onto their existing place. The door was open and led into a small hallway and on to a large oak-beamed living room, which was completely empty other than a television and speaker system already fully installed and occupying one end. He could hear a commotion from halfway up some stairs to his left, Shauna was chastising Godfrey for not keeping his end up, which had caused Godfrey to collapse in a fit of giggles. He wandered into the room and then up the stairs, his steps echoing through the building as he ascended. Will followed them up. There were three doors off a small landing and Will went into the one from which the giggling came.

"Hi Will," came Shauna's lilt from inside, "come on in." He entered to see that most of his possessions were now lying in the middle of the floor. He looked at them a little blankly.

"How's Tamsin," she asked, the levity gone from her voice.

"She's stable. We'll just have to wait and see," he said. "What's going on?"

"Ah, well, you, we, er, decided to move house," said Godfrey.

Shauna intervened before Godfrey could launch into one of his convoluted explanations. "The thing is, the landlord came round this morning," she began, "and told me that he was selling our house and could we move out as soon as possible. I was a little disappointed, I have to say, and went outside to get a bit of fresh air, where I met the cleaner who does the pub."

Will nodded, his tired brain just about following.

"We got talking, and it turned out that she had been asked to sort out this house, 'The Beeches', around the corner, ready for renting. She let me have a look around and I took an executive decision, phoned the owner, and now we're just moving our stuff round."

"OK," said Will, slightly bemused.

"And the really good bit," said Godfrey, bouncing like a puppy, "is that there are three rooms."

"Oh, I get it," said Will smiling, "we're getting another housemate."

"Yes," said Shauna. "Conveniently, one turned up just as I'd finished on the phone to the landlord."

Godfrey had a grin on him wider than that of the Cheshire Cat.

"Do you like your new house?" she asked.

"I'm not sure," said Will, the corners of his mouth curling up slightly. "I mean, is there any sticky lino in the kitchen and an all-pervading smell of mildew throughout the house. And is there a risk of getting lung cancer instantly from just taking in one breath of its air?"

Shauna and Godfrey grinned back at him, shaking their heads.

"It'll be great," he said. "Well done."

A few hours later all the clutter from Southside had been transferred to The Beeches, including, Will noted, Godfrey's milk churn, which sat by the front door. It suited its new position, added character to the place. Shauna had gone inside to put the kettle on, and Godfrey had nipped out to get a "bottle of something sparkling" to celebrate with, given he'd received his exam results that morning and managed to scrape a pass. Will walked back to Tamsin's car to retrieve his wetsuit. He would go back to the hospital later that evening when she should be being taken out of her induced coma.

He flung the wetsuit over the clothesline in the garden, even though the stillness of the air meant it wasn't great drying weather. A knotted piece of rope dropped to the ground. It was *that* piece of rope. He picked it up and began fiddling with it as he walked back to the house. One of the knots dropped out. A massive gust of wind hit him from nowhere, flattening him to the floor and sending the milk churn clattering across the cobbles in front of the house, grazing his head as it passed. Will lay there, his head spinning only dimly aware that the wind settled as quickly as it had come. But as the last whispers of air blew through, he thought that he heard the voice again.

"*You must prepare and decide who to trust,*" a voice said, "*the Nexus Divide is approaching. Then you must choose your path.*"

And the world plunged into darkness.

Epilogue

A **1997**

He peered through the one-way glass of the Intensive Care Unit nursing station and watched as Will kissed the forehead of the now extubated and conscious medical student, Tamsin Trevelyan. He had done what he needed to be done and hoped that it was enough for her to recover fully. She had after all, had the purest, most refined batch yet, but he had seen enough to know what damage the elixir might do.

Alarms sounded, and his eyes flicked to the other side of the unit. Concerned doctors and nurses walked briskly over to a middle-aged man in bed three. He was ventilated and just down from theatre after a repair to his abdominal aortic aneurysm. Humans were so fragile, life so precariously balanced. His jaw tensed as he recalled from personal experience just how fragile. So much loss, so many young lives... and then there was Jen... and his parents. So high a price to pay.

He stared at the small, red, dragon-shaped scar under his left eye, reflected in the glass. He knew who and what he was now, felt time pressing on him, but even so his path was far from clear. Maybe it was up to these two people, the visionary, and the enigmatic witch, to help him understand who he was and what he was to do.

Cadan Metern, or "King", were the Cornish words translated, turned to leave the room, the white, doctor's coat flaring and flashing off the mirrored glass creating the illusion of cloaked armour; perhaps the modern armour of a warrior born again of sacrifice and of dragon-fire.

The series continues with **Witchcraft, Science, God: Science.**

Cover design Darwin Kaitiff

Printed in Great Britain
by Amazon

62630169R00184